BLOOD BROTHERS
A Family Saga

M.J. Akbar

For Brinda
Affectionately

LOTUS COLLECTION
ROLI BOOKS

10 · XII · 08 Kolkata

Lotus Collection

© M.J. Akbar, *2006*

First published in 2006
The Lotus Collection
An imprint of
Roli Books Pvt. Ltd.
M-75, G.K. II Market, New Delhi 110 048
Phones: ++91 (011) 2921 2271, 2921 2782
2921 0886, Fax: ++91 (011) 2921 7185
E-mail: roli@vsnl.com
Website: rolibooks.com
Also at
Varanasi, Bangalore, Jaipur & Mumbai

Cover design : Sneha Pamneja
Layout design : Narendra Shahi

ISBN: 81-7436-439-0

Typeset in ACaslon Regular by Roli Books Pvt. Ltd. and
printed at Syndicate Binders, Noida (UP)

BLOOD BROTHERS

~

To the next generation,
Mukulika and Prayaag

~

CONTENTS

1	PRAYAAG	1
2	DREAMS	6
3	CONVERSION	17
4	PLEASURES	29
5	DREAD	44
6	DERVISH	59
7	APHRODISIAC	73
8	DESIRE	89
9	KRISHNA	108
10	WORDS	124
11	SAHIBS	141
12	BRIDGES	160
13	BLOOD	181
14	BRAHMA	214
15	FRIENDS	236
16	STARS	259
17	OFFERING	278
18	BIKINI	301
19	BROTHERS	318

PRAYAAG

MY GRANDFATHER DIED WHILE I WAS PLAYING ON HIS CHEST. That was my first stroke of luck. My elder aunt, dark, wise, hunched against her corner of the courtyard, promptly declared that his soul, seething with miracles, had passed into me. My younger aunt, widowed, and a flitting presence at home because she was often possessed by raving spirits, promptly agreed. The motion, having been moved and affirmed, became established family fact.

I was about a year old, fat and indeterminate of face in the manner of babies with enough to eat. My grandfather was fond of me, possibly because I was not yet old enough to ask for money. He was a miser. The thought of parting with cash wrought great misery upon his soul, now possibly transmigrated to me. He had his reasons. The most important one was that he nearly died of hunger when he was eleven.

Starvation is a slow fire that sucks life out in little bursts, leaving pockets of unlinked vacuum inside. Death comes when the points of emptiness suddenly coalesce; there is a silent implosion. The worst is in the beginning, when the body still has the energy to rebel and the mind enough hope to fear. When hope fades, fear evolves into a dazed weariness. You turn numb, and it no longer matters whether you are alive or dead. Dadu, our affectionate term for grandfather, had drifted into that zone when a short bald man in a vest and a sarong, known locally as a lungi, shook his lifeless shoulders and offered him a thick home-baked biscuit softened in tea.

The escape from death began three days earlier in the Bihar village where he was born, near the squalid town of Buxar. The great moment in Buxar's history had come about a hundred years earlier, when the splendidly colourful soldiers of the East India Company, led by Major Hector Munro, defeated the joint forces of the Emperor Shah Alam of Delhi, Nawab Mir Qasim of Bengal and Nawab Shuja ud Daulah of Avadh on 16 August 1765. Till that point, the East India Company was known as the English Company. After Buxar, admirers renamed it Company Bahadur, or the Heroic Company. It was extraordinary how Indians became transformed when they switched sides: disciplined, unwavering under the command of the white man, and pathetic buffoons under the green and black-and-white standards of Muslim dynasties in decline. One old man could still do a wondrous imitation, learnt from his forefathers, of a Mughal champion who swung his heavy sword in thin air so vigorously before battle that he was utterly exhausted when actual fighting began. He was fortunate. He survived. But why cast aspersions on a mere braggart? Most of his compatriots preferred to disappear rather than die, after an initial, very brief surge of heroics. The white man passed into local legend: he stood his line against the charge, and left it only to go forward. The Muslims were high on bravado and short on bravery. They carried too much baggage around the waist: their bellies sagged with curry and sloth.

British rule was a welcome relief from gathering chaos. It took one lifespan for optimism to change to apprehension: British stability was soon interspersed with famine. The British were individually more honest than the Mughals, but collectively more greedy. Taxes were too high, and their middlemen, the class known as zamindars, took pleasure in adding insult to extortion. The peasant did not have the surplus to resist a drought, so drought degenerated into famine. Fighting hunger became a full-time job. There was not much strength left to fight a government.

My grandfather lost his parents to a famine that started around 1870 and emptied his village within five years. Those who could, migrated. Some were shipped out by British merchants to plantations across the seven seas, in the West Indies or Mauritius or Fiji. They were not called slaves since slavery had been abolished by Britain. They were given another name: Indentured labour. It was a polite term invented for similiar conditions.

~

My grandfather was born a Hindu and named, rather grandly, Prayaag, after the confluence of the holy rivers, Ganga and Jamuna. The grandeur reflected his caste, for he was a Kshatriya, born of the arms of Brahma. His mother taught him his faith: the universe was once a dark vacuum, which the Eternal Creator injected with energy. From energy emerged light, and then water. Water flowed from the Lord's body, and in it the Lord's semen. That semen turned into a golden egg brighter than the sun, from which, after one year, emerged Brahma, the originator of mankind. With the power of his thought, Brahma divided himself into two, and opposites were born: earth and sky, and the four directions. He meditated and the "I" evolved, both the self and the senses. Brahma divided mankind into four castes to establish order: the Brahmin from his mouth, the Kshatriya from his arms, the Vaishyas from his thighs and the untouchable Sudras from his feet.

Famine had no caste. Funnily enough, famine was kinder to the Sudra than to the Brahmin, for the scum of the earth were familiar with hunger while the salt of the earth were not.

Prayaag had heard stories of the jute mills of Bengal from his father. The stories were told in driblets, as if to ease the pain as they watched their land slowly become sterile. They owned some four bighas; nothing substantial, but not worthless either. They once lived comfortably on an income of about seven rupees a month, and he fondly remembered one year when the family income crossed one hundred rupees. Drought had reduced that to two rupees a month if not less, and that wretch of a rent-collector had sunk so low that he demanded taxes even from caste-brothers in a season of hunger.

Jute mills were the powerful engines of a new economy that swelled along the banks of the Hooghly, a tributary of the mighty Ganges that swung south and flowed through Calcutta on its way to the Bay of Bengal and the Indian Ocean. Prayaag had heard that a new mill, named after the Great Queen of London, Victoria, had opened in a place called Telinipara. He knew an important landmark. The nearest railway station was not in British territory, but in Chandernagore, the French outpost in the east, some thirty miles upstream from Calcutta.

After cremating his father, the last in the family to die,

Prayaag climbed onto a train and slept on the floor of the compartment. The ticket collector left him alone. Sleep was Prayaag's only nourishment. It was dark when he got off at Chandernagore. Determination took him to his destination. A long journey ended in a scrawl of mud roads beyond which lay the huge iron doors of the Victoria Jute Mill, a blur of green paint between thick walls.

He collapsed against a tin sheet. He was fortunate that the sheet was the door of a tea shop, and therefore opened at four in the morning, when a blast from the high chimney told workers to prepare for the first shift. He might or might not have survived till sunrise. The owner of the tea shop, Wali Mohammad, like the ticket collector, was not demonstrative, but retained a stony sympathy for the wrecks of famine. He gave Prayaag a couple of baked biscuits, tea and a mat to sleep on before his wife, Diljan Bibi, fed him a meal of rice and dal. Then he gave Prayaag work, washing dishes.

Later, perhaps much later, whispers suggested that a street dog had sat beside my grandfather as he lay unconscious that night, and then barked to wake up Wali Mohammad a bit earlier than usual. However, such stories are always told about those who succeed. But this much is true: there was always food at home for strays, and they romped through our lane like free children when grandfather was rich enough to build the first double-storied brick house in Telinipara, ten yards from that tea shop.

DREAMS

THE ASCENT FROM POVERTY IS THROUGH FIVE CLIFFS: FOOD, roof, marriage, wealth, esteem. On the first cliff, Prayaag kept his head up and eyes down. His high cheekbones framed glowing, deep eyes; he knew his stare could be disconcerting, and therefore disrespectful to elders.

Wali Mohammad's kindness was sustained by business instinct. Prayaag was the solution to a dilemma. Famine in Bihar had brought job-seekers to Telinipara, and with it the prospect of more customers. He did not have much to offer: tea, home-made biscuits and, for those with a taste for luxury, boiled eggs. But food was a sensitive matter to many Hindus. Some upper castes treated Muslims as *yavana*, or outsiders, the term originally used for Alexander's Greeks when they invaded a centre of Hindu civilization, Taxila, and later applied to Muslims. All outsiders were *mleccha*, unclean. Hindus might happily converse with a Muslim, work with him, conspire with him, but not eat with him. But they might eat if served by a Hindu Kshatriya boy.

Prayaag was uninterested in reasons for his good fortune. He had found shelter, and a life. He did not expect money. Wali

Mohammad was childless, and his wife, Diljan Bibi, grew fond of this quiet, intense boy. She had nursed him when he was dying, and began to believe that Prayaag was Allah's answer to her prayers for a son. She would occasionally slip him a few cowrie shells to buy carrots or a mango in an abundant season; on some weekends she gave him as much as an anna, a sixteenth of a rupee. Life became comfortably routine.

Victoria Jute Mill sat heavily on the western bank of the Hooghly, some thirty miles north of Calcutta, the political and industrial heart of the British Empire. On both sides of the river Scottish entrepreneurs were constructing massive factories to spin rich jute from Bengal's fields into products like gunny bags. Victoria, the youngest child of Thomas Duff and Company (headquarters, Dundee), was protected by walls one foot thick and eight feet high on three sides, with the river marking the fourth boundary. The western gate opened towards a huge field, called the maidan, that separated Victoria from its sister, the Champdani Jute Mill.

Telinipara's mud and thatch huts were spread randomly between the southern and eastern gates. Facilities were rudimentary. Water came from wells, and light from the sun. The jute mill continued production beyond sunset with the help of four-foot high gas-lit lamps that shed a heavy, white glow through the fluff of jute that floated like smog. Outside the factory, the darkness was occasionally disturbed by the flicker of a pallid wick placed in a *dibiya,* a small tin box filled with kerosene. The workers went to the further edge of the maidan, called the *bhagar math,* for their ablutions; and then to the river for a bath if they wanted to. Women needed the darkness.

In winter the sun set by five; in summer by six; by eight or nine the day was over. It resumed at four in the morning, with a blast from the factory's siren, attached to a towering brick chimney, so that sound and smoke gushed out in atonal harmony. Prayaag generally woke up half an hour earlier to get the shop ready for the first customers. Workers sipped tea from small earthen cups, and sometimes slipped a thick biscuit into the top knot of their lungi, to eat later. Those privileged enough to get credit from Wali Mohammad chalked a white mark on a slate to confirm their purchase. Accounts were settled every Saturday, on payday. Occasionally disputes arose, but Wali Mohammad's reputation for honesty was rock-solid. He would not serve a defaulter until accounts had been settled, and he could sit for hours outside a difficult debtor's home moaning for his money.

Prayaag got his one break for laughter on Saturday evenings, when the weekly fair, or *haat*, gathered on the sprawling Victoria maidan. The open expanse and cool river breeze made this *haat* an epicentre for workers from half a dozen jute mill colonies on either side of the river: Shamnugur, Gondalpara, Angus, Titaghur, Champdani, Kankinara. Women gossiped around stalls full of ribbons and bangles. Men enjoyed the preening of wrestlers as they challenged known and unknown foes: the winner was assured a decent collection, enhanced by those in the audience who had made the right bet. Amateurs preferred hand-clasp competitions. Children screamed and played gilli-danda, with short sticks and a puck sharpened at both ends that was tapped into the air and then hit as far as possible. Fried food was the preferred delicacy: Narayan Teli's *pyaaju,* an onion *bhaji* cooked in boiling mustard oil, would always sell out. Local medicine men, ayurveds and hakims, some knowledgeable, some quacks, displayed a range of strange powders and oils, and sometimes a whisper would wander through the fair that oil from the fat of a tiger had come to the market and could do your sex life some good. Acrobats walked the tightrope, and charmers made snakes rise to the music of a *been,* a short bulbous gourd whose sound was manipulated by fingers dancing on holes in the stem to produce a sweet, swaying wail.

Prayaag loved the storytellers. His favourite was Talat Mian, who laughed through his spiky beard at all his jokes just before he told them. He wore the same clothes whenever he came, which was not often. They were styled in the Lucknow fashion: the *chau goshia,* or the light, four-cornered cap; *angarkha,* the knee-length-shirt with a crescent necklet attached to a buttonhole towards the left of the neck, edged with lace at the hem; wide linen pyjamas and light, velvet shoes called *khurd nau.* The joke was that he put these shoes into a bag the moment he began to walk. The clothes, clearly hand-me-downs from an indulgent aristocrat, gave credibility to his claim that he lived in Matiyaburj (the Mud Fort), a riverside locality about four miles south of Calcutta, where the British had resettled the last of the Nawabs of Avadh, Wajid Ali Shah, after they stole his throne.

"This happened," said Talat Mian, "about a year before the Great Patriotic War of 1857, which frightened the British so badly that, more than twenty years later, they still quiver at the sight of any Indian with a moustache." His sigh was audible beyond the circle of listeners. "But you should know why the British rule us. Because we are more loyal to them than we are to Indians. Our people have become servants and our kings have gone mad. Wajid Ali Shah, ignoble son of a noble dynasty, danced while his kingdom was lost! This man, who built Lucknow's Qaiser Bagh, a marvel of its age, now feeds off the crumbs of the British table and lives in a house that once would not have been fit for his barber. Do you know that his barber, Azimullah, owned a house called Chau Lakhi because it was worth four lakhs of rupees? Do you? Do you?"

No, of course they did not; and suppressed their disbelief with a giggle. The only barber they knew was Wahabuddin, who sat on his haunches, sharpened his razor on water and stone, shaved or snipped hair from any part of your body and was an expert in circumcision, for which the Muslims were truly grateful.

"Let me tell you about Qaiser Bagh!" continued Talat Mian, refusing to indicate whether he had merely heard about it or seen the glories of this palace himself. "The flowers of its Chinese Garden were imported from Japan, and scattered among pools and pavilions with strange, curving roofs. It had a Mermaid Gate, and don't tell me that there are no mermaids just because you do not see them in this wretched river of yours. Through Mermaid Gate you reached Hazrat Bagh, whose exotic flowers came from either a hidden valley of Kashmir or the famous Kewbagh of London. The roof of Chandi Wali Barah Dari was made of silver. The founder of this dynasty was Nawab Saadat Khan; but its greatest ruler, Shuja ud Daulah, was a true warrior of the faith who lived in the best Islamic tradition – in a simple, rented house! Allah rewarded such virtue, for he, with the help of the Afghans, saved the Mughal empire when he defeated the Marathas at Panipat in 1761. Alas, four years later, what Shuja had saved in the west, he lost in the east, when the British demolished him in Buxar."

Prayaag's ears perked up when he learnt he had been born so close to history.

"The defeat of Shuja marked the birth of the British Empire. When Shuja died, the power of Muslims was buried with him. His successors were miserable pygmies who fought each other rather than Christian infidels. I have seen their portraits in Matiyaburj. Each one's arse is as fat as his belly. Shuja was tall, erect and stern. His son Asaf ud Daulah was so fat he overflowed from his chair like an overfed baby elephant. As for Saadat Ali Khan – he was the first in the family to wear English boots, trousers and coats: shame!

"Shuja employed 22,000 messengers to bring him news: every seven days from Pune and every fifteen days from Kabul. That is how you rule a kingdom! Asaf employed 22,000 cooks and wastrels! They say there were 1,200 elephants in his son Wazir Khan's marriage procession and his bejewelled coat cost Rs 20 lakhs! And Wazir was not even his own son, for Asaf was impotent despite a diet of the best aphrodisiacs made from Himalayan herbs. Imagine how much he would have spent if the bastard had been legitimate! But, as they say in Lucknow, Asaf spent many fortunes when alive, but his funeral cost only seventy rupees...

"The debauch Wajid Ali Shah betrayed his faith, betrayed his heritage, and his misery today is Allah's justice. He would strut and swagger before his soldiers and insult them by calling them women or homosexual. He named one regiment Banka. You know what that means? Bent. Another was called Tircha, which is a sly term for a eunuch. Is that how you address brave soldiers?

"The Holy Quran has said that a tyrant will be sent to destroy any Muslim king who forgets Allah. Changez Khan's grandson Hulegu was sent by Allah to destroy the Arab rulers of Baghdad. The British were sent to destroy Nawab Wajid Ali Shah. Allah gave Wajid one last chance to redeem himself with martyrdom. During the Great Patriotic War sepoys in Calcutta sent word secretly to Wajid Ali Shah that they would revolt if he agreed to be their leader. But he preferred to be a beggar! And now enough for one day…"

Talat Mian looked discreetly skyward while those who could threw small coins onto the cloth he had spread for his reward. It was impolite, by the standards of Lucknow culture, to look at money.

Prayaag did not have any money to give. Talat Mian would not have spoken any less if he had not been there, he rationalized. A story is wealth-neutral; like nature, it belongs to both the rich and poor.

~

If one obsession was fantasy, the second was magic.

He was entranced by magicians, wild men who lived on that strange precipice which was the home of both human beings and spirits. It was said that there were beneficial sorcerers and evil ones. As far as Prayaag was concerned, they were either charlatan, and entertained you, or genuine, and terrified you.

One afternoon, a fugitive with matted hair raked in ash and missing front teeth turned up at the fair. There had been havoc at the last village that gave him shelter: soon after his arrival, cattle died from a mysterious disease, accidents multiplied and women became barren. The villagers blamed his malevolent powers. A learned Brahmin was hired to spy on him, and he reported that the outsider used to chant the awesome *Atharvana Veda: Om Sri Hsan Hgita Ramaya-namah!* Sages had forbidden its recitation because the verse was so destructive that it could cause the death of kings and destroy the even tenor of social life. The Brahmin suggested a solution.

The key to any mantra is correct pronunciation. If you mispronounce a single syllable, the mantra turns ineffective. His advice was simple and effective. Break the bastard's front teeth. The malign mendicant would never be able to chant any mantra correctly again, and the world would be safe. The villagers did so before they drove him out.

Prayaag was fascinated by his eyes, which seemed to be as big as a god's and changed shape, strength and personality on some inner command. He went warily to the shed that the magician had made his home.

"I come from the line of Solitary Brahmins," the magician said, his eyes rolling violently, as if they had no socket. "My ancestor was the illegitimate child of a Brahmin widow. He learnt, through his devotion, the secret of *shrum, craum, hrim, hrum, hru* and *hu* from Lord Shiva. Those who know the various combinations through which these words become incantations, have power over life and death. Some foolish Brahmins did not invite my ancestor to a wedding because he was illegitimate. He entered the wedding tent, and, using just two syllables, turned the food into toads. The terrified Brahmins begged for his forgiveness. He reversed the order of syllables and the toads turned into food again!"

He told stories of unseen worlds. "I am in touch with spirits who live between the first and second skies, in the company of powerful djinns, where souls of the dead rest on the first stage of their journey to the beyond. From there, they are permitted to communicate with the living one last time, and return to visit the one person they have loved the most – before they travel beyond our reach."

He was indifferent to heat and cold, he said, to wind and rain, delicacy and disgust: milk and excrement tasted the same to him; neither destruction nor creation mattered anymore. Illusion was the only reality he enjoyed.

And so one monsoon evening, when the sky swarmed with fluffs of gray cloud and the sun changed into a dark flush in the west, the magician stood between two bamboo staves planted some ten feet apart, and boomed:

Jai Kali Calcuttewali
Tera wachan na jaaye khali!

Oh Kali of Calcutta
Let not your oath be barren!

In the deepening twilight a rope rose from between his feet like a thin, climbing snake, to the level of bamboo stalks, still and erect. From a basket behind the magician a child of perhaps four crawled out, then sprinted quickly up the immobile rope. The magician looked up at the boy, a blur in the dusk, and shouted: "Are you there?!"

"Yes, master," replied the boy in a thin but audible squeak.

"Then die!" screamed the magician, and the boy seemed to

explode against the fading light, and little parts of his body fell to the ground while the air was stained with dark patches of blood. Voices gasped in the crowd; fear and bewilderment turned to horror. The magician laughed like a maniac, in sustained roars that rolled in airborne waves, one after the other. "Come back, boy!" he screamed: his voice spread across the maidan, and became an invisible roof that had sucked up all sound from the earth. The world became still.

A gurgle interrupted the thrall.

From somewhere in the crowd the child came racing towards the magician, chuckling with joy. The magician picked up the boy triumphantly, placed him on his shoulders and began to dance slowly, happily, three steps forward and then three back, to some rhythm in his soul. Someone in the crowd twittered nervously and the spell was over.

Diljan Bibi was restless when Prayaag returned home that night. "Why are you so late?" she asked angrily. Prayaag bit his lip and his chin sank into his neck in shame. "Why? Why? Why? Don't you think I get worried?"

It took a while for Prayaag to answer. "Forgive me, Mai." He had used the endearment "Mai" for the first time since his mother died. She looked sternly at him. "Don't do it again as long as I am alive." Then she hugged him. "You are my son. Don't ever go away."

Prayaag wondered a great deal about the magician and his last performance. He knew it was a trick, and was unable to comprehend its power on his imagination, or his dread that it was an omen.

It was at the *haat* that Prayaag learnt, from the fear on faces and the hush on the tongue, that the *Kali Dain*, or Black Witch, had reached Champdani on the outskirts of Telinipara. Later, the government would write a monotonous report explaining that the cholera epidemic of January 1883 that took seventy lives in Champdani was due to filthy sanitation in unplanned, choking, unlit slums. The workers explained that cholera was the curse of the Black Witch who struck suddenly, quietly, arbitrarily and would not be appeased until she had supped on enough lives to sate her appetite.

Wali Mohammad had gone to Champdani to meet a newly-arrived relative from Bihar. His mistake was to stay overnight. When Diljan Bibi heard that he had succumbed to cholera she began to moan softly, incessantly. They would not bring his body to Telinipara for fear of contamination. Prayaag ran all the way to the funeral. Wali Mohammad's body, covered in a shroud, lay next to a freshly-dug grave. A handful of people had gathered for the last prayer: *From Allah we come, to Allah we go.* Prayaag did not understand this, nor had he ever given a thought to any form of prayer. At the grave of Wali Mohammad he lifted his hands up towards God, and broke down.

3

CONVERSION

"I WANT A CHILD." THE SENTENCE DROPPED FROM DARKNESS AND probed Prayaag's insecurity. He was sitting on the floor of their hut, eating his day-meal of rice, dal and a spicy potato mash called *chokha,* while his mother gently fanned off flies. Another child? How? Why? Didn't she have faith in his ability to provide for her? He did not readily voice his dreams, for they might seem outlandish, but he was certain that while such an unlit, airless room might be acceptable for Wali Mohammad's wife, it was not fit for his mother. But he needed time to make money. He felt confused, threatened. Did she want to marry again? Angrily, he asked, "Am I not good enough to be your son?"

Diljan Bibi began to laugh gently. "Oh my darling boy, I mean I want you to give me a son. This room is too lonely; it needs a baby."

Prayaag flushed and did not know what to say.

"It's time you got married," she continued. "You are too old already. You have crossed twenty and should have been married five years ago. How much time do you think I have left? Even if disease does not take me away, old age will. How many poor women cross forty…? That is why we marry early. If you start a home at twelve or thirteen at least you get a chance to see a grandchild for a few years."

Prayaag lowered his head further towards his plate; he had stopped eating. "Whatever you say, Mai."

She beamed. "My handsome young man! Now I must find a good girl for you from your caste."

Prayaag looked up. "What do you mean from my caste? If I marry anyone, it will be from your caste, Mai."

"My caste? What's wrong with you? We are Muslims. How can a Hindu boy marry a Muslim girl?"

Prayaag looked steadily at her, conscious that she should understand that this was a deliberate, considered decision. "Mai," he said, "you are my mother. Your religion is my religion."

Diljan Bibi stared back at her son, and in a moment her tears had reached lips that were smiling.

She sorted out options and made a decision. Her cousin Saira had three pretty daughters and nothing to eat. The eldest, Jamila, was twelve and had crossed her puberty. If all went well, she would be nursing a grandson in less than two years. They would have to rent another room, of course. She fantasized about spoiling the child. When she returned from her reverie she noticed that Prayaag was still motionless. "You can continue eating," she said sharply, "you will need your strength now!"

After a pause she added, "I have selected your bride."

Prayaag's head dipped.

"Her name is Jamila."

The head went further down.

"She is pretty."

His nose touched his plate.

"But of course you cannot marry for a few months after you become a Muslim."

He shot up. "Why?"

She laughed. "You'll know why after they have made you a Mussulman."

Such things could not be kept hidden. They had to be done properly. She asked Maulvi Taslimuddin, imam of the Big Mosque, the Bari Masjid, who always wore a small green conical straw hat in the middle of his turban, to perform the conversion.

Maulvi Taslimuddin shuddered with delight. The conversion of one infidel to Islam was enough to ensure a place in the first of eight heavens, the Jannat ul Khuld (Garden of Eternity). He was satisfied. It was a garden and it was eternal. His betters might hope for Jannat ul Firdaus, the highest of the glorious abodes of the Almighty, but if a believer could reach Khuld with Telinipara as his starting point, it ought to be considered achievement enough. Houris with large dark eyes luminous as pearls, bearing silver flagons of drink tempered by *zanjabil* (ginger) from the fount of Salsabil, or the intoxicating waters of the eternal spring, Tasnim, floated in a blur before him. No one had told him at his seminary in Deoband that the houris were not only virgins but destined to remain so, but that was an unnoticed detail in his delirium.

Taslimuddin was a graduate and missionary of a new seminary situated north of Delhi that was already attracting attention across the country, the Dar-ul Ulum at Deoband, shortened, in common usage, to Deoband.

Deoband was born in 1867, under a beautiful pomegranate tree inside the Chatta Mosque, when the first teacher, Mullah Mahmud, gave a lesson to the first student, Mahmud Hasan. It was considered auspicious by some, and merely fortuitous by others, that both master and pupil had the same name. Taslimuddin, whose father was an impoverished imam of a small mosque in the city, went to the madrasa after Maulana Rafiuddin became *mohtamim,* or chancellor, in 1872 and began to convert an idea into an institution. The new seminary sought to be different from existing schools like the family-run Farangi Mahal in Lucknow, whose syllabus and style were oriented towards churning out future government servants. Deoband's founders had fought the British during the Patriotic War of 1857, and their motive was reform within the defeated Muslim community through a renewal of faith. They set up a modern administrative bureaucracy with a rector, known as *sarparast,* as the head and patron; a *mohtamim* as the chief executive; and a *sadr modarris,* or principal, responsible for faculty. In 1892, its stature established, Deoband added a mufti to supervise the growing demand for fatwas, or judgments on matters of Islamic law that were treated as binding by those who sought them.

Deoband created a growing community of men trained in Islamic law to look after the daily needs of Indian Muslims through a network of schools and mosques from Kabul in Afghanistan to Chittagong in Bengal. Arabic, the language of theology, took precedence over Persian, the language of government. The spirit was puritan. Poverty was a virtue. The founders rejected all offers of financial assistance from the British, and left worry about finance to Allah: they were serving

Him, and He would provide. It worked. Local Muslims sent food for teachers and students every day; other expenses were met by donations large and small. The school expected its students to carry such values into life beyond its walls.

The reputation of the Muslim clergy at that time was mud. Any Urdu poet in search of applause at a mushaira, or poetry-reading, had but to make a sly reference to the hypocrisy and pomposity of the mullah and the largely-Muslim audience would applaud in agreement. Mirza Asadullah Ghalib of Delhi, the newest literary star, was particularly provocative; his couplets were repeated with much relish by Deoband's students when they had wearied of poverty and discipline. The favourite doing the rounds during Taslimuddin's term went:

Kahan maikhana ka darwaza Ghalib aur kahan waaiz,
Par itna jaante hain, kal woh jaata tha ke ham nikle.

The tavern door is at one end, the priest at the other
But this I know, yesterday he was entering when I was leaving.

Taslimuddin always asked Allah for forgiveness by adding "*Tauba, tauba*" (I repent, I repent) whenever by chance or mischance he used a word like *maikhana* (tavern) or *sharab* (wine), for the very mention of the forbidden could be a sin. He had an arithmetical approach to eternity. The fewer the sins the quicker the journey to Paradise. The Holy Quran says that the moment of death is written in one's destiny, and no one can change it; if Allah had to punish men for their sins in this life, life would be impossible. The accounting begins immediately after Malak ul Maut, the Angel of Death, squeezes your soul like water from a bag, and two white angels with piercing blue eyes,

Munkan and Nakir, enter your grave, tell you to sit up and begin checking the sin-roster. Huge swathes of sin would be erased by bringing an infidel to the true faith.

This also meant one more Muslim in Bengal. Taslimuddin recalled the frisson of excitement in Deoband when, as a result of the 1871 census, people learnt for the first time that Muslims were in a majority in Bengal. Before 1871 no one knew and no one cared. Hindu zamindars across the huge rural hinterland, and their genteel upper class cousins in Calcutta were horrified at the implications. The Muslim elite from Dhaka to Delhi, sheikh and sharif, delighted in having stolen a province away from Hindus. Till 1871, Bengal's social conflicts were largely between the powerful and powerless: rich and poor; landlord and peasant. European Sahib, Anglo-Indian, Hindu Baboo, Muslim peasant and Bihari labour formed shifting patterns of coexistence. After the census, rift lines sharpened between Hindus and Muslims as they gradually acquired another layer of identity. Hindu revivalism, already visible in earlier reform movements, found a new momentum from powerful and lyrical writers of Bengali prose. Less dramatically, more slowly, the Muslim peasant became conscious of the strength of numbers, making Hindu landlords apprehensive.

Deobandis arrived with questions for the community: did they know enough about Islam? Did they have the guidance necessary for a meritorious life? Taslimuddin was among those sent to provide answers, and so became head imam in Telinipara when only a little more than twenty.

~

A tiny kerosene lamp on a ledge in the wall produced large

shadows but little light. Maulvi Taslimuddin and Prayaag looked evenly at each other.

The priest's opening question was direct. "*Bismillah ir Rahman ir Raheem* (In the name of Allah the Merciful and Benevolent): Are you here out of your own free will?"

"Yes," replied Prayaag.

"Has there been any pressure on you from anyone to convert?"

"No."

"I have to insist on these questions because in the Holy Quran, and by the precepts of the Holy Prophet Muhammad, peace be upon him, it is illegal to forcibly convert anyone to the true faith. You are welcome into the redeeming radiance of Allah only if you come by free will. It is said clearly in the Holy Quran – and remember that every word in the Quran is sent by Allah, it is Allah's book – in Verse 256 of the second chapter: *La ikraha fi ad-deen.* Let there be no compulsion in religion. If you do not see the light, then the Quran lets you go your way. *Lakum dinakum wa-la-yeddin:* Your religion for you and mine for me.

"Who could be more powerful than the last Prophet of Allah? Could he not have forced his persecutors in Mecca to bow to his will? But no: he preferred to leave Mecca for Medina. He was a man of peace; Islam is a religion of peace. The Quran welcomes Jews and Christians as people of the Book; they hate us, but we do not hate them. Christians, Allah forgive us, have turned Jesus into a son of God! *Tauba, tauba.* Could anything be more preposterous? Is Allah a man that He can have children?"

Prayaag, who could recognize a sermon when he saw one coming, was bored. A little more ritual would have been welcome.

Maulvi Taslimuddin took out a copy of the Quran from a

made-to-measure green cloth jacket and asked Prayaag to place his hand upon the holy book. "I must explain to you that in our religion," he continued, "there is only one God, and not hundreds as among Hindus. This is the basis of our faith. Do you understand and do you agree?"

"Yes."

"We never worship idols. The Prophet personally destroyed 360 idols when he cleansed the Holy Kaaba. You must never even look at an idol anymore. Do you agree?"

"Yes, I agree."

"Now say after me: *Ash-hadu la ilaha ill-al-Allahu wa ash-hadu anna Muhammadan abduhu was rasuluhu.*" I bear witness that there is no god except Allah, and Muhammad, peace be upon him, is His servant and His apostle.

Prayaag repeated the words.

"No, no, no, no... You mispronounced *hadduanna.* These are words from the Quran, they are the words of Allah. Not a single word can be changed in the Quran, nor a single word mispronounced."

This was getting a bit tough, thought Prayaag. But he concentrated and got the pronunciation right, or at least up to the Maulvi's satisfaction. Then came the *kalimah,* the creed of Islam. "This," intoned the Maulvi, "is what you must repeat every day when you get up, and every evening before you sleep, to keep the devil away. It asserts two truths: the first is known as *nafi,* or rejection of any deity other than Allah, and the second as *isbat,* or affirmation of the Prophet as the Last Messenger of Allah. The two parts do not appear together in the Quran, but we Muslims always say it together because we believe equally in both. Repeat after me, thrice, *La ilaha il-Allah, Muhammad ur-*

Rasool Allah! " There is no God but Allah and Muhammad is His Apostle.

Prayaag did so, and was pleased that he got the pronunciation correct this time.

"*Allah-o-Akbar!*" exclaimed the Maulvi. "This is the first of the five principles of Islam. The others are *namaz*, prayer, *roza*, fasting during the month of Ramadan, *zakat*, which is compulsory charity but not meant for you since you have no money, and haj, which, if you are fortunate enough, you will perform at least once in your lifetime. But prayer and fasting don't cost money; make sure you observe them. Come to the mosque after a few days and I will teach you the prayers."

The only Muslims who prayed five times a day were those without work, or those whose work it was to pray, thought Prayaag, but let it pass. He was too new a convert to argue. Maulvi Taslimuddin turned slightly towards Diljan Bibi, sitting in a dark corner, her face half covered with a fold of her sari. He did not look directly at her when he asked: "What shall we name him? He has to have a Muslim name now."

She kept quiet.

"I have some suggestions. We can call him after one of the Prophets: Muhammad, peace be upon him; Ibrahim, after our greatest prophet before Muhammad, peace be upon him; Moosa, after Moses; Yusuf, after Joseph; Yunus, after Jonas, or Isa, after Jesus. Anything. Or we can link him directly to Allah. Saifullah means the sword of Allah; it is a good name for troubled times. If that is too strong, then maybe Barkatullah, or the gift of God; or Rahmatullah, he who has been blessed with the mercy of Allah."

Prayaag interrupted the chatter. "Just call me Rahmatullah."

"Good. There is nothing more blessed than the mercy of Allah. Very good. From today you are a Mussulman with the name of Rahmatullah. Do you willingly confirm that?"

"Yes."

"Now there are many things you must learn, about the Prophet, about Allah, about the faith. I will tell you all, I will teach you the prayers. You don't know how to read; so you come to me whenever you have a question or a problem, and I will solve it for you because I have studied in India's best madrasa. Our Prophet, Muhammad, peace be upon him, was born in Mecca. His mother's name was Amina, daughter of Wahab; his father Abdullah died before he was born, and Amina died when he was six."

Prayaag stopped the Maulvi: "My Prophet was an orphan at six?"

"Yes, and he was brought up by his grandfather..."

Prayaag felt a sudden affinity with his new faith.

Maulvi Taslimuddin cleared his throat. "There is still one thing to do before you become a proper Mussulman. Now, you see, it was not our Prophet Muhammad, peace be upon him, who ordered this. You can't blame him for this. This was decided by the father of the prophets, Abraham." As if to ease the coming blow, the Maulvi launched into a short narrative.

"Prophet Abraham was born thousands of years ago at the time of King Namrud, who had turned away from the true God and begun to worship idols, stars and planets. Abraham challenged Namrud. Idols, he said, were only the creation of man, while man was a creation of Allah. Abraham asked Namrud if a mere king could make the sun rise. Namrud was so angry that he threw Abraham into a huge fire, but the angel Gabriel appeared and saved Allah's believer. When the people saw that Abraham was unscathed they began to believe in Allah. Abraham had three sons, Ishmael, Ishaq and Yaqub. Our Prophet is a descendant of Ishmael."

Prayaag was wondering where this rigmarole was leading when Taslimuddin came to the point.

"Now, let me be frank with you. It is not written anywhere in the Quran that every Muslim should be circumcised. But Abraham was circumcised and the Prophet, peace be upon him, said that one of the marks of faith is *khatna,* which is the Arabic for circumcision. We know this from the book written by Imam Bukhari, the great sage and scholar who collected verified stories and sayings of the Prophet. We call circumcision Mussulmani because this is proof that you have become a Muslim; although I must add that Jews are also circumcised. Normally this is done when a boy is between four and seven. But take heart: Abraham was circumcised at the age of eighty and had sons only after that; he was 100 years old when his elder son Ishmael was born. Some scholars say that seventeen of our Prophets were born circumcised, including Adam, Noah, Moses, Solomon, Joseph and Jesus. However, you were not born circumcised, so… Don't worry. The pain will pass quickly."

Maulvi Taslimuddin hurried away, a jump in his step at the prospect of Paradise. The barber, Wahabuddin, was waiting at the door.

Prayaag shuddered with fear. Mai looked away, burnt some rags and kept the hot ash on paper. Wahabuddin lifted Prayaag's lungi, and, using a six-inch stick probed the penis to estimate the extent of the foreskin. Prayaag froze. He had barely touched his own penis in all these years; another man was now in its vicinity. Wahabuddin took out a pair of forceps made from split bamboo, caught the foreskin with it firmly, and Prayaag screamed. The scream had not ended when with a swift circular movement, Wahabuddin sliced the foreskin off with a glistening razor. A little blood began to flow from the cut, but not much. Wahabuddin took the hot ash prepared by Mai and wrapped it around the wound. Then he smiled and waited for his reward.

Prayaag was dazed. It took a while for relief to set in.

His mother shuffled up to him, put his head on her breast, and stroked him to tired sleep. She took out a small copper tube attached to a string, and tied the string around his upper arm. Inside the tube was a piece of paper on which was written a prayer from the Holy Quran, *Ayat al Kursi: There is no God but Allah, the Living, the Self-subsisting, the Eternal. No slumber nor sleep can seize Him. His are all the things in the heavens and on earth. Who can intercede in His presence except as He permits? He knows the past, the present, the future; He cares equally for all; He in His knowledge grades his creations. His throne extends over the heavens and earth; He is the Guardian, He is the Preserver. He is the Highest, He is Supreme.*

The Verse of the Throne would protect her Rahmatullah.

4

PLEASURES

"ANY OLD WOMAN CAN PRAY FIVE TIMES A DAY. TO BE A MAN you have to do something more," said Bauna Sardar to my grandfather.

Abdul Ghani was called Bauna Sardar because he was four feet six inches tall; *bauna* means a dwarf. *Sardar* means chief, and was equally accurate, for he was the lord of the millhands. You could not get a job in Victoria Jute Mill without paying a premium of at least five rupees to Bauna Sardar plus two annas a week until confirmation. He was five years older than Rahmatullah, and already a luminary.

His official designation was head *mistry*, or chief mechanic, but he was not expected to work. He was the link between British managers and Bihari workers, the key that kept communication lines open. He worked both sides of the divide, and was good at it. Anyone who could ensure peace in the spinning department, traditionally the most turbulent part of the factory, was worth whatever money he made. He was silent with Sahibs and taciturn with Biharis. If the managers, prompted by heaven knew what considerations, were in a mood to improve working conditions, he made sure that he first voiced it as a demand so that he could pass it off as a victory. There was for instance the confusion over children in 1882. The Sahibs started to get mild qualms about children aged four and five helping their parents in the batching department, and those of eight and nine at the looms. The workers did not give a damn about children's rights and wrongs; what they saw was their work being done at half the wage. The Sahibs could not afford to alienate adults, so they promised child-reform. Bauna Sardar staged an elaborate demonstration, after which management agreed that every child would need a certificate from inspectors proving that he or she was above seven. It was welcomed as a great working class victory.

Bauna Sardar never stood while speaking to a worker. He either sat on a bench, or lay on his string-bed, the charpoy, his bed at night and settee during the day. No worker was an equal, so he had no friends. He had watched Prayaag emerge very slowly from isolation, convert his tea shop into a canteen and metamorphose into Rahmatullah, generally shortened to Rahmat. Since Rahmat was the one man in Telinipara who had never asked Bauna for a favour, a muted friendship had developed.

Rahmat ignored the light taunt. Bauna continued, "I am only repeating what my elders have told me, and what you should know now that you have become a Mussulman like me. By the way, did it pain terribly when they chopped you up?"

Rahmat ignored the wit. "Can I complete all the obligatory needs of life before I become a heroic believer?" Rahmat responded.

"Like?"

"Getting married, for instance."

"Wonderful, wonderful, wonderful! So you are finally going to use that thing of yours for something other than pissing, are you? Congratulations, congratulations, congratulations! Has it healed?"

"None of your business! Just try and pray seven times a day instead of five for that is your only hope of finding any girl willing to marry *you*."

"Marry? Me? When this township is full of wives whose husbands live at my mercy! God has given me a field of flowers to choose from and a maidan near the river in which to enjoy their fragrance."

"Thank God that none of the workers can hear your lies, otherwise instead of giving you a weekly bribe they might bribe Wahabuddin to castrate you. You can then sing at weddings. That's an idea! I won't be bothered by eunuchs demanding money at my wedding!"

The banter did not stop till Rahmat, a veil of flowers flowing down from his forehead, sat solemnly before Maulvi Taslimuddin for his *nikah*. The wedding procession was short; only five friends accompanied him: Bauna Sardar; Girija Shankar Pande, a lean, gaunt Brahmin who had never shaved in his life, the results of which were showing; Zulfiqar Khan, a Pathan from Kabul who had wandered this far on the back of a fruit truck and built up a moneylending business; and Thakur Bhagwan Singh, the young and handsome chief of the durwans, the doorkeepers posted at the vast gates of Victoria Jute Mill. Girija and Zulfiqar spent more time at Rahmat's canteen each day than they did at home.

Singh was a distant relative from Bihar, and they had got on well once they discovered each other.

Diljan Bibi prepared her son for his wedding by rubbing turmeric paste over his body, then scrubbing it off with pumice stone and buckets of deliciously warm water. He put on a new lungi and shirt, his friends placed the *sehra* of flowers over his head, and while they moved solemnly towards the bride's home, Diljan Bibi flitted over. There was a single touch of extravagance. A large gas lamp had been rented.

The only hitch that evening was Maulvi Taslimuddin's passion for sermons, and since he knew he would not get any attention after the ceremony he launched into one before. *"Bismillah ur Rahman ur Rahim!"* In the name of Allah, the Compassionate, the Merciful! "The Prophet, peace be upon him, has said that a marriage is not legal unless both the man and the woman give their consent. If a woman, out of modesty, prefers silence, then her silence should be taken as consent. All men, he said, should marry, because marriage prevents sin. All marriages should be simple. The Prophet, peace be upon him, says that the best wedding is that which costs the least, and the worst feast is one in which the rich are guests but the poor are not invited – "

Bauna Sardar was trapped into silence by his taciturn public image; Girija Pande and Bhagwan Singh could not interrupt since they were unaware of the niceties of another faith. But Zulfiqar Khan had no inhibitions. "Maulvi, are you going to get on with the marriage, or shall I marry the two myself?"

Rahmat scowled, uncertain whether the interruption had interfered with the sanctity of the occasion. But Zulfiqar knew what he was talking about, and the Maulvi knew that he knew. A marriage in Islam is a civil contract whose validity is confirmed by *ijab*, the declaration of intent, and *qabool*, the acceptance, in front of two male, or one male and two female witnesses. Taslimuddin tumbled off his high horse, a dower was agreed at ten rupees, the groom was asked if he consented, witnesses were sent into the hut to check with Jamila. A cry of *"Qabool!"* rose, and all hands went up towards Allah. A loud *"Ameen!"* closed the prayer. Zulfiqar Khan took out a packet of dried dates, put one into Rahmat's mouth, and threw the rest with a celebratory fling over the heads of guests. Bauna Sardar caught Rahmat in a warm hug, the others embraced him in turns. Diljan Bibi's excited chatter accompanied glasses of sherbet. Dinner was placed before the guests: biryani for Muslims, and dishfuls of savouries for the Hindus purchased from a Hindu sweetmeat shop. It was the best available. Rahmat knew that, because he had paid for every expense. Jamila burst into tears when she left her mother's house, but they dried very quickly.

~

Marriage became a spur. Rahmat devised new ways to increase his income. The tea shop expanded into an eatery, providing *khoraki*, or daily hot meals to regular clients. He found a formula for payment. Wali Mohammad's methods had been emotional. Rahmat was professional. He extended credit to those who could not, or did not, pay for an extra thirty days but charged ten per cent interest on debt. This quietly expanded into moneylending, and since he charged the lowest interests, business grew rapidly. Some Muslims whispered that usury was forbidden, but Rahmat shrugged and said he would sort it with Allah on Judgment Day.

He comforted himself with the thought that, unlike Zulfiqar Khan, he did not stand outside the gate of the mill on payday with a stick in his hand, or hover over the gambling den to encourage a loser with a loan, and charge twenty-five per cent a month. He was honest. Most workers simply had no idea how much they owed, in principal or interest, and became victims of extortion.

His mind was practical, and restless. He saw an opportunity in miserable living conditions. Charity was not high on the agenda of jute mill owners, but even they could see that filth was a source of disease. Epidemics got headlines, but a much bigger problem was the debilitating effect of low fever on production, which nullified the advantage of low wages. The government established a municipality in 1884 to improve sanitation, but it was soon seething with politics.

Rahmat dreamt of building the first double-storied home in Telinipara for himself and, for workers, well-lit, roomy huts in planned rectangles, around a courtyard and at least one latrine for every two plots. He thought he could charge a quarter rupee a month per room, and checked out the investment needed for land and construction. There was no point keeping money at home; there was no question of saving it at the post office, since he did not trust anyone else with his money. The duty of money was to make money.

~

Jamila was happy, childish, obedient to Mai, and a good cook. They had begun to eat egg curry every Saturday, and chicken once a month. With over fifty regular *khoraki* clients and Rs 100 on the money market, he could afford to improve the family diet.

A brainwave lifted his eatery into a new class. Regular pay was adding a perceptible dimension to the quality of workers' lives. They still sent part of their salary to families in Bihar, but were ready to spend more on themselves. Some of the fun budget went to toddy shacks and Ayub Mastan's gambling den. My grandfather offered a more respectable option.

Bengal is famous for the magic of its women and the sweet tooth of its men. The Bihari tooth is different: it prefers the dry laddoo, made from gram, or the twisting, syrupy jalebi, made from near-liquid flour poured in small ringlets through a hole at the bottom of a metal tumbler and fried in boiling oil. Rahmat suspected that class-consciousness kept Bihari workers averse to delicacies like the shandesh created by sophisticated Bengali confectioners. They would not go to Chandernagore to buy Bengali sweets. Why not bring Chandernagore to them?

Surjya Modak's reputation had spread throughout the district. All the zamindars, with their fancy homes along the river at Gondalpara and Chandernagore, patronized him. Some said that he had once been employed in the kitchens of the Viceroy's Palace in Calcutta. Even if that was a rumour, it was a healthy rumour. My grandfather made enquiries, and learnt that Modak was an affable sort of chap who sat late into the night stirring the milk till it had fully curdled, the first step in the complicated process that mixes milk, corn flour, sugar and essence into a shandesh.

He walked one night to Modak's shop, and sat on a bench till all the customers had left. Modak separated whey from water, lifted it from the fire, strained the thick concoction in a clean piece of muslin, wet the cloth, squeezed out excess water and hung the bundle of lacerated milk, called *channa*, on a wire. Then he turned to Rahmat and asked, kindly, if he wanted anything.

Rahmat replied that he wanted to learn. Modak smiled. "You are not a Bengali. How can you make shandesh?"

Later, when they had become friendlier, he would explain many things to Rahmat. Bengalis loved their sweets so much, he said with perfect seriousness, that in their age of glory they had named their capital Gaur, a variation of the word for both delicious date juice and molasses. Gaur disappeared from history when Laksmanasena, the last of a noble dynasty, abandoned the city. He was eating dinner when he heard that eighteen horsemen from the cavalry of the Turk, Mohammad bin Bakhtiyar Khilji, were heading towards his palace. He fled to Dhaka in eastern Bengal, and preserved the ancient arts of Bengal. Making sweets like shandesh was one of the great secrets that had passed through generations within select families. He could think of only one new sweet. A genius from Baghbazar, Calcutta, Nabin Chandra Das, was in his twenties when he created the luscious rossogolla in 1868. Rahmat made a deal. Each Friday night he would come to Modak's shop and purchase a payday-supply at wholesale rates.

The upward mobility of his tea shop was greeted with mild hilarity from friends like Zulfiqar, who thought that Rahmat was going soft in the head. Girija considered any deviation from a jalebi a betrayal of the motherland. But Rahmat knew he had won the battle for taste buds when Zulfiqar paid for the second rossogolla after treating the first one as a brotherly gift. Soon, every worker going to his village made it a point to take a packet of Bengali sweets for his family: it became a signature of pride, a mark of success.

~

The high point of Rahmat's life during those years was a visit to Matiyaburj. Talat Mian had not visited Telinipara for some time. Was he dead? Were his stories true? Did Nawab Wajid Ali Shah of Avadh actually live in Matiyaburj? What did a palace look like? Very early one Saturday he left his shop in the care of two assistants, picked up a bundle containing a new lungi, kurta and leather slippers, and headed towards the station to take the train to Calcutta. With him were Jamila, barely able to contain her excitement, and Mai, who blushed at the thought of going anywhere. Calcutta was dreamland.

Rahmat felt a sharp pang when he learnt the cost of hiring a hackney at the railway station in Calcutta, but there was consolation in the wonder on his wife's half-covered face, and the contentment on his mother's.

The carriage followed the course of the Hooghly river to the south, past warehouses and offices of great industrial and trading firms. The driver pointed out the square and stolid Writer's Building, from where Bengali clerks helped the British govern their massive empire. An artificial tank separated the seat of government from the seat of authority, the magnificent Viceroy's Palace, an English country home planted in the middle of an Indian quagmire. Then came the vast maidan, an expanse of unspoilt green, the river on one side and the glitter of Chowringhee's shops and theatres on the other. They crossed Fort William, headquarters of the British Indian Army on Red Road, and made their way through the crowded docks and slums of Kidderpore and Garden Reach. Beyond it lay Matiyaburj. From the clothes and sprinkle of meatshops, it was apparent that the population was largely Muslim. The true vocation of the place seemed to be tailoring. A bit naively, Rahmat asked a man stitching noisily inside a room, not much more than four feet wide, why there were so many tailors.

"You are a visitor, are you?"

Rahmat nodded.

"This is because we Avadhis taught Bengalis to wear stitched clothes. Before we arrived from Lucknow Hindus would wear a dhoti and Muslims a lungi. The upper garment," he added contemptuously, "was a vest with three holes, one for the head and two for the arms. Women wore saris. We introduced the art of tailoring. Now all the Baboos want their kurtas stitched and embroidered." Rahmat could not argue with such historical certainty. He asked about Talat Mian.

The tailor snapped, "There are ten Talats in every corner out here, and every Muslim is called Mian."

"He wears a beard."

The tailor giggled, "Who has money for a barber these days?"

There was only one other thing my grandfather knew about Talat Mian. "He used to tell us beautiful stories."

"Oh, you mean Talat the *dastan-go.* He was once quite a star in *phabti,* pleasantries, and *zila,* double meaning. His asides were hilarious, and double entendre wicked. He was not too bad at *tuk-bandi,* rhyme competitions in which, as you know, you can get as coarse as you like. But he has become bitter these days, so no one gives him any money. He only abuses the crazy Wajid Ali Shah now."

"That's the one!"

Talat Mian was dozing on a charpoy in the warm shade of a tree, in faded lungi and torn vest, unperturbed by flies flitting across his back. Diljan Bibi and Jamila waited on the other side of the tree, their faces turned away, while Rahmat prodded Talat Mian awake. He looked up and scowled. It took him a while to connect, and then his face flushed with pleasure. "You mean to say that you have come all this way just to see me?" He had the unambiguous excitement of a man with nothing to do.

"Yes," Rahmat said, and gave him the bundle of clothes and sandals he had brought as a gift.

Talat Mian's joy soared, and landed on the edge of uncertainty. He did not have enough money to be hospitable. The laws of courtesy were, however, supreme. "You must come to my humble home."

Rahmat reassured him immediately. "You are most gracious, and it would be an honour. But my mother insisted on cooking food for you; she knows how much you enjoy her cooking," he lied. "We would be honoured if we could share what little we have with you."

Talat Mian's relief was unsentimental. The women went to meet his wife, and served the men before they ate themselves. After lunch, Talat Mian repaid his guest in the only way he knew, with delicious stories about the fallen dynasty.

"Did I tell you about the Nawab of Avadh who thought he was a Roman emperor? He married a white Italian woman and ordered tiger fights because he had heard Romans liked lion-fights. His queen lived in a palace called Vilayati Bagh, European Garden. He gave all his wealth to the British as a loan; in return they called him a king! What he really enjoyed was inventing new ways of sleeping with women. He became a lesbian!"

Rahmat did now know what a lesbian was, but he was too fascinated by his first taste of pornography to interrupt.

"He dressed like a woman in his harem, and that is only the start of the story. Every so often he would get it into his head that he was pregnant, and a great charade would begin, ending only when, after a series of contortions, he delivered an imaginary child. He once claimed that he was giving birth to an imam! Can you imagine such heresy? He was so busy producing fake imams, he had no time to govern. Fortunately, he was poisoned by well-meaning friends.

"Wajid Ali Shah is his grandson, now loitering in Matiyaburj. When he was king, our Wajid attacked anything in pyjamas: servants, courtesans, female palanquin-bearers who were hired to lift up his huge frame by day and his thirsty cock by night. Harlots and singing girls were the jewels of his court. He had no time for his people. And so the British took over – in the name of law and order, naturally! They only act in the name of law and order; their orders become the law! It was February, in the year before the Patriotic War of 1857. A general called Outram delivered a letter to Wajid Ali Shah saying that his kingdom was now part of the British empire. That's it. They didn't even have the courtesy to conquer our King of Kings with a proper army. Wajid Ali Shah began to cry. The British brought him to Calcutta, and locked him up in their fort. There was really no need. A coward creates his own prisons. His mother, Nawab Hazrat Mahal, and his son, Birjis Qadar, were braver than him: they deserved the Mahi Maratib, the Order of the Fish, the highest Mughal honour for bravery, for the courage they showed in the war of 1857, when we Indians threw the British out of Lucknow and placed ten-year-old Birjis on the throne. Alas, the infidels took the city back in 1858 with the help of Punjabis and short men from the Himalayas. Birjis Qadar's life was saved by a mullah from Faizabad called Shah Sahib. He had the *junoon* of a believer when he scattered the infidels in 1857. But success led to the sin of arrogance. Since he was a Sunni, he misbehaved with us Shias. Whenever Muslims are divided, the infidels win. Shah Sahib engaged the enemy long enough to enable Birjis Qadar and Hazrat Mahal to escape. He was caught and killed by the Raja of Puwain at Pilibhit, who sent his head to the British to claim a fabulous reward.

"Strangely, Wajid Shah has become very devout after his banishment to Matiyaburj. This must be due to old age, when prayer becomes a sort of insurance policy. Faith has not stopped his debauchery; but he now insists on marrying all his women. If a girl who has not reached her puberty catches his fancy he marries her and then sends her off to await her turn for the royal consummation. We Shias have this system of *muta*, or pleasure marriage: we can marry at night and divorce in the morning. That is very useful for our king. He once married a water carrier and gave her the grand title of Nawab Aab Rasan Begum, or Her Highness the Water-Giver. A young sweeper woman became Nawab Musafa Begum, the Queen of Cleanliness.

"The British gave him two houses, but of course that could never be enough. We starve; he builds more palaces: Sultan Khana, Asad Manzil, Qasr ul Baiza, Gosha-e-Sultani, Shahenshah Manzil – what a name! Emperor's Palace, when the

King has become a beggar! Then there's Murassa Manzil, for his consort; Asad Manzil, Shah Manzil, Nur Manzil, Tafrih Baksh – yes, the name means what it says, this was a special house for pleasure. This is not Telinipara, Master Rahmat! This is Matiyaburj, the Paradise of exiles! You will find more dancers and cooks in Matiyaburj than anywhere else in India."

The muted roll of a drum reached them. "That," said Talat Mian, "is the *naubat* (drum) of Sultan Khana. This is how we mark time: the day is divided into eight *pahars* (parts), four at night and four during sunlight, and each part is divided into eight *gharis*. One of these days," he pointed our wryly, "they will discover that sensible people use clocks, but not in this generation."

In the afternoon, Talat Mian took his guests to the extraordinary zoo that Wajid Ali Shah had created on the parks of Nur Mahal, said to contain the most fabulous collection of birds and animals in the world. Talat Mian was as blasé as any resident of Eden; but Rahmat was astounded by such wonders.

There were hundreds of buck, spotted deer and antelopes, turkey, peacocks. In the centre a large water body became the habitat of cranes, geese, herons, flamingoes and a stimulating variety of exotic birds that hopped from pool to tree. Magnificent cats growled for space in the tiger cages. Monkeys teased the cats from the safety of mesh-and-wood cages, and amused visitors with their antics. Small ponds were heavy with fish that had become fearless enough to leap across the top of the water to catch crumbs. Rahmat stood hypnotized before the Hill of Snakes: a circular mound of earth raised around a pit with slippery sides, in which lay thousands of large and small snakes like untouched spaghetti. He swayed and thought he would fall.

Rahmat felt a timid hand on his back, steadying him. It was the first time Jamila had reached out to touch him.

All the way to Telinipara, on the hackney, the train, and then the rickshaw, he had just one thought, one emerging passion. When Jamila gave him a son, his child would live like a prince.

5

DREAD

IT WAS THE SORT OF YEAR THAT INTIMIDATES ASTROLOGERS: first came the miracle, then catastrophe, and finally dread.

The evening had settled into silence, broken only by the faint murmur of muted conversation and the chatter of crickets that filled the grass and flickered through the clumps of trees on the expanse between the huts and the river. Girija Maharaj made a minor ceremony of his first, deep drag on the short, stemless hookah called a chillum: the opium burned sweetly inside the tobacco. Fumes seeped down through his lungs even as their glow spiralled ever so slowly up towards the imagination. Bauna Sardar took an occasional drag, generally cloaking guilt with humour, but today he was pensive. That was unusual.

"The English are bringing bottled fire to the mill," he said.

"What is that?" asked Thakur Bhagwan Singh.

"It is a magic fire that gives light but neither dances nor burns. The fire is still. Its white glow turns night into day. It lives on the edge of an iron thread through which it travels for miles and miles without being seen."

"You and your stories."

Bauna Sardar shrugged, and Girija Maharaj stirred.

"Does the Englishman think he can challenge Agni, our preserver, the god of fire?" asked Girija Maharaj.

"This is the age of the white man's gods, my friend," replied Bauna Sardar.

"And we have to accept it? Do the English understand Hindu gods? Do they know the wrath of Agni, born from the mouth of the creator Prajapati, who bears the sacrifices of Brahmins to the lords of heaven; Agni, riding on a ram, with red eyes, two faces, three legs, seven arms; Agni the imperishable, the sun in the sky, lightning in the air, fire on the earth, and heat in the belly!"

"They think Hindus and Muslims believe in nonsense, while their religion builds factories and invents cold fire."

"Fools," said Girija Maharaj softly, and took another deep drag. "They do not know the power of Agni. A great war broke out in the heavens between gods and demons. The demons, led by Taraka, won. The gods, in a panic, rushed to the abode of the mighty Shiva in the Himalayas. Alas, they had chosen quite the wrong moment. Shiva was making love to his wife Parvati when they knocked on his door. Shiva's seed fell to the ground. Parvati's anger shook the Himalayas. The terrified gods turned to Agni. Agni took the form of a dove and ate up the seed of Shiva. Parvati, livid, cursed his soul to eternal torture, which is why flames always dance in pain."

"You tell too many stories, Brahmin, particularly when you smoke," responded Bauna Sardar, taking another puff himself.

Rahmat was lost in thought: tobacco had given him an idea. There was money to be made from addiction.

"You dare doubt the word of a Brahmin?" Girija Maharaj was not incensed, merely incredulous. He stared at Bauna Sardar. "Do you know how a yawn was created? During the great war in the heavens, Vritra the demon challenged Indra, king of the gods, to individual combat, pinned him down, picked him up, opened his mouth – and swallowed the king of gods! A clever Brahmin found the solution. He created a yawn. Vritra yawned, and Indra, seeing his chance, jumped out of the demon's mouth and ran to safety. What have you swallowed Bauna, that you are yawning? Go home!"

On the evening that the first electric bulb was lit in Victoria Jute Mill, the three friends went to witness the white man's miracle. Thakur Bhagwan Singh welcomed them proudly at the gate. Bauna Sardar, on the side of the English and progress, looked smug. As he happily told his friends, electricity meant night shifts and night shifts meant fun. Rahmat added this luminous magic lantern to the list of fantasies that would decorate his double-storied home when he built one.

Girija Maharaj acknowledged the beginning of yet another age in the cycles of time, but insisted that it would begin in sorrow. When the rains failed in 1896 and 1897, he pointed out that the curse of Agni had begun. He warned his friends to await the assault of the dog of Yama, the god of death; the dog that had four eyes, wide nostrils and belched disease.

The terrible plague that killed thousands and emptied Bombay, hit Calcutta in the summer of 1898. Maulvi Taslimuddin heard the news on the mosque network and passed it on in a whisper. It stood to reason that only a Sahib could have brought the plague from Bombay to Calcutta. No rat could travel for thousands of miles, could it? No Indian could afford such a long journey, could he? The British, concluded Taslimuddin, had started the plague to kill Muslims. He had evidence.

Sheikh Delu, a syce in the stables of Cook and Company in Calcutta, had written a pamphlet that explained why. *"The Government is determined to kill every Mussulman it can because the Russians are coming to India. Russians are a friend of Turkey, and are coming with the permission of the Caliph. The English are afraid that if they reach India all the Muslims will rally around the standard of the friends of the Caliph."* The advance of the Russians, it said, had been reported in nationalist papers like the *Amrita Bazar Patrika* and blacked out by pro-British papers like the *Statesman*.

Hindus were not safe either, the pamphlet continued; Maulvi Taslimuddin glanced at Girija Maharaj as he read on. Hindus were being forced to inhale a deadly gas or given a lethal injection in the so-called medical camps. Bodies were dumped beside one another with no consideration for caste, in the carts which transported the dead. British soldiers entered Hindu homes and took away wives and daughters – to be inoculated, they said, but could anyone trust them? In Bhawanipore one European had actually dared to enter the home of a Brahmin. He would have been lynched if he had not taken out a revolver and killed two innocent men. The British kept the real plague antidote only for themselves. Sheikh Delu urged Indians to beat up Sahibs and rape their wives: only then would this arrogant race remove their sola hats, fall at the feet of Indians, and beg for mercy.

Individual stories built upon collective anguish. A worker picked up courage and confronted Bauna Sardar. A sweeper had heard a Memsahib singing a song to celebrate the death of Muslims. Twice during that song she made a sneezing sound, *A-tishoo! A-tishoo!* It was common knowledge that a sneeze was the death rattle of a plague victim.

Zulfiqar Khan claimed he had personal information from relatives in Afghanistan that the Russians had reached Herat. The next city to fall would be Kabul, opening the road to Delhi via the Khyber Pass. Millions of Muslims would become mujahideen and join the jihad against the British.

Rahmat tried to reason with Zulfiqar Khan. "Do you really believe what you are saying?" he argued. "You think the British have no guns? Delhi is not the capital of the British; their capital is Calcutta. The Russians will have to capture Calcutta. If Muslims support the Russians, might there not be a reaction? What if the Hindus join the British?"

Zulfiqar Khan had the answers. "What do you know of world politics? Just because you once went to Matiyaburj you think you know how kings behave? Nawabs have become beggars and their women are singing in whorehouses. The people of the mosque are the only ones who know the truth about the modern world; they have secret networks and dervishes who relay information from Dhaka to Peshawar." Rahmat was silenced.

I am writing this story comfortably ensconced on the lap of hindsight. I therefore know the explanations: in the absence of medical relief, the small, nerve-wracked British community at

Victoria Jute Mill sought comfort in grandmothers' remedies. Cigarettes were ordered in bulk when someone helpfully remarked that Etonians were flogged during the Great Plague of 1665 if they refused to smoke: tobacco was considered an antidote. Nursery rhymes were talismans. *Ring around the rosies* was the circle of red spots around the buboes; *A pocket full of posies* were flowers meant to freshen the air; *A-tishoo,* the sneeze, was the deadly symptom, and *We all fall down* meant precisely what it said. That was the *A-tishoo* heard by the sweeper. There was no Russian army in Afghanistan, and anti-British fever was only a symptom of recurrent Muslim anger at the loss of the Mughal crown after defeat in the war of 1857, when the last Mughal, the melancholic poet-emperor Bahadur Shah Zafar, was deposed.

The plague in Bombay and Calcutta, however, was real enough. It took nearly a million Indian lives over a decade before it was brought under control. Some imperial voices, notably that of journalist-author Rudyard Kipling, blamed the newly-empowered chatterbox Indian commissioners on municipal boards. The British government did its best, which included hiring the services of the son of a Jewish schoolmaster from Odessa.

Vladimir Aronovich Khavkin was born in 1879 and studied physics, mathematics and zoology at the Odessa Malorossiysky University, where he came in touch with Elie Metchnikoff, the microbiologist who would win a Nobel Prize. Khavkin was denied a teaching position at the Zoological Museum in Odessa because he refused to convert to Christianity. He shifted to Switzerland in 1888, and Paris in 1889 where he joined Louis

Pasteur. In July 1892 he tested a cholera inoculation he had discovered on the ultimate guinea pig, himself. This brought him to the attention of India. He was invited to stop the virulent cholera epidemic in Calcutta in 1893. He did. Somewhere along the way he changed his name to Waldemar Mordecai Haffkine. When plague broke out in Bombay, he was sought again. He returned in October 1896. In February 1897 he successfully tried a vaccine based on dead bacteria on criminals lodged in Bombay's Byculla jail. It was this vaccine that reached Telinipara in April 1898.

The man who carried that vaccine was an Austrian with a missionary heart and a martial temperament, Dr Johann Laing. He was the doctor involved in the incident at the Brahmin's home in Bhawanipore, and had no regrets about shooting two hysterical natives. He came to calm British nerves in Victoria and other nearby jute mills, and then sent word through Bauna Sardar that he would be happy to offer the same inoculation to workers.

But my grandfather was not blessed by hindsight, and his vision, like that of others, was blurred by fear and sharpened by suspicion. Zulfiqar Khan, who now claimed that he was in direct touch with Sheikh Delu, proclaimed that there were three kinds of serum. The first one saved lives and was administered to the white people. The second, meant for Bengali babus, led to high fever that might or might not be fatal. The third killed, and was reserved for Muslims. What happened inside the jute mill therefore was no indication of what would happen outside. He would rather leave his fate to Allah than to an infidel. It was a persuasive argument.

Rahmat observed such anxiety in habitual silence. He

recognized the source of the problem, filth. A worker's hut was a dark, airless, unventilated square box, perhaps nine feet by nine, the walls mud, the roof tiled and tilted. After the cholera epidemics, a makeshift latrine had been added to a corner of some compounds, serviced by untouchables who removed the waste in large mud bowls. Children defecated where they wanted. Irregular drains were haunts of flies. Seven out of ten babies died in childbirth, and every mother knew that each pregnancy was also a notice of her death, for nothing was certain in childbirth. The worker had no roots in Telinipara, for he went to Bihar to die. His possessions were minimal. A charpoy to sleep on; a thin blanket, the chadar, to cover with; a metal pot, the lota, for water. Rahmat had nowhere to go, so he was determined to make Telinipara a place which a community could call home.

He felt deeply about cleanliness. He wanted to remove filth with his own hands. His mother was wiser. Plague invoked passions, Mai told her son, and if it became known that he had done a sweeper's work, the clientele at his hotel would disappear. There was already competition from Narayan Teli. Rahmat tried a second argument: Jamila had lost two children already, one in childbirth and the other within the first week, to infection. Both were girls, but supposing one had been a boy? It was as strong as an argument could get, and yet it did not get very far. To clean filth would make him unclean.

Rahmat decided that he would take Dr Laing's injection. Mai, predictably, wept copiously when informed. Jamila, stoically, said that she would do exactly what her husband did, whatever the consequences.

Dr Laing walked down from the jute mill. The train of children behind him soon included adults. Word had spread about Rahmat's stupidity. Men and women, standing or sitting on their haunches, filled the courtyard outside his hut, and Dr Laing had to push his way through. Rahmat's close friends, uncertain and apprehensive, were sitting on the charpoy that had been brought out of the room. The silence was broken by the bustle of Maulvi Taslimuddin, who rebuked Rahmat for being naïve: he was a convert, a new Mussulman, and did not know what the British had done to Muslims after 1857. They had turned Shah Jehan's glorious mosque, the Jama Masjid of Delhi into a stable for their horses, sold the Fatehpuri mosque to a Hindu, Lala Chuni Mal, and turned the Zinat mosque into a bakery. How could Rahmat trust such people?

Dr Laing sensed the Maulvi's argument, and Taslimuddin withered beneath his look. The doctor opened a large bag, wiped a syringe with cotton dipped in antiseptic, rubbed a patch of Rahmat's left arm with fluff, drew vaccine into his syringe from a small glass bottle with a red rubber cap rimmed in tin foil, and plunged the needle in. Murmurs broke out, punctuated by a gasp or two.

Dr Laing explained in broken Hindustani that he was leaving his bag with the vaccine behind to prove that the medicine would not be changed. In two hours everyone would know whether Rahmat was alive or not. He hoped that when he returned others would follow Rahmat's brave example.

Zulfiqar Khan broke the tension. "Okay. Enough! If Rahmat is the first, I will be the second. Now. Not two hours later."

Dr Laing smiled indulgently and left. Mai began to wail. If

the doctor had been so confident, why hadn't he given an injection to Zulfiqar as well? Jamila could not restrain herself, and the women, who rarely missed a chance to cry collectively, were soon in mass mourning. My grandfather had never received an injection before. He waited for after-effects. Nothing happened. He told Mai to stop crying.

He was not yet thirty, but after his example had been emulated eagerly they gave him the title of "sheikh" or leader. Maulvi Taslimuddin accorded the honour formally during the *khutba,* or sermon before Friday prayers. He congratulated Sheikh Rahmatullah for being a true jihadi for he had offered his life in the cause of the Greater Jihad, *Jihad-e-Akbari,* the struggle to cleanse oneself of ignorance. The other jihad, of battles and war, was only the *Jihad-e-Asghari,* the Lesser Jihad, he explained. Old Muslims, Taslimuddin noted wryly, had been taught a lesson in true faith by a new one.

Girija Maharaj's pessimism abated but persisted. Only a quarter of the year had passed, he warned; the almanac was crowded with inauspicious days.

~

They thought that Talat Mian had come with another bag of dramatic stories when he turned up suddenly, a little before the festival of Bakr' Id, but he had only one to tell. He looked frail, and his smile had thinned. Rahmat told Jamila to move in with Mai so that a charpoy could be laid out for Talat Mian in their room. He could not sleep in the open for April showers had broken, bathed the air and washed the leaves of the numerous neem, mango, guava, lichi and tamarind trees till they glistened with new life.

Talat Mian slept well and welcomed the morning with a nourishing breakfast of paratha (baked in ghee by Mai now that a guest had given her an excuse which her abstemious son could not deny), pickle, curd and eggs with large orange eyes fried in a brass cup teetering on the edge of a long handle. Properly fed, he sat back on a cushion to talk. His story, he began enigmatically, was not about the past but the future. He came with bad news. The past was unhappy, but the future was ominous. He had heard Telinipara being mentioned when Rishra was being discussed in a mosque at Matiyaburj.

They understood at once what he was talking about.

The trouble had begun two years before, during the Bakr' Id of 1896, when some Muslims in Rishra, a jute colony some ten miles south of Telinipara, began to insist that their religion demanded cow slaughter. Hindus were equally vehement that they would protect the holy cow. On the eve of Bakr' Id police discovered a letter written by the imam of the Rishra mosque, Nazir Mian, to a Calcutta businessman, Haji Muhammad Zakaria, seeking the latter's help against "Hindu obstruction". It was an appeal for toughs. Nazir Mian was arrested.

Nazir Mian was persistent. The following year he sent a formal petition to the government for permission to sacrifice a cow during Bakr' Id. The subdivisional officer, John Craven, decided to be a Solomon. He permitted one cow to be killed, but in the loneliness of the Muslim burial ground, unseen by any Hindu.

Talat Mian had heard that this year Haji Zakaria wanted to help Telinipara's Muslims in their "struggle for self-respect" by sacrificing a cow on Bakr' Id.

"You know why we Muslims sacrifice an animal on this day, don't you?" asked Talat Mian. Girija Maharaj and Thakur Bhagwan Singh, being Hindus, did not know; neither did Rahmat; and Bauna Sardar had only a vague idea.

"It's a great story. The Prophet Abraham is father of Jews, Christians and Muslims. His very loving and devoted wife, Saira, had only one drawback. She could not bear sons. She nobly offered her Ethiopian slave, Hajr, as a second wife to Abraham. Ethiopian genes were clearly more fertile, and within no time at all Hajr gave birth to Ishmael. Abraham was delighted; unfortunately, Saira was not. Does a wife persuade or order? Anyway, she urged Abraham to banish Hajr and Ishmael. Being a prophet, Abraham did nothing without consulting God, even when he knew that he had to listen to his wife. And so it was that the Angel Gabriel led Hajr and infant to a desolate spot in the Arabian desert. Hajr wept and pleaded, but Abraham had his alibi... God.

"They almost died of thirst and hunger before the good Angel Gabriel returned. Gabriel touched the sand, and water began to gush out. Thus appeared the spring called Zamzam, around which grew up the city that is known as Mecca, where Abraham and Ishmael built the Kaaba. The water of Zamzam, Gabriel said, would flow till the day of judgment. And so it does. Every Haji still brings back water from the spring of Zamzam. I wish the story could have ended here, but there is one more twist.

"Once a year Abraham would visit Mecca, travelling on the heavenly horse, called Barraq, which moves at the speed of lightning. On one of those visits, Allah asked Abraham for proof of his faith – by sacrificing his beloved son. Tough, but there it was. Abraham wavered for three days, but on the fourth he told Ishmael to bring a cord and a knife, and go with him to the mountain to collect some wood. At a place called Shab he revealed his intent. Calmly, Ishmael replied that Allah's command was above all other considerations. Abraham placed the sharp knife to his son's throat, but, strangely, it would not cut. And then a voice was heard saying that Allah was pleased by such faith, and Abraham should release Ishmael and sacrifice whatever animal he saw behind him. This animal turned out to be a large ram, which had pastured in the gardens of Paradise for forty years. Abraham uttered the great cry, the *takbir: Allah-o-Akbar!* (Allah is Great!), and sacrificed the sacred ram at a place called Mina. That is why each year at Bakr' Id, the time of Haj to Kaaba, we Muslims sacrifice an animal to Allah."

"All this is very good," noted Girija Maharaj drily, "but where does the cow come in?"

Talat Mian shrugged, "It doesn't."

"Then why do you Muslims insist on killing a cow? Kill all the goats and rams you like, we Hindus will have no objection."

Talat Mian was phlegmatic. "You are right. There were no cows in that desert. They either sacrificed rams or camels. Muslims began to kill cows only when beef-eaters converted..."

"Then why do Muslims create so much trouble now?"

"The answer is obvious," said Talat Mian. "Not because they want to worship Allah, but because they want to create trouble."

"Bauna," Rahmat asked his friend sharply, "you keep your ears to the ground. Is anything happening?"

"Something has happened. That young man who can never resist insolence, Mangu Qasai, has opened a butcher's shop near the mosque. I heard talk that he was going to sell beef – not to us here, but to the Sahibs in the mill. He argued that the Sahibs bought their beef from Chandernagore, and it made better sense for them to buy it outside their gates. I thought that a reasonable explanation. But…"

Mangu Qasai, of medium height, had curly hair, broad biceps and a thin moustache that curved like scimitars from either side of the nostril. Four days before Bakr' Id, while drinking tea in a shop outside the mosque, he told anyone who would listen that he did not have money to buy a goat or a ram, but he had a cow, and he would sacrifice this cow. He added that if a butcher, who killed animals every day, did not sacrifice one on Bakr' Id, there would be, literally, hell to pay.

My grandfather felt burdened by the trust that the illiterate, uncertain community had placed in him. He was their sheikh. Bakr' Id was just three days away, long enough to incite hatred, and insufficient to find answers. There had never been any trouble between Hindus and Muslims here; there would inevitably be a first time.

Talat Mian had seen a motley crowd around an old man sitting under some trees. Was it what he thought it was?

"Oh," replied Bauna Sardar, "you are talking about that old madman. He is even called that, Burha Deewana. He turned up some months ago from nowhere. Or somewhere. He calls himself a fakir, a dervish. There is no shortage of holy men using God to justify their laziness."

"I don't know… such chaps can be useful," answered Talat

Mian. "You, my friends, are now the new nawabs of Telinipara. That holy man belongs to the poor. I saw men and women, Hindus and Muslims, at his feet. We should talk to him."

Talat Mian was firm. "He will know what is going on. He might even know what to do."

6

DERVISH

"I AM THE COOK AT THE FEAST OF MUHAMMAD'S POVERTY," HE said, and Rahmat was satisfied that the mystic was not a fraud. "Call me a dervish, a beggar who goes from *dar* to *dar*, door to door; or call me a *goshanishin*, one who disappears from sight, for I am both. I am a sufi! The seeds of my faith were sown in the time of Adam, took root in the age of Noah, flowered under the care of Abraham, bore fruit in the garden of Moses, reached maturity in the spirit of Jesus, and became pure in the glow of the purest of them all, Muhammad. There are four kinds of believers: the wise, who are obedient; the penitent, who fear the fires of hell; the devout, who seek heaven; and the ecstatic, who want only the love of Allah! Only poverty is real, all else is accident. My master would ask his companions, 'Is there any food in the house?' If the answer was no, he would thank Allah. If the answer was yes, he would get perturbed and say, 'The smell of wealth is coming from this house'."

Professionally suspicious of anyone else's claims, Talat Mian asked, "Who was your master?"

"My master died seven centuries ago in the Turkish city of Konya, at the age of sixty-six, just after he completed writing the epic of the age, his *Mathnawi*," the old man answered with a slight smile. "His name was Maulana Jalal al-Din Rumi." He addressed the urbane doubt in Talat Mian's eyes. "He was born in Balkh, Afghanistan, in the seventh year of the thirteenth century by the English calendar. When he was seven, the savage Mongol Changez Khan descended on their homes and his family fled to Turkey: hence the title Rumi, which means 'of Rome', for Turkey at the time was a Christian country known as the Eastern Rome Empire. His father Bahaeddin Walad, a learned sheikh, took his son on a pilgrimage to Mecca when Rumi was only twelve. There they met the mystic-poet Sheikh Farid al-Din Attar. When Sheikh Farid saw father and son, he remarked, 'Here comes the sea followed by the ocean'. The venerable Sheikh Farid blessed my master, and gave him the *Book of Secrets*. When he was thirty-seven Rumi turned from scholar to divine, and joined the Chishti sect of sufis. In a sufi's freedom he found poetry. I, a small ring at the end of a long chain, became one of the millions who have been intoxicated by that wine.

"My spiritual lord is Syed Muin al-din Hasan al-Husain al-Sijzi Chishti, born in Ispahan in the first half of the twelfth century. He was nearly fifty years old when he travelled to Mecca, where, in a dream, God commanded him to show the people of Hindustan the way, the *tariqa*. And so, resplendent in the cloak of poverty, he journeyed from Mecca to Baghdad and then to Delhi, sleeping in cemeteries along the way. He reached Delhi in the reign of Maharaja Prithviraj, one year before the armies of the

Afghan, Mohammad Ghori, defeated the Rajput king. Rajas and sultans play games of war. Muinuddin was the emperor of hearts; his titles, *Nabi al-Hind,* and *Aftab-i-mulk-i-Hind,* the messenger and radiance of India, were given by the people. He is *Gharib Nawaz,* Lord of the Poor: a glance from his hidden eye could reform a sinner. Each time he recited the whole Quran from memory a voice told him, 'O Muinuddin, your recitation has been accepted!' He was a true fakir, free from the three addictions: eating, drinking, sleeping. He fasted during the day and prayed at night. At sunset he broke his fast with one cake of bread dipped in water. His only possession was a patched robe, for he personally mended every tear; but that tattered robe was more magnificent than Joseph's coat. Whatever he received he distributed among the poor. A dervish, he said, is one who never disappoints anyone in need. This is the highest form of worship. A king of a realm dies and is forgotten; a king of the heart rules beyond his grave. Muinuddin was ninety-four when he left this world. His shrine, in Ajmer, in the deserts of Rajasthan, is a place of pilgrimage for Hindu and Muslim, an altar where the prayers of the poor are answered."

Talat Mian retreated, and Rahmatullah found himself drawn towards a new space opening up before him.

"To answer your next question before you have asked it." The old man's eyes sparkled with fun as Talat Mian winced. "I have come to Telinipara because it is anonymous. A forgotten spot is closer to God, and therefore an excellent place to die.

"This grotto is my last halting point on the journey towards Allah. The Quran says, 'We are all returning'. My turn has come, and I pray to Allah each day that He may take me back to His heart, to absorb me within Himself. I have come here to seek the liberation of my soul from this cage called the body, to seek annihilation in Allah." His eyes were now nearly closed, a smile suffused his light-brown face marked by a fading beard, his head sank on to his right shoulder, and he sat on legs bent back from the knees. He wore a rough woollen robe and frayed rubber sandals. "But you did not come to hear me talk about myself. You came with a problem."

"Yes."

"Khwaja Muinuddin Chishti used to say, 'Mere talk of peace will not bring you peace'."

"How did you..." began Talat Mian, and then shrugged. "Well, at least we've come to the right man."

The old man heard them out patiently.

"There is no evil more malignant than a poisoned heart," he sighed. "God does not divide men. Men divide God. God is one: alone, eternal, indivisible. The Jews call Allah Elohim, the Hindus know Him as Brahma. Let men kill each other over wealth, women, property, prejudice and power, but not over God. Bakr' Id is a day when your heart must open its door to others. Who dares to shut hearts with hate! Sufi Hamiduddin of Nagaur, a companion of Muinuddin, ordered his devotees to bring him only vegetarian food out of consideration for his Hindu followers."

"Well, Mangu Qasai is no sufi, I can tell you that," remarked Bauna Sardar. "We need a solution, Burha Deewana, not a sermon."

"Well, in that case, I must first go and pray, isn't it?" His eyes twinkled as he added, "I've got the women on my side already; now I've got to get God."

He answered the scepticism. "Have faith in God. When you are ill, you show faith in the doctor; why can't you have faith in the One who created the doctor?" He chuckled, and added, "Allah will never accept a cow that was bought for the English!"

The chuckles were beginning to irritate Talat Mian.

Burha Deewana assuaged him. "The butcher thinks he is a true believer. Show him Verse 32 of the fifth *Sura* of the Holy Quran, where Allah condemns Cain for the murder of his brother Abel and forbids Muslims from taking another life. The Quran says that to kill one person is akin to killing the whole community, and to save one person from death is like saving the whole community. Bauna, give this warning to Mangu Qasai: 'When you play with mice, the cat will find you'."

The old man paused. "Our problem is not the butcher. A butcher kills helpless animals; it is a coward's calling. Ask a butcher to face a man who can fight back, and his knife will tremble like unset pudding. But beware of Taslimuddin, for a Maulvi's support can give legitimacy to mischief. Rahmatullah, remind Taslimuddin that Prophet Muhammad once said, three kinds of people hurt faith: a scholar who is bad-tempered, a leader who is a tyrant, and a theologian who is ignorant. Our biggest problem is Ayub Mastan. The Maulvi might create tension. Mastan will draw blood."

They knew Mastan: middle-aged, of medium height, with curly hair and the build of a former wrestler, flesh sagging over the fold of the lungi around the waist; pugnacious; steel eyes on a pockmarked face; owner of a toddy shop that opened each evening at sunset and turned into a gambling den on payday.

"Zulfiqar Khan," the dervish ordered, "tell Mastan: 'An axe does not care how much it wounds the branches, but it never hurts the leaves'."

Zulfiqar Khan, always practical, asked, "We can tell them both, but will they understand?"

"They will, they will. Each to his own level..." The chuckle resumed. "Jesus was intoxicated by the spirit of God; Jesus' donkey got drunk on barley!"

He disappeared into his cave, and they soon heard the regular, rhythmic beat of *dhikr jali:* literally, the remembrance of God. Remembrance begins with repetition. Voice merges into heart. The dervish chants, the chant takes over the dervish, and then God chants through His worshipper. The old man turned west towards Mecca, sat in the posture of prayer, and breathed the word "Allah" drawing the sound first from the left of his throat. He next bent his head to his left knee, and said "Allah", a little louder than before; repeated the sequence on the right side, and continued alternately, left and then right. He straightened, closed his eyes, and uttered *La,* raising the sound from his navel to the left shoulder; he drew *ilaha* from his head towards the mouth, and then with a final burst of energy shouted *il-Allah-hu!* Each stage of the process, called *zarb,* was recited hundreds of times late into the night while in his consciousness swirled verses from the Quran about Allah: *He is the First and the Last, the*

Evident and the Hidden, He who has full knowledge of all things... He is with you wherever you may be... [Says Allah] We are nearer to man than his jugular vein... To Allah belong east and west, wheresoever you turn there is the face of Allah... All that is on earth will perish, but there will be forever the face of thy Lord, full of Majesty, Bounty and Honour...

"Either this man is the purest of gems or the biggest fraud I have seen, and I have seen a few frauds in my time," sighed Talat Mian after they left.

"We will find out soon enough," said Bhagwan Singh.

Girija Maharaj and my grandfather were entranced.

~

They stayed up late that night listening to stories about the old man from his disciple and companion of twenty years, Fareed Jang. Fareed was proud of his sole indulgence, his beard, which Wahabuddin groomed, free, every week. He was content to care over the limited needs of the old man. He enjoyed the unexpected attention he was now getting from the powers of Telinipara.

"I met Burha Deewana when he was already old. His face, his bearing, his sharp mind, nothing has changed in the two decades I have known him – except that his smile has become younger! Do not underestimate him just because you discovered him in Telinipara. I suppose you think that only a beggar or a criminal on the run from the law would come to this wretched place. Do not be fooled by his simple ways. He is a learned man. He learnt Islamic law and Persian in Delhi Madrasa from the son of the great sage, Shah Waliullah. He is a Rumi scholar, an expert in the six books of the *Mathnawi* and the quatrains of his *Diwan*. He is fluent in Persian. He is truly wise, for he never puts his learning on display. He only wants to change men, not the world."

That, explained Fareed, is the nature of the Chishti order: they have no structured organization, no political programme, no declared objective. They show no particular desire to convert non-believers, although their personal example often leads to conversions. They give spiritual guidance only if asked. They are fearless: they glory in the fate of their hero, Sarmad, who cried out to his executioner: "Come, come! I recognize you, no matter which form you adopt!"

"A dervish," said Fareed, "starts as *talib* (seeker, student), moves to *salik* (one who begins to walk on the spiritual path); reaches *abudiyat* (happy slavery to Allah); graduates to *arif* (the knower); aspires towards *marifat* (knowledge of God), and only then may he find the joy of being a *wali* (one near to Allah). Only a *wali* can attain *jazb* (divine attraction) and reach the stage of *hol* (divine ecstasy) as he strives for his *maqam* (goal); and only through true *ishtiaq* (ardour) can *farq* (separation) give way to *jama* (union), and the last stage, *sakinat* (serenity). Burha Deewana is serene."

~

The rustle of workers getting ready for the first shift in the pre-dawn darkness broke the enchantment. Ghosts seemed to slink between the irregular lines of workers heading for the factory that morning. Chatter was subdued, as if an unguarded remark might scrape unrevealed wounds. A shiver erupted when a man was seen running, a blur against an awakening horizon.

It was Wahabuddin. A barber has composite functions in a small community, but flitting between huts that early was still unusual.

Rahmatullah dozed fitfully. Girija Maharaj slept soundly, and it was nearly noon before the friends met again. Talat Mian was the first to grumble. "Hell will be on our doorstep tomorrow morning, and the saint is still with God!"

Bhagwan Singh wondered if they should tell the authorities so that arrests could be made in time but Talat Mian warned them that a white man would complicate the problem rather than resolve it. Rahmat was apprehensive that he might have been charmed out of his senses the previous evening.

At about two they heard the friendly babble of a group of women walking down the mud path, a rolling pin in every hand. Their leader was Mastan's wife, Zubeida, who strode a step ahead of the others. As she swayed past she challenged the inertia of Zulfiqar Khan with a betel-red smile as others in her group giggled. Zulfiqar Khan turned crimson; his friends watched, bemused. It was common knowledge that Mastan's machismo stopped at his own doorstep. Inside the home Zubeida was monarch. Beyond the threshold she was spice, and did not give a damn what Mastan thought about her saucy amiability towards good-looking men like Zulfiqar Khan.

Passing concern turned to astonishment when Rahmatullah discovered his mother-in-law, Saira, looking very determined, at the head of a second, larger group, again with rolling pins in hand but, reflecting the character of the leadership, more subdued. He went home to Jamila and asked what was going on.

"I wish I had gone too," she said, "but I was afraid you would be angry."

The story was fascinating. While the men of Telinipara had been busy being manly, most of the women had become devotees of Burha Deewana. His message was revolutionary. Husband and wife, he explained, should be like a pair of boots, equal; if one was too tight the pair was of no use. "He tells us," said Jamila, "never to despair. If you want a pearl, he says, you have to go to the sea – and even if you do not find the pearl, at least you will find water! Good, isn't it? He says that a sin committed out of love brings more merit than prayer without love. He can also be very funny. I laughed loudly when he said that a donkey with a load of holy books is still a donkey! It reminded me of Maulvi Taslimuddin!"

"Don't be disrespectful to your elders, Jamila!"

"I don't show disrespect in front of them, but I have every right to say what I want behind their back."

Burha Deewana taught women songs that they could hum along with their daily chores, the *charkhanama* while spinning cotton or the *lorinama* while putting babies to sleep. The lyrics looked at love and life from the woman's perspective – the pain of separation from parents, to the joy of a new life in marriage. The beat harmonized with the tempo of the work: the circular action of the wheel, or the gentle sway of the child. Images linked life with faith: the feminine hand that spun the cotton was never seen by the many who wore the cloth, just as Allah was never seen by the millions who got sustenance from Him.

~

Zubeida stopped at her husband's shop, and Saira at Mangu Qasai's. They spread mats, squatted at the door and declared that they would let neither establishment do business till their single demand was met. Mangu Qasai would have to swear upon the Holy Book that he would not sacrifice a cow on Bakr' Id. They had launched, said Zubeida, a non-cooperation movement.

The ridicule of women is sufficient to destroy the bravado of men. Mangu Qasai, a bigot, had no convictions; Ayub Mastan, a bully, knew only bluster. The workers, unable to hide their laughter, told the two to stop being obstinate. Maulvi Taslimuddin, switching sides in a hurry, proclaimed that offence to a neighbour was an offence to God. By sunset Mangu Qasai had pledged, hand on Quran, to sacrifice a goat the next morning. Saira, sensibly, took home his cow and returned it only after the festival was over.

Relief doubled the elation of a festive eve. There was laughter, gossip, and generosity under a sky lit by a ten-night moon. Vendors brought gas lamps that lent a glow to their colourful bangles and ribbons. Those who could purchased new clothes. Animals were trotted out for examination and praise. There would be a feast in every home the next day, for meat sacrificed to God has to be shared with the less fortunate. Rahmatullah, leaving all arrangements to the care of his mother, returned to Burha Deewana that night, alone.

"You are called Rahmatullah, son, but for me you shall also be Fazlullah, for I see the grace of Allah upon you. The people of Telinipara are like your children. You must look after the worst of them with affection. If a child is not reasonable, it does not mean that elders should behave childishly. Men are not evil, but temptation comes easily to them. Remember this: Satan never really tempts you. He simply exploits the faith that you have thrown away."

"You achieved a miracle, Baba," Rahmatullah said.

The old man smiled. "A sufi must believe in miracles. People laugh when they hear that such and such a dervish claims to have flown from Delhi to Ispahan. But what is miraculous about flying? Do you see that little mosquito? Even that insignificant creature can fly through the air! If Allah can make a mosquito fly, why not man? Men will fly easily the day they want to. That is not a miracle. Changing the course of hate is a miracle..."

"Is this change permanent? Does hate ever disappear?"

"No. But hate is so much more exhausting than love. Jesus, who is called Ruhollah, the spirit of Allah, in the Quran was once insulted in the marketplace. A disciple asked him, 'You pray for your fellowmen. Don't you get angry at their ingratitude?' Jesus replied, 'I can only spend what is in my purse...' Jesus had no anger in his purse."

"We cannot all have the patience of prophets..."

"You have seen this new light in the factory, the light they call electricity? So many bulbs live on one wire. Spiritual teachers are like bulbs on that wire, but the light comes from one source, God. He is before the beginning and after the end. He needs nothing and owns everything. Where do you find Him? In your heart. That is where the Brahmin discovers Him, that is where the sufi finds Him. Religions may seem different, but only on the surface.

That surface is made by man. A sufi goes beyond the surface through many routes: love, devotion and knowledge; through poetry, music, dance, meditation and above all through prayer. As our Prophet, the living Quran, said, 'God made a polish for everything that rusts, and prayer is the polish for the heart'."

"You talk of God all the time, as if you knew Him personally, but God has become invisible to me!"

"One day some Israelites told the Prophet Moses, who used to talk to God, that they wanted to see Him, and invite Him to dinner. Much to Moses' surprise, God accepted. In great excitement, the Israelites were cooking the finest feast for the Almighty, when an old beggar appeared and asked for something to eat. Irritated, they shooed him off. Time passed and there was no sign of their honoured guest. The next day an irritable Moses asked God, 'Where were You? I do all I can to convince sceptics that You exist, and then you do not turn up for dinner after accepting the invitation!' God replied, 'But I did come. If you had fed the beggar, you would have fed Me.'

"A dervish has two reasons to live: to love God, and give what he has to the poor. Everyone has something to give. When some poor people came to Hazrat Ali, son-in-law of our Prophet, and asked what they could give when they did not have a single coin, he told them to smile. A smile is also a gift..."

"But before you give, you must find yourself, isn't it?"

The old man answered affectionately. "Very good. You are young. There is enough time to find out who you are." The smile returned. "Have you heard of Mullah Nasruddin of Bukhara, the man who discovered a problem in every solution? The Mullah was wandering aimlessly after a long night in the tavern when a policeman stopped him and asked, 'What are you doing on the streets at four in the morning?!' Nasruddin replied, 'If I knew the answer, I would have been home'."

A prolonged laugh followed. He looked at my grandfather and said, suddenly in earnest, "If you ever want anything very badly, and what you seek means as much to you as life itself, then go to Ajmer and fall at the feet of the Gharib Nawaz, Khwaja Moinuddin Chishti."

7

APHRODISIAC

THE SNUB WAS GENTLE. "SOMEONE, PASSING BY A MENTAL asylum, jeered, 'How many madmen are in there?' An inmate answered, 'First, tell me how many sane men are out there in the world and then I will tell you how many mad men are in the asylum!'"

The old man laughed at his joke; it was a signal for the loyal to follow.

The rituals of Bakr' Id, a congregational prayer followed by sacrifice, were over. Maulvi Taslimuddin had delivered a powerful sermon in praise of harmony. Normally, Hindus remained indoors till after the bloodletting; the sight of flashing knives is hardly an invitation to a feast. But that morning a small group led by Girija Maharaj and Thakur Bhagwan Singh waited outside the mosque to offer my grandfather an embrace that was reciprocated with quiet joy, as if exhibitionism would sully the gesture. By nine, the slaughtered animals had been skinned and the first smell of kidney and liver being fried rose from select kitchens. Volunteers took small platefuls of raw meat to the homes of the less fortunate. As usual street dogs gathered in front of my grandfather's hut. Food was given to his favourites every day; on festivals they turned up from all over Telinipara. It was party time.

By noon, enough people had gathered in Burha Deewana's grove to constitute an audience. A quick shower had mellowed the heat, and a light breeze from the river played among the trees. For Rahmat and Girija Maharaj, the soft lilt of the old man's voice was perfect music for a beautiful day.

"You must confront madmen who roam among us, disguised in masks of virtue. Their strength lies in your fear. You are afraid because you think you are weak; but you are weak only because you think you are afraid. Look how strong my sister Zubeida and my sister Saira became when they rose above fear. Women are the true guardians of life because they give life. They will remember me after I go to my grave…"

Eyes grew moist as he let thoughts of his death simmer in the hearts of women, who outnumbered the men across an informal aisle. "Do not hesitate to weep," he encouraged, "for tears are a form of speech."

"Kindness to an evil man is as harmful as injury to a good man," he continued, after a pause for those tears. "Human beings are hypnotized by Shaitan, the Satan. The Prophet Muhammad, peace be upon his pure soul, used to say that if men were forbidden to make porridge out of camel's dung, they would have cooked it every day." His laugh had the thrust of admonition.

"Our Prophet gave us a religion of peace. He said, 'If a man rejects war when he is wrong, he will go to Paradise. But if a man rejects war when he is *right*, he will sit beside Allah!' Why then do some Muslims seek war in the name of their faith? Allah has ninety-nine names: *Al-Rahman,* the beneficient; *Al-Rahim,* the merciful; *Al-Salam,* the peaceful; *Al-Haq,* the truth; *Al-Wadud,* who loves me; *Al-Mubdi,* the creator... Not one of ninety-nine names describes Allah as a warrior. Allah is a creator, not a killer.

"There are Hindus who enjoy washing a wound with blood. They exploit what divides brothers, and are blind to what is common. The supreme God of the Vedas is Brahma. Brahma has no form; Allah also has no form. The Hindu philosophy of *mimansa* says that idols are only a means to assist the mind towards Brahma. The Hindu seeks release from life in nirvana, I seek assimilation in Allah. Both sufi and sannyasin reach God through meditation. The Hindu's *kravana* is my *sama,* we both listen; his *manana* is my *muraqaba,* we both obey; his *nididhyanasana* is my *tawajjuh,* we both contemplate. The *buddhi* of the Brahmin is my *ilm;* we both learn; his *jnana* is my *marafat,* we both seek emancipation through knowledge. What you call *maya,* illusion, I call *alam-i-khyal,* the world of fancy."

My grandfather felt vaguely reassured, as if he had not travelled too far when he converted.

"It is not the fault of the sun that the blind cannot see. Today is the day of the Haj. Every faith has a destination. The Muslim goes to Kaaba in the desert, the Hindu travels to Kashi on the Ganga. But I tell you, you who are poor and can go nowhere, that the greatest pilgrimage is the journey into yourself. As my master Hazrat Maulana Rumi used to say: when you are away from Kaaba, you must turn towards it, but if you are inside Kaaba you can pray in any direction.

"If prayer is sincere, it will find its way to God, even if it be the prayer of a demon. Diti, the queen of demons, lost all her sons in the great war against the gods, and wanted vengeance. She told her daughter to enter a forest, light four fires in the four directions, sit beneath a fifth, the sun, and meditate till a boon was granted. Impressed with her penance, the sage Suparsva came to the forest and sired a son through her. This child, Mahisa, with the body of a man and head of a buffalo, grew up to be so powerful that he drove Indra, king of gods, out of heaven. Brahma, Vishnu and Shiva were stunned. What did they do when they wanted to destroy evil? They did not create a new god, but a goddess! Thus was Durga, who is worshipped in every home in Bengal, born. Shiva created her head, Vishnu her arms, Brahma her feet. Her waist came from Indra, her hair from Yama, her breasts from the moon, her thighs from Varuna, the god of rain and the seas; her hips were from the earth, her toes from the sun, her fingers from the eight radiant Vasus, her teeth from Prajapatis, the seven sons of Brahma, her eyes from fire, her brows from the two twilights, her ears from the wind."

As they left, Girija Maharaj wryly commented that the old man had overdone his thank-you note to women.

At about three in the afternoon, four men appeared outside Rahmatullah's hotel with *dhol tasha,* a combination of large and half-drums, trumpet, bugle and cymbals, and struck up that furious rhythm that generates instant excitement. The stick becomes a blur against the taut skin of the small drum, and notes shift at stimulating pace from bass to treble and back. The band was a gift from Thakur Bhagwan Singh. It led a happy procession to the maidan, which was coming alive at myriad points. In the *akhara* a huge wrestler offered to accept any challenge. His wispy bagman bragged that the champion drank forty pounds of milk each morning and ate a small kid goat every afternoon.

"Where have you been all day?" Rahmatullah asked when he saw Talat Mian flying a kite near the river. He had quite forgotten his guest. Talat Mian ignored the question and dwelt on kites. "This one is only an ordinary kite with a double bow; next time, my flying lantern will compete with the moon. I will show you what a disciple of the great kite-master, Ilahi Baksh Tundey, can do with paper and a string!"

"I am sure you can fly a magic carpet on a string."

"Here is an idea, given free. Start a kite competition, offer a prize of five rupees and let us see who becomes the Champion of Telinipara!"

"Five rupees! You think I have five rupees to waste on kite-flying?"

"Waste money? On a kite-flying competition? The sky is free, the wind is free, the earth is free. Each competitor brings his own kite and string sharpened with crushed glass. So what will it cost you? Only the prize money, isn't it? Will the five rupees really come out of your pocket? I expect about a hundred competitors in the first year and twice that number in the second. Then there are spectators. Let us say that there are 200 people, and they spend about half an anna each on food from your hotel. You are looking at revenue of over 100 annas minimum. Sixteen annas make a rupee, so your gross revenue should be over six rupees. I know what the cost of your food will be – not more than two rupees. Food always makes a healthy profit, isn't it? Your loss in the first year therefore will be no more than one rupee. So there you are. Hero of Telinipara for one silver rupee!"

My grandfather laughed along with the others and changed the subject, but that autumn, during the puja of Lord Vishwakarma, architect and artisan of the gods, and therefore a favoured deity of Hindu workers, he launched a kite festival that became the pride of the district.

When they reached home at dusk he discovered what Talat Mian had been doing: cooking. His tribute to Burha Deewana was a splendid Lucknow meal, prepared in conspiracy with Mai and Jamila; my grandfather was not told for fear that the miser in him might growl. Talat Mian's culinary skills were unexpected. Over a lifetime of chequered employment, Talat Mian had picked up diverse abilities.

There was a spread of biryani, *roghni* roti, *qaurma*, dal and zarda. Biryani, a rice and meat dish flavoured in saffron and spices could be a meal in itself but this was not an occasion for the abstemious. *Roghni* roti was unleavened bread, about half a foot in diameter, soaked in milk and clarified butter. This was really a breakfast bread, but *shir mal,* which Talat Mian wanted to bake, needed a special oven, and Telinipara was not equipped for high cuisine. The mutton *qaurma* had been cooked till the water evaporated leaving the meat wafting in the perfume of burnt butter and sixteen spices. Dal, or lentil, might seem a simple dish, but only the finest chefs knew how to turn it into a gourmand's delight. Zarda, a sweet rice mixed with saffron and raisins, completed the meal.

Burha Deewana beamed. He did not eat much, but his delight was evident as they squatted on a large mustard-coloured sheet with a simple line border known as a *dastarkhwan.* Girija Maharaj sat slightly askew of the others so that he would not have to look at the meat; that was the only concession he made to his vegetarian Brahminism. His presence was a veritable social revolution, for he was eating, for the first time, in the company of Muslims. A splendid yogurt had been brought for him to augment the lentil, bread and zarda. Bhagwan Singh archly pointed out that since he was a Thakur, he was not compelled to be vegetarian.

Bauna Sardar sniffed, "What is dal doing in such company?"

"Do not look down upon lentil! It is not as humble as you think," cried Talat Mian. "Butter dal is one of the most difficult dishes to get right, and nothing is tastier than it. What do you understand about food, you ignorant Biharis!"

Zulfiqar Khan flared up: "I am a Pathan from Kabul!"

Talat Mian responded with a withering stare. "Kabul. Ah, Kabul. The land of Pathans who roast dry meat on a rusty spit and make naans twice the size of their turbans and a hundred times the size of their brains!"

~

That evening Talat Mian was cultural ambassador of Avadh, perched on the highest rungs of civilization.

"Let me tell you a story from the time of Nawab Asaf ud Daulah. As you are well aware, I never make up anything. A cook presented himself for employment before His Majesty and was asked his speciality. 'I only cook lentils,' he replied. And what did he want as a salary? Five hundred rupees. The gasp could be heard all over Lucknow. Remember this was more than a hundred years ago, when a rupee could actually buy something! But Asaf ud Daulah's brains lived in his stomach, so he said yes. The cook had two more conditions. He would prepare lentils only if given a day's notice, and the preparation would have to be eaten the moment it was ready. Some months later His Highness suddenly asked for dal. He was talking to a courtier when informed, a day later, that it was ready. Two reminders were sent, but His Fatness continued talking. The cook picked up the bowl of dal he had prepared, threw it on a withered tree and disappeared. Asaf ud Daulah was in deep distress when he heard what had happened, but the cook could never be traced again. In a few days, however, that withered tree had begun to blossom!"

"What a liar you are!" remarked Bauna Sardar, licking his fingers before he picked up another roti.

"You have no imagination, Sardar! How will you ever know what truth is! Do you know that there was a *rakabdar,* a chef, who made a pomegranate pilau, so-called because one side of every grain of rice was red while the other was white? The physician, Hakim Banday Mehndi, placed such herbs in his special pilau that you were full after a mere mouthful! My friends, how can I explain to you the Lucknow I have seen? Nobles left their palaces and came down to the street to eat Mahamdu's *nihari,* the breakfast soup that is beyond my capability to make, at his foodstall in Firangi Mahal. Mahamdu saw Hindus fry flour in ghee to make puris, so he put ghee on the dry Persian bread of Muslims and turned it into a paratha. From this he evolved the smaller, more delicate *shir mal.* That bread is his creation. When you mix Kabul and Lucknow you get India!"

The banter continued as Wahabuddin cleared the plates. The barber had eaten with them, for everyone was equal on a *dastarkhwan.* Equality ended with the meal. He picked up the plates and brought water and lime for the guests to wash their fingers. No one seemed in a mood to leave so Fareed Jang fed some kerosene into the lantern. Burha Deewana, his eyes sparkling, made a suggestion. "Junayd of Baghdad used to say that divine mercy descends on the sufi on three occasions: when he eats, for the sufi does not eat without hunger; when he meditates, for his mind is clear of everything but Allah; and when he hears music, for music transports him into the presence of God."

Wahabuddin disappeared, and returned minutes later with an old harmonium whose white keys had faded into brown and whose black keys had been scratched semi-white. Fareed placed the instrument on his lap and said, "Baba, let me offer you a taste of Hazrat Amir Khusro!"

"Khusro..." murmured the old man. "Who can understand the ways of the Almighty? Changez, that bloodthirsty tyrant who sent Rumi to Konya, also sent Amir Khusro to Delhi. Khusro's father, Saifuddin Mahmud Lachini, a Turk from Central Asia, took refuge in India and became an officer in the armies of Sultan Shamsuddin Al-Tamash. His son could have been a soldier but he chose poetry, laughter and mysticism; Khusro became a disciple of the great saint Hazrat Nizamuddin Auliya of Delhi. There has never been a disciple like Khusro. When Nizamuddin Auliya passed away, Khusro, clad in black, sat by his grave on folded knee and did not move till death could take him away as well, in six months. He is buried by the side of his master. Khusro, Khusro... the voice of my country, the voice of my people. *Kishware Hind ast bahishte bar zameen,* he said. Hindustan is a Paradise on earth." He remembered a couplet:

Kaafir-e ishqam Musalmani may dar kaar neest
Har rag-e man taar ghashta haajat-e junnar neest.

"I will have to translate that for you, for it is in Persian. Love, Khusro says, has made him an infidel, he no longer needs the appearance of a Muslim; and since every vein of his body has become a cord, he does not need the cord of a Brahmin either... Fareed, let us hear Khusro; it has been a long while since my heart sang to his music."

In a powerful voice that was never loud, Fareed sang of the lover who begs his beloved not to punish him further for he no longer has the strength needed for separation:

Zi haal-e miskeen makun taghaful, duraay-e naina, banaye batiyaan
Ki taab-e hinza na daaram ai jaan, na lehu kaahe lagaye chatiyaan.

Talat Mian turned nostalgia into melancholy. Night became an appropriate metaphor for the lyric poetry of the last Muslim emperor of Delhi, Bahadur Shah Zafar, banished to Burma after the defeat of 1857: an elegy of empire, a curtain of romance between glory and despair, a dividing line of so many lives, including perhaps of the old man.

Mera rang roop bigarh gaya, mera yaar mujhse bichar gaya
Jo chaman khiza se ujar gaya, main usi ki fasl-i-bahar hoon.
Na kisi ki aankh ka noor hoon, na kisi ke dil ka qaraar hoon...

My countenance is lost, my friend has left
I am the harvest of a barren field.
No longer the light of any eye, no longer the wish of any heart.

Umr-e daraz maang ke laaye the char din
Do aarzoo mein kat gaye, do intezar mein.

I brought four days from the giver of life
Two went in hope, two went in waiting.

He paused theatrically, for the contemplation of sorrow and a little applause.

Kitna hai badnaseeb Zafar, dafn ke liye
Do gaz zameen bhi na mili, koo-e-yaar mein.

Misfortune is your destiny, Zafar, you could
Not find two yards for a grave in your homeland.

"After music, silence and stillness are required," said the old man. They left.

The next day, Girija Maharaj proclaimed that the curse of Agni was over. Every fortune seemed to lift in Telinipara. My grandfather prospered more than others. No one grudged him success. His most profitable business coup was tobacco.

~

The East India Company, which managed the finances of its empire with the emotional range of an accountant, began tobacco cultivation in 1829. Firms like Dunlop and Peninsular Tobacco were soon doing business with agents from Turkey and the United States, makers of the finest cigarettes and cigars. Leaf from Rangpur in East Bengal fetched a special premium. By the end of the century Indian companies like A.C. Dutt from Nadia, India Cigarette Manufacturing from Murshidabad and Naidu Cigarette Company from Howrah were competing with British firms. But jute workers were not interested in the high end of the tobacco market. They wanted bidis, a pinch of tobacco deftly wrapped in the leaves of the *tendu* tree; or zarda, a heady, black extract that heightened the potency of the betel leaf; or the no-frills, high-voltage *khaini,* crushed from raw tobacco, mixed with lime, and savoured in the pouch between the front teeth and the lower lip. My grandfather bought cheap tobacco, stocked it in a warehouse and supplied it to a string of *khaini* shops through the jute belt. He bought an iron safe for his new money. The old tin suitcase with a heavy lock that had served so far was thrown away.

Home expanded into a series of huts around a compound; family grew to include Jamila's relatives; and the kitchen served an ageing Talat Mian, who had moved in from Matiyaburj after his wife died. My grandmother became a quiet patron of women in difficulty; my grandfather preferred the ignorance of generosity. His focus narrowed to two objectives: the double-storied home of his early fantasies, and a son of his dreams. The house he knew was a matter of time. But time seemed to be running out for a son. He was now entering his forties, and Jamila was over thirty. He had no idea what could be done. He overcame his natural reserve and confided in Girija Maharaj.

The Brahmin was brisk. He sought the advice of Surjya Modak, their window to the world. Modak referred them to a doctor of ancient Indian medicine, a *vaidya* who had acquired a reputation by curing the local zamindar, Satyajit Banerjee, of premature impotence.

Vaidyanath Brijbhushan Trivedi had a chin as sharp as a V and a laugh that left itself open to interpretation. "The purpose of life," he intoned, "is to achieve three goals: dharma, righteous action; *artha,* money; and kama, desire. I gather you have made enough of the second through suitable application of the first. The first two are your companions till death, but kama is a temporary guest. The penis of an old man is like moth-eaten wood. It disintegrates on touch. But you are still young. Sex for a man must begin before twenty and should be possible, with the right advice, till seventy. Don't gape, that is what I get paid to ensure.

"I gather you want a son. One solution is to try another woman, although I must inform you that according to our ancient texts, sex with the wife of an enemy, friend, teacher, student, or with any old lady is prohibited..." Rahmatullah cut short the ramble with a curt assertion that he was not interested in anyone except his wife.

"In that case, do you want me to treat your wife first? I could suggest *artava sodhaka* to purify her ovum, or perhaps the *yoni srava stambhaka,* which prevents any excessive secretion from her vagina – *yoni* means vagina – which could be diluting your male chromosomes."

Rahmatullah was horrified at the thought, almost as much as Jamila might have been. He had never seen his wife get angry, but the suggestion that a *vaidya* might probe her vagina was a certain trigger. "Stick to what you can do for me."

"All right, all right. I will have to ask you a few questions since the mind plays the most important part in sex. Bitterness, anger can kill the sexual drive, as can gluttony."

My grandfather reassured him that he had no such excesses, nor gonorrhea or syphilis, which kill generative ability. He was not suffering from any deformity in his sexual organs, he did not masturbate, and he did not have sex during his wife's periods.

Trivedi looked at his potential patient thoughtfully. "The best aphrodisiac is an untroubled heart. Perhaps the intensity of your desire for a son is making you too tense... There are two classical views on sex. Manu, our lawgiver, said that the pleasure of sex was children. Vatsyayana, the philosopher who wrote *Kama Sutra,* thought that the pleasure of sex was sex. I would put you in the Manu camp."

Rahmatullah wished he would just get on with it.

"I can see that you do not need to improve your *sukra*, your semen. I am not so sure about your *ojas*, the vital essence of life. Ideally, there should be eight drops of *ojas* in your heart, which travel, in minute portions, through your blood into your penis when you make love, determining your virility. It is good that you do not drink, for alcohol kills *ojas* and reduces virility. *Ojas* is heavy and cool, alcohol is light and hot; *ojas* is smooth and sweet; alcohol is rough and sour; *ojas* seeps, alcohol rushes; *ojas* is uplifting, alcohol is a depressant. That is what I had to get through to the fat head of the stupid zamindar. You can't be high on alcohol and hope for an erection."

He paused for breath.

"You must drink cow's milk. The sage Charaka recommends it. However, it cannot be any old cow. It must be either black or brown, have pointed horns, and get fattened on gram and sugarcane. Add sugar or honey to her milk and it becomes a good aphrodisiac. You eat meat. I could recommend a soup made from the testicles of a he-goat, to be drunk every morning, although you will appreciate that as a Brahmin I cannot make this myself. Add clarified butter, some salt, coriander, ginger and cumin to the soup."

Rahmatullah listened without expression.

"You can also fry the testicles in butter, sprinkle some sesame seed upon it and wash this down with fresh milk. Now, if you drink milk boiled with crushed asparagus and sugar, your penis will remain erect even after intercourse."

Rahmatullah did not yet doubt Trivedi, but he had begun to doubt his own qualifications as a patient.

"If you find this difficult to prepare for any reason, I can suggest oils," continued Trivedi, "but they will be more expensive. There is the Sri Gopala oil made of sesame, asparagus – you notice how often these two recur in sexual recipes? – mallow, cherry, saffron, musk, amber and the testicles of a civet cat. You need to massage your penis as well as your wife's breasts with this."

Girija Maharaj, as sombre as a penitent so far, burst out laughing.

Trivedi continued, icily. "I cannot recommend the *purna chandradayarasa* pill because it will be too expensive for you. Only the richer zamindars can afford it. It is made from a sulphur base on gold leaf. Add the juice of the red cotton flower, place this in a bottle wrapped in cloth smeared with mud. Heat it on a mild fire, keeping the mouth of the bottle open till the sulphur has been smoked out. Seal the bottle with calcium and paste of jaggery and lime, and heat again. After it has cooled a second time, scrape the powder, add camphor, musk and pepper and enjoy it with betel leaf. Watch your penis rise!"

"Listen," asked Rahmatullah, "can any of these medicines ensure a son?"

"I know what I know," answered Trivedi enigmatically. He considered. "Look, there is one method mentioned in the ancient texts. In the second month of pregnancy a particular puja can be performed while the juice of certain herbs is squeezed through the vagina. This is called *purusvanakarma* and can change the sex of a child in the womb..."

Rahmatullah left behind a silver rupee, which was excessive. The only explanation was guilt. He was paying for the *vaidya's* silence. Girija Maharaj shrugged off the experience. No one could fault them for trying. They stopped at Surjya Modak's shop to chat and test a new specialty, puffed puris with a curry of spiced pumpkin and potato followed by shandesh. Modak listened sympathetically. His expansive mood reflected his expanding frame, a by-product of his vocation. "When science fails," he advised, "return to God."

Burha Deewana scolded my grandfather. "You have forgotten what I once told you. If you ever want anything that means more to you than life itself, then go to Ajmer and fall at the feet of the Gharib Nawaz, Khwaja Muinuddin Chishti. I have decided not to die till I hold your son in my arms."

8

DESIRE

THE ARRIVAL OF BEGGARS WAS CONCLUSIVE EVIDENCE OF prosperity. They lived on the line between wandering fakir and wandering pest, adopting whichever identity suited an immediate purpose. They were generally draped in saffron, tattered at an edge or two; their necks were heavy with colourful glass beads and white cowrie shells that glistened off dark chests below wild beards. They addressed their lamentations to the skies rather than the street, on the fair assumption that alms reach the poor through the hands of God. Muslims and Hindus differed in style. Hindus chanted, and Muslims sang, sometimes mellifluously. The most successful beggar came at about eleven each morning, his neck tilted forty-five degrees north, with a song that became something of a local hit: "*Gareeb jaan ke,*" he warbled to Allah, "*hum ko na tum bhula dena... Tumhi ne dard diya hai, tumhi dawa dena..." Don't forget me because You know me to be poor; You gave the pain, You provide the medicine...*

For reasons that escaped the non-unionized workers, demand for jute packaging began to rise in the second decade of the twentieth century, and with it wages and workforce. Jute, flexible and durable, was a traditional resource of Bengal, for the finest hemp in the world came from the eastern part of the province. Handloom weavers turned it into twine that was used for a variety of needs, from the intercrossed rope that formed the soft bed of a charpoy to tough fabric that clothed the poor. Two wars brought luck to Indian jute. The Americans restricted cotton supplies to Britain while they fought for independence; and the Russians stopped exporting flax to Britain during the Crimean conflict. The East India Company sent Indian jute samples to England where British technology softened it with oil and water, and spun it on flax machinery to create a thread that withered like powder but became formidable in a knit. Dundee's flax factories were converted into jute mills. By 1900 a third of Bengal's exports came from jute.

Over a drink in the club by the river, the managers of Victoria Jute Mill, all Scotsmen, occasionally raised a toast to a Liberal who was first elected MP in 1908 from Dundee, once the royal city of Robert Bruce but now more famous for jute, jam and journalism. His name was Winston Churchill, and he was too grand to protect an industry as scruffy as jute. But it was the profit line rather than Churchill that shifted the base of the industry from Dundee to Bengal. Raw materials were nearer, labour was cheaper and profits higher. Dundee had no chance. From one mill in Rishra with no looms in 1855, Bengal had, by the first decade of the new century, fifty-nine mills with 30,685 looms. In 1914, a world war kicked in. War meant trenches. Trenches meant sandbags. Sandbags meant jute. Jute meant smiles all around Telinipara. In a good month Bauna Sardar might earn up to forty rupees between pay and commissions. The average wage was higher than that of coal miners in towns like Asansol and Dhanbad. Doleful miners, who got twenty rupees a month if skilled and less than half if unskilled, had a saying: If you came up you got a coin; if you went down they got a corpse.

Thomas Duff and Company, owners of Victoria, were so pleased by their profits that, in 1913, they served a grand feast to celebrate the visit of King George V to Delhi, designated the new capital of Imperial India, in 1911. The discrepancy in time was meaningless to workers who had little sense of time, except when it was time to die. Two tents were constructed on the maidan, one for Muslims and the other for caste Hindus. Muslim cooks were brought from Matiyaburj, and Hindu cooks from Orissa. The mill managers could not resist triumphalism: they hired a musician to sing a stirring ode which, they had been told by a newspaper appropriately called the *Englishman,* was composed in honour of King George V by Rabindranath Tagore. The poet thought otherwise, but distinctions between Emperor and God were thin in Telinipara. The opening lines, *Jana gana mana adhinayak-e jaya he, Bharata bhagya vidhata,* lauded George V, or God, as the architect of India's destiny and applauded the British for conquering Punjab, Sind, Gujarat, Maratha, Dravida, Orissa and Bengal. The paean ended on a drum roll of a distinctly military character: *Jaya jaya jaya hey!* Victory, victory, victory! The workers did not understand the Bengali in which it was written, but if it came with free food it had to be a good thing.

Leftovers, along with an impressive quantity of toddy, were sent to untouchables, who had not been invited. There was fulsome gratitude and substantial drunkenness among the untouchables, who were astonished that the British considered them human. Telinipara's feel-good factor was bad only for moneylenders, who preferred business for more compulsive reasons. My grandfather, nagged constantly by Jamila, for Islam prohibited usury, had reluctantly reduced his rate of interest to five per cent a month against the average of twelve per cent or more charged by Zulfiqar Khan or Bhagwan Singh. Jamila ignored his sulks.

Girija Maharaj marvelled at British rule. "*Yatha Raja,*" he often said, quoting a Sanskrit proverb, "*thatha praja!*" As the ruler, so the ruled! It was not only the jute mill, a fortress that fed the poor rather than an army, giving life instead of taking it. He surveyed the queue waiting to be inoculated outside a makeshift dispensary and recalled the year when everyone thought Rahmatullah was going to die. The British believed in preventive action. Ten miles away, in a village beyond the Hooghly Madrasa, a dead rat had been found in a grain storeroom. Word reached the English health officer. Government machinery went into motion. The region was fumigated. White lines of disinfectant appeared along drains and latrines in Telinipara. A plague camp was set up.

Over the past fifteen years the curse had been controlled but not eradicated, and periodic scares were one reason why Rahmatullah did not embark on his cherished pilgrimage to Ajmer. Fear became a reason for inertia, and inertia a stimulant to fear; travel was tainted with too much uncertainty. Mai would burst into tears each time a plan was made for the journey, and his daughters joined in till they were pacified with jaggery or *sattu*, flour kneaded in butter. Burha Deewana was philosophical. One did not go to the shrine of Khwaja Muinuddin Chishti, one

was called there by the spirit of the saint. When the summons
came no force would be able to prevent the pilgrimage.

Everything, explained Girija Maharaj, was written in the
stars. The almanac confirmed that India was passing through an
inauspicious period that would end only with the arrival of a great
comet, whose appearance in the sky would mark the high point
of misfortune. Less fatalist friends offered other remedies.
Zulfiqar Khan brought news from Calcutta that the medicines of
the famous Indian doctor, Hakim Ajmal Khan of Ballimaran in
Delhi, had reached Bengal. The hakim, scion of a family that
came to India with the Mughal emperor Babar, was son of a *rais*,
the noble Hakim Mahmud Khan, friend of the poet Ghalib and
epitome of the prime virtues of Delhi: honour, culture, education,
honesty. Both Hindus and Muslims left their valuables in his safe
custody when they fled Delhi after defeat in 1857. The British,
suspicious of the father, were persuaded to recognize the merits
of the son and honoured him with the title of *Haziq-ul-Mulk*, or
The Skilled One of the Kingdom. Hakim Ajmal Khan had
revived the science of *yunani tibb*, the system of medicine that
the Abbasid Arabs had learnt from the Greeks, Galen and
Hippocrates, but which was now seen as "oriental" because it was
patronized by Muslims. His first factory of Indian medicine, the
Hindustani Dawakhana, at Ballimaran, was ceremonially opened
by Raja Kishan Kumar and offered both yunani and ayurvedic
potions in its range. Word spread that all profits went to a
madrasa; that the hakim did not take a fee from the poor, but if
he had to call on a Nawab he charged nothing less than an aston-
ishing thousand rupees! Not only could he cure every known
disease, he could also rid a possessed man of spirits. With such

powers, he would certainly find a way of ensuring that Jamila gave birth to a son. My grandfather was tart: he would rather go with a begging bowl to God than to a doctor. That did not prevent him from opening a yunani-ayurvedic shop in Chandernagore.

Girija Maharaj heard from Surjya Modak that a very renowned astrologer from the southern French settlement of Pondicherry had paused in the sister town of Chandernagore on his way to the holy cities of Benaras, Hardwar and Badrinath; and thence to Gangotri, source of the Mother Ganges, the holy lake of Mansarovar in Tibet, and Mount Kailash, abode of Lord Shiva. Sarevapalli Iyengar, a short man who improved his height with a high, white turban and his face with a brown beard, was cool and businesslike. He asked Girija Maharaj to return after the meteor had passed, pointing out that he had suspended his own travels. He would charge four rupees as his fee.

On the night of the meteor, Girija and Rahmatullah went to the river bank, and were amazed by the peacock dancing against the sky, its tail a huge mass of glittering light that remained in their vision long after the head had raced away towards the unknown expanse of an eternal universe. The starburst was fading when a panting boy informed them that Talat Mian had died, suddenly, without even a cough as a warning. Girija Maharaj sighed in relief. This, he said, was Talat Mian's way of thanking them, for with his death Talat Mian had taken with him all the misfortune that the comet might have visited upon Telinipara.

Sarevapalli Iyengar pocketed four rupees and made a general prediction that nine years of prosperity would follow. He asked for the specific time and place of Rahmatullah's birth so that he could cast a horoscope. My grandfather had no clue, so Iyengar politely asked for another rupee for additional services. He took out a large brass plate, filled it with oil, and told my grandfather to shut his eyes and concentrate on his deepest desire. He applied mascara on my grandfather's drawn eyelids, saluted the plate with a long mantra, and asked him to open his eyes and look at the oil. All three men saw a baby lying on steps that rose towards a marble platform on which rested a massive arch that formed the entrance to a wide courtyard and a mosque. The astrologer pronounced, expertly, "Four years." That startled them a bit. No one had heard of a four-year pregnancy. "You will take four years to reach this mosque to pick up the baby."

Burha Deewana identified the picture as the mausoleum of Khwaja Muinuddin Chishti and shrugged off the four-year wait. "The longer the night, the more dreams one has…"

A long journey was possible only when the weather had cooled, for summer was an invitation to discomfort and disease. The British had improved trains. There were now lavatories even in compartments used by Indians, but the risk was considered unnecessary. When plans were ready for departure in September they learnt from Bauna Sardar that a big war had broken out between the English and the Germans. A sense of urgency entered factory life. Demand for bags rose, taking the price of raw jute up with it. War was good for Bengal. A labour shortage induced the mill managers to hire short men from Madras with lean bodies glistening in oil to work new looms. This was also insurance against any potential Bihari blackmail on the production floor. The Madrasis were given facilities that became the envy of Biharis, including a colony with brick lanes and safe toilets. They brought with them stories of how the rich Tamil

Brahmins had fled Madras when a huge German warship called *Emdem* entered the seas off the port city. Laughter brought the two communities into passing contact, but they remained separate in all other matters.

My grandfather started construction of a house suitable for an heir. He was architect, builder and occasionally mason as well. His design was simple. At the centre was a courtyard open to the sky. Rooms rose on two stories around it. His bedroom, embellished by a magnificent replica of the four-poster bed he had seen long ago in Chandernagore, faced south on the first floor. It was common knowledge that the breeze was best from the south, for Kama, the god of desire, took the form of a southern breeze when he wanted to deceive the guardian bull, Nandi, and enter the abode of the ascetic Lord Shiva. A door opened to the living room which connected to a landing and the public staircase to the street. The kitchen was beside the courtyard. Mai slept with the children in her bedroom to the north. There was a bathroom on the eastern side. A hall on the ground floor was his office as well as a community centre. Everyone was welcome.

A flat one-dimensional pyramid rose above the roof, bisecting the ledge facing the street. A crescent rested on the tip of the triangle. On its base, nestling among carved sunflowers, lay what looked like the sacred Vedic syllable, *Om*. The whispers, floated by a mason, were not loud but Maulvi Taslimuddin was heard muttering a few times that his chances of reaching Paradise could be jeopardized if the rumour was true. A convert's loyalties are always suspect.

No one else bothered. Burha Deewana left his grove to bless

the home and attached a warning to his prayers. Sultan Alauddin
of Konya, he said, had built a palace so magnificent that it was
the wonder of his friends, and so powerful that it was the awe of
his enemies. A visiting dervish asked the Sultan: did the palace
have walls high enough to protect him from the poor and
oppressed, whose sighs were unseen arrows that could leap across
the tallest towers and destroy the mightiest monarch? Burha
Deewana looked at my grandfather, opened the Holy Quran and
read verses 18 and 19 from Surah 31, named after Luqman the
Wise: *"And swell not thy cheek with pride at men, nor walk in
insolence on the earth, for Allah loveth not the arrogant boaster.
Be moderate in thy pace, and lower thy voice; for the harshest of
sounds, without doubt, is the braying of an ass."* Only trees that are
fruitless, like the pine, are tall and erect, he reminded the master
of the house; trees that bear fruit like the mango have low
branches.

~

It might have been rising self-esteem rather than pride, but one
morning, to the amusement of his companions and the
bewilderment of his family, my grandfather announced that he
was going to learn how to read and write. A distinguished teacher
from the Hooghly Madrasa, an esteemed seminary founded in
1817 a few miles upriver, would come once a week. And thus did
the bright and energetic Syed Ashfaque Alam, a graduate of
Persian and Arabic from the class of 1910 of Calcutta University,
enter the life of Telinipara.

He bounded up the stairs with all the enthusiasm of a young
man about to make his first bit on the side. Six new cane chairs
glistened against the walls of the living room, but my grandfather,

his body bare, sat against pillows on a cotton mattress that covered most of the floor.

"*Assalamalaiqum!*" Alam said, wishing peace all around. It was ten on Friday morning and Wahabuddin was administering, with care and affection, his twice-weekly combination of shave, head-rub and neck-massage. The greeting was returned, a little guardedly. In rapid fire, Alam exhausted all the ways in which an Urdu sophisticate could enquire about his host's health: *Mizaj-e-aali?* How is your exalted well-being? *Mizaj-e-mubarak?* How is your blessed well-being? *Mizaj-e-mualla?* How is your eminent well-being? *Mizaj-e-aqdas?* How is your sacred well-being?

During the course of his brief but intense education my grandfather often wondered whether the correct pronunciation of alphabets like *sheen, seen, swad, dwad, ain* and *ghain* would make him any richer; but apparently such knowledge would make him more civilized. The British, rulers of India, were content with one kind of "Sir". The Muslims, losers of India, had at least six shades of class in one honorific: *Janab,* Sir; *Janab-e-vala,* Honourable Sir; *Janab-e-aali,* Exalted Sir; *Hazrat,* Respected Sir; *Hazrat-e-vala,* Respected and Dignified Sir; *Qibla,* Most Eminent Sir.

Lessons were a conversation rather than a lecture. Text was enhanced by context. Alam introduced my grandfather to the nuances of Urdu. "As the Prophet said, wit is to speech as salt is to food. Frankly, I don't know if the Prophet actually said this or not, but who is going to argue? This much I do know – you cannot understand, or speak, Urdu without wit. Not laughter – wit. A belly laugh is too coarse for our language. Wit is the smile of an equal. Even a repartee must never be unkind, for rancour is foreign to the spirit of Urdu. You may pierce your opponent's defences, but you cannot wound him; it is a duel with blunted rapiers." It was also full of bathos: "He who feeds on majesty becomes eloquent. He who feeds on eloquence becomes majestic." My grandfather once asked why anyone would waste his time on Urdu when English had become the language of power. Alam, in rueful agreement, quoted from his favourite poet, the satirist Akbar Allahabadi who, though ageing, was still alive:

Gaye sherbet ke din yaaron ke aage ab to ay Akbar
Kabhi soda kabhi lemonade kabhi whisky kabhi tea hai!

The days of sherbet are gone, my friends; ahead, oh Akbar
Lie soda, or lemonade, or whisky or tea!

When my grandfather heard he was going to get lessons in guttural, palatal, lingual, dental and labial enunciation he decided he had had enough. Alam found a genteel explanation. He announced that he was unworthy of being my grandfather's ustad, or teacher. But my grandfather enjoyed Alam's company, and devised reasons for regular visits as well as discreet forms of compensation that would protect the delicate balance of mutual respect. Gifts replaced an emolument. The boat that took Alam back to Hooghly at the end of a weekend now contained provisions, or "gifts" from Jamila Bhabhi, the affectionate Indian term for sister-in-law. It was fast-track graduation to the status of a younger brother.

~

Alam brought the high drama of political news to Telinipara, for his seminary subscribed to two Calcutta papers, the pro-British English daily, the *Statesman,* and, while it lasted, the trenchant

Urdu periodical *Al Hilal*, edited by a young man called Abul Kalam Azad, an owner-editor who was so vehemently anti-British that he was imprisoned for sedition at the start of the First World War. Inevitably Alam, the leading local authority on world affairs, became my grandfather's travelling companion when he sold his usury business to Thakur Bhagwan Singh, and set off for Ajmer in the winter of 1915.

"You have come on Thursday night, the night of victory, the night of miracles: he who prays on this night at the feet of Khwaja Muinuddin Chishti, Gharib Nawaz, Lord of the Poor, never returns empty-handed, for tonight he will intercede on your behalf at the court of Allah," said the elderly servant of the shrine, who welcomed them effusively when he learnt that they had made the difficult journey from distant Calcutta. They sat in the flicker of a lamp, wrapped in blankets, outside the decorated room with four heavy silver doors in which lay the grave of the emperor of sufis.

"There has been no king more powerful in India than Akbar the Mughal," he continued, "but even a fly does not visit his grave in Agra. The shrine of Khwaja Muinuddin in Ajmer is never empty.

"Ajmer was founded by the great Rajput king, Raja Ajsa, who ruled over the whole region up to Ghazni in Afghanistan and built this city on the mountains as his capital. Mir means mountain, and so the city was called Aj-Mir, and then Ajmer. Astrologers had warned the Raja that no harm would come to him from kings but he should beware of a wandering mendicant with forty unarmed followers. Orders were proclaimed that if such a person were found he should be put to death on sight.

"The Raja's men found the Khwaja on the banks of the Ana

Sagar lake. The first assault was led by a royal magician called Shadi Dev. But instead of conquering, he was conquered; when he saw the inner power of the Khwaja, Shadi Dev became a believer and gave his own home to the Khwaja to live in. We are today sitting in what was once Shadi Dev's home. Raja Ajsa now summoned Ajaipal, the most powerful magician in India, who set out at the head of 1,500 disciples, 700 of whom were magicians as well. He came flying through the air on the skin of a deer.

"Khwaja Muinuddin drew a circle and recited the Ayat-al Kursi, the Verse of the Throne, the Verse of Power, from the Quran: '*Allah! There is no God but He, the living, the self-subsisting, eternal. No slumber can seize Him nor sleep. His are all things in heaven and on earth. Who is there who can intercede in His presence except as He permits? He knows what appears to His creation, before, or after, or behind them. Nor shall they compass His knowledge except as He wills. His Throne extends over heavens and the earth, and He feels no fatigue in preserving them for He is the Most High, the Supreme Glory.*'

"Ajaipal sent snakes in their thousands, but the moment they reached the edge of the circle they froze. The Khwaja's followers hurled the snakes back and a tree sprouted wherever a snake fell. Defeated, Ajaipal, snakes clinging to his body, flew off. The Khwaja picked up his slippers and threw them into the air. The slippers chased Ajaipal, caught him, and began to slap his face incessantly. Ajaipal returned, bowed in submission before the Khwaja and asked for a boon, the gift of eternal life. The wish was granted – with a caveat. Ajaipal would live till the day of judgment, but he would not be visible to men. And so Ajaipal wanders in those woods on the hills and every Thursday night, he comes to pay homage at the radiant tomb of Khwaja Muinuddin Chishti... Ask and it shall be given."

Rahmatullah told him of his desire for a son, adding that age was not on his side.

"Allah is The Creator! He created Adam by breathing life into a mound of earth, and Jesus from a virgin. It is in Allah's power to give life when He chooses. Recite after me, this prayer of prayers: *Qul ho wallah o ahad; Allah hussamad. Lam yalid wa lam u-lad. Wa lam yakullahu kufuwan ahad.*" Say, He is Allah, the One and Only, the eternal, the absolute. He begetteth not, nor is He begotten. There is none like Him.

The grave, covered in green velvet scented with rose petals, was laid out west to east, with the Khwaja's feet pointing east, away from Mecca. Jamila and Rahmatullah knelt down, touched the floor with bowed heads, then rose, raised their hands, and prayed for a son, Jamila unable to contain her emotions, Rahmatullah permitting only the hint of a tear to moisten his eyes.

Alam greeted Rahmatullah with a reassuring laugh, and Akbar Allahabadi's verse, when they awoke late the next morning:

Raqeebon ne likhwai hai ja ja ke thane mein
Ki Akbar naam leta hai Khuda ka is zamane mein!

My foes have reported to the police in rage
That Akbar takes the name of Allah in this age!

Some two years later, in September 1917, my grandfather proudly took into his arms a dark and stubbornly silent baby. He was pleased that his son had his complexion rather than Jamila's brown wandering towards light brown.

The people of Telinipara could not hide their disappointment.

Dark was a poor man's colour. It suited Rahmatullah, but not his son. My father had sharp features that promised a handsome future: my grandfather's broad forehead, deep eyes, high cheekbones, and his mother's straight nose rather than his father's slightly bulbous one. Alam, displaying singular lack of imagination, insisted that the child should be named after Akbar, the poet. My grandfather, displaying singular diplomacy, said he would be named after Akbar, the emperor. Burha Deewana pointed out that neither emperor nor intellectual would achieve much without the faith and heroism of the Prophet's son-in-law Ali, and so my father became Akbar Ali.

On *chatti,* the sixth day after his birth, mother and son were bathed in hot water while the women, each gifted a new sari, celebrated the survival of the baby with song and music. Rahmatullah presented Jamila with a heavy, 22-karat gold *hansli,* a heavy flat round necklace made at express speed by the jeweller with a rising reputation, Hazari Babu. Jamila wore the necklace till she died. My father got enough rattles to create a din for a decade. Eunuchs turned up to demand their share. On the eighth day, in a rite that went back to Abraham, the *aqiqa* was performed. As Wahabuddin began to shave the hair on the baby's head, two goats were sacrificed in the courtyard. Sandalwood ointment was rubbed on the clean scalp, and meat was distributed to the poor. Five months later my father, dressed ceremonially in a silk brocade shirt and tasseled cap, was given a fingerload of rice pudding. It was his first touch of solid food, *khir chitai.* The family got its first taste of his temperament when he snatched the cap off his head.

My father was the first spoilt child of Telinipara.

My young aunts were delighted with a baby brother. My father's birth cleared a psychological hurdle, and sure enough, within six months, on the same day, both were married to sturdy young men from Telinipara. The couples were given spacious huts, cupboards, beds, jewellery, clothes and a cow and a calf as dowry. Bauna Sardar ensured that the husbands got jobs in the spinning department of the mill.

~

The tranquillity of Telinipara was disturbed when Maulvi Taslimuddin discovered Gandhi. Gandhi had been promoted to the status of a holy soul, a Mahatma, after his great victory against British indigo planters on behalf of Bihari peasants in Champaran. The sceptical view was that while Gandhi was undoubtedly sincere, he had simply got lucky. When great kings and generals had crumpled before British guns and discipline, how could one man in a dhoti challenge the most powerful empire in history? Some Indian idiots thought that the king of Germany could defeat the English emperor. Germany was taught in 1918 what Indians already knew.

One November afternoon in 1920, during that eunuch phase between monsoon and winter, Maulvi Taslimuddin delivered, without warning, a disjointed, excited, call to non-violent arms in his Friday prayers sermon. "The hour has come to throw the British out of India!" he exclaimed. There was more than one exclamation mark in every sentence as words and thoughts tripped over one another in their excitement. "Under the Mughals, Hindus and Muslims were equals in Delhi. Delhi was a city of *admiyat*, humanity, and culture. Every week the best poets patronized a mushaira at Ghaziuddin Madrasa, the school started by Aurangzeb

Alamgir ten years before he died. Hindus flourished under Muslim rule. The biggest bank, Delhi Bank, was owned by Lala Chunna Mal. The British tried to divide us, or to convert us to Christianity, but only Dr Chiman Lal and Master Ram Chandra changed their faith, the latter, I am sure, just to get government advertising for his Urdu newspaper. What did the British do when they conquered Delhi? They massacred innocent Muslims! Our women were driven out of purdah into humiliation and worse! Even the British were better before the British came! It was the city of the brave Colonel Skinner, whose father was English but whose mother was Indian, and who knows how the Great Uprising might have turned out if Colonel Skinner had been loyal to his mother rather than his father in 1857! What greater example of Hindu-Muslim unity can you find than 1857? Our enemies laugh and say that the only thing that the last Mughal emperor Bahadur Shah Zafar had in common with his great ancestor Akbar was that both of them were experts in flying kites. Both believed in Hindu-Muslim unity. Bahadur Shah ordered Muslims not to slaughter cows during Bakr' Id when the British incited Muslim butchers to divide Indians. I am happy to tell you, my brothers, that I have received word that all over our country Hindus and Muslims have united under the leadership of Gandhi and Maulana Mohamed Ali to destroy the British. Hindus have decided to support our jihad for the restoration of our holy cities, Mecca and Medina to Muslim rule, to the Caliph of Islam, the Sultan of Turkey. And Muslims have decided to abandon cow slaughter! Gandhi has given the call, *Karo ya maro!* Do or die! Of course he has told us to be non-violent," he ended lamely. He would have much preferred an immediate distribution of swords.

Who knew there was so much anger inside old Taslimuddin,

commented Rahmatullah thoughtfully to Bauna Sardar as they left the mosque that afternoon.

Alam was sardonic when he heard the news of Taslimuddin's conversion to Gandhi. "I know these mullahs only too well," he said, "I live with them. Their friendship is as dangerous as their enmity. Gandhi is lighting a fire with religion; if it ever goes out of control...!" With his familiar laugh Alam recited:

> *Mussulmanon ko lutf-o-aish se jeene nahin dete*
> *Khuda deta hai khana, Sheikhji peene nahin dete.*

> *They never let Muslims live in joy and comfort*
> *Allah gives us food, the Mullah denies us drink.*

Distant events never seem an immediate reality. In the summer of 1919 rumours began to circulate that innocent Hindus, Muslims and Sikhs had been massacred in Punjab when they were celebrating the spring festival of Basant in a public garden called Jallianwala Bagh. The British had jailed thousands for merely talking about it. Indians were made to crawl on their bellies and shot at point blank range on the orders of a mad general called Dyer. Instead of punishing Dyer, the government had rewarded him.

Nothing happened for a long time and suddenly everything began to happen. Gandhi the alchemist had conquered fear; Gandhi and the mullahs would vanquish the British. Alam continued to insist that this fire would burn the home. "Gandhi is a Hindu. He has no idea what mullahs are like... I tell you, this Muslim leader called Jinnah may not be much of Muslim – he wears English clothes and I gather he drinks gin and whisky; well, good luck to him! – but Jinnah understands that the politics of religion will destroy us before it destroys the British. That is what he has told Gandhi."

But India was with Gandhi.

As events built up to a climax, Alam brought news of history as it was being made:

Gandhi returns Kaisar-i-Hind Gold Medal granted for humanitarian work in South Africa!

Gandhi returns Zulu War Medal for services as officer in charge of Indian Volunteer Ambulance Corps in 1906 during Boer War!

Gandhi returns Boer War Medal for services as assistant superintendent of the Indian Volunteer Stretcher Bearer Corps during Boer War of 1899-1900.

"I stopped bloody revolution in 1919": Gandhi

Gandhi tells Indians to rise, reject British rule!

Gandhi, Ali, Azad greeted by delirious crowds during Punjab, Sind, Madras tour!

Gandhi gives three slogans for Hindus, Muslims: "Allah-o-Akbar!", "Vande Mataram!", "Hindu-Musalman ki jai!"

Gandhi crushes anti-Khilafat heavyweights at special September Congress session!

Indians ordered to resign British jobs, leave schools, boycott foreign goods, wear handspun cotton!

Hakim Ajmal Khan, presiding over annual session of the Muslim League in Amritsar, calls on Muslims to stop cow slaughter!

British will be thrown out in one year, promises Gandhi!

A dread fell over Telinipara.

The workers of Telinipara did not want the British, who had built their jute mill, to be thrown out of India.

9

KRISHNA

Om bhurbhuva swaha!
Tat Savitoor varenyam
Bhargodevasya dhimahi
Dhiyo yo nah prachodayat!

GIRIJA MAHARAJ STOOD STILL AND STRAIGHT, WAIST-DEEP, IN the river. His hair, flowing back, and his beard, flowing down, ended at the same level, a finger-length above the water. His eyes were shut; his face searched for warmth in the twilight that gently precedes sunrise. The seasons had changed, for it was the day after the colourful spring festival of many origins, Holi, on the fifteenth day of the Hindu month of Phalgun. The young, as they might, celebrated Holi with the god of love, Kamadeva, for flirtation of many nuances was condoned. The more pious destroyed evil by hurling cow dung into a bonfire, in symbolic rage against King Hiranya who had ordered his daughter, Holika, to burn her brother Prahlad because he dared to worship Lord Vishnu instead of his father. Girija Maharaj's Holi was more relaxed. He indulged in a few glasses of milk laced with bhang, complemented the heady potion with half a dozen shandesh from his friend's hotel, and slept. The next morning, he returned to the river to welcome the warmth of spring.

His calendar, the *panchangam,* viewed time through five concentric mirrors: the lunar month, the week, the zodiac, eclipses, and the movement of planets. From these variables Brahmins calculated auspicious and inauspicious hours and days; predicted the fate of monsoons; prophesied whether locusts would devour the crop, and, in case of war, the direction from which an enemy would advance. They determined days and hours auspicious for travel, weddings, ceremonies, and fixed the dates of festivals, which might, as a consequence, vary from year to year by as much as a fortnight.

In every season barring winter, Girija Maharaj walked from his hut to the Hooghly in the last span of fading night to offer the Brahmin's prayer to the sun god, the Gayatri Mantra. The twenty-four syllables of this mantra were the holiest of the 10,500 verses of the *Rig-Veda:* they had emerged from the mouth of Brahma and constituted the supreme creed of the Brahmin, a chant so powerful as to make the gods themselves tremble. Only a Brahmin was permitted to recite the Gayatri Mantra.

Girija Maharaj tightened and shut all the openings of his body, held his breath and whispered so that no person of a lower caste might hear him. *"Tat Savitoor varenyam, bhargodevasya dhimahi dhiyo yo nah prachodayat!"* We meditate on the unique light of the divine Sun, with which we illuminate our minds!

He repeated this twenty-four times, until a slice of sun began to climb over the brink of the horizon. He addressed the rising god: "The face of fire is Brahma, the head of fire is Vishnu, the heart of fire is Shiva... You are Brahma when you rise, Shiva in the middle of your course, and Vishnu when you set. You are the jewel of the air, monarch of the day, eye of the world, the divider of time, Lord of the nine planets..."

Thus, each morning, did he destroy the sins of the night. Each sunset, in the silence of his home, he recited the prayer till the first stars became a sprinkle on the western sky; thus did he destroy the transgressions of the day.

His morning *shlokas* completed, Girija Maharaj began to calm, through the science of yoga, the ten winds lodged in the human body: *prana,* which rises from the anus, moves to the head and then descends to the nostrils; *apana,* which settles in the navel and expels waste; *vyana,* which digests food and bursts out through the anus; *samana,* which ensures tranquillity; *naga,* which causes hiccups and retching; *kurma,* which makes the eyelids flutter involuntarily; *khled* which produces sneezes and phlegm; *devata,* which leads to convulsions; *mukha* which excites laughter and tears; and *jananjaya,* the deep wind of the head which is the last to leave the body after death. Girija Maharaj did not possess the discipline to keep all ten winds under control, so he limited his exercises to *prana* and *apana.*

The transition from ecstasy to reality was through a buffalo.

When Girija Maharaj opened his eyes, he found, staring impassively at him, a huge dark languorous beast with empty eyes and arrested IQ. Its back was being massaged with wet hay. It was not a particularly appetizing sight, but he could not find fault with it. Dawn held one meaning for a Brahmin, and quite another for a cowherd. The Brahmin cleansed himself, the cowherd cleansed the buffalo. Cowherds, called *gawalas,* knew that an early bath induced the animal to give more milk.

Girija Maharaj muttered contemptuously that the buffalo and its master seemed to be on the same intellectual level, and was moving away when he glimpsed a thread that made his Brahmin blood simmer.

He recognized the challenge. This must be Govardhan Ahir, newly arrived from Patna. People who dropped by in the evenings to share his chillum (his combination of tobacco and opium was an acknowledged hit) had begun to whisper about the newcomer.

Govardhan Ahir was wearing a *janeyu,* the sacred cord, across his body, from his left shoulder to his right hip. The sacred cord was the mark of a Brahmin. It was inconceivable and unforgiveable that a mere Vaishya, a lower caste *gawala,* should wear it. The three strands of a Brahmin's cord were woven from cotton gathered by Brahmins, and therefore unpolluted by the touch of a lower caste. The thread ceremony of a Brahmin boy at the age of seven was the defining moment of his identity. It initiated his *brahmacharya:* the years of learning, devotion and abstinence from sex. The cord was thickened to nine strands when a Brahmin married and entered *grihasta,* the family phase, and lived on his body through the last cycles of *sannyas,* and *vanaprastha,* meditation and seclusion.

Girija Maharaj knew that Brahmins had lost their ancient purity, but faith was nothing if not the defence of principle by deviants. Long ago, the aristocratic Kshatriyas, backed by the sharp edge of swords, had extracted the right to wear a sacred thread. But compromise could not be permitted to degenerate into decay. If a mere cowherd could flaunt the sacred thread, the caste system might as well be abandoned. Without caste, there could be no social order. Without social order there could be no peace. It was reason enough to summon the *panch,* the group of five whose decisions had the power of law in Telinipara.

They gathered in Sheikh Rahmatullah's living room that afternoon. The host sat in front of a low, black, wooden box with a sloping top that functioned as both a depository and a desk. Bauna Sardar took a corner, and covered his small face with a thin red piece of cloth called a *gamcha* cutting off visual traffic in all directions. His authority over workers was now absolute, for the British owed him more than one favour. If militancy had not entered Victoria Jute Mill, in the manner of places like Kankinarrah, just across the river, where workers had physically attacked a Sahib, it was because of Bauna Sardar.

The turbulence let loose in 1920 had not quite ceased with the failure of India's first mass movement and Gandhi's arrest in 1922. Gandhi, with his dhoti, smile, wile and conviction, had not changed India, but he had changed Indians. He had promised freedom within a year. When 1921 ended with freedom still a mirage, the first taunts began to be heard. Gandhi implied that the fault lay with his followers, who had let violence corrupt the struggle. For instance, nationalist anger burst into anti-government riots in Bombay on 17 November, and Hindu-Muslim wars erupted in Kerala. On 5 February in a small northern village called Chauri Chaura constables, all Indians, opened fire on nationalist demonstrators till their ammunition ran out. The furious mob torched the police station; twenty-two constables were burnt to death. Gandhi blamed Satan, halted the mass campaign and went off to jail. Victoria's Scotsmen laughed, at least one of them publicly. Maulvi Taslimuddin went into political coma. He emerged a few weeks later, embittered. The Muslims had committed a horrendous sin in the eyes of Allah, he preached. They had entrusted their jihad to a Hindu. There would be divine retribution, of that he was certain. Indian Muslims would suffer. He did not know how, but, as had been said, a crime might take a moment; the price would be paid through centuries.

Bauna Sardar, not as close to God as either Gandhi or Maulvi Taslimuddin, had cooled hotheads in more practical ways. As long as they listened to him, he told workers, their wages were secure. They would never be able to earn in their villages the kind of money they were getting from Victoria Jute Mill. Moreover, was it wise to confront the British? They had witnessed the fate of India Jute Mills No 2 in Serampore, just ten miles south of Telinipara. Millhands struck work in November 1923 because the bad quality of yarn reduced their output and diminished their earnings. The workers were right, but what happened? The management shut down the factory, and a month later the millhands returned, hungry and defeated. Turbulence touched factories on both sides of the river. But Victoria Jute Mill was quiet. Bauna Sardar kept it so.

Girija Maharaj sat to the right of Rahmatullah and Thakur Bhagwan Singh to his left. The fifth man was Head Constable Lal Dhari Singh, from the newly created police station at Telinipara. His uniform gave implicit legitimacy to a kangaroo court.

Govardhan Ahir arrived punctually at four in the afternoon. He had sensed hostility on the street and knew that the *panch* could order a social boycott of his caste. He had seen this happen in Patna. He sat only upon being told to.

Girija Maharaj did not wait for civilities. He exploded: "*Abey Ahira!* Who gave you permission to wear the sacred thread?"

"I have taken an oath," mumbled Govardhan.

"Oath? What kind of oath was that?"

"Before my brotherhood…"

"And is that a Brahmin or a Thakur brotherhood?" sneered Girija Maharaj.

"No. But it is a brotherhood that is loyal to Lord Krishna. This is not an oath before men. It is an oath before God."

"Lord Krishna? So you rascals have begun to use the Lord himself to destroy the Hindu faith?"

"Destroy our faith? No, Maharaj. We are the ones who have sworn to defend the faith! Why do you sneer at us cowherds? Lord Krishna was also a cowherd. The cow is our mother. For a thousand years we impotent Hindus have allowed our mother to be slaughtered before our eyes and done nothing."

"Allowed our mother to be killed? What is this nonsense?"

"It is a long story, Maharaj."

"Then you better start telling it quickly, isn't it?"

They had not expected an introductory lecture from an upstart cowherd but they got it. He was illiterate, but educated.

"Our religion is Sanatan Dharma, the Eternal Faith. Hinduism was born on the golden, lotus-shaped Mount Meru beyond Tibet in the Himalayas, the home of our gods. In the great age of Hindu glory, all castes were equal: *varna* (caste) was a simple allotment of responsibilities. Brahmins were given charge of prayer; Kshatriyas were entrusted with war; and we

Vaishyas were given the greatest responsibility of all, that of providing food and milk. Can you worship God or go to war on an empty stomach? The Shudras became untouchable only because they were too stupid for any social responsibility other than the management of filth. Brahmins trace their lineage to Brahma; Kshatriyas to either the Sun or the Moon. We cowherds are descendants of Lord Krishna."

"So you are children of Lord Krishna, are you?" asked Thakur Bhagwan Singh with a quick laugh. "Shouldn't you be better-looking? Krishna was the most handsome of all our gods, the love of every girl in Mathura... Your looks don't quite make the category, I am afraid."

Govardhan, used to upper-caste insolence, ignored the taunt. He had a different story to tell. "We live in Kaliyug, the Age of Evil. That is why beef-eaters, first Muslims and then Christians, have conquered our holy motherland, massacred us, molested our women. Why must Muslims kill my mother in the name of their God? Conquerors take everything. We know that. The defeated are left with only their faith. Must Muslims take away my faith as well? The first thing a Muslim does if he gets any money is to go to a butcher. Meat and women are his only pleasures. Muslims even have a separate festival for eating meat. Every year, on the day of Bakr' Id, they shout the name of Allah and slit the throat of a cow. They call it *qurbani* – they kill our mother and call it a holy sacrifice! I die in shame at the impotence of Hindus each year.

"Today, we Ahirs are the vanguard of the new Hindu army that will make our faith virile. This was only possible because of the Arya Samaj, started by the great Gujarati saint Swami Dayanand Saraswati. I do not know how to read, but I have kept a small book given to me by the Arya Samaj, written by Babu Navratan Das, called *Apna Sanatan Dharm Pehchanon (Know Your True Religion)*. It proves that Hindus have been corrupted by Muslims. But there were other impurities too, perhaps worse. The Swami found we had polluted our ancient texts to such an extent that in the tantras incest was allowed with mothers, daughters, sisters and, worst of all, low-born untouchable women. We had succumbed to the five temptations: *madya*, liquor, *mans*, flesh, *meena*, fish, *mudra*, worship in the nude and *maithuna*, sex. The sixth evil also begins with 'm': Muslim. Arya Samaj monks reminded us that we were children of Lord Krishna. They gave us coloured prints of Lord Krishna playing the flute in front of a cow. We pasted these holy pictures with rice glue on the walls of our huts.

"I was a young man when Hindus at last began to stir. I was among those in Patna in 1911 who surrounded Muslim bustees at Dost Mohammadpur in order to stop cow-slaughter during Qurbani. The police came to help Muslims. You will not believe it, Babu, but we drove the police back. Those were heroic times, like the Mahabharata.

"In four or five years, all the higher castes, Brahmins, Rajputs, Kayasthas and even Marwaris, who take the first road to safety in any conflict, joined our holy war. The Maharaja of Rewa went to the famous cattle fair at Sonepur and bought up all the cows so that they could not be sold to Muslims. Can you think of a more noble way to spend your wealth? Muslims tried every trick at Sonepur, sometimes using untouchables to buy cows on their behalf. One untouchable was caught with a pair of cows he said he had bought for seven rupees and one anna: tell me, which untouchable has seven rupees? Most of those swine do not have one anna.

"The strategies for our holy war were planned by some of the noblest names of Patna, lawyers like Keshri Prasad Singh and Babu Nirsu Singh; and great zamindars like the Dalippur Babus. Secret meetings were held, cells were formed. Men were called to battle through *patias* – marked leaves used as chain letters. Teams were given responsibility for oiling staves and sharpening swords and spears. Some 5,000 of us assembled at Kanchanpura, in Patna, in 1915, armed and ready for martyrdom. The police had to shoot at us! Oh – what glory! The earth of our motherland was once again wet with Hindu blood!"

There was an anxious silence in the room. Bauna Sardar was immobile. A little gleam appeared in the eyes of the head constable. Girija Maharaj played with a thought, but waited before he reached a conclusion. My grandfather was calm; any reaction would either be a sign of weakness, or open to misinterpretation.

"I was sent the next year to Jagdishpur in Barh, where more than 10,000 brave warriors from some forty villages collected on the night before Bakr' Id. I remember that night. The season had shifted; it was a bit cool. The Muslims, as is their practice, did not sleep on the eve of the festival. Do you know that for Muslims, the day begins at night…" He began to chuckle. "What else can you expect of a people who are the opposite of all that is right? We face the east in prayer; they face the west. We begin our day by worshipping the rising sun; they begin their day by sighting the moon. The Muslim begins to ebb by sunrise!"

His voice rising with each word, Girija Maharaj snapped,

"When we want to hear jokes from you, we will let you know!"

Govardhan lowered his head but his face glowed with memories. "Such was the grace of Lord Krishna that even the police joined our holy war in Jagdishpur. The local constables helped us when we attacked Muslims while they were returning from their Bakr' Id prayers. We sprang up from a hundred points as if we were erupting from the womb of the motherland. Our best *lathials,* stave-masters, and swordsmen surrounded their bustee, set their homes on fire. You know that a Mussulman becomes a coward before fire: he believes that if he dies in a fire he will not be buried, and angels will not be able to come to his grave to carry him to his heaven.

"They were unprepared. They fled. I know some of us behaved badly, looting their goods and raping their women, but in a war you cannot ensure total purity. I am sorry to say that some Hindus protected their Muslim neighbours... everyone is not a good Hindu: that is our weakness. Our war cries made Jagdishpur tremble: '*Jai Hanuman!* Victory to Lord Hanuman!' and '*Angrez Raj uth gaya!* English rule is over!' and '*German ki jai!* Victory to the Germans!' We thought that the Germans would defeat the British and hand over India to us Hindus. Maybe that is why the British came and chased us away."

The five men were hypnotized. Bauna Sardar stirred beneath the *gamcha* on his face, but did not speak. My grandfather knew that he would have to think out his response; this was a slow walk on burning coal. Head Constable Singh was in awe of an activist who had participated in such wondrous events. Banter disappeared from Bhagwan Singh's eyes. Girija Maharaj had questions: Govardhan was not a cowherd; he was a missionary. Who had sent him to Telinipara? What did all this have to do with wearing the sacred thread?

The missionary's voice suddenly dropped to a whisper. "And then Gandhi appeared out of nowhere.

"No one recognized Gandhi when he first came to Bihar. When he got off at Patna in 1917 on his way to Champaran, there was no one to receive him at the railway station. He took a rickshaw to the bungalow of the famous lawyer Babu Rajendra Prasad. Rajendra Babu was away, on holiday at Digha. His servant threw Gandhi out of the house. Gandhi then went to have a bath at the home of his fellow-student in London, a Muslim, Mazharul Haq. After he defeated the British at Champaran, Gandhi became a god. I was thrilled when I heard that, like a good Hindu, he dreamt of turning India into Ram Rajya, the kingdom of Lord Ram.

"Then I learnt that Gandhi wanted to include Muslims in Ram Rajya. This puzzled me. What did Muslims have to do with Ram? He was not their god. I was told that Hindus and Muslims had signed an agreement. What did this mean? Would Muslims stop killing cows?

"I could not understand what Muslims wanted. I wanted freedom for my India. They wanted freedom for their Caliph in Turkey. Why should their Caliph be in Turkey and not in India? The Turkish Sultan had lost the war, so he lost his kingdom. That is the law of history. So what if the British now ruled Mecca and Medina? Didn't Muslims rule over our holy cities, Ayodhya and Kashi and Varanasi? But Muslims will always be more loyal to Mecca and Medina than to India," he said bitterly.

"Enough!" Girija Maharaj was not loud, but harsh.

My grandfather intervened for the first time. To understand, he had to know. "Go on," he said. "What happened next?"

"I was perplexed by what happened next. The Muslims stopped killing cows, even during Bakr' Id! The price of goats shot up! Gandhi launched Satyagraha, his fight for truth. Since no one knew what truth was, each community believed its version of the truth. Hindus thought they were getting India from the British, Muslims thought they were getting Mecca and Medina. Peasants said that Gandhi would give them free cloth. Even untouchables thought they were getting something – I don't know what, but something. Maybe they thought we would begin touching them!

"I went to one public meeting on the banks of the Ganga in Patna and heard Mitter Lal of Masaurhi, who used to be my leader in the Arya Samaj, say that a Hindu who did not join Gandhi would be committing a sin equivalent to eating the flesh of a cow, and a Muslim the flesh of a pig. How could any Hindu even utter such a thought? Had Gandhi become more important than our religion? Had he become holier than the cow?

"I saw Gandhiji from a distance – I am an insignificant man – when he came to Patna in the winter of 1920. Women from my village went in their bridal saris to glimpse their Mahatma. Peasants claimed that the British might have conquered Germany with cannons but would be defeated by one man with a walking stick. I heard a story that was travelling from village to village to the beat of a drum: Gandhi, a Brahmin, a cow and an Englishmen were thrown into a fire. Gandhi, the Brahmin and the cow survived, but the Englishman was burnt to death. Every village that heard the story was told to spread it to five others; failure to do so would merit the same punishment as killing five cows.

"But I always knew in my heart that this Hindu-Muslim unity was fake. When Gandhi failed, everyone went back to their old ways. The Arya Samaj returned to *shuddhi*, the self-purification programme. Frankly, I was not so enthusiastic about the Arya Samaj now. You cannot switch a holy war on and off as if it was water from one of these taps that the municipality is now giving.

"I turned towards reform in my own caste. People called us fools because we were illiterate. Thakurs and Brahmins laughed at us. Even vermin like untouchables, *chamar* and *chamains*, barbers and washermen, jeered. Our caste held a big meeting at Patna. I was so proud when I was invited. We took an oath to wear the sacred thread to show that we belonged to the family of Lord Krishna. We vowed to send our children to school; to stop child marriage; to open shops so that no tradesman could blackmail us by refusing to sell us grain and oil. We decided never to work free for any Thakur or Muslim landlord. Everyone who owned land promised to donate one anna per bigha to a scholarship fund. We vowed to spread this message. Since I am unmarried, I was sent to Telinipara to work among our brothers in the jute mills. I got two shirts, two *gamchas*, bedding, thirty rupees and a sacred thread to set up a new life. That, Maharaj, is why I am wearing the sacred thread."

The uneasy silence settled down and became its own comment. Govardhan had nothing more to say. Girija Maharaj was pensive, till he framed his question. "Do you know who killed Lord Krishna and started the Age of Evil?"

Half-convinced that it was a trick-question, Govardhan kept quiet. Girija Maharaj's voice rose steadily. "Do you know why you are cursed to be imbeciles? Because rascals from your caste, drunk on *maireyaka,* a liquor that makes you arrogant and idiotic, killed Lord Krishna! You thought you could play a practical joke on the great Brahmin sage, Viswamitra, so you dressed up Krishna's son, Samba, as a pregnant woman, and asked the sage to predict what the sex of the child would be. Viswamitra was so furious at your cheap lies that he uttered a terrible curse. Samba, he prophesied, would give birth, not to a child but to a metal club that would destroy the whole race! Not even Lord Krishna could reverse the curse of the Brahmin! Deprived of reason by your fate, deprived of your senses by alcohol, your sons slaughtered fathers, and brothers killed brothers. You attacked Krishna himself and assaulted his brother Balaram. Appalled by this self-destruction, Balaram, using yoga, merged his atman with the eternal soul. Heartbroken, Lord Krishna, dark as a cloud and lustrous as gold, sat under a banyan tree, placed his foot on his right thigh and waited for the destined hunter to pierce him with an arrow formed out of the club that his son Samba had given birth to. Thus began Kaliyug, the Age of Evil. And today you want to kill again, and – confound you! – do so in the Lord's name? You are the voice of utter folly!"

My grandfather broke the heavy stillness that followed by calling out for sherbet. A tray appeared. He offered Govardhan a glass.

Govardhan did not lift his head or move.

Girija Maharaj understood why. He roared. "Didn't you see the glass?"

Govardhan replied evenly, "How can you force me to drink water in the house of a Muslim when you, a Brahmin, do not drink water touched by me, a fellow Hindu? You buy my milk, but not drink my water!"

Girija Maharaj was now livid. "That is because milk comes from the cow and water from your vessel. If I, a Brahmin, can drink Sheikh Babu's sherbet who are you to refuse? Drink!"

Govardhan looked at my grandfather, paused, thought, snatched the glass, drank the sweet sherbet in one long gulp, got up, folded his hands, and turned to go.

"Wait!" Bauna Sardar spoke for the first time. "You are a zealot. Just remember one thing: I do not want any trouble between Hindus and Muslims in Telinipara. We have lived in peace so far. If anyone starts any trouble, anyone – I don't care who, and I don't care why – I will personally come and break every bone in your body."

Bauna Sardar's threat was not empty. My grandfather, however, understood that it was not enough.

Girija Maharaj sighed, "The nine years of prosperity are over."

10

WORDS

"WHERE DO BIRDS GO TO DIE?" MUSED BURHA DEEWANA AS HE looked up at branches cackling with life. He lay on a cot in the grove, feeble in everything but spirit. My grandfather sat at his feet. "Each year nests cackle with the demands of newborns. But we never see a sparrow fall to the ground, dead of old age. Where do sparrows go to die?"

Rahmat would listen, and leave when the dervish fell asleep.

A fortnight earlier, my grandfather had received peremptory summons. "It seems you are too busy to see me! When I am dead you will weep at my grave! See me now, when I am still alive!"

In those two weeks, Burha Deewana offered his disciple wisdom leavened with laughter. Knowledge, he said, is like dough; it becomes too heavy without the yeast of wit. "Trust in Allah," he would giggle, then drop his voice and add, "but tie the camel's leg!"

At other times, he was instructive: "Behind every palace there is a garbage pit, and the straightest arrow flies from a bent bow."

Or philosophical: "There are four stages of life, Rahmat: first, there is yours and there is mine. When we begin to understand, then mine is yours and yours is mine. When we reach the truth, *haqiqa,* there is neither mine nor yours. And when we reach *marifah,* gnosis, there is neither me nor you... The beauty of life lies in submission to love; there are a hundred ways in which to kneel and kiss the ground... Before he died Muhammad told his companions that he would leave behind two teachers. The speaking teacher is the Quran. The silent teacher is death."

Or enigmatic: "What did the duck say to the fish? 'After death what does it matter whether our world was a sea or a mirage?' When Rumi reached the door of departure, he said, 'I used to want buyers for my words. Now I wish someone would buy me away from words'."

Or concerned: He advised Rahmat and Girija Maharaj: "Do not provoke the enmity of one honest man for the support of a thousand. Honesty is always evident: the trees will tell you if it rained last night. Remain friends and there will be harmony in Telinipara. What is harmony? How do two washermen work together? One wets clothes to wash them, the second dries the washed garments. Your ego is your only enemy. Jesus said that the virtues of the pious are erased by pride. Remember these words, for words from the heart travel to the mind; words from the tongue get stuck in the ears..."

Or testy: "How are you?" Rahmat once asked. "How am I compared to what? Compared to Fareed, standing there, who is more depressed at the thought of my death than I am? How am I compared to what I was yesterday? Better, far better, for I feel closer to Allah."

One quiet evening he first made a request, and then gave a command. He asked my grandfather to give Fareed money to return to Hyderabad and settle down, for he had nothing to give. "All my life I have done nothing, and now I have nothing more to do."

He commanded that henceforth Muslims and Hindus should together commemorate, each year, during the month of Muharram, the martyrdom of Imam Hussain, son of Ali and grandson of the Prophet, killed by fellow-Muslims in the battle of Kerbala on the tenth of the month. Hussain raised his sword against tyranny; in his death lay the victory of principle. Hussain belonged to Hindus as much as to Muslims, for what is right is right in every faith.

And so my grandfather and Girija Maharaj took equal ownership of the Muharram procession. A splendid paper-and-bamboo model of Hussain's tomb, called a *taazia,* was built before Burha Deewana's weak and watering eyes. Women immediately invested it with magical properties, believing that any barren wife who walked through its arch would be blessed with child. Hindu fakirs arrived, their mouths sealed with locks that would be opened only after the *taazia* had been immersed. On the seventh day of Muharram, men gathered for the *dupahariya maatam,* the afternoon atonement, and beat their bare breasts to the rhythm of ancient memory: *Ya Ali! Ya Hussain!*

On the tenth, people poured in from the mills across the river, some with ardour reinforced by toddy, waving large banners in green and black. Drums kept time to a martial beat, in atonal harmony with the wail of mourners. The more passionate, a handful, took out large iron rings on which small blades hung like glistening silver confetti and lashed their backs, each stroke leaving a splay of sharp cuts from which blood oozed and dried.

The procession started with mock combat between my grandfather and Girija Maharaj, who used wooden staves instead of swords, and stopped every two hundred yards or so for set-piece displays by experts, young and middle-aged men who had mastered the traditional martial arts of north India. The simpler skills came first: swinging the long stick, the lathi, on either side to force one's way out of an ambush. There were two forms of this art, *ali mad*, in which the fighter keeps his left foot entrenched to one spot and manoeuvres only with his right foot; and the freewheeling *rustamkhani*. There was *pata hilana*, in which a long sword becomes simultaneously a weapon of offence and defence. An expert martial artiste could ward off five arrows at a time, then, using his sword as a lever by resting its point on the ground, leap over the heads of his assailants.

There were Brahmin specialists in *bank*, who used wrestling holds to disarm an opponent and then pinned a straight, double-edged knife to his throat. The best practitioners considered a knife inelegant. They carried a solid metal key on their sacred cords with which they choked their opponents with the utmost politeness. Muslims with fierce beards wielded the *barcha*, either flexible long spears with triangular heads or short spears with conical ends. The *taazia* was carried by volunteers who nudged each other out for the honour of lending a shoulder. It was dark before they reached the river, immersed the tomb, and dispersed.

The seasons shifted and brought the month of Ramadan. Towards its end, in the stillness of the cool air they sensed the coming of the night of mystery, the night when all creation, including the animal and plant kingdoms, bows in adoration to Allah, the night that transcends time, and Allah forgives sin at the intercession of His angels; the night when Gabriel appeared before an unschooled forty-year-old, Muhammad the *al-Amin*, the faithful, in the cave of a mountain called Hira and commanded: "*Iqra!* Read! *Inna anzalnahu fi lailatil qadr. We have revealed this message in the Night of Power. Wa ma ad raka ma lailatul qadr. What will explain to thee this Night of Power? Lailatul qadr-e khairumminalfe shahrim. The Night of Power is better than a thousand months. Tanazzalul malaekato wa-ruho fi ha be-izne rabbehim min kulle amrin. There come angels and the Spirit by Allah's permission, on every errand. Salam! Hiya hatta matla-el fajr! Peace! Until the rise of dawn!*"

Burha Deewana's eyes were closed. My grandfather and Girija Maharaj sat on the earth in the posture of prayer. Fareed stood in the shadows. "I have surrendered and am now free," the dervish murmured. "An ocean takes care of every wave till it reaches the shore... Allah, my sister Rabea's prayer is my prayer. Allah, if I worshipped Thee for fear of hell, burn me in hell; if I worshipped Thee in hope of Paradise, exclude me from Paradise. But if I worshipped Thee for Thine own sake, then do not exclude me from Your grace."

He held my grandfather's hand and passed away, a child's happiness on his face. Fareed sobbed. My grandfather hid his tears but would not release the dead man's hand until it was gently prised away.

Burha Deewana was buried where he lived, in the grove. My grandfather built a small shrine. The inscription was a verse from the Surah on the Prophet Jonah: *Allah calls to the Home of Peace, and guides whom He pleases to the straight path.* On Thursday nights a green sheet would be placed on the tomb. In the morning, women soaked the sheet in a pail of water, and took home the water in small earthen cups for good luck.

~

At the end of the month in which Burha Deewana died, a stranger came to Telinipara. To those who see signs in events, it seemed as if peace had died with the dervish.

Maulana Jauhar Kanpuri was a missionary of the Tablighi Jamaat, a movement launched by some of the more militant clerics of Deoband to purify Muslims from the stains of coexistence with Hindus.

Maulana Jauhar, a guest of Maulvi Taslimuddin, overflowed. His homespun robe reached beyond his hands, climbed over a sumptuous stomach, and went over his sandals in anticipation of future expansion at the waist. His thick black beard started over the ears and flourished till the neck, but was carefully patterned, forming a hirsute coastline from an inch above the cheekbone down to lower lip. There was no moustache.

Young Kalyan Singh, the teenage son of Bhagwan Singh, whose naiveté was punctuated by sharp darts of perception, pointed out that it must take more effort to preserve such a beard than to shave every day. The witticism, repeated frequently, was noted by Govardhan Ahir. When Syed Ashfaque Alam saw the visitor he recalled a couplet from Akbar Allahabadi:

Mujh ko khush aati hai masti, Sheikh ji ko farbahi
Main hoon peene ke liye, aur woh khane ke liye.

I am happy when in ecstasy, the Mullah when obese
I was born to drink, and he was born to eat.

Maulana Jauhar was polite, soft-spoken, and quickly enthralled believers with his sermons. He had a large whisper that echoed through the hall of the mosque. "I am blessed," he introduced himself at the start of the Id sermon, "to have been a disciple of all three masters of our age: the founder of Tablighi Jamaat, Maulana Ilyas Khandalwi; the friend of Gandhi, Maulana Husain Ahmad Madani; and the revered Hazrat Shaikh ul Hadis Maulana Muhammad Zakarriya, who taught me the sayings and deeds of the Prophet, may peace be upon him."

The theme of his sermon was the miracle of the Quran.

"Allah," he intoned, "creates what He wants, erases what He pleases; with Him is the *Umm-al Kitab,* the Mother of the Book. He created the Divine Throne, the Divine Chair, Heaven and Hell, Earth and Sky, the Tablet and Pen, angels, man and djinn. The Holy Quran is the treasure house of all knowledge, the Complete Book, sufficient for this life and the next. There is no knowledge outside the Quran. It was revealed over twenty-three years, and compiled long after the Prophet's death, and yet so superbly crafted that not a line can be shifted or a word changed. Great scholars have discovered a divine balance in its structure that is a message of equality. *Man* is mentioned twenty-four times, *woman* twenty-four times. *Duniya,* the world, appears 115 times; *akhriyat,* the end, 115 times. *Angels* are mentioned eighty-eight times in the holy verses, *Satan,* eighty-eight. There are 145 references to *life* and *death* is mentioned 145 times!"

"*Subhanallah!* Glory to Allah!" cried Taslimuddin.

"*Museebah,* misfortune, is written seventy-five times; and *shukrah,* gratitude, seventy-five times. *Zakat,* charity, appears thirty-two times and *barakah,* blessing, appears thirty-two times." The admiring refrain got louder. "*Hardship* is mentioned 114 times by Allah, and how many times do you think *patience* appears? 114. There is a message in the Quran even for me," he ended with a nasal flourish. "*Tongue* appears twenty-five times and how many times does *sermon* appear? Twenty-five! Let me tell the British, so proud of science, that all secrets of nature were written in the Quran long before their scientists 'discovered' them. *Day* appears 365 times in the Holy Book, and *month* twelve times. Do you get it?"

They got it, and responded, their voices high with excitement. "Learn the Quran, O believers, and tear apart the 72,000 veils between man and Allah!"

~

Maulana Jauhar, who was an activist during the Khilafat movement against the British, was horrified when Gandhi suddenly, arbitrarily called off the struggle. Shock turned to despair, despair to restlessness, restlessness to questions. Answers came in the ideas of Maulana Kandhalwi and the introspection of the Tablighi Jamaat. Muslims were weak because they were afraid to be Islamic. Allah had not forsaken Muslims; Muslims had denied Allah. India's Muslims were in a double-trap, either sycophants before the conquering Christians or ensnared by the idol-worshipping Hindus.

Mangu Qasai, now much nearer to his grave, became his principal ally, particularly when he heard that the eventual objective was to usher in an Islamic *nizam,* or rule, although no date was set for world power. A committee of three, two clerics and a butcher, drafted a reform pamphlet and a common minimum programme for Telinipara's imperfect Muslims:

1   Correct recitation of *kalimah*.

2   Prayer, five times a day; petition to be sent to Victoria management to permit Muslims to do so in mill compound.

3   Islamic appearance and behaviour (*shakl-o-surat*) among men: viz., heavy beard (preferably dyed in henna), light moustache, ankle-length pyjamas.

4   Elimination of "Hindu" practices among women, like vermilion in the parting of their hair, or music and dancing; insistence on the veil.

5   Compulsory madrasa for children.

Money was raised and pamphlets printed on a lithograph press in Chandernagore before anyone realized that the target audience could not read. Mistakes did not dampen zeal. Alas, Telinipara's women laughed, and men showed little interest in growing beards. The five-point programme thinned to one, when Maulana Jauhar decided that Mangu Qasai's less theological agenda might have more impact. The cow would establish the difference.

The Maulana built up a careful case, and sold it assiduously. The sacrifice of a cow on Bakr' Id was lawful in Islam. Pressure from Hindu militants had curtailed the practice. Why should Muslims live in fear of Hindu wrath? Were they equal citizens with equal rights or not? If they ceded space on religion, they would be in retreat everywhere. The call to prayer could be banned, as it was banned in Christian Europe. To prevent cow sacrifice on Bakr' Id was illogical as well. Beef was sold through the year. The British ate beef. If Hindus did not agitate to prevent the British from eating beef, why should they stop cow slaughter, a holy duty, during Bakr' Id?

Govardhan Ahir was the natural leader of the response.

His immediate circle consisted of Kalyan Singh, and Mohan and Vishnu, sons of Narayan Teli, whose fried vegetables had lost out to my grandfather's hotel half a lifetime ago. Under protection of darkness, others would join his strategy sessions. His most important recruit was Head Constable Lal Dhari Singh.

"You consider Muslims pious because they go to a mosque five times a day, isn't it?" laughed Govardhan. "They don't go to a mosque to pray. They go for military training. Have you seen how they pray? They stand in straight lines, like soldiers. They do not allow any gaps. They bend and kneel and touch the floor with their heads; these are all military exercises. Obedience is compulsory. Each year, for one month they fast without drinking even a drop of water from sunrise to sunset. Why? To learn military discipline – because the Quran orders them to fight and kill! Hindus also fast, but do we go crazy like Muslims, who don't even let saliva down their throats even at the height of summer? Muslims are peaceful only when powerless – as they shall be when Mother India rediscovers her glory and Hindu India rises from the ashes of foreign rule!

"Muslims will tell you that Islam is a religion of peace. Bunk! There are two kinds of verses in the Quran, those uttered in Mecca and those uttered in Medina. In Mecca the Prophet of Muslims was not in power, so in Mecca he said things like, your religion for you and mine for me. But in Medina, he became a king. What happened then? His Allah suddenly began to send verses saying that all non-Muslims should be slaughtered in a jihad. Muslims call us kafir, which is the worst abuse in their language: we will be burnt in unceasing hell fire, they say, because we worship idols of Lord Krishna and Radha, and our skins will be replaced over and over again so that our suffering never ends. If you do not believe me, ask Taslimuddin. Or ask the fat mullah he has brought to create trouble!"

The wide-eyed young men were eager to believe and had no intention of cross-checking with the enemy.

"That is why there are so few Hindus in India. There used to be 600 million Hindus before the Muslims came. Today we are only 200 million! When the accursed Afghan invader Ghori defeated Raja Jaichand of Benaras, he massacred 50,000 Hindus in one day and converted 1000 temples into mosques. When Babar defeated Maharana Sangram Singh of Mewar at Khanua he killed 100,000 Rajput prisoners and another 100,000 innocent bystanders. How many Muslims came with Babar? Only 10,000. And I don't have to tell you how many Muslims there are today! There are more Muslims than Hindus in Bengal!"

"But how did so few Muslims manage to kill so many Hindus?" asked Kalyan, who could never resist a question.

"Because," answered Govardhan persuasively, "Muslims are trained to kill from the age of seven, when a boy is sent to say his *namaz* in a mosque. Didn't you see how they were brandishing swords and spears at the Muharram procession? Islam is like an army, with Allah as its commander-in-chief and but a single aim, to establish its empire all over the world. Every mosque is a camp of this army, where men are trained for jihad. Their Prophet ordered eighty-two jihads from his mosque in Medina. Whenever Muslims want to start a riot they first gather in a mosque. That is why Swami Dayanand Saraswati says in *Satyartha Prakash* that if Allah was a true protector He would not have ordered Muslims to kill people of other faiths. A

Muslim does not go to a mosque because he wants to go to Paradise. A Muslim is promised Paradise in any case, whether he prays or not. He is guaranteed houris in see-through garments who will always be sixteen, always be virgin, and with whom he can make love for forty hours."

"Forty hours?!" asked Lal Dhari Singh, incredulous. "Won't he get tired?"

"Maybe they will get a different kind of body. I heard that they will be able to eat everything and digest it completely so that they don't have to shit."

"That's not too bad an idea," said Kalyan Singh, who tended towards constipation. "But tell me, how can a houri make love for forty hours and yet remain a virgin?" The young man had been married a year earlier and knew all the facts of life.

"When Badshah Akbar captured Chittor," said Govardhan, changing the subject, "the number of Hindus slain could not be counted. When he ordered the sacred threads from fallen bodies to be weighed, it came to seventy-four and a half *maunds*! Firoz Shah Tughlaq butchered 120,000 Hindus, including those who had taken shelter on an island, when he desecrated the temple of Lord Jagannath in Orissa. Muslims give you only two choices: either conversion or death!"

Kalyan Singh persisted. "In that case why are so many Hindus alive today?"

"Because Lord Krishna will never allow Hindus to perish completely. It is our duty to arouse Hindus from their long sleep! We must never let a butcher spill the blood of our mother cow on our motherland!"

Head Constable Lal Dhari Singh nodded sagely.

Maulana Jauhar permitted himself an amused look when someone in his group suggested that Sheikh Rahmatullah would protect the honour of Muslims.

"Rahmatullah," he said, "is a recent convert, and who knows how many old convictions still lie in his heart. They say that there is an *Om* hidden among the decorations of his fancy house. If Rahmatullah wants to prove that he is a genuine sheikh of Muslims, he should sacrifice a cow on Bakr' Id. The blessings of Allah are five times as great in the case of a cow as compared to a goat."

This casual thought developed a life. Would Sheikh Rahmatullah prove that he was a genuine Muslim, or would he prove to be a *munafiqeen,* a hypocrite, or worse, a *murtadd,* an apostate? Maulana Jauhar explained, without any display of emotion, that the Quran condemned the hypocrite to hell, while the punishment for apostasy was death.

The moon of the month of Dhu al Haj was sighted; Bakr' Id was ten days away. Rumours circulated among Hindus that cows had been kept across the river, and would be brought by boat on the eve of the festival to be slaughtered en masse by the hand of Maulana Jauhar. Men became apprehensive, women fearful. Lal Dhari Singh, wearing the pastemarks of puja on his forehead, strode into Hindu homes and made a promise: as long as he was alive, he would defend Hindu honour. Bhagwan Singh and Zulfiqar Khan suggested to my grandfather that perhaps he should send his son and Jamila to a safer place, provoking his irritation and anger. Privately, Taslimuddin was miserable at the frenzy he had inadvertently let loose, but hapless in the grip of Maulana Jauhar's personality.

The friends met to compare notes, and found they had no

ideas. Muslims answered Bauna Sardar's admonitions with downcast eyes and sullen silence. Hindus accused Girija Maharaj of polluting his caste by eating with unclean outcastes. Zulfiqar Khan swayed from one suspicion to another, and wondered why Hindus were making such a fuss about Bakr' Id unless it was a conspiracy to attack Muslims with the help of the police. Better safe than sorry, he quietly sharpened the two swords and three knives he possessed. The authorities, advised by their Head Constable, posted policemen near the mosque, raising tension a few notches higher. Forty-eight hours before Bakr' Id, Muslims began to whisper that Lal Dhari Singh had supplied Hindus with kerosene to burn the huts of Muslims. Kalyan Singh talked openly of slitting the throat of anyone who slit the throat of his mother. Men began, behind latched doors, checking their weapons.

Girija Maharaj resisted doubt, increased his intake of ganja to calm his nerves, but the question grew from a tiny nag to an overpowering worry: there were only forty-eight hours left to Bakr' Id and Rahmat had still not purchased any goats. Each year he bought the animals with a great deal of fuss, their size and looks scrutinized for the minutest flaw. Henna would be applied on their foreheads, and they would be fed the finest gram. But this year not a word had been said and no one dared to ask why. Ashfaque had not shown his face for a fortnight, which was unusual: did Ashfaque know something that he did not?

Girija Maharaj was reluctant when he received a message to come over to his friend's home on the eve of Bakr' Id. He would have preferred the numb comfort of opium to the strain of dread. But he could not find the courage to refuse. Bauna Sardar was already with my grandfather when he reached. No one spoke. Girija Maharaj sat listlessly against a wall. His heart began to hammer against his senses when he saw Maulana Jauhar and Maulvi Taslimuddin climb the stairs some minutes later. What price was friendship going to demand this night?

Sheikh Rahmatullah welcomed the two clerics politely, correctly. Sherbet and tea were offered. Girija Maharaj refused tea with a trembling hand.

"Maulana Jauhar," my grandfather said gravely, "we Muslims of Telinipara have the highest respect for your knowledge of the Holy Quran and the life of the Prophet. You have enlightened us with your sermons, you have brought back the young to the mosque. Maulvi Taslimuddin is an old friend of mine, and he will pardon me if I say, with due respect, that you have done in a few months what he has not been able to achieve in the decades I have known him."

Maulana Jauhar resisted the urge to beam.

Maulvi Taslimuddin could not hide his relief. All would be well. Rahmat would not let Islam down. "Tomorrow is the Id of Haj, and the sacrifice of an animal to Allah is obligatory on every Muslim with means," continued my grandfather. "Tell me, Maulana, which animals are lawful for sacrifice?"

"The sheep, the goat, the cow and the camel."

"And, in the eyes of Allah, the sacrifice of which animal is the most meritorious for a believer?"

"The camel, of course; a verse in the Quran marks out the camel as an example of God's wisdom and kindness, and Allah honours the sacrifice of that which He loves best."

"It will be my privilege, Maulana, to honour your presence in

Telinipara during Bakr' Id this year by offering a camel as a sacrifice, and I hope that you will do us Muslims of this humble place the favour of slaying the camel by *nahr,* in the hollow of the throat near the breastbone where the three blood vessels are combined so that death may be as painless as possible to the animal that will go to Paradise."

"A camel?" responded Maulana Jauhar in mild panic for he had no idea how camels were killed. "Where are you going to get a camel in Telinipara?"

As if on cue, they heard the sound of children's cries and cheers from the lane. Maulana Jauhar sensed that something was happening which he could not comprehend. Syed Ashfaque Alam bounded up the stairs. His laugh broke the tension.

"*Adaab... tasleem... assalamalaiqum wa rahmatullah wa barkat-e-hu!*" he saluted, in typical multiplex style, distributing peace in all its forms. "Maulana Jauhar, a very special welcome to you on this holy evening! Rahmat Bhaijan," he shouted, "your camel is at the door! But this is the last time I get you a camel from Calcutta! The next time you want a bloody camel, get it yourself!"

Maulana Jauhar recognized defeat, and got up with dignity. Sheikh Rahmatullah had drawn a large circle around his small one. A cow would not be slaughtered the next morning. And no fatwa could be delivered on the purity of Sheikh Rahmatullah's faith.

"Let me help you get up, Maulana," Ashfaque offered breezily. "Sometimes this beast of a body can be demanding. Tomorrow is going to be a big day for eating. You will need all the rest you can manage to do justice to tomorrow's cooking."

Girija Maharaj grinned like a schoolboy when he heard the

full story from Ashfaque. Arranging a camel was not a joke. Moreover, they had to keep it a secret for who knew what new demand Maulana Jauhar would come up with were he given time.

In the ladies' quarters, a second party was in progress. Women crowded around Jamila, cradled my father, called him a lucky omen. Mai sat imperiously on a chair and repeated till she was roundly condemned as a bore that they must remember whose son Rahmat was.

"It was Burha Deewana's wisdom, not mine, Girija," explained my grandfather as they talked through the night, unwilling to sleep, welcoming anyone who dropped in to celebrate their release from danger.

"And how was it Burha Deewana, may God be pleased with him, this time?" asked Girija.

"You forget what he once said! 'Trust in God, but tie the camel's leg!' That gave me the idea…"

Let it be recorded that the scholarly dissertations of Maulana Jauhar, who soon took his mission elsewhere, had some influence on the oratorical skills of Maulvi Taslimuddin. He explained the return of peace in his first Friday sermon after Maulana Jauhar's departure: "Angels are the hierarchy between man and God. God created angels from intellect without sensuality, and beasts from sensuality without intellect; but human beings from both intellect and sensuality. When our intellect prevails over passion we become better than angels; when our sensuality conquers intellect we become worse than beasts."

No one really understood what he was saying, but it sounded good.

11

SAHIBS

What men call gallantry, and gods adultery
Is much more common where the climate's sultry.

Mathew Horne claimed that these lines were written by Lord Byron. There was no argument. He had taken a degree in English.

"The ideal of Western beauty," continued Matthew, lounging upon a sofa, "is the Perfect 3. Three features must be white: skin, teeth, hands; three black: eyes, lashes, brows; three red: lips, cheeks, nails; three long: body, hair, hands; three short: teeth, ears, legs. Add three large: breasts, forehead, brows; and three slender: waist, hands, feet. Throw in three plump: arms, hips, thighs; and three thin: fingers, hair, lips. Mix and stir. That is your Perfect 3."

"She certainly does not live in Victoria Jute Mill," responded Simon Hogg, who had studied engineering in Dundee rather than English at Edinburgh. "Or anywhere, I dare say, in the British empire, except your imagination. I'll settle for large breasts, plump thighs and slender waist."

"If you wait for that combination in a British woman, you

will remain a virgin as long as H. Meyer Esq. According to a personal ad I read in the *Statesman* he was sixty-four when he wed Miss Casina Coupers, sixteen, after five years of courtship. Child-molester! Miss Coupers must have been eleven when he started wooing her."

"I rather admire the famous Begum Johnson who married at twelve, got her fifth English husband at nineteen and was given a state funeral when she died at the age of eighty-seven in 1812. They should have played Tchaikovsky at the funeral," responded Simon.

Colonel White was over 40,
Jane, his bride, was 17;
She was also very naughty,
For she loved a Captain Green!

They laughed.

Mathew rose, placed one arm behind his back in the best Parliamentarian manner, and delivered a speech.

"You are aware, I trust, that the honourable British Empire has an official policy on sex in the tropics. Abstinence is good for freezing Britain but unhealthy in hot India. The Portuguese obtained a firman from the Emperor Shah Jehan to keep Bengali women in summer. Their needs were, it seems, seasonal. We British turned sex into a year-long discipline. The Indian Army, therefore, maintains a red light area, Lal Bazar in native lingo, next to every cantonment. The supply-demand ratio is one whore to forty-four men. Who worked this out, I don't know, but it brought an end to the age of the papaya as a cock-calmer: useful, I suppose, but not very elegant, what? Be it noted that the British army whorehouse is run on exemplary Marxist principles: from each according to his ability, to each according to his need. A trooper pays one rupee, a corporal two and the sergeant pays five. I applaud sexual socialism! The Lal Bazar at Agra cantonment is situated opposite the church, and on Sundays you can hear evensong and soliciting simultaneously. Calcutta has its own stories to tell! I hear that when the city's most famous courtesan retired in 1903, during the durbar of Lord Curzon, after thirty-three noble years of service to the Empire, she kept open house for five hours that night as a thank-you gesture."

"Who do you think was last in that queue?"

"Someone with the patience of an empire-builder. India was won by the best of the British, our mavericks. When the British are boring they are good. But when they are mad, they are superb. Clive, our great ancestor, father of Bengal, had a massive stalagmite and picked up the pox regularly in Madras. The favourite British toast after his victory at Plassey was to 'a lass and a lakh a day'. Colonel James Skinner, hero of the Mutiny, admitted to fourteen children from a flourishing harem. About eighty claimed his paternity after he died, and who knows, they may have all been right. David Ochterlony, the British resident of Delhi in 1803, would take his thirteen wives, each on a separate elephant, for an airing every evening along the Jamuna river. They called him Loony Akhtar, but it was an utterly sane thing to do. There would have been fisticuffs if they were all on the same elephant, methinks. George Dick, the governor of Bombay a little more than a hundred years ago, had an Indian mistress who spied for the Marathas. If that wasn't the original Mata Hari! Bishop Reginald Heber, my boy, the first Bishop of Calcutta! He used to stare longingly at beautiful young women bathing in the Hooghly river: their deep bronze skin was more agreeable to the human eye, he wrote, than the fair skins of Europe. That's my kind of Bishop! What was good for the lord in 1823 is good enough for me in 1932!"

Simon raised his eyes in mild disbelief.

"Absolutely true, absolutely! Check out his journal, *Narrative of a Journey*. We called our Indian wives, Bibis. Sir Charles Metcalfe brought one from the court of the Sikh, Maharajah Ranjit Singh and had three healthy sons. You might imagine that Lord Teignmouth, our governor-general in 1793-98, might have been less randy, given that he was the founder of the British and Foreign Bible Society. But no, there he was, banging away a brown Bibi! Our most famous international pornographer, Sir Richard Burton − he served in the Indian Army for seven years and managed to get out just in time, two years before the Mutiny − did extensive studies to prove that Indian women had contempt for the haste and clumsiness of Europeans. In matters of sex, we're just big mouths, I'm afraid, and not very big anywhere else…"

"Was all this in your university course?'

"If you can't pick up good gossip in a university, what is the point of education? Jemdanee, the Bibi of our first journalist, the muckraker William Hickey, was greatly admired by his English friends for her wit, although, being a good Muslim, she never touched a drop of alcohol. What utter prigs we've become! There was a time when the King's birthday would be celebrated with an evening of nautch. Why have dancing girls disappeared from our lives, I ask! I blame it on the damn Suez Canal, which brought memsahibs and morals into our lives. Mark my words. The decline of British India will be traced to 1905, when the government cancelled the nautch at the official reception for the Prince of Wales in Madras!"

Simon Hogg was thereby persuaded by Mathew to accept an invitation from Baboo Satyajit Kumar Banerjee, zamindar of Mankundu and Bhadreshwar, to a nautch evening, for Sahibs only, to celebrate the grand festival of Durga Puja. The card, on white hardboard paper with a border of gold dust, said:

10 October, 1932   GRAND NAUCHES
Durga Pooja Holidays

BABOO SATYAJIT BANERJEE
of Mankundu and Bhadreshwar

Begs to inform Honourable Guests, of limited variety, that a Grand Nauch shall be conducted by Nicki & Party of Lucknow, with warble by exquisite Anjuman & Party, in front of Great Goddess Ma Durga, on 10th thereof, of repertoire viz. Kathak Nauch, Bearer Nauch, Kite Nauch, Snake Nauch etc., etc., etc. in Apsara Fashion. It is humbly beseeched that every attention will be paid to the Gentlemen who are respectfully solicited to grace the occasion with their presence, and it is mentioned that tiffin, wines, dinner will be furnished and also, entertainments afterwards, during their stay at the humble riverside abode of

Yours Truly
Baboo Satyajit Banerjee.

Satyajit Baboo's admiration for the white man was unqualified, and he reserved one evening of puja festivities for Sahibs. He understood their qualms. They were comfortable only without either wives or natives.

Satyajit Baboo had clear views on Gandhi. Gandhi was an unmitigated disaster. He regretted signs that British resolve was weakening. It had been a mistake to let Gandhi meet King-Emperor George VI in Britain. A naked rebel had been given implicit equality with the sovereign of the greatest empire in history. Too many Indians were spreading the story, surely incorrect, that Gandhi had snubbed the King. (King to Gandhi, who was wearing a thin loincloth: "Aren't you a trifle underdressed for London?" Gandhi to King: "Your Majesty, you are wearing enough clothes for both of us.") Gandhi had blackmailed the British into announcing a Communal Award by which the dregs of native society – Hindu untouchables and Muslim peasants – would now be able to contest elections and enter legislatures. Such classes, dark and illiterate, were meant to take orders, not give them. He respected the fair-skinned Muslim aristocrats of the north with Turkish blood in their veins, poetry on their lips and a sword at the side. They were a handsome ruling class. The British were more than worthy successors. He was proud of the fact that his son, Adheep, was studying law in London.

~

Victor Matheson, general manager of Victoria Jute Mill, did not forbid Mathew and Simon from taking the company boat for a nautch evening, since the District Collector and Superintendent of Police would also be there, but made his disapproval evident. In a formal letter he regretted his personal inability to attend a function to which wives had not been invited.

A friendly breeze floated across an extended balcony and through a French window into a hall dominated by a sparkling chandelier, and further illuminated by electric bulbs encased in shaded, frosted glass decorated with small flowers. Persian and Afghan carpets ran over one another on the polished wooden floor, past imitation Greek marble statues. Satyajit Baboo sat on a chair, very dignified, the tube of a hookah in one hand. Next to him rose an imposing image of the Goddess Durga, wife of Shiva, daughter of the Himalayas, armed with Shiva's trident, the *trishul,* Vishnu's discus, the *sudarshan chakra,* Brahma's prayer beads, the *rudraksha,* Varuna's conch and noose, Agni's dart, Vayu's bow, Surya's arrows, Indra's thunderbolt, Kuvera's mace, Kali's sword and Vishwakarma's battle-axe, astride her father's lion, slaying the demon Mahesha, created in the latest style by the master craftsman, Gopeshwar Pal.

He wore the traditional Bengali dress of gossamer-thin kurta and dhoti, spun from the finest cotton. On his shoulders lay a Kashmiri shahtoosh, popularly admired as a "ring shawl" for it was soft enough to pass through a finger ring, woven from the hair of the throat of a Tibetan antelope that lives at 20,000 feet in the Himalayas. There were less than a dozen guests, a few of them French. Pleasantries were exchanged, in which the host played a minimal part. Each guest was offered a chair and a hookah. An attendant, the *hookahburdar,* squatted next to the bowl at the base, filled with water perfumed with the essence of rose. He offered the long, looping tube to the Sahib when required, and refurbished the burning tobacco in the cup at the top of the stem, the silver-rimmed chillum.

"Grab a Cream Can," urged Mathew as the two settled

down. "Cream Can" was British colloquial for hookah in the belief that it had been invented by a Persian called Karim Khan Zend.

The nautch girls, relieved that no wives were present, were at their seductive best. The owner of the troupe, affectionately called Khalajan, or Aunty, by the girls, sat with the musicians, chewed betel leaf and smiled decorously while Anjuman warbled, as advertised. The gentlemen sipped Scotch, gin, brandy, wines or port, passed around on silver trays by young men in white turbans set off by a sharp red slash. The evening started with Nikki's snake dance: lissome, long-limbed, she took the edge of a scarf in her mouth, puffed it into the shape of a gourd, and swayed like a snake on hashish. The mood got more sinuous. Two women, with a sash around their loins, a turban on their heads and their long hair over their bosoms, danced the *kaharka*. Towards the end, a girl who could not have been more than eighteen, came within six inches of Mathew, glanced at him through the dark outline of antimony, and brushed his face with her sky-blue skirt six mesmerizing times as she swirled without a pause. She laughed as she moved away, while he turned purple. Dinner was eaten in a haze of smoke and wine. When Mathew lingered over the cognac, Satyajit Baboo courteously invited him and Simon to stay over rather than, as he put it, risk a boat journey in the dark. The others had come by car. Bearers led Mathew and Simon to two spacious, well-appointed guest rooms on the other side of a sprawling garden, across the pond.

Khalajan entered Mathew's room noiselessly, and, her head bowed, suggested that he must be tired after such a long day. Could she send young Gulab – surely he remembered the swirl of her skirt? – to massage his feet? Would Simon Sahib also like some attention to his feet?

Simon was clear: he would not like. He slept uneasily and slipped away much before dawn, vaguely unable to face his host. He left a note of thanks which also indicated that the boat would return for Mathew. Satyajit Baboo was either discreet or asleep. He did not appear in the morning when *chota hazri,* the small breakfast, was brought to Mathew's room at six. Gulab had slipped away once Mathew, sated, fell asleep. She was feeling a bit grim, for he had made all the mistakes attributed to Englishmen and Pathans: bitten her lips, squeezed her nipples, scratched her neck and made love like a man setting off a gun. But he was young, always an advantage, and sincere, always a bonus. When he returned ("if" never entered her mind; she was confident he would seek her out at the boudoir they ran in Chandernagore's Urdi Bazar) he would get a few lessons along with his whisky.

~

Summoned by a small handbell, Ghulam Rasool brought tea in fine company china. Simon sat on the balcony of his bungalow and watched the first hint of light change the colour of the river. It was five in the morning. In the haze, about two hundred yards to his right, three figures emerged.

Two middle-aged women entered the water; their young companion sat for a while on the edge of the bank, one foot playing with the ripples. The drape of her knee-length sari swept up across her breast, turned over her shoulders and across the back till it was tucked at the waist. The curve of her breasts fell heavily against the soft cloth. Simon stared, transfixed by her beauty. She had an oval face; her left eye tilted upwards towards the line of a mischievous eyebrow. She wore a ring in the nose; and the tinkle of her glass bangles reached him with sensuous faintness. She stood up, supple, slender with well-rounded limbs. Her expression was playful. She looked up and down on either side of the bank, found her moment of secrecy, loosened the top of her sari and plunged into the river in a blur. She seemed hidden for an eternity. She rose waist-high above the water, protected by semi-darkness, drew her fingers through her tresses like a half-immersed mermaid, her wet sari clinging to her breasts. She waded towards the bank, picked up a dry sari from the bank, turned her back to unseen eyes, shook off the wet sari and folded herself in the dry one, stepped on to land and walked away, her full breasts swaying with the confidence of youth.

Simon Hogg was woken from hypnosis by a less than discreet cough. Ghulam Rasool's stare locked into space above the master's head. Later, when he checked on the servants' grapevine, he was impressed by news that his master had refused the services of a dancing girl. He was not a prude. He did not buy the silly rant of moralists who saw the furies of hell in the eyes of a nautch girl. He did not expect young men to be priests, and from what he had heard of priests that might not be a suitable analogy either. But he had become fond of Simon and expected higher standards.

It became a ritual. Simon, who had rarely woken up before seven, was now on his balcony each morning at five. The girl did not return.

It is possible that Ghulam Rasool also got tired of being woken up so early. One morning, while serving tea, he whispered gently into the master's ear, in the limited Urdu that Simon had picked as part of his training.

"She will not come to the river," said Ghulam Rasool.

Simon was astonished. When he recovered, he dropped pretence and asked why.

"She is an honourable woman."

"I am an honourable man," replied Simon, with some vehemence.

"Our women are afraid of white men," Ghulam Rasool responded.

"All white men are not alike, just as all brown or black men are not alike."

Ghulam Rasool's voice was soft against Simon's ear: they were exchanging a confidence, after all. "Sahib, the work in this house has become too much for me. It is a large house, and I cannot cook and keep house as well."

Simon was not abstemious. Others might worry that the value of the rupee had declined from two shillings to one shilling sixpence; he did not. But there were cogent reasons for limited staff. The company provided a range of services. The untouchable *mehtar,* sweeper, not only cleaned the house but also polished his shoes (upper-caste Hindus would not touch leather, and Muslims considered it beneath their dignity). Security was provided by company durwans. The company dhobi turned up for the laundry. In the old days status-conscious cooks would demand the services of an attendant to carry bags from the bazaar, but these days cooks preferred to keep the change from the shopping bill to themselves. A salary went only so far. An assistant meant sharing the swag.

"If Sahib has no objection, I would like to bring a niece to help with the housekeeping and wash the dishes."

Simon shrugged and said yes. That was how he met Hasina, the girl he had seen by the river.

Ghulam Rasool was deadpan; Hasina's eyes were fixed on the floor. Simon mumbled. He did not know how to thank his cook, until the obvious occurred to him. He handed Ghulam Rasool a large tip. Ghulam Rasool slipped the baksheesh into the folds of his coat, and said loudly to the girl, "You will have to work very hard here."

Within a week Simon asked Ghulam Rasool to recommend a teacher who could educate him to speak proper Urdu. Ghulam Rasool went to my grandfather's home. Syed Ashfaque Alam was delighted to accept a well-paid reason to visit Telinipara. "Give me food and drink," he exclaimed in remembered doggerel, "and then see what I think!" At long last, he thought, his university degree might actually come to some use. According to classicists at his madrasa, basic Urdu could be learnt in seventeen one-hour lessons; naturally, he intended to take much longer. But this assumed that master and student had at least one language in common. Syed Ashfaque decided to take my father along as interpreter since my father was the first Bihari in Telinipara to speak English.

Abbaji, which is how we addressed father, had been spoilt with the kind of consistency that only a strong grandmother can ensure.

Every detail of his health, from the first sign of constipation as a baby to the first sign of acne as a teenager, was addressed with maximum fuss. The medication for acne was almost ceremonial. Clarified butter was heated to scalding point, then poured into kneaded flour, which was applied over each acne spot till the heat inflamed and burst the minute boils. His diet was based on a legendary prescription designed by the great Hakim Babar Ali Khan for the Nawab of Rampur in the 1850s.

Every morning from the age of seven, he ate a concoction of gold leaf, white ambergris, essence of the *kewra* flower, specially made with white crystallized sugar, swallowed with a mixture of vinegar, lime-juice, honey and rosewater. He ate plenty of chicken, and lightly-done eggs, but it was considered unhealthy to eat chicken and eggs together. Bowlfuls of goat's foot gravy were made every Friday for breakfast.

His education began when he was four years, four months and four days old. He was dressed in the finery of a bridegroom and seated on a rug. Maulvi Taslimuddin stroked his beard and told the young man to recite after him: *"Bismillah...* In the name of Allah..." He asked my father to repeat the first Arabic alphabets after him: *Alef, bey, tey, sey, jeem, hey...* "Oh Allah," he prayed, "make learning easy for this child so that by knowledge he may conquer the world." Basketloads containing four kinds of *halva – papri,* dry and hard, *habshi,* so soft it crumbled, *jauzi,* equally soft but not as black, and *dudhia,* made with milk - were distributed to every home in Telinipara along with the sweet barfi, as white as the snow that gave its name.

In that instant, my father also became the first literate member in family history. Friends beamed, gave presents and promised a great future. But my grandfather realized that Arabic and Urdu alone would not enable him to conquer the world. He had two options. St Joseph's Convent, on the Strand in Chandernagore, was run by Irish priests and nuns for the children of French officials, but was outside his horizon. He went instead to Baboo Akshay Mookerjea, principal of the Bengali-medium Bhadreshwar Municipal School, established by the government in 1921.

My grandfather had only one query: would his son learn English? Baboo Akshay Mookerjea, a Bengali Christian, asserted with quiet confidence that he took English classes twice a week himself. He proudly pointed out a framed quotation from a speech delivered by the empire-builder Thomas Macaulay during the debate on the renewal of the East India Company's charter in 1833: "By good government we may educate our subjects into a capacity for better government; that, having become instructed in European knowledge, they may, in some future age, demand European institutions. Whether such a day will ever come I know not. But never will I attempt to avert or retard it. Whenever it comes, it will be the proudest day in English history".

When my father learnt that he would be calling on a Sahib at the Victoria Jute Mill, he made the first of a number of demands. And so a low-mount bicycle made by Rover of Coventry, fitted with detachable Edouard Michelin tyres, was added to his personal possessions. He also wanted a white cotton suit, tailored by Barkatali Brothers of Park Street, Calcutta. Wealth had not made my grandfather any less a miser. He cringed and muttered.

Surjya Modak often came over to play cards, a local variant of bridge called 29. Modak had left his shop to a competent son, and taken up pilgrimage and gossip to fill his time. The choicest bits were inevitably about local glamour, the family of Baboo Satyajit Banerjee. The zamindar, he sighed, was addicted to English whisky and had left his estates to sycophants and adventurers. His unctuous manager, Pulluck Sanyal, stole the rent, slept with the mistress, and took the air on the strand in the family's large Raj Cadillac car, driven by an Eurasian chauffeur.

He was said to be worth lakhs of rupees while the expenses of the zamindar's son in London were not met. Baboo Satyajit Banerjee was once again in need of a loan. Could Rahmatullah help?

My grandfather, eyes glistening, asked with a smile that twisted upwards, "Will the great Bengali Baboo take a loan from a Bihari coolie?"

Modak laughed: "A drowning man is not troubled by rain."

Pulluck Sanyal ushered my grandfather into the hall with the aplomb of a grandee doing a supplicant a favour. The terms of a loan of Rs 10,000 had been settled. My grandfather did not want interest, which was surprising, but demanded the ownership deeds of a garden home with three ponds off the Grand Trunk Road in Bhadreshwar as collateral in case the loan was not repaid within two years.

Baboo Satyajit Banerjee hid his embarrassment with discordant aggression. Speaking Hindustani was beneath his status, and Bengali was above my grandfather's, so he unconsciously descended into pidgin to reach the assumed mental level of an illiterate. "We Bengalis race of brilliant men. Our textiles, pottery, cutlery, leather, paper, brass, handicrafts best in world before bloody Marwari came brought cheap phoren stuffs from England. That is why glorious Lal-Bal-Pal call for boycott phoren stuffs in glorious year 1905 after Mother Bengal divided by unpatriotic Muhammadans. All you outside peoples – Marwari, Bihari, Punjabi, Parsi, Gujarati, Madrasi, Chettiar, Jew, Parsi – came to Bengal after Palashi, when Clive threw out rascal Siraj ud Daulah, shaved Bengal. But even in deep darkness shining Bengali culture and brain shone. Ramdulal De! Have you ignorant heard that glorious name?" He shifted to pidgin Bengali for emphasis. "*Naam shona hai? Koishe shonega? Tum log bilkul* backwards thinking. (Have you heard his name? How could you have? You people are backward thinking.) Babu Ramdulal sent ships fool of hot-shale goods to America in great American civil war, and richesht man in Bengal after Englishman. Dwarkanath Tagore! Dwarkanath Tagore have huge business in opium, indigo, sugar, silk, coal, moneylending, shipping. Englishman make him partner in everything. Now Marwaris build big big mills – Birla Jute Mills, Hukumchand Jute Mill, Hanuman Jute Mills, Mathuradas Mills, cotton mills owned by Birla, Dalmiya, Goenka. But brain belong to Bengali." With a satisfied growl he slumped on his sofa and turned his face away. Pulluck Sanyal hurried my grandfather and Surjya Modak out. Their audience was over. My grandfather, who understood not a word, made no comment but clutched the agreement signed on stamp paper.

~

My father and Syed Ashfaque crossed an invisible line when they entered Simon's bungalow as his guests. The only non-whites permitted were brown and black maids who sang *Umpti Dumpti gir gaya phut!* (Humpty Dumpty fell down phut!) to babies while parents had a drink at the club, and household staff like Ghulam Rasool. Victor Matheson worried about the implications. Familiarity, he had been taught, bred contempt.

Matheson believed in order, honesty, discipline, decency, trade, law and civilization. His views on the economy had been shaped by a visit to the Empire Exhibition at Wembley in 1924; he believed that he was creating wealth for natives, and that Victoria Jute Mill was an integral element of a noble mission.

He did not loll on the sofa reading poetry; he sat upright with the heroic tales of G.A. Henty, published by Blackie & Sons in the half-crown series. He had as many of the India books as he could find: *With Clive in India, Through the Sikh War: A Tale of the Conquest of Punjab; Colonel Thorndyke's Secret, A Tale of the Mahratta War, Through Three Campaigns: A Story of Chitral, the Tirah and Ashanti,* and, best of them all, *The Tiger of Mysore* which exposed the Muslim hero, Tipu Sultan, as a bloodthirsty tyrant who took pleasure in the torture of his prisoners and revelled in massacre. The contrast between the oriental despot and the British soldier explained why one was subject and the other ruler. Who but the British officers of John Nicholson's garrison could have played cricket at the gates of Delhi during the siege of 1857?

Running India needed, as Kipling wisely noted, a cool head, an unbroken soul and an untiring body. Just 30,000 white men ruled 300 million Indians because Indians trusted British justice and feared British authority. If millhands lost this fear, how could five white men command the loyalty of a thousand?

Simon and Mathew, expecting polite conversation about golf and Bobby Jones over a long-awaited friendly drink, were surprised when he shifted to the ethics of power.

"Justice, legal and social, is the bedrock of our Empire. What was India before we came? A land infested with cholera, malaria, enteric fever and sloth. The only thing Indians get passionate about, believe me, is religious violence. Nothing else stirs them. We brought civilization to a people incapable of self-rule."

"Civilization? I often wonder what it is. Eating with spoons and forks? India had a university when Alexander reached Taxila." Simon was not combative, merely conversational.

"Had. Indians always *had* everything. Well, what have they become? We created a country out of decay, disease, corruption and confusion, because we knew our strength and they learnt to understand their place."

"Oh it was not so bad, you know. They gave us a lot of nice phrases," interrupted Mathew, trying to be his familiar jolly self. "Did you know that 'big cheese' is derived from the native *'barhi cheez'* or big thing. And Worcestershire sauce was first made in India, not Worcestershire!"

Matheson ignored him, Simon smiled.

"*Four and twenty blackbirds baked in a pie... When the pie was opened the birds began to sing. Wasn't that a dainty dish to set before a king?*" trilled Mathew. "Did you know that such pies were actually cooked in India? I kid you not. This culinary marvel was first seen on the table of Nawab Nasir ud Din Haidar of Lucknow, and then taken to Hyderabad by the chef Pir Ali. The Nizam of Hyderabad used to delight high English officials at dinner with a triumphant display of live birds twittering out from a pie. Personally speaking I wouldn't touch such a pie, given the crap that the shit-scared birds must have left inside."

Matheson refused to be diverted. "India contains one-fifth of humanity, and we rule it because of strength of character. There is an iron law: let white remain with white, and black with black. There must be courtesy, but never intimacy. There are better minds than mine who have suggested this. You've read H.G. Wells, haven't you, and if not, buy his *New Republic* tomorrow. The future, he writes, belongs to western civilization, which represents the fine and efficient in humanity. Base and servile people, will either die out or serve the efficient.

Indian soldiers turned their backs on the enemy in the Great War!"

"The Indian Army?" Mathew could not disguise a sudden rise of irritation. "When we wanted to save Natal, or rescue white men in Peking, or fight the Mad Mullah in Somaliland, or defend the coaling stations of Empire – Aden, Mauritius, Singapore, Hong Kong – or guard the rubber plantations in Malaya or defeat the Turks in Mesopotamia, who did we send? Indian soldiers. When we wanted to exploit the plantations of Demerara or Jamaica or Fiji, who did we send except Indian labour?"

"I am afraid, young man, idealism is not a substitute for facts. Indians are good at what they are good for. Coolies. Would an Indian soldier face fire for a minute on the battlefield without the steadying hand of the British officer? This is what I mean. We must have a dividing line in Victoria Jute Mill."

"An Indian won the Nobel Prize for literature. That wasn't given for being illiterate!" Simon thought he had a point, and drove it.

"You mean Tagore? That Bengali Baboo? Kipling was right about him, when he called Tagore an anti-climax."

"Well, Kipling learnt Hindustani from his maid," replied Simon drily.

Matheson quoted his hero: "*Oh, East is East, and West is West, and never the twain shall meet, Till Earth and Sky stand presently at God's great Judgment Sea.*"

"*But there is neither East nor West, Border, nor Breed, nor Birth, when two strong men stand face to face, though they come from the ends of the earth!*" Mathew responded and they all laughed, which was a very civilized thing to do.

12

BRIDGES

"ALEXANDER THE GREAT DIED OF INVINCIBILITY. WHEN A conqueror has no enemies left, he becomes his own enemy," remarked Syed Ashfaque Alam. "Negligence is the thief of empire," he ended, on a slightly grander note.

"Very wise," replied Simon, in Urdu. Conversation had become the preferred means of instruction.

"You have surely heard of Mahmud of Ghazni, whose conquests extended from India to Iraq. An old Iraqi woman came up to him when he was hunting and complained that she had been robbed. Mahmud brushed her aside with the remark that he could not protect every citizen from theft. She answered swiftly: 'In that case why do you conquer so much land? Rule only those you can protect'."

Simon retorted, "One of your leaders, Rammohun Roy, said, 'Conquest is very rarely an evil when the conquering people are more civilized than the conquered, because the former bring the latter to civilization'. You have to admit that we have brought the modern world to India. What has the Hindu or the Muslim produced that we use in the twentieth century? Electricity? A printing press? A fountain pen? An aeroplane? A bomb? A motor car? A razor blade?"

"Alas, those who have wealth also assume that they have happiness."

Simon Hogg asked his tutor to elaborate. Syed Ashfaque Alam cleared his throat in the best professorial manner and opted for delicacy. "The Western ideal is achievement; a man is only as great as his glory. Success is measured by levels of praise. Praise becomes an addiction. We believe that happiness can come from culture and human relationships. Sultan Harun al Rashid saw Bahlul, his wise fool, striding past and asked where he had gone. To hell, replied Bahlul. Why? To get some fire, Bahlul answered. So why had he returned empty-handed? Explained Bahlul, 'You see, there is no fire in hell. Everyone takes the fire in which he will burn with him'."

Tactfully, Simon asked for the point of the anecdote. The answer was oblique. "Urdu is not a string of alphabets that grow up to become a sequence of words; it is the expression of a unique sensibility. You cannot do bookkeeping in Urdu; you can, however, write poetry. The poetry of love is the soul of Urdu, and, love, like God, demands complete obedience. As Ghalib, our poet, said of the legendary Majnu, who was pelted with stones by a crowd when he cried out for his beloved Leyla, 'When I picked up a pebble to throw at Majnu, I became vulnerable'."

It was a conversation between two worlds with few bridges. A less persistent mind might have given up, or dismissed Urdu as a nonsense, but Simon Hogg enjoyed what he heard, for he was in love. Since his love was hopeless, he was certain it was an Indian passion.

"The moral order of the priest is barren, for life must lead to something more than applause from God, is it not?" asked Syed Ashfaque.

This was deliciously heathen.

"The poet does not discover truth on my behalf. He deftly draws strokes on a page and leaves me to complete the portrait, for in the unwritten lies the reader's freedom. Ghalib was less than fifteen when he began writing or, as he put it, was old enough to be immoral. Ghalib had the wit to forgive his own sins before God could forgive them!"

Ashfaque praised Ghalib but quoted Akbar Allahabadi. Simon did not know whether to be amused or entranced by lines such as these:

> Hum aah bhi bharte hain to ho jaate hain badnaam
> Woh qatl bhi karte hain to charcha nahin hota.
>
> I have but to sigh and blame descends
> She kills me, and not a word is said.

My father's stiffness began to melt and his English improve after the third lesson. He also discovered, with some help from Hasina, the pleasures of blackberry jam, Scottish marmalade and Polson's butter. His grandmother sneered at foreign butter, but would not deny him, and so Polson's began to arrive at home in low, round tins.

"The charm of Urdu lies in its teasing metaphor. The maikhana is a tavern, but not a pub where you English people go to lose your senses. It is a meeting place for the ultimate intoxication, the total surrender to love. That is why the poet condemns abstinence as hypocrisy. Are you confused by our contradictions?" It was a rhetorical question.

Syed Ashfaque explained differences between Muslims and Hindus. Muslims obey a defined law, Hindus accept a defined hierarchy. The Muslim has a linear mind: he believes in life before, during and after death. The Hindu has a circular mind, because he believes in rebirth. But together they create the culture of India. The greatest contemporary exponents of Hindu ragas were Muslims. The music never stopped at Shah Jehan's Red Fort, a fortress designed to bring the world in, not to keep the world out. The British divided Hindu and Muslim by creating stereotypes: the Muslim became a violent, masculine, despotic sword-wielder; the Hindu a passive, indolent, cunning intriguer.

At the end of three months, Simon Hogg paid a very cultured fee for his education: six gold sovereigns, worth Rs 14 apiece. He gave my father Charles Lamb's *Tales from Shakespeare* and a copy of *Twelfth Night* with the suggestion that English was synonymous with Shakespeare. He also invited them to a meal.

Hasina was cook and part-hostess; power in the household had shifted subtly from Ghulam Rasool to her. Ghulam Rasool observed his master's silent passion with a benevolent and patient eye. Time was a great arbiter of emotions and instinct would tell him when the moment was right to intervene.

Mathew and Simon were sipping punch when my father and Syed Ashfaque came over for Sunday lunch. My father had added a sola topi to his attire, which he kept carefully on the hat stand. The Scotsmen were in golf shirts. It was the first time my father had seen alcohol, and felt a minor thrill at the sight of sin. As they mangled each other's languages, often with a self-deprecating laugh, conversation turned to the audacity of words that hopped through cultures. Paradise, observed Syed Ashfaque, was an Arabic word, Pirdaus. Simon pointed out that the British used to once sleep on the same kind of charpoy that Telinipara's workers used, which explained the origins of the familiar phrase, "Goodnight, sleep tight!" Sleep was comfortable only if the ropes that secured the frames had been tightened. And it "rained cats and dogs" because people were "dirt poor". Animals found warmth under the thatch of a roof during stormy nights, and if it became slippery on a particularly rainy night, cats and dogs fell off their perch. Only the rich, a thin slice, could afford stone floors; the rest slept on mud and were called "dirt poor". Abbaji imagined a Britain full of Teliniparas, and flushed when he realized that his was the only family which could not be called "dirt poor". Mathew, tempted by erudition after his third punch, mentioned that Red Indian Algonquins had no word for "time" and some Australian aborigines never used "because" since they had no concept of cause and effect. After his fifth punch he informed Simon that fuck was an acronym of Fornication Under the Consent of the King, since marriage in the old days needed the permission of the King. Simon, relieved that his Indian guests had no idea what he was talking about, asked for lunch.

Hasina offered "Hurry-Scurry", a variation of French toast, thin bread slices bathed in egg and milk, fried in ghee, and eaten with or without jam from Keventer's in Calcutta. There was prawn *dopiaza* and kidney toast, Madras-style: fried, crumbled kidney spread on crisp toast. There was pilau, kebab, roast chicken and Simon's Sunday favourite, a dish he called kedgeree, which the others recognized as good old khichdi with fish and chopped eggs instead of mutton. Hasina did not retire modestly into the kitchen while they ate, but encouraged my father to take more, ordered Mathew to eat kebabs with his fingers instead of a knife and fork, and, wordlessly, pulled the plate away from Simon when he sought a third helping of the sweet rice-and-milk pudding called firni. My father concentrated on caramel custard, nicknamed 365 because it could be counted upon to be on an Anglo-Indian table 365 days of the year.

"The Czech proverb is very wise," suggested Mathew over coffee. "To learn another language is to become a different person."

~

Unobtrusively, a new generation began to cluster around my father. Thakur Bhagwan Singh's son Kalyan inherited the job of durwan, but some sons were less amenable to tradition. Zulfiqar Khan's son Mustafa refused to continue his father's usury business since it was forbidden in Islam. The old rogue Ayub Mastan's son, Gauhar Ayub, embellished his family skill of theft with a splendid imagination. He claimed that he had been trained by a master pickpocket of Delhi, inside a house hidden in the labyrinths of the old city around the great mosque of Shah Jehan, by a wizened old man with a long beard below a long face. His first lesson was exotic. He was asked to extract a rupee noiselessly from the folds of a silk garment. Whenever he failed hidden bells began to chime. He observed a golden rule: no crime in Telinipara. He would disappear for months to make money, and return home to spend it. There were differences of wealth in this group but none of class.

My father was part of this set as well as beyond it. His best friend in school, Benoy Chowdhury, introduced him to the strengths of Bengali middle-class culture, with its deep commitment to education: daily life revolved around the schoolchild rather than the adult. The only priority of the morning was to feed, dress and send the children to school. At ten the men ate a substantial brunch and left the house. Those with jobs carried insurance against afternoon pangs in a tiffin packed with shandesh. After 10.30 the women relaxed, enjoyed an oil massage, had a bath and ate. Around 11.30 vendors bearing carts turned up to haggle. The siesta ended punctually at three when women hawkers armed with trinkets descended on the doorstep for business and gossip, after which they began to prepare a repast for the children who would return from school by 4.30. At sunset, the grandmother monitored lessons before the child was returned to the affections of the mother, and the comfort of a mosquito net for a night's sleep. My father saw books like Upendra Kishore Ray Chaudhury's *Chotto Ramayana* (*Ramayana for Children*) and Kasiramdasa's *Mahabharata* in Benoy's home, but, unsure of how to deal with holy texts, left them alone.

During the day, our home, with its courtyard and cool rooms, became the gathering point of the neighbourhood women, a club presided over by Mai, ageing gracefully, and her deputy, my grandmother Jamila. There were strange incidents. There was the much-hushed story of the yogi and a coconut bowl. A bristling, aggressive holy man, beard burned in ash, brought to the courtyard by a wide-eyed neighbour, asked for a coin, whispered at it, and turned it into two. On the second day he doubled a silver rupee. On the third day he made an offer: he would double all Jamila's jewels with his mantra if she placed them into his shawl. He then told the women to wait while he went to the river to fetch some holy water, and would have doubtless disappeared had my grandfather, who could smell any interference with his wealth, not intercepted him outside the door. The charlatan was thrashed by a couple of sturdy young men while children applauded.

~

There was much excitement in the jute mill when Mathew bought a Minerva. It was an eight-cylinder, 40-horsepower Belgian beauty, described in brochures as "The Car of Kings and Queens" and the choice of Hollywood stars. The company did not advertise the fact that the 1930 model, hyped as the "Goddess of Automobiles", had flopped, making the Minerva excellent value in the second-hand market. Mathew explained that he needed the car to drive to Calcutta on weekends.

Each Saturday afternoon he would drive through the factory gates, and turn left on the Grand Trunk Road towards Calcutta. After a few miles, he would make a U-turn and head back to Chandernagore. Monsieur Francois Dupleix, the proprietor of Hotel de Baron, tucked away on a quiet street parallel to the strand, was charming and discreet. He had become rich by leaving his guests alone. Mathew signed in as M. Horne. He could have been A. Bugle or Y. Trumpet for all Monsieur Dupleix cared. Mathew occupied a small suite on the first floor. He carried his own supply of Bell's, and his favourite waiter, Nazakat Ali, brought up the ice and soda. At about nine, when dinner had been cleared from the tables on the ground floor, and the foyer was largely empty, Gulab arrived, shielded by a gossamer dupatta, the light cotton scarf worn over the head, ending below her eyes.

Nazakat Ali brought up the tiffin filled with meats and savouries that she had cooked for her Sahib.

Mathew's instincts were reformist. In the first flush of their relationship, he wanted to rescue Gulab and was upset that she had no desire to be saved. She was not morose about her past: she had food, shelter, the kinship of colleagues, an education in Urdu and, most important, the captivating power of beauty.

She knew what they called her in the trade: a "red carpet", a girl of the highest value. She had no trace of self-pity, and sought her identity in forms of beauty: her own, of her verse, and of her dance. She was a virgin when she entered Khalajan's household, and could not help adding, with modest pride, that her nose-ring had cost Rs 10,000. She laughed when Mathew did not understand: the nose-ring was the euphemism for the money paid for her first night. She was lucky, she said: her first man was a son of a zamindar. She had known of girls given to rich old men who were either too drunk to perform or got drunk because they could not. She told Mathew that she continued to dance for other men, but had stopped sleeping with anyone else despite insistent demands for her favours. She said this without sentiment. Khalajan kept the money she made from dancing, and left her alone with Mathew.

Characteristically, she revealed her strengths first and her memories later. She was not waiting for a prince to marry her. "Marriage," she said, "does not make two persons one. And if it did, a husband would expect submission. I am loyal, but not subservient." She would rather be a victim of circumstance than victim of a marriage contract.

Mathew could not help being British. He lapsed into

honourable intentions, particularly when lost in her large, dark eyes touched with smoke and dew. He fantasized that he would find a job as a manager in the tea gardens of Assam, and she could become a teacher at the local school, where no one would know her past. Gulab would nudge him out of his reverie with a smile. "You take your pleasures too solemnly, Sahib. Laugh. There is so much to be cheerful about when we are young. Time and duty will make their demands soon enough."

She was calm when he announced that he would be going on leave for a month. She would wait for three months, she said, adding nothing.

Hasina felt a faint sense of dread when she heard that Simon had also applied for leave so that the two friends could be together in Britain. London was certain to be full of beautiful women who kept fluttering around men, like Maureen, daughter of the Burra Sahib. who had come to stay with her parents after finishing school in Scotland. Hasina did not hide her satisfaction when Simon was denied leave, on the grounds that two British managers could not be away at the same time.

One morning, Ghulam Rasool placed tea on the table, lifted his head, adopted a determined look and delivered the first of a series of much-deliberated lines. "Sahib, you once said that you were an honourable man."

"Have I done anything to change your view?"

"You keep staring at my niece."

"I like her, dammit!" Simon flared up. "I am good to her!"

"Yes, Sahib. But are you honourable?"

"Damn! What more do you want me to do to prove it?"

Ghulam Rasool paused. "We are Muslims, Sahib, Shia

Muslims. For Muslims marriage is a personal contract between consenting adults. The Prophet said, 'Marriage prevents sin'. Those are very wise words, Sahib... In this world, temptation is the mistress of virtue."

Simon was flummoxed.

"Marriage among us does not need a public ceremony. It is a simple agreement of *ijab* and *qabul*: declaration and acceptance, made before two witnesses. A dower is fixed, so that if a man divorces the wife will not starve. That is most important, Sahib: a good dower must be fixed. That is a true guarantee of a woman's self-respect. A Muslim may not marry an idol-worshipper, but we are allowed to marry people of the Book, Christians and Jews. Both of you are young, and it is impossible to say when impetuous youth will cross that boundary which defines the difference between legitimate bliss and sin. Hasina is a good and honest girl, but she too is young. Who knows when storms of the heart might scatter prudence? We know that you will not want the Burra Sahib to know anything. Hasina will be dutiful and I will be discreet. But whatever is done must be done lawfully. That is my plea."

Simon Hogg was stunned by the simplicity of the proposal. He asked for time to think, and tension gathered like a thin impenetrable gauze through the home. Life would change whatever the answer. Sleepless, he got up from bed around midnight, and heard a barely-audible murmur in the kitchen. He walked softly towards it. Hasina was sitting still, her knees bent behind her, her head covered, her hands cupped towards Allah in prayer. She turned her eyes towards him, and looked at him steadily. Both knew that if he refused the next morning she would leave, and they would never see each other again.

"The best wedding is that which is the least expensive. I didn't say it: the Prophet did!" Ghulam Rasool chortled. "I don't need a priest; I can preside over the ceremony myself. I know enough. Don't worry about a second witness. I will get the sweeper's thumb impression on this blank piece of paper later."

He recited the *fatiha,* the opening verses of the Quran. "Repeat after me," he told Simon, "I desire forgiveness from God." Simon duly desired forgiveness from God. Ghulam Rasool recited four chapters of the Quran that begin with *Qul.* He then took Simon's hand, and asked if he consented to take Hasina, daughter of Abdullah Haq, niece of Ghulam Rasool, as his wife, with the promise of a dower of one hundred rupees. Simon, whose Urdu had become useful, repeated: "With my heart and soul, on the dower settled, I consent, I consent, I consent." Ghulam Rasool went to his niece in the kitchen, her head bowed under the wrap of a new sari, the parting of her hair glistening with the red of vermilion, and asked her if she consented. She blushed and smiled. "It is accepted," said Ghulam Rasool. "A smile is acceptance." He lifted his hands and prayed, "O Allah! Grant love between Simon Sahib and Hasina Bibi as You did between Adam and Eve, Abraham and Sarah, Joseph and Zuleikha, Moses and Zipporah, Hazrat Ali, *Radi Allah-o anhu,* God be pleased with him, and Fatima, and Muhammad, peace be upon him, and Ayesha." Simon was touched by the prayer. The next day, he opened an account at the post office in Hasina's name and deposited a thousand rupees. It was a fortune, but that was his estimate of a proper dower.

He could not, of course, resist telling Mathew on the latter's return from England. Mathew's eyes widened in amazement and delight, and Hasina blushed when she bowed in a salaam towards her husband's friend. For just a while he was tempted to reveal his own secret, but did not. He changed the subject, to prices in London: he had picked up at Simpson's Daks trousers at twenty-five shillings each; striped shirts with detachable collars for eight shillings each; a homburg for a guinea and a Harris tweed jacket for two guineas. Hasina heard their laughter and was content.

~

The high points of our family history during those placid years, were, in chronological order: my father's first cigarette, to celebrate passing out from high school; my aunt Najiban's djinn; an election in which no one from Telinipara voted; my father's twenty-first birthday; and the purchase of zamindar Satyajit Banerjee's car.

The cigarette, a Capstan Navy Cut, came with a lesson. "History," Simon explained, as my father coughed on his balcony, "belongs to victors, which is why the British put it about that they had introduced smoking. But nicotine, the core element in tobacco, comes from the name of Monsieur Nicot, the French ambassador to Portugal in 1559. Portuguese traders introduced tobacco to the Chinese in the sixteenth century."

The evil spirit, an unholy djinn, an *ifrat*, no less, who seized my childless, and by now widowed, aunt Najiban was hungry, angry and prone to the most curious pranks. One night she suddenly jumped over a six-foot wall, screaming for food. An exorcist was summoned. The old man, Murad Ali, had an extremely foul tongue. He looked hard at my aunt, who sat facing a wall in her hut like a docile, repentant schoolgirl, and pronounced that food worth fifteen rupees should be cooked. He placed the food in a small hole in a corner of the mud floor, covered it with cloth, took out an empty bottle from the folds of his robe, put it near the hole and started to pray. The food began to disappear. He suddenly stood up and with a triumphant cry clamped the lid shut on the bottle. Two childlike images were dancing inside. He was disappointed. He had managed to trap two servants of the *ifrat* but the master tormentor had escaped. He would return and battle would resume. There was nothing to worry about, however. The spirits which roamed the space between earth, heaven and hell, often took their frustrations out on human beings. He would deal with the nuisance if the djinn returned to worry my aunt.

The elections of 1936 were an important British step on the road to Indian self-rule but they meant very little in Telinipara since the only person with a vote was my grandfather, and he preferred law and order to nationalism. The franchise was restricted to a tax-paying elite: landlords, lawyers, doctors, professionals and government servants. Eleven per cent of India voted. My grandfather did not. Freedom as a concept left my grandfather bemused. No one had restricted his freedom, he argued. But it was characteristic of youth to demand what it could not fully comprehend. The Chinese dentist who had started a practice in Chandernagore once told him, while filling a gap with gold, "Be careful about what you want, for you might get it."

My father, despite his admiration for Simon, was entranced by the heady idea of freedom. On a hot day in May 1937 he went with Benoy Chowdhury to a Congress rally on the dusty Calcutta maidan and heard the slightly nasal oratory of Jawaharlal Nehru, who promised great wheels of heavy industry, socialism, equality between Hindus and Muslims. Benoy Chowdhury, who had become convinced that the secret of Muslim and British rule was diet, was more interested in sneaking away to taste beef. Muslims and Christians were tall and strong because they ate beef, he thought, and could therefore lord over the physically weak and stunted Hindus. He urged my father to take him to a restaurant called Nizam's, near the maidan, which specialized in *kathi* kebab, roasted beef rolled in succulent paratha. My father told him not to be stupid.

Benoy Chowdhury dreamt of admission to Presidency College in Calcutta. My father let it be known that he would prefer college to marriage. My grandfather dismissed the thought of his son living away from home and no more was heard on the subject.

A strange aspect of the elections of 1936 and 1937 was that the two politicians of Telinipara, Maulvi Taslimuddin and Govardhan Ahir, were in broad agreement over Gandhi. The Maulvi had not forgiven the Mahatma for betraying the Khilafat movement, and Govardhan was convinced that Gandhi's touch was a curse that killed. As a child he had been betrothed twice; both girls died. When he finally got married, at the age of thirteen, he almost killed his father! The coach bringing his father from Rajkot, where he was working as a high official of the prince, to Porbandar, where the family lived, for Gandhi's marriage overturned. His father barely survived. Gandhi had now touched India; he would kill India.

The Maulvi nodded and added that Gandhi was a sex-maniac, went to brothels and was making love to his pregnant wife when his father died in the next room.

"Who told you?" Govardhan knew that Gandhi was bad news, but this bad?

"Gandhi himself," answered Taslimuddin with a sneer and a laugh. "He has written all these things and much more in a book about himself that you could have read if your father had the sense to make you literate!" Govardhan clutched his forehead with his palms in despair.

Simon turned my father's twenty-first birthday into an event. My grandfather did not quite understand why twenty-one should be special, for he had not waited till twenty-one to become an adult. His only concern was my father's obstinate refusal to get married. My father did not want a bride; he wanted a car. My grandfather balked, and my father threw a tantrum of epic proportions. He picked up fistfuls of currency notes from the till at the tobacco godown and began tearing them to shreds. Unable to bear such torture, my grandfather succumbed. Satyajit Banerjee's car was purchased.

A crowd gathered as he stepped into the grand limousine for the short distance to Simon's home for his twenty-first birthday party. Syed Ashfaque Alam sat by his side, trying hard to look unimpressed.

The other guests were Mathew, Victor Matheson, his buxom and faintly pretty daughter Maureen (in place of her mother, who did not relish an evening with the natives), and Simon's cousin, Colonel Ian Hogg, who had come down from the army headquarters in Calcutta, Fort William, for a weekend of golf.

Colonel Hogg's other passion was Arthur Wellesley, who, along with his brother Richard, turned the East India Company from a regional force into the dominant power with victories over Tipoo Sultan, the Marathas and the nominal Mughal emperor chained to Delhi, Shah Alam II.

"Mark the date," the colonel said, "we are discussing December 1803 not December 803. When the Hindu-Maratha warriors defending the fort of Gawaligarh against Lord Wellesley decided to fight to the last man they first slit the throats of their wives. Our troops were horrified at the sight of dead and dying women when they entered the fort. Now measure this against another fact. We were equipped with the latest sixteen-inch EIC bayonet, a triangular spike of steel that punctured the body and twisted the flesh inside. We captured 2000 such muskets in pristine condition from the fort – unused! Why? Why did the Marathas, brave enough to take the lives of their women before they gave their own, not use the latest muskets that could have defeated Arthur Wellesley!? That is a mystery between the Indian and his gods."

"Just a cock-up from the high command, probably, the sort of thing that happens in war," suggested Simon.

Matheson was not troubled by uncertainties. "Defeat comes with decadence, and if there is one thing in common between Hindus and Muslims it is moral decay. It is remarkable that the heaven of both Hindus and Muslims is full of nymphs: that is all they can think about. The armies of Lord Rama were promised millions of apsaras and Muslims, as you know, dream of houris in Paradise. The greatest Hindu sage, Vishwamitra, succumbed to a nymph called Menaka when Varuna, the god of wind, blew her clothes away in front of him. This is scripture in India..."

Simon asked mildly, "How do you know so much?"

Colonel Hogg, who had no idea how a discussion on Lord Wellington's military strategy had turned into a dialectic on sex, retired quietly into his Scotch.

Matheson stepped up his rhetoric. "If it wasn't for Lord Bentinck they might still be throwing widows into the funeral pyre. Can you imagine something more inhuman than suttee? It took another ninety years after Bentinck to end prostitution in temples: we passed the law finally only ten years ago. Concubines for priests! Is that the behaviour of a proper religion, I ask you!"

"Some of our Popes were not much better..."

"Young man, that is disingenuous. The degeneration of the Catholic Church was temporary and vigorously resisted by reformers. Where is the reform among Hindus and Muslims? They still live in their dark ages."

"What do you think, Ash?" asked Mathew, conscious that it had been a European conversation so far.

When he had recovered from his nickname, Syed Ashfaque Alam suggested, with a light laugh, "If you are the moon, the world will inevitably point its finger at you."

"Hindus search for answers in fate, and my learned teacher looks for alibis in poetry. It won't do, Ashfaque Sahib, it won't do," remonstrated Simon. "This was a legitimate question and you must give a legitimate answer."

"We lost power when we lost knowledge, not when we acquired prostitutes," answered Syed Ashfaque carefully. "Ibn Batuta, the social scientist who came to India with the conqueror

Mahmud of Ghazni and stayed back to study Sanskrit, analysed the weakness accurately: the Brahmins lost their edge because they refused to share knowledge. They kept it confined to their caste. And so a people who had given the world the idea of zero could not withstand small bands of horsemen from the wastes of central Asia. In 1232 the Sultan of Egypt gave Frederick II, leader of the bloodless crusade, an astronomical clock that was the wonder of the thirteenth century. By the eighteenth century, Egypt could not compete with the cuckoo clock. Babar, with 10,000 men, twice destroyed armies many times that size because of better technology – his *rakhale,* a horse-drawn gun mounted on a cart. As long as the Mughal matchlock was superior to the British musket, Mughals treated the British with contempt. Today you have better guns, so you treat us with contempt."

"By God, that's true!" exclaimed Colonel Hogg. "The slower burn rate of gunpowder gave the Mughal long barrels an edge. The Mughals had a powder chamber in the barrel which accommodated air and facilitated the burn rate, giving the gun increased velocity and range. We did not know this until Colonel Anderson of the Ishapore Gun Factory conducted tests. Well spoken, Ash, well done!"

"Surely it's a question of character as well," Victor Matheson argued. "Clive said a dozen times if he said it once, that he could conquer India with 2000 men. Hindus, he said, were indolent, ignorant, cowardly, natural tricksters in love with luxury. And Muslims did not know the meaning of gratitude."

"Was Clive a god, a prophet or a pope? Or was he the man disguised as a woman who struck a devil's pact with Mir Jaffar to betray Nawab Siraj ud Daulah?" Syed Ashfaque's smile had thinned considerably.

"Clive's heirs have been good for India," responded Matheson. "Consider what the quiet British administrator has done for India – a road built, silently, a desert irrigated, silently, a forest saved, silently. All we have to do is appease the noisier Congressmen and we can rule this country for a thousand years."

"Don't underestimate Gandhi," argued Simon.

"Gandhi!" Matheson exploded. "He is mischievous, mysterious and as cunning as a cartload of monkeys."

Ashfaque smiled the seasoned smile of a conquered race. "British rule will survive as long as it is just. We have a word in Urdu called *iqbal*. It is a moral word. Justice is a two-way street; the ruler passes judgment on the people, but the people also judge the ruler." He wondered if he had overstepped: You can always tell a king, but you cannot tell him too much.

Simon tried to calm the waters. "Mr Matheson did not mean it personally, Ashfaque Sahib."

"Faith and morality: I have often wondered what they mean. Does conscience have anything to do with faith? Conscience cannot be superior to faith, for that would be an invitation to anarchy. A century ago, Christian conscience coexisted with slavery; Muslim conscience accommodates it in some places even now. This young man who is twenty-one today might have been born in Fiji or Mauritius: half his father's village was taken there as indentured labour, the polite word for slavery."

"Ashfaque Sahib," said Simon, "we have a right to be eloquent for I am on my third gin, and Mathew on his fifth. You have no right to be so persuasive without touching a drop!"

"We must never forget that alcohol is an Arabic word," interrupted Mathew smartly. "Al Kohl."

My father joined in the laughter. He was too young to have a viewpoint, and though he was expected to have the occasional view he was too much in thrall to express it. This was the civilized conversation of his dreams, a conflict between warriors, each determined to hold his ground with maximum valour, minimum rancour.

My father drove home in triumph and went straight to his grandmother. Her lap had been his comfort since a child. He kissed her gnarled face, and rested his head on her shoulder. He did not notice that she seemed tired as he narrated every detail of the evening.

Ghulam Rasool retired, discreetly. Simon and Hasina began to clean up. Mathew poured a strong cognac for himself and broke into song: the words were from a minor poet, but the music was his.

Life can little else supply
But a few good fucks and then we die.

Hasina did not understand what he was saying and Simon knew that it was only a matter of minutes before Mathew fell asleep on the sofa.

13

BLOOD

"WAR! WE'VE GOT TO HAVE A WAR – WE'VE ALREADY PAID RENT on the battlefield!" Mathew shouted; and Simon laughed as they walked down the Chowringhee on a warm July evening in 1939, cooled by spurts of thin rain. It was the perfect finale to the happiest day of my father's life, and he often thought later that the unceasing laughter was ominous, a kind of compensation before a decade of unrelieved confusion and relentless pain.

Duck Soup had been made by the hysterical Marx brothers five years earlier, but took its time to reach the Metro theatre in Calcutta. As devotees of intelligent farce, Mathew and Simon booked seats for the first Saturday and invited my father to his first film. Cinema was no longer a novelty. In 1931 the Imperial Movietone Company had advertised *Alam-Ara* as "The only INDIAN TALKING Complete Drama so far produced in India... All living, Breathtaking 100% Talking... Peak of Drama, Essence of Romance... INDIAN SONGS! INDIAN MUSIC! INDIAN DANCES! INDIAN STARS!" But my father was forbidden cinema because my grandfather heard that there were kissing scenes in movies. Syed Ashfaque Alam assured him that the Marx brothers were chaste.

As ever, preparations were made for the Event. My father wore a beige linen suit tailored by Barkat Ali Brothers of Park Street, a gleaming white Favre Leuba watch, and brown leather boots made by Henry, the bespoke shoemaker from Chinatown, whose shop was ten minutes of dark bylanes away from Statesman House, the imposing newspaper office that dominated one end of Calcutta's glamorous main street, Chowringhee. My father insisted that they travel to Calcutta in his chauffeur-driven Raj Cadillac. Mathew asked him to leave his sola topi at home; it had become unfashionable.

My father took deep puffs of Capstan cigarettes – the deeper the puff the more adult he felt – at the bar of the Metro theatre, sipping his lemonade as casually as his English friends tipped their Scotch before and after the film, when one-for-the-road became two-for-the-movie and conversation a stream of sentences from *Duck Soup* and half-remembered Marx hits from the past: "You can leave in a taxi. If you can't leave in a taxi, you can leave in a huff... You talk so much it seems you've been vaccinated by a phonograph needle... Who you gonna believe? Me or your own eyes?... If you want to see a comic strip, you should see me in the shower!... Perhaps I might tuck you in, if I may end a sentence with a proposition... When were you born? I don't remember, I was just a baby... You're a brave man. Go and break through those lines. And remember, while you're out there, risking life and limb, through shot and shell, we'll be in there thinking what a sucker you are."

They left the theatre singing:

They got guns,
We got guns,
All God's chillun got guns.
We gonna walk all o'er the battlefield,
Cause all God's chillun got guns.

They took their time as they ambled towards Prince's, in the Grand Hotel, a far more splendid establishment than the ageing Great Eastern Hotel nearby. To their right pretty gas lamps encased in frosted glass lent a glow to the Eden Gardens. They window-shopped at Whiteaway Laidlaw and Company and the boutiques in the arcade of the Grand. Here was an example of what Indians could achieve, said Simon, if they set their minds to it: a young Indian called Oberoi owned the hotel. My father reminded his friends that another young Indian called J.R.D. Tata had flown an aeroplane alone from Karachi to Bombay, and now owned an airline. At Prince's they watched graceful couples in evening dress match the rhythms of the band. They slept in the car on the long ride home, and my father, rested, described every detail to his grandmother long into the night. When he had finished, she whispered to him, "Get married, son. I want to see your bride before I die."

Mathew and Simon had laughed at war in July; in August, war was sneering at them. The Second World War did not come to Telinipara, but a newspaper did. Simon insisted that my father subscribe to the *Statesman*: to read history in the making, and improve his English through the editorials. It was brought to our doorstep by a sturdy Bengali lad called Mithun who wore clasps on his wide khaki half pants, and became a self-contained world with magical cities, legendary names and photographs that eliminated distance. My father was entranced by information and fascinated by politics, although so much of it seemed to defy common sense, and so little of it seemed honourable.

Newspapers also sidestepped time; the past slipped seamlessly into the present. Articles on writers who had just died, like Sir Muhammad Iqbal, the Urdu poet, and Saratchandra Chatterjee, the Bengali novelist, sat beside reviews of books etching a new vision: *The Dark Room* by R.K. Narayan, *Kanthapura* by Raja Rao, *The Village* by Mulk Raj Anand. He thrilled to the promotion of Squadron Leader Subroto Mukherjee, the first Indian to command a squadron in the air force, and felt the glow of national pride when Calcutta University, instead of asking a Viceroy or a Governor to address the annual convocation, invited Rabindranath Tagore to do so. Eager for more news, my father bought a huge GEC radio, which came to life slowly in the form of a deep green light in the right-hand corner, before it began to crackle. He would search for the BBC's Empire Service and All India Radio. The rest of the family discovered other pleasures: the voice of K.C. Dey, R.K. Boral and, above all, Kundan Lal Saigal. The family would crowd around the set and stare at it while listening until Mai reminded them, sharply, that you did not have to look in order to hear.

The radio was switched off between October and November in deference to Ramadan, the holy month of fasting. The Id moon was sighted at sunset on 12 November. The next morning, my father learnt from the *Statesman* that the Viceroy had asked the leader of the Muslim League, Mohammad Ali Jinnah, to send an Id message over All India Radio to India's Muslims. Jinnah told young Muslims in immaculate English that they would "have to bear the burden of our aspirations". The Viceregal gesture raised Jinnah's prestige. My father was vaguely reassured when Jinnah recommended a book by someone called John Morley, titled *On Compromise* for this suggested that in compromise lay the solution. Syed Ashfaque Alam agreed. There was a scheme called Pakistan in the air, he said, but noted that Jinnah had ignored it. He added that the power and eloquence of the speech did not suggest that Jinnah had fasted for a month. He sounded too robust.

"I see that you have become a slave of English when the rest of us are getting ready for freedom from the English," Syed Ashfaque told my father, as the latter pored over his newspaper. "The language of an Empire dies with the Empire: who remembers Persian now? A language needs the support of the state. English will die when the English leave." My grandfather's friends were in the drawing room, sipping tea and sherbet while waiting for a festive Id dinner. All eyes turned on my father. He fought his corner. "English does not belong to the English alone. Americans also speak English. If the British cannot protect English, the Americans will."

They beamed. Syed Ashfaque's smile was the proudest: "Man's only true friend is knowledge – it is far better than wealth. You have to take care of wealth, while knowledge takes care of you. But be careful, knowledge without discretion is dangerous. Some Israelites went to Jesus, and begged him to teach them the art of raising people from the dead. Jesus was reluctant, but gave in. The Israelites saw a heap of bones in the desert and decided to test their new-found knowledge. A lion came to life and ate them up." They laughed.

My father enjoyed the invective of domestic politics: Jinnah called the penniless Gandhi a "Bania" implying that like any trader he was less than reliable; the Congress accused the wealthy Jinnah of being a "Dictator of Malabar" after the fashionable district of Bombay in which he lived. If Jinnah was a dictator, no one was taking much dictation as yet. One of his admirers in Calcutta, the industrialist M.A. Ispahani, wrote to Jinnah that he had become a reactionary and a "jee-huzoor" of the British. My father could not resist a smile. The only man he knew who kept saying "jee-huzoor" was Ghulam Rasool, and it was weird to think of Jinnah as some Ghulam Rasool. But Jinnah, he noted, had the support of some interesting Hindus, like Periyar E.V. Ramaswami Naicker, leader of the anti-Brahmin movement in Madras, and Dr B.R. Ambedkar, hero of the untouchables.

The sparring between Jinnah and Gandhi never stopped. Before the Lahore session of the Muslim League in March 1940, Gandhi wooed Jinnah and called him "my brother". Jinnah responded, "The only difference is this, that brother Gandhi has three votes and I have only one." At Lahore Jinnah made Pakistan his horizon. India, he said, should be demarcated into regions, with two of them, one in the west and the other in the east, both Muslim-majority, becoming autonomous and sovereign. My father checked the dictionary for clarity, and could not decipher how autonomous was synonymous with sovereignty. If this was Pakistan, then it was still vague and contradictory. He was more interested in the photographs from Lahore in the

Statesman and a report that Jinnah's hands trembled when he lit a cigarette on the podium. He thought: Gandhi is thin, but Jinnah is ill.

Jinnah, however, had unhinged Gandhi: what else could explain Gandhi's open letter to the battered but unbowed British suggesting that they confront Hitler "without arms" since weapons were "useless for saving you or humanity. You will invite Herr Hitler and Signor Mussolini to take what they want of the countries you call your possessions. Let them take possession of your beautiful island, with your many beautiful buildings. You will give all these, but neither your souls, nor your minds. If these gentlemen choose to occupy your homes you will vacate them. If they do not give free passage out, you will allow yourself, man, woman and child, to be slaughtered..."

Being a saint was clearly no guarantee against stupidity. Politics was the flavour of the time, amid a dim but growing sense that history had taken a curve and blocked the view.

Hooghly district saw its first Indian Superintendent of Police in the summer of 1940. He was a middle-aged, handsome Kashmiri from Punjab called Syed Shah Bukhari. His family preferred to live in Amritsar; Bengal was too humid for them. Syed Ashfaque introduced him to my grandfather's weekly salon.

"If Pakistan is created," asked Syed Ashfaque, always ready to ride a nuance, "will it happen by Allah's will or Jinnah's wilfulness?"

"Men's deeds are of three kinds: obligatory, meritorious and sinful. The first, like haj or prayer, is by the command of Allah; the second is according to His will; and the third is within His knowledge but not according to His will," responded my grandfather, who had started to think of God when his teeth began to weaken.

"That distinction releases Allah from all obligation!" protested Ashfaque.

"What about *ikhtiyar*, choice?" asked Bukhari.

"Allah's knowledge does not predetermine all human conduct; that is why He is the judge on Judgment Day," suggested my grandfather.

"Can man's determination shape God's will?" asked my father.

"Good question, young man! Asking good questions is half of knowledge!" said Syed Shah Bukhari. "The Quran says, never will Allah change the condition of a people until they change it themselves. You know the lines from Iqbal: *Khudi ko kar buland itna ke har taqdeer se pehle Khuda bande se yeh pooche, bata teri raza kya hai!*" Make your will so strong that before writing your destiny, God asks man, tell Me what is your wish!

"That is merely the illusion of a poet," said Syed Ashfaque, "I find a distinct advantage in leaving all decisions to God. It releases me from the bondage of men! Allah is merciful, unlike the mullahs. The pig is forbidden, but no punishment has been prescribed for eating it. Indeed, you can eat pig if you are starving."

"Really? I didn't know that," said Bukhari.

"I eat no meat whatsoever. Hindus and Muslims have two laws. Does that make them two nations?" asked Girija Maharaj.

"British India today has more than 600 nations. So what if India tomorrow becomes two nations?" asked Bukhari.

"Do you know what it means?"

"Yes," replied Bukhari evenly. "Hindus and Muslims will rediscover each other only when India is divided. I live in Punjab now, but I am a Kashmiri. I know my Hindu brethren, the Kashmiri Pundits. Very charming, very suave, very educated. But they treat us Muslims as untouchables. They talk to us, but won't touch us. If by accident they do so, they forgive themselves with a proverb, *'Yath na pus, that na dus.'* When one is helpless, one is blameless. How can I live with someone who treats me as an untouchable?"

"You are turning human faults into a national crisis," replied Girija Maharaj. "A nation is not the sum of human weakness; India is an ideal, the land of Bharata."

"Forgive me if I am wrong, but wasn't King Bharata an illegitimate child?"

Girija Maharaj was unfazed. "It is true that his father, Dushyanta, abandoned his mother, Shakuntala, after he married her in the forest, but he repented and accepted both son and mother. Bharata ruled from Peshawar to Bengal, and any subject could travel freely to any part of Bharatvarsha. I am a Brahmin from Bihar, living in Bengal; if I want to go to Punjab I can go in peace. Will that be possible when Muslims create their Pakistan? How does Punjab become a Muslim country? The Vedas were revealed on its sacred soil; they are my Quran. The Rishi Vaishampayana first recited the *Mahabharata* in the Punjabi city of Takshila at the time of King Parikshit. Punjab is the home of our sacred language, Sanskrit, and the Sapta Sindhu, the seven rivers, Kabul, Indus, Jhelum, Chenab, Ravi, Beas and Sutlej; rivers are not Muslim or Hindu. The river hymn of the *Rig Veda* names the ten sacred rivers of India, Ganga, Jamuna, Sarasvati,

Satuduru, Parushni, Marudvridha, which is today the Chenab and Jhelum, Asikni, Vitasta, Arjikiya and Sushoma, another name for Indus. How many of my rivers are you taking away from me?"

"That India is long gone," said Bukhari gently, as if reluctant to hurt an old man's romanticism. "Today's India holds one-fifth of the world's population. Social scientists say that there are at least seven different physical types, fourteen different languages with their own literature, as many as 150 distinct tongues, and nearly 550 separate dialects. There is more than religion that divides us. India itself is only an artificial name that the Persians gave to the land beyond the Indus."

"The seven sacred cities, Ayodhya, Mathura, Hardwar, Kashi, Kanchi, Ujjain and Dwarka are spread across the country. The three sun temples are in Konarak, Surat and Multan: Orissa, Gujarat and Punjab. How can you divide Bharatvarsha?"

"Well," laughed Syed Bukhari, "the border of Punjab stops short of Hardwar, but I am sorry about Multan. Anyway, how does it matter? Pakistan does not mean that a Hindu cannot worship in Multan or Lahore, or that I cannot come to the Jama Masjid in Delhi or visit the Taj Mahal!"

Syed Ashfaque laughed, but uncertainly. "Whenever I hear of a Promised Land, I begin to tremble. Whether it's Moses or Jinnah, their dreams always seem to be preceded by famine and plagues of locusts, lice and frogs. Water turns to blood. There is death everywhere."

"Suffering never comes to one people alone, Ashfaque," said Girija Maharaj softly. "Violence, famine, plague, water, blood, death have no religion. When Rahmat as a young man risked his life to stop plague, he did not save the lives of only Muslims. If such is to be our fate, both Hindus and Muslims will suffer. We live, after all, in Kaliyug, the fourth age of Time, an age of evil that began with the death of Lord Krishna and will last 1200 divine years or 432,000 human years. It is written in the *Vishnu Purana* that virtue has four legs. In the first age, Krita, she walked on all four; in the second age, Treta, on three; and in the third, Dwarpa, on two. In Kaliyug she stumbles along on one."

My grandfather, apprehensive, intervened to change the subject and asked Bauna Sardar when he was due to retire. Bauna Sardar, a *gamcha* as ever across his face, grumbled that the Sahibs kept asking him his age, but since he did not know this himself, how could he tell them? Bauna Sardar was happy with old age. He had adopted his brother's grandson, Mustaqim, who became the son he never had. When Mustaqim was ten, Bauna Sardar told my grandfather that the boy's future was his responsibility, and Mustaqim became a part of our family.

That was the year Girija Maharaj learnt, by postcard, that his granddaughter-in-law, Laxmi, had become pregnant, and left for his village to ensure, through rituals, the birth of a son.

Towards the end of the second month of her pregnancy, Laxmi sat behind a fire, facing east, while a twig of the *soma* plant, pounded to a paste, was placed in her right nostril amid the chanting of prayers. This was the Purnasavana ceremony. In the fourth month, Laxmi performed the *garbharakshana* for the welfare of the foetus: her limbs were massaged with purified butter blessed by priests. Laxmi entered, for her labour, a special hut at whose door burnt a holy fire. A son was born, and named Kamala. Rock salt and butter were placed on the child's tongue, two stones moistened with water were rubbed close to his ear, oil was poured on his body, a cloth soaked with purified butter laid on his head and the traditional Sanskrit *shloka* wishing him a hundred years of life was whispered in the ear. For ten days the hut echoed with music and laughter.

On the third day of the third fortnight after his birth, Girija Maharaj went out at night, worshipped the moon, returned, picked up Kamala from his mother's lap and took him out of the hut for the first time. He repeated this at an auspicious hour during the phase of the waning moon. In the fourth month, he showed the baby the sun. In the sixth month the child ate his first morsel of solid food. When Kamala had learnt to walk, he was sent to Telinipara. His parents would have to be content with their other children: Kamala became Girija Maharaj's love and responsibility.

~

Perhaps too much happened in 1940. Mathew's "trips to Calcutta" ceased when Gulab told him, very lovingly, one weekend that she was nearly thirty and wanted to return to her family in Lucknow. She would explain to the inquisitive that she had returned from a defeated marriage: people were adult enough in her old neighbourhood to avoid questions. She had sufficient money for her limited needs; and in a sense their relationship was a defeated marriage, wasn't it? Mathew took shelter behind self-pity, which Gulab indulged, and then dismissed with two lines from the Urdu poet, Zauq:

Qismat se hi lachar hoon, ai Zauq, wagarna
Har fun mein hoon main taaq, mujhe kya nahin aata!

My fate is my misfortune, O Zauq, or else
I am master of every art, perfect in every skill!

Love must adjust to its limitations, she suggested, as Ghalib, the master, knew.

Chand tasweer-e-butaan, chand haseenon ke khutoot,
Baad marne ke mere ghar se yeh saamaan nikla.

A few pictures of goddesses, a few letters of love,
It was all they found in my home upon my death.

Gulab held his face in her warm hands, kissed Mathew lightly on the forehead, and swirled out of his life.

Mathew lost his car a few months after he lost Gulab. The government ordered the mobilization of private vehicles for the war effort. But he saved our car. He arranged that it be kept in the custody of Monsieur Dupleix, who, as a citizen of Vichy, France, was outside British reach.

The Mathesons did not celebrate Christmas in 1940, and Maureen spent most of her time with Mathew and Simon. They gifted one another gin bottles on Christmas eve, and sat down to empty their gifts. Hasina watched them for a while, and went to sleep after dinner had been served. Simon asked Ghulam Rasool to leave enough tonic and ice on the tray, and bade him good night. Conversation did not sparkle.

Gin, unlike whisky, is a hunter, not a warrior. Gin stalks, while whisky overpowers you step by step, in frontal combat. You can feel the whisky rising. Gin is sly.

Mathew tried to fill another pause. "The five greatest inventions of man are, in my considered opinion, fire, wheel, printing, electricity and the condom. No one knows who gave us fire and the wheel, and everyone knows of Gutenberg and Benjamin Franklin, but I challenge you to tell me who invented the condom!" Pause; dramatic. "Gabriel Fallopius, that's who: born 1523, died 1562, and in those brief forty-one years this professor of anatomy in Pisa saved the world. Should have been more famous than Galileo, for my money. He also coined the term 'vagina'. I wonder what they called it before…"

Maureen turned up her nose. "Clever. Or not."

In the light of subsequent events, Mathew's speech was ironic. If Mathew had a condom in his pocket, his life might have been different. With barely half of a bottle of gin left from the three, Maureen announced that she was going to bed. Instead, she slumped on the sofa before she had finished the sentence. Gin, the stalker, had found its prey. Mathew picked her up and staggered towards the spare bedroom. He took a long while to get back.

A week later Maureen went to his flat for tea and told him that she had missed her periods. Within a fortnight, they were married at St James' Church in Calcutta. Mrs Matheson beamed, but Victor Matheson maintained a grim look in view of the wartime news. To smile publicly might seem unpatriotic. Two weeks after the marriage Maureen announced, sadly, that she was not pregnant after all. Mathew said nothing. Simon recalled a line from Kipling: "The silliest woman can manage a clever man, while only a clever woman can manage a fool."

Simon and Mathew marked the fall of Singapore by purchasing weapons. Simon bought a Webley & Scott revolver, and Mathew a Manton shotgun. Indians were more excited by the dramatic escape of Subhas Bose from Calcutta to Germany and his meeting with Hitler. The destruction of the American fleet at Pearl Harbour confirmed the impression that Bose had chosen the winning side. War came to the subcontinent in 1942 when the Japanese, after taking Rangoon, bombed Chittagong and rattled the eastern door of India. Colonel Ian Hogg went to fight with the Chindits on the Burma front.

Benoy Chowdhury graduated from Presidency College, where, he told my father in hushed tones, Bengali women wore sleeves cut at the elbow and necklines that stopped just short of their cleavage. In 1941 he became the first Indian to be offered a job as a junior management trainee in Victoria. Bauna Sardar's methods were outdated and war demands made a British replacement impossible; Benoy was slotted for the labour officer's responsibilities. From cynosure, he became an icon. His family added duck's eggs to his breakfast to make him stronger. His marriage was arranged. My father was at his friend's home when his prospective wife's relatives came to inspect Benoy. A starchy old woman, counting beads from a *kunrojali* (cloth bag), was leader of the inspection team. A scattering of middle-aged men hovered around her. Benoy entered the room, touched the feet of all his visitors, and stood against the wall, his back towards the elders. Questions were asked. His answers were brief. In effect, he gave a test in grammar, learning, deportment, and demeanour. He was careful about his views of the British because he had been told that they were a nationalist family who bought Turkish bath cake soap from Bengal Chemical and cloth from Bangalakshmi Cotton Mill, companies owned by Indians, rather than British manufacture from Lever Brothers. Benoy passed his test, married Swapna, and Mai wept that my father did not have the sense to obey his elders.

"Why does the white man drink?" asked Tapeshwar Prasad Singh.

"To forget that he has to live with us," answered my father courteously.

"No! No! No! No! To kill mosquitoes. When do mosquitoes swarm towards us in search of our blood? At sunset. When does the Sahib order his first drink? The moment the sun goes down. That is why he mixes his alcohol with a bitter liquid like tonic. Tonic has quinine, which protects him from malaria."

"Do you just make these things up?"

"Who knows more about the British than I?" Singh asked, with a touch of world-weariness.

T.P. Singh was younger than my father, but had the track record of a revolutionary. As a student leader of Allahabad University, from where he graduated in political science, he went in a delegation to the All India Congress Committee session in Bombay in August 1942 and heard Gandhi tell his restless followers, "We shall either free India or die in the attempt; we shall not live to see the perpetuation of our slavery... Lay down your lives in the attempt to achieve it! He who loses his life will gain it. He who will seek to save it shall lose it. Freedom is not for the coward or the fainthearted... Nothing should be done in secrecy. This is an open rebellion!"

Gandhi's rebellion resolution was adopted on 8 August 1942. The next morning, the Mahatma rose at his usual hour, four, and told his secretary Mahadev Desai that the British would never dare arrest him. He finished his prayers and found the police commissioner at the door. Gandhi was given half an hour to get ready. He breakfasted on goat's milk and fruit, sang his favourite hymn, *Vaishnav Janato*, read verses from the Holy Quran, packed a copy of the Bhagavad Gita, a Quran, an Urdu primer and his spinning wheel, and was politely escorted to the special train that would take him to the last jail sentence of his long life.

T.P. Singh took the first available train to his village in Ballia, near Allahabad, ready to die.

He found his district in flames, and, like thousands of other angry Indians, fed the fire. He was part of a mob that torched the office of the absent deputy commissioner, away in the capital, Lucknow, for meetings. The British officer returned with troops. The revolt dissipated and T.P. Singh fled the province to escape arrest. He got off the train in the safe haven of Chandernagore, and slipped into Telinipara. My father was quickly drawn to the first Bhojpuri-speaking graduate he had met, and cemented their friendship with the gift of a comfortable three-room hut that was very useful when they wanted to play cards.

Every morning TP, my father's nickname for his friend, would come home to read the *Statesman*, and often stay on for lunch. A Thakur, of the warrior caste, he sniffed at vegetarian Brahmins and enjoyed eating meat at the large dining table with my father, while mother and grandmother fussed over them. "You know, Akbar, the smell of the kebab could make me into a Mussulman!" TP would sigh. Simon's influence enabled him to get a job as a wartime rations inspector, and he was soon known as Inspector Sahib.

"One has no control over one's enemies, so we must choose our friends with care," remarked Syed Ashfaque with approval. "Akbar has made a good choice."

The friendship had practical advantages. T.P. Singh solved the mystery of my father's bachelorhood. My father wanted to marry a fair-skinned girl but did not have the courage to tell anyone this. My grandfather held his head in his hands and moaned, "Now where am I going to find a white woman for this son of mine!"

Syed Shah Bukhari knew where. "Rahmat, look at my skin," he said, raising the sleeve of his shirt. "You have this curious notion that only the British are white. We Kashmiris, like Pathans and Afghans and Iranians, are as fair as any Englishman. Akbar will get a wife from my family. I know just the girl. My niece is fifteen, pretty, and has learnt Urdu in school. She is always reading some book or the other. Her father was a prosperous carpet merchant in Amritsar, but he passed away two years ago, leaving three sisters unmarried. Her two elder sisters are married."

Then he teased my father. "Young man, are you sure your British friends approve of your inclinations? Lord Curzon permitted the tall and fair Maharaja of Patiala's marriage with Miss Flory Bryan, but when he heard that the dark Raja of Pudukkotai was going to the funeral of Queen Victoria only to bring back a white bride, he forbade the Raja to leave Indian shores!"

My father's fancy gave way to fantasy when he learnt that his prospective bride's name was Imtiaz. What a cultured name, he thought.

Matters moved quickly. Syed Bukhari wrote a letter to Amritsar to say that he had found, for Imtiaz, a prince who owned palaces and cars, and neighbours came over to stare at her and wonder at her extraordinary fortune. My grandfather said that he was now too old to travel the distance to Punjab. Syed Bukhari solved that problem as well: the marriage would take place in Amritsar, but the celebrations would be in Telinipara. This would also save, he thought, my mother's family money they did not have. And so a delegation of six, consisting of Girija Maharaj, who insisted that he had not aged, Syed Ashfaque, Syed Shah Bukhari, T.P. Singh, Jamila and Mustaqim boarded the Frontier Mail along with my father.

A wedding guest is within his rights to expect the finest hospitality. On the evening of the marriage they were offered a full *wazwan*, the traditional Kashmiri dinner of thirty-six courses, prepared by a *Vasta Vaza*, or head chef, assisted by two *vazas*. Twenty dishes were meat-based, the rest of vegetables. The rice came in a large plate called a *tarami*. The food was eaten at a slow, leisurely pace. My father, warned in advance, took care to limit each helping; TP was not so discreet, and stretched his appetite to accommodate the last, and best dish, *goshtaba*. Girija Maharaj later bored the good folk of Telinipara for months with his descriptions of spinach and peach, and said no Hindu could make vegetarian food better than Akbar's in-laws. T.P. Singh proudly claimed on his return to Telinipara that he had gained three seers in weight in just two days.

My mother sat in a separate compartment with her mother-in-law and Mustaqim on the train to Calcutta, her young, bowed face shielded by the heavy *zari* of her dupatta, over which she wore a warm, light pashmina shawl; her hands brilliant with henna; her neck laden with jewellery gifted by her husband; her eyes soaked in tears; her mind echoing with the *babul*, the song of departure that was her farewell as she left home. Marriage was inevitable; but did fate have to take her to a strange country and strange people? A large and loud musical band playing popular film tunes on trumpets, clarinets and drums welcomed her at Chandernagore. A procession formed. My father, in a glistening sherwani, was at the head, seated on a horse; my mother, on a palanquin, was at the back. Songs in a strange language rose above the din of the crowd as she neared our home in Telinipara, and she was suddenly terrified at the thought that her husband might not know Urdu. There seemed only one point of reassurance: the smile of the young boy, Mustaqim, who guarded her till Mai enveloped my mother in her arms. My mother was taken to a room buzzing with flies and strewn with sweets, jaggery and flowers. She was seated on a low stool and put on display. She was not expected to talk or look at anyone. Every minute or so a woman would bend down, peer at her and whoop with admiration at her white skin and delicate features. She sensed the hostility of relatives who resented her status as a fairy princess.

Outside, long rows of guests formed on both sides of carpets laid out on the street. By midnight, more than a thousand people had been fed (some, twice). My father came to a bed heavy with flowers around midnight, accompanied by the twitter of women until they were shooed away by Mai. It was a scene that my father had practised a hundred times in his imagination. My mother's eyes were fixed on the sheets. He lifted her face. She half-opened her eyes and could not restrain a startled, shocked cry.

Later my father dismissed that half-shriek as the nervousness

of a virgin. My mother never told him the truth. She had never
seen a black man before.

~

Her last wish fulfilled, Mai died within a few months, in her
sleep, at peace with herself, a soft smile on her face. The family's
sadness lingered, but it was apparent that age had become a curse
for Mai.

Girija Maharaj was depressed at the funeral; he had seen the
almanac and the stars were askew. "It is written in the Jyotisha
Shastra," he quoted, "*Pancha griha hanti samasta desan, Shasta
griha hanti samasta bhupan, Sapta griha hanti samasta lokan,
Nirmatyam ashta griha samyutena.*" If five planets enter one of
the houses of the Zodiac in any month, countries shall be
destroyed; if six planets enter, kings shall be finished; if seven
planets enter, the whole world will suffer destruction; if eight
planets combine it will signal the end of mankind.

Astrologers were soon counting planets against the wail of
hunger and the thud of bombs. In October 1942 a severe cyclone
devastated more than 3000 square miles of Bengal. Crop disease
followed crop damage. The winter harvest was short. The fall of
Burma to the Japanese in early 1942 ended rice imports. The
price of grain, which had been rising quietly, began to jump. The
hoarder-profiteer, already in play, took command of supply and
demand.

Since jute production was treated as part of the war effort,
ration shops opened quickly in Telinipara to guarantee food
supplies. (My grandfather inevitably got the permit.) Rural
Bengal was not so fortunate. On 20, 22, 23 and 24 December
1942 the Japanese bombed Calcutta, and grain disappeared in

anticipation of an imminent invasion. Rice, which had been selling for Rs 6 a *maund* (about 35 kilograms) in January rose to Rs 15 by the last week of December. One end of the chain in this reaction was fear, the other, greed, and in the middle was a callous government. British officials insisted on *exporting* huge quantities of rice from Bengal. Muslim League ministers handed out procurement contracts to corrupt cronies. Hindu traders became millionaires when the price of a *maund* of rice was rigged up to beyond a hundred rupees. The real deficit, economists on the Famine Inquiry Commission later confirmed, was only about three weeks' requirement, and could easily have been met by honest governance. By early 1943 the poor began to die in eastern districts like Chittagong; by July death had spread to every district. On 28 September 1943 the *Statesman,* which did splendid investigative reporting, commented, "This sickening catastrophe is man-made. So far as we are aware, all of India's previous famines originated primarily from calamities of Nature. But this one is accounted for by no climactic failure; rainfall has been generally plentiful." In October the new Viceroy, Lord Wavell, expressed his disgust publicly at the complacency of the Bengal government. Only then was rationing introduced in Calcutta and camps set up for the destitute. By December between 3.4 and 3.8 million Bengalis had died of hunger.

My grandfather did not wait for Wavell's conscience to stir. For obvious reasons, nothing affected him more than famine. He cursed the British government for doing nothing and, unusually, opened his own purse. He asked the ailing Maulvi Taslimuddin to offer the *Nimaz-e-Istisqa,* the special prayer for relief from famine. Taslimuddin added *Salat-ul-haja,* the four *rikah* recited after night prayers in times of dire calamity. My grandfather set aside his reservations, called on Satyajit Banerjee for help in setting up a kitchen, and heard wailing at the wrought-iron gates of the mansion. Muslims cried out to their zamindar, "*Khudawand!* You who are blessed by Allah, help us!" Hindus chanted in a piteous monotone, "*Annadata!* Giver of food!" But those imperious gates remained shut, to the hungry as well as to my grandfather.

He went on to visit his bedridden friend Surjya Modak, still the best source of news in the district, and heard stories of a brigand called Ram Chatterjee, who lived in Chandernagore. Chatterjee's methods were uncomplicated. He stole from the British and took refuge with the French. He looted grain from wagons at the railway station and sold the food in the black market. There was no sin higher than this in my grandfather's code. He confronted Syed Shah Bukhari, and angrily dismissed his legal helplessness as immoral. "An empire may last if the ruler has no religion," he said, "but it will never last if the ruler has no morals. Honour your badge, Bukhari! You are an Indian. You cannot claim helplessness when Indians are dying in front of your eyes."

Syed Shah Bukhari ordered an agent of his secret Criminal Investigation Department to find out when Chatterjee would strike next. That night he went with three jeeploads of armed policemen, ignored the feeble and corrupt gendarmerie at the gates of Chandernagore, arrested Chatterjee, confiscated stolen grain and threw the thief into a British jail. Chatterjee remained in prison as long as Bukhari was superintendent of police of Hooghly district.

Abbaji was entranced by my grandfather's passion, and worked hard at the food camp set up on the premises of the Hooghly Madrasa. Simon was appalled that Indians would die in millions, but not step across some imaginary line and storm the godowns and shops. Was India timid in its genes, he asked. Mathew was cynical. As usual he had a theory. Lord Cornwallis, who became Viceroy in 1793 and created the rentier-class of zamindars which assured the British of regular revenue, and opened the land to the theft of India by Indians, justified his exploitation with a dry sentence: "Every native of Hindustan, I verily believe, is corrupt." Mathew recalled James Mill's conclusion, based solely on the yardstick of utility, that Hindus had never possessed a high degree of civilization. Maureen sighed and quoted Hillaire Belloc:

> The Poor Indian, justly called "The Poor",
> He has to eat his Dinner off the floor.
> Moral?
> The Moral these delightful lines afford
> Is: "Living cheaply is its own reward".

Mrs Matheson sniffed and went as far away from famine as she could, for an extended holiday in the British summer capital in the Himalayas, Simla (city motto: "For rule and rest, Simla is the best"). Victor Matheson looked glum and quoted Kipling. "There is too much Asia and she is too old. You cannot reform a lady of many lovers, and Asia has been insatiable in her flirtations."

~

The excellent winter crop of 1943, and the arithmetic of death, ended famine. There were at least three million fewer mouths to feed. My grandfather was convinced that the Raj was on its deathbed, for the British had lost their moral right to rule. The British had only one asset left: the suicidal tendency of Indians towards violence. Gandhi, he suggested, demanded non-violence not because Indians were non-violent but precisely because they were inherently violent.

"I agree with you," said Syed Ashfaque, stroking a virtually non-existent beard: it was so wispy now that you could count the hairs. "Moses wanted God to destroy Pharaoh but God would not do so as long as Pharaoh fed his people. God had to balance Moses' prayer against those who prayed for the Pharaoh's welfare. God abandoned Pharaoh only when famine came to Egypt."

They were chatting in the familiar drawing room on the day of Id in the autumn of 1945. The mood was relaxed. Famine and war were over: the American bomb that had annihilated obstinate Japan into submission was the signature of a new world power.

"Gandhi will get his freedom from the British," Syed Ashfaque continued, "but will Jinnah get his freedom from Gandhi?"

"Gandhi learnt politics from his mother," laughed Syed Shah Bukhari. "As a child he had a friend called Uka, who was an untouchable. His mother was horrified that Gandhi would bring pollution to their upper-caste home. So she suggested that Gandhi should touch a Muslim on his way home, so that Uka's pollution could be transferred to the Muslim! Gandhi preserves his purity no matter what happens to anyone else. Jinnah has a more difficult problem. His dream is in the air; it needs to settle down on land."

"You always see what is wrong with Gandhi; why don't you see what is right about him? He gave us Indians *abhaya*, freedom from fear, and fear was the principal weapon of the British," responded Syed Ashfaque.

"A hundred caravans have come to rest in India; why should one of them want to leave after a thousand years?" asked Girija Maharaj.

Perhaps in an unconscious answer, Thakur Bhagwan Singh said, "That crafty Govardhan Ahir has been arguing at the tea shop that the age of Hindus has finally dawned, that India will become an Akhand Bharat once the British go. Do you know the strange part? Some of the mullahs wandering around are frightening Muslims with the same thought. They are saying Islam is in danger! Do you think there is a conspiracy between the two?"

"How can Islam be in danger?" asked Zulfiqar Khan, hissing through missing teeth. "Islam is the true faith. How can the true faith be in danger? It is heresy to say such a preposterous thing."

"Well, the biggest beards in the business are saying so. I do not know if these mullahs are creating Pakistan or not, but they are certainly creating the need for one," answered Bhagwan Singh.

"It is strange that those who talk most of faith should understand it the least," Syed Ashfaque reflected. "Muslims are a brotherhood, not a nation. I wish someone would persuade Jinnah Sahib to read the Quran. The Quran is clear – it says, I think in the sixteenth *sura:* 'If God had willed He would have made you one nation; but He leads astray whom He will, and guides whom He will, and you will surely be questioned about the things you wrought'. *You will surely be questioned about the things you wrought...*"

"The Quran also says that a small group of believers can overcome a great host. But let's leave God out of this; this is an argument between men," answered Syed Bukhari.

"What does Pakistan stand for?" asked Girija Maharaj.

"The word was coined by some chap in Cambridge University, I understand," replied Bukhari. "It is actually Pakstan: P for Punjab, A for Afghans on the Frontier Province, K for Kashmir, S for Sind, and Tan for Baluchistan..."

"There's no Bengal or Bihar in it then," interrupted my grandfather.

"You are talking of old India," suggested my father. He did not speak often in front of elders, out of respect. "There is a new generation of Indians with different hopes, different ambitions. J.R.D. Tata gave us an airline; he is now building cars in a new factory and training scientists at the Tata Institute of Fundamental Research. Writers like R.K. Narayan and Mulk Raj Anand are teaching the English how to write English. They are dreaming of a new India, not a new Pakistan!"

"Our child is a statesman," punned Syed Ashfaque.

They did not know it then, but the Id festival of 1945 was the last time they laughed together.

The long season of whispers started soon after. Telinipara was now almost a township, and strangers melted into the population. Men with saffron draped over their shoulders, in baggy knee-length shorts, from a still mysterious organization called the RSS, began to assemble children for drill and indoctrination at early morning classes. Muslims wearing green scarves, claiming allegiance to a new organization called the Jamiat-e-Islami, told their brethren to oil the rust out of their swords. Stories of

Hindu-Muslim violence began to fill the city pages of the *Statesman*. They leapt to the front page after a demonstration by Calcutta's Muslims on 11 February 1946. They were protesting against a seven-year sentence given to a Muslim officer of Subhas Bose's defeated Indian National Army. Bose had died a year before in a mysterious air crash in Formosa. His force was taken prisoner and tried for desertion. By some inexplicable alchemy, the anti-British rally turned against the city's Hindus. A fuse was lit.

Eight days after the Calcutta incidents, Prime Minister Clement Attlee sent a mission of three Cabinet members that talked and argued its way from Karachi to Delhi. Plans and schemes for post-British India crawled and raced through the media, some dying at birth, others strangled by deadlock. Syed Ashfaque, irrepressible, still attempted a feeble joke or two (Gandhi had a solution for every problem and Jinnah a problem for every solution) but humour fizzled out in uncertainty. In May, the improbable happened.

A plan for a federal India with three zones, a Muslim-majority northwest including the whole of Punjab; a Muslim-majority east, including Bengal and Assam; and a Hindu-majority bloc in the centre of the subcontinent was accepted by both the Congress and the Muslim League. Good news had to be deceptive. In June the newly-elected Congress president, Nehru, reneged on the agreement at a press conference in Bombay. Jinnah was furious. On 29 July 1946 he declared, "The time has now come for the Muslim nation to resort to Direct Action Day to achieve Pakistan." A date was fixed – 16 August, a Friday.

On 14 August Nehru accepted the Viceroy's invitation to form an interim government to facilitate the transfer of power. On 15 August he met Jinnah in Bombay to get Muslim League cooperation, but failed. In Calcutta, the Muslim League chief minister Hussain Shaheed Suhrawardy declared 16 August a public holiday, ostensibly to reduce tension. Gandhi, a little bereft of events, was in his ashram in Sevagram, wondering how he could test his non-violence in the furnace of communal riots. He would not have to wonder too long.

A pamphlet published by the Muslim League reached Telinipara in early August. Its message was unambiguous: "The Bombay resolution of the All-India Muslim League has been broadcast. The call to revolt comes to us from a nation of heroes… The day for an open fight which is the greatest desire of the Muslim nation, has arrived. Come, those who want to rise to heaven. Come, those who are simple, wanting in peace of mind and who are in distress. Those who are thieves, goondas, those without the strength of character and those who do not say their prayers – all come. The shining gates of Heaven have been opened for you. Let us enter in thousands. Let us all cry out victory to Pakistan." A second followed, even more specific: "Be ready and take your swords… We shall show our glory with swords in hands and will have a special victory."

Syed Ashfaque had but a single comment, a quotation from the Quran, before he retreated into unfamiliar silence: "Allah pronounces doom and no one can reverse it."

Doom came to Calcutta on 16 August. Mobs began operating from a little after dawn; curfew was not imposed till nine at night. Policemen were invisible, even traffic policemen.

By the nineteenth, the only civil force in the city, the army, was wearing masks to mute the stench of dead bodies piled on carts and shoved into drains. The government offered five rupees per corpse. Nearly 16,000 were killed, and if the Muslims were the "victors" of the opening bouts of frenzy then proportions had evened out by the second and third day.

Victor Matheson had one objective: to ensure peace and continue production. He summoned Bauna Sardar from retirement, and telephoned Bukhari to ensure that police were deployed at sensitive points like the butchers enclave around the mosque and the road through the bazaar on the east that led to the river. There was peace, couched in doubt.

The next few months seemed to pass in a strange twilight. No one knew where he would land when the world stopped spinning. The British wondered whether they would retain their jobs after India became free. Simon's Christmas party of 1946 was uneasy and unhappy. There was too much drunkenness. Hasina did not appear. Mathew and Maureen fought. The Mathesons barely spoke. Benoy Chowdhury was too obsequious. Colonel Ian Hogg dominated the evening with dismal stories about senior officers, particularly the commander of the Burma front till an air crash killed him in 1944, Major General Charles Orde Wingate, leader of the Chindits, the soldier Churchill called a "man of genius who might have become a man of destiny". Wingate, said the colonel, held briefing sessions in the nude, rubbed his body with a toothbrush since he considered conventional bathing unhealthy and thought that the best way to cool down in the tropical heat was to eat raw onions. The evening ended with Colonel Hogg singing:

Come you back, you British soldier
Come you back to Mandalay...

Events brought no relief from uncertainty. The British announced in February 1947 that they would leave by June 1948. A handsome Viceroy, Lord Mountbatten came in March for the funeral ceremonies of the Raj. In May the *Statesman* wrote an editorial saying, "Calcutta, once the most lively if never the most comfortable city of India, is becoming unbearable to its inhabitants. Under the blight of communalism, it is from dusk onwards a city of the dead... If Calcutta passes two 'quiet' days in succession, hope revives to fall again as the third day brings news of fresh outrages." Gandhi had become little more than a preacher of homilies: "When the Ganges is in flood the water is turbid. The dirt comes to the surface." With so much dirt soaked in so much blood, no one had any appetite for excessive celebrations when my mother gave birth to her first child, a son. To my father's delight, he had a small sixth finger on his left hand. They named him Zaigham. My mother wanted to show her child off to her mother, her sisters and her friends in Amritsar, but everyone advised against travel.

Hope disappeared on 3 June, when it was formally announced that India would be partitioned to create a divided Pakistan, half of it in the west, and the other half in Bengal. My grandfather answered consternation with simple logic: "Pakistan has been formed for the Punjabi Muslim in the west and the Bengali Muslim in the east. No Pakistan has been offered to Bihari Muslims." There was nowhere to go, he concluded, with obvious relief.

Syed Shah Bukhari did have somewhere to go. He wanted to

return to Amritsar. He did not know how Bengalis would behave during the separation but he was confident that the Sikhs, Muslims and Hindus would never fight. He took his leave with great dignity, and everyone believed his promise to return for a few weeks every year.

Independence came on the strangest of all days. My father never left the controls as elders and friends clustered around the radio to hear India's first Prime Minister Jawaharlal Nehru. Nehru spoke in English, and my father had to effect a random translation. "Long years ago," said a slightly quavering, nasal voice, "we made a tryst with destiny, and now the time has come when we shall redeem our pledge, not wholly or in full measure, but very substantially. At the stroke of the midnight hour, when the world sleeps, India will wake up to life and freedom."

"Why isn't Gandhi talking to us?" asked Girija Maharaj.

Gandhi was not in Delhi. His struggle for freedom had killed the India he knew. While Nehru celebrated freedom in Delhi on 15 August, Gandhi was protecting life in Calcutta.

That was why it was the strangest of all days, for nothing happened in Calcutta. On 9 August Gandhi came to Calcutta. On 11 August he suggested to the leader of the Muslim League, Suhrawardy, that they move into the deserted home of a Muslim widow in a locality called Belliaghata, which Muslims had abandoned after being attacked. Gandhi would not accept police protection, and invited Suhrawardy to share the trust. A crowd of Hindus hurled stones, smashed windows and stormed into the house to ask Gandhi why he was protecting Muslims rather than saving Hindus. "How can I," answered Gandhi, "who am a Hindu by birth, a Hindu by creed, and a Hindu of Hindus in my way of living be an enemy of Hindus?" Slowly, hypnotized by the Mahatma, the crowd dispersed. The next day, Hindus and Muslims, still suspicious of each other, came separately to narrate bitter grievances. On 15 August, in front of incredulous newspapermen, Hindus and Muslims embraced one another before Gandhi. Just after freedom came Id. Gandhi celebrated the Muslim festival with a public prayer meeting at the Calcutta maidan, at which the Quran was recited in an affecting, sonorous warble in the presence of thousands.

Telinipara heard the periodic clamour of tension bursting through its controls: an argument that threatened to become a squabble, a rumour that grew into dire fact under the protection of the night. But after Gandhi's miracle Syed Ashfaque was convinced that Gandhi and Gandhi alone could reverse the doom that had been pronounced.

14

BRAHMA

"THEY KILLED ASHFAQUE?" ASKED MY GRANDFATHER IN AN incredulous whisper. "But he was always for India!" His mouth opened and froze, as if his whole life had suddenly sunk into uncertainty. He stared at nothing for a long while, until my father, who had brought the terrible news, tiptoed away and Jamila came to the drawing room and held him in her arms.

There had never been a winter as bereft of hope as the one they had just seen. Gandhi's peace held in Bengal, but paled before the havoc in north India, from Bihar to Punjab. Syed Bukhari had left for Amritsar in the belief that Hindus and Muslims would remain brothers in Punjab; instead Punjab discovered wells of hatred that were filled each day with fresh blood. Bewildered caravans wandered through the province in search of new nations, each bearing scars of violence so vicious that even Europe, still numbed by seventy million dead in a world war, might have wondered if death could be more pointless.

My mother looked at the pictures on the front page of the English newspaper, and wept. She asked for an Urdu paper, and the *Azad Hind* was ordered, but it was nervous about facts. The

Statesman was more informative. She read and heard about her city, Amritsar, and broke into spasms. Images of her sisters, her family and the avuncular Syed Shah Bukhari appeared and reappeared, magnified into terrifying aspect by ignorance. Her husband was by her side only late at night, the one time it was decorous for a couple to be alone in a joint family. He was often nervous and moody and with little patience to listen. Alone and miserable, she found comfort in her baby, speaking to the wordless child whenever she could be alone with him. She talked to her baby even while he slept, for Zaigham, with her features and her fair looks, was one of her own in a land of dark strangers. In timid steps she sought out her own space within this distant and hostile world. She changed its language. When Zaigham crossed the gurgle stage, she taught him to call her Ammiji rather than Mai. It was no longer the Bhojpuri Mai and Baba, for mother and father, but the Urdu Ammiji and Abbaji.

The first letter, from her eldest sister, Khaleda, came in late October. The postman had never seen a Pakistani stamp before and showed it around before he delivered the letter. She went to the roof to read it alone and cry in relief. Her mother and her sisters had reached Pakistan safely, but the letter was weighed down by what might have been as it described the horrors they had seen on the brief journey between the sister cities, Amritsar and Lahore, now separated into two nations. Syed Shah Bukhari's uniform, they said, had kept them safe as the carts they hired drove at whatever speed mangy, tired and frenzied horses could manage. It was Allah's will that they were alive. In Lahore Syed Bukhari had found them rooms in a tenement in a lane across the Shah Alam market. Syed Bukhari, God be praised, said the letter, had moved into a bungalow vacated by Hindus in the Krishnanagar locality. Ammiji wanted desperately to be with them, to talk in Punjabi, to hear each detail of their story, and to find out whether her five-year-old nephew Infishar had faced turmoil with courage. She sought comfort on the roof, as if the open air brought her closer to those who lived so far away. Mustaqim would sit on the stairs behind the door, shielding her loneliness with a son's fierce love.

By the end of August street battles resumed in Calcutta. In the first week of September Gandhi returned to his familiar bed of nails: he began a fast to death. It took three days of penitence to tame rabid dogs. On the fourth day, Hindu and Muslim "resistance" groups surrendered weapons at the feet of their Mahatma and pleaded for punishment. Bengal, and Telinipara, were quiet.

It was cold on 30 January. The sun set before five. Shivering slightly, my father wrapped himself in a shawl and idly twiddled the knobs of the radio. The women were in the kitchen for winter dinners were early. At five minutes to six, the music stopped. My father froze instinctively at half-heard words. The announcement was repeated. Mohandas Karamchand Gandhi had been shot dead as he was about to begin the evening prayer at Birla House in Delhi. Anger, fear and sorrow filled his heart. Then came relief, implosive in its impact. The second sentence of the special news broadcast was shorn of every detail except one: The assassin was a Hindu. Then pain overwhelmed him. He said loudly to no one in particular, "They've killed Gandhiji." A sob arose from the kitchen and cooking pots were taken off the fire. They placed the radio on the balcony and turned up the volume so that those on the street might also hear Nehru's lament into the night: "Friends and comrades, the light has gone out of our lives and there is darkness everywhere. I do not know what to tell you and how to say it. Our beloved leader, Bapu as we called him, the father of the nation, is no more. The light has gone out, I said, and yet I was wrong... For that light represented something more than the immediate present, it represented the living truth, the eternal truth..."

Telinipara joined the hush that fell over India. Gandhi's death was his last miracle. The civil war that had taken some two million lives in five months, suddenly ceased. Numbed by guilt, Hindus and Muslims sought repentance, barring the fringe that would never cease hating.

Ram Chatterjee, surrounded by mute, obsequious cronies in Chandernagore, drank rum and gloated. "Gandhi is dead!" With an exaggerated swivel, he asked the room, "Who will save these Muslim bastards now?" He did not expect an answer. But Chatterjee was confused. Every event in the past few years had induced a rampage. Gandhi's death had led to calm. No one wanted to kill Muslim bastards anymore. Why, he asked himself repeatedly, had not a Muslim killed Gandhi? Life would have been so uncomplicated.

The idea emerged from the fertile mind of Pulluck Sanyal, manager of Satyajit Banerjee's estates, once-proud sole occupant of the Raj Cadillac that was now in my father's garage. The rich tend to accept shifts of fortune better than their employees. Satyajit Banerjee would never have approved had he been told about the scheme. Such niceties did not interest Sanyal.

Ram Chatterjee flourished in free India. Surplus war

revolvers and ammunition had flooded the black market, part of which he controlled; Chandernagore remained with the French, who, unlike the British, were in no hurry to leave. A monthly stipend to the Bengali gendarmes served as guarantee money.

They met at night in the first fortnight of February. Pulluck Sanyal did not get up, or even acknowledge his visitor as Ram Chatterjee was escorted into the outhouse where Mathew had once spent the night. Chatterjee was not offered a chair. "I know a great deal about what you are," said Sanyal carefully, and lifted his eyes so that Chatterjee could see the sneer in them. "But I never thought you were a fool."

Chatterjee knew his place, and accepted it; but this did not extend to abuse. "What do you mean?"

"How many years did you spend in jail?"

"That swine. That Muslim swine!" Chatterjee thought of Bukhari when he thought of prison.

"That is why I call you a fool. Your anger is three steps ahead of your intelligence. Where is Bukhari now?"

Chatterjee was not sure so he kept quiet.

"Pakistan. That makes him a Pakistani bastard instead of just a Muslim bastard! You were kept in jail by a traitor!"

Chatterjee's eyes gleamed. He did not know that he had been part of the national struggle for Indian unity.

"What is our duty? The Muslims wanted Pakistan. It is our duty to send all traitors to Pakistan. Is it, or is it not?"

Chatterjee nodded vigorously.

"Who persuaded Bukhari to send you to jail? That Telinipara crook who gave Satyajit Baboo a small loan and stole a large estate, Rahmatullah. Who is his daughter-in-law? Bukhari's niece! What does this mean?" Sanyal had lost the measure of his tones and was half-screaming. "It means that Rahmatullah's son Akbar has married a Pakistani! The first letter from Pakistan has come to his family. What does this make him? A traitor! Chatterjee: what is your duty?"

Chatterjee was beginning to get the idea, but remained uncertain about its limits. He kept quiet again.

"What is your duty? Your duty is to rid our holy land of Pakistanis!"

Chatterjee got it. Whatever his limitations in knowledge and logic, he was ahead of the street on loot. A deal was struck. The garden estate would be returned to Satyajit Banerjee. Sanyal would get the Cadillac. Chatterjee could keep all the cash and jewels. Chatterjee asked for clarifications. What if blood had to be shed? And then there was a pretty young wife at home. Could he...

Sanyal pondered briefly. "I don't care what you do," he answered. "There are only two places for Muslims now: Either Pakistan or *kabristan!*"

Chatterjee smiled. "*Kabristan*. Graveyard. You have a great way with words, Sanyal Babu."

"Pakistan or *kabristan*," Sanyal repeated, very pleased with his own Muslim solution.

~

A bedridden Surjya Modak picked up the first murmur. Modak's restaurant was a natural magnet for gossip. He heard talk that Ram Chatterjee was planning to kill my grandfather in revenge for sending him to jail. Bhagwan Singh learnt, from his son

Kalyan, who picked this up from the *gawala* colony, that there would be trouble during the Holi festival.

The spring festival of Holi, a day of frolic for gods and men, occurs during the full moon on the fifteenth of Phalguna; it corresponded to 25 March that year. Girija Maharaj and Bhagwan Singh proposed that in view of Gandhi's assassination Hindus should not celebrate Holi. Govardhan Ahir, the undisputed leader of the *gawalas,* agreed, but made it clear that he expected Muslims to be similarly abstemious when Id came around a few months later. Three days before Holi Govardhan Ahir explained that while there would be no frolic, his caste would perform the ritual burning, on the night before Holi, of an effigy of the evil monster that devoured little children. A day later, he announced that they would take out a bonfire procession after sunset.

That afternoon Syed Ashfaque Alam boarded a bus to spend, as was his preference, the holiday at our home. Just after sunset he got off at the corner on the Grand Trunk Road from where a bylane turned towards Telinipara. For some half a mile the lane passed through deserted, uncultivated fields overgrown with high grass, punctuated by the occasional clump of trees. Syed Ashfaque negotiated a fare with the nearest rickshaw and set off.

His assailants were either aware of his schedule or were patient. Within about five minutes two men, their faces half-hidden by large handkerchiefs wrapped below the nose, stopped the rickshaw. They pulled Syed Ashfaque down.

"Check whether he is a Muslim," said one.

"He has a beard. Only Muslims have beards," replied the other.

"I said check him out! Strip him!"

Syed Ashfaque understood. He faced the moment with serene dignity. "My name," he said, speaking clearly and without the least tremor, "is Syed Ashfaque Alam. I am a Muslim, a believer in Allah and His last Prophet, Muhammad, *salle-ala-alaihe-wa-sallam,* peace be upon him."

"What is he saying?"

"He says he is Ashfaque. He also spoke some gibberish in a Muslim language."

"Well, then, what are you waiting for?"

Syed Ashfaque cupped his hands and raised his eyes towards Allah. "Ya Allah, You have given me a full life, blessed with bread to eat, knowledge to impart, and friends to love. My birth was Your will, my death is Your will. I thank You for the comforts of this lifetime, and seek a place by Your side in the afterlife. *Inna-lillahi-wa-inna-Ilahi-rajaoon."* From Allah we come, to Allah we return.

"He is still talking!"

"Well, shut him up then!"

A good bullet makes no more sound than the snapping of a dry twig in the silence of a forest.

They threw the body into a dip in the grass off the road. Only then did they notice the shivering rickshaw-puller.

"What do we do with this terrified idiot?"

"Check whether he is a Hindu or a Muslim."

They lifted the rickshaw-puller's lungi to find out whether he was circumcised, discovered he was a Hindu, warned him that they would cut off his tongue if he opened his mouth, and disappeared on a motorbike towards Chandernagore.

The body was found next morning. Word spread in a series of anonymous whispers. Two young men, Gauhar Ayub and Mustafa Khan, were the first to reach the murder spot, and brought the body to our drawing room. The rickshaw-wallah was traced, interrogated, and each detail was repeated till it grated on every Muslim nerve. The local police inspector came, saw the anger, and retreated; since no one had filed a complaint or a First Information Report, the murder did not exist. My grandfather, Girija Maharaj, my father and T.P. Singh were the first to place the four corners of the bier on their shoulders as the funeral procession left our home. A community prayer was offered at the new railway track that had been laid during the war to facilitate the movement of supplies to and from Victoria. Govardhan Ahir sat on the bench at his favourite tea shop and said loudly and often that the Bihari *gawalas* of his locality were blameless. The killers had been speaking in Bengali. It was the smug look on Govardhan Ahir's face that removed any trace of doubt from the minds of Gauhar and Mustafa. They conferred with Zahid Qureshi, owner of the biggest meat shop on the Bazaar Road, and agreed upon the place where the Holi procession would be attacked that evening.

It was only when the flares lit up, and, a little later, screams were heard, that the elders realized that Telinipara was out of control. Stones had been thrown at the procession, and three men stabbed. Govardhan Ahir began wailing at the top of his voice that Hindus were being killed in the land of the Hindus. My grandfather felt numb and helpless.

Bhagwan Singh, as head of durwans and chief of security, hurried off to Victor Matheson to make a detailed report. For the first time in anyone's memory Matheson walked into the workers' colony. The Burra Sahib's presence had immediate effect. He spoke to both Muslims and Hindus, promised justice without specifying what he meant by it, and there was calm when he headed back to his bungalow in Victoria. Matheson was not fooled by his success. He deputed Simon, who was upset by Syed Ashfaque's death, to find out more. Simon, using the telephone, learnt that a smokescreen had been set up for the main event.

He was restless all night, and the pre-dawn phone call came as a relief, for it was a reason to get out of bed. Surjya Modak, his voice quivering, was at the other end. Simon panicked when he heard that Chatterjee had sent two jeeps to the petrol pump to fill up. He woke Benoy Chowdhury. Chowdhury came over to my home and told my father that he must leave Telinipara with his family at once.

My grandfather was blank. "Go where?" he asked, as if there was no place on earth apart from the home he had built two and a half decades ago. No one had slept through the tense night, and people peered out upon Benoy Chowdhury's arrival, sensing that something dramatic was happening, but unsure of what precisely it was.

T.P. Singh paced up and down, Bhagwan Singh by his side. He spoke loudly, to no one in particular, "Anyone who comes for Akbar will have to deal with me first!" Benoy Chowdhury caught my father's shirt and began to plead like a child, "Go away, go away, go away, Akbar, go away for my sake, for the sake of my children, for the sake of your children! TP's lathis will not stop Ram Chatterjee. He has guns." My grandfather moved to the safe in which he kept his money, and clung to the metal that contained all his wealth. No one in the family stirred; they would not move, unless he did.

A second phone call informed Simon that Chatterjee had left with two jeeploads of men. He rushed out, drove his own jeep to our house and shouted from the street, "Come on, Akbar, let's leave!" There was no answer. He ran upstairs. "This fire has no judgment. It is a lunatic fire! Get out, I tell you, get out!" Simon was shouting into my grandfather's ear. My grandfather understood nothing. He would not have understood even if he knew English.

"Akbar! For God's sake leave! Get your father out! Chatterjee is a killer. He is on his way. You have a young wife! My revolver will not be enough to stop them. Please, in the name of all that's holy, please!" Simon's scream was heard across a silent Telinipara.

My father moved. He rushed towards my grandfather, and, with the help of Mustaqim and Simon, clawed him out of the metal embrace, picked him up and dragged him into Simon's jeep. My mad aunt decided at this point that another djinn had descended upon her and rushed back to her hut. My other aunt, Nasiban, had already packed whatever she could, a few clothes, and all the cash and jewels, for us to take. She took out a *tabeez*, a prayer wrapped in a small silver container, blessed at Burha Deewana's grave, and tied it on my father's arm for his protection. T.P. Singh told my father not to worry about his sisters, who were staying behind: they were his sisters and no harm would come to them as long as he was alive. My grandmother, my mother, Zaigham and a maid were huddled into the family car, waiting ahead of the jeep.

"I don't want to leave Telinipara," whimpered my

grandfather. "Let me be… please let me be… I am an old man… Let me be."

From the jeep, my grandfather suddenly shouted, "Bauna! Where are you, Bauna? I am not leaving without Bauna!"

"Now what? For God's sake, let's go!" Simon was frantic.

Bauna, looking older than his countless years, shuffled towards the vehicle, and said, "Go, Babu. May Allah be with you, your family, may Allah keep you safe… You have family and wealth; you have something to protect. Mustaqim is the only wealth I have, and I have given him to you. I have nowhere to go. Don't worry, the Sahibs will protect me." And then with a sudden twitch of the old spirit, he lifted his head and said, "Plus, someone has to look after your home while you are away, isn't it? Go!"

The street dogs were barking in a discordant chorus, waiting at the corner for intruders. The street was nearly empty. Muslims had retreated into the courtyards of their rectangular blocks of huts, seeking safety in numbers, the men guarding narrow entrances with swords and knives. Hindus crept into their homes, waiting for the calamity to pass: no one knew the strength of the coming storm. T.P. Singh, in perpetual motion, dared any mother-fucker to cross his path. When he saw my father climb into Simon's jeep, he rushed up and said, "Akbar, this is the madness of a moment. Maybe the Sahib knows better and is taking you to safety, but this will always be your home. You can't live in Calcutta or – or, anywhere else." My father reached out, clasped his friend's hand tightly, and said nothing.

Simon bellowed and the cars moved ahead. "Take the shortcut through the factory," he ordered the driver of the Raj

Cadillac. At the factory gate he instructed the durwans not to let any other vehicle through.

Bhagwan Singh was not there to say goodbye. A few minutes before, acting on an idea, he had gone to the police station to plead for a special picket at our home. The inspector said he had not received any orders to do so. Bhagwan Singh was still arguing when, about fifteen minutes later, Ram Chatterjee's jeeps sped past the police station.

My mother was utterly distraught, for Zaigham had fallen very ill the previous night with high fever. Trembling violently at the thought of unknown horrors, she cowered in a corner, hidden by a heavy chadar. Zaigham was on her inert lap, numb. My father sat beside Simon, who drove with one hand and held his Webley & Scott revolver in the other. Mustaqim wedged himself between my father and the window, to protect him from a stone or a bullet. They swerved through the factory gates and hit the Grand Trunk Road.

Ram Chatterjee reached my house, cursed his luck, and ordered the jeeps to turn around and give chase. It was a holiday, the Grand Trunk Road was empty, and Chatterjee knew that my family could have gone in but one direction, towards Calcutta.

Some six miles along the highway, at Baidyabati, there is a railway crossing. Trains were infrequent then, so normally passage was unimpeded. The gates of the crossing were shut. Vehicles halted, and hearts turned to ice. Simon jumped out, waving his revolver, and shouted in his limited Hindi, "Open! Open!" The bored railway attendant looked contemptuously at Simon, suggesting that the latter had not heard of the demise of empire, and returned to his vigil. Fortune was on our side, albeit barely.

Within three minutes an engine puffing black smoke went past and the barriers lifted.

At Sheoraphuli they heard the sound of pursuing jeeps. Simon sought in vain for a policeman, even a traffic policeman. One revolver was not sufficient to stop Chatterjee. They were near Serampore when jeeps appeared in Simon's rear-view mirror. He took his eyes off the road, turned and sent a single bullet into the windshield of the Chatterjee jeep, which swerved, halted and lost precious minutes. But Calcutta, and safety, was still more than fifteen miles away. Despair was giving way to desperation when they saw the huge headlights of a military truck approaching them. Simon threw his hands away from the wheel, hitting my father in the face as he did so, and shouted in triumph: "Thank God!"

Before he left Victoria, Simon had phoned Ian Hogg and appealed for help. The colonel had come from Fort William with eight soldiers. He drove past the Cadillac and Simon's jeep, turned the army truck and straddled the highway, blocking traffic. His men were in position when Ram Chatterjee turned up. They ordered Chatterjee to halt. Chatterjee did not wait to be arrested. He stopped, turned around, and, anger evident in large bloodshot eyes, returned to Telinipara.

Bauna Sardar was sitting alone, his *gamcha* across his face, in the drawing room, when they slit his throat with a Nepalese kukri before looting our home. The safe was Chatterjee's personal reward.

It took a few hours for people to venture cautiously out of their safety nets. Workers buried their Sardar's body beside the fresh grave of Syed Ashfaque. T.P. Singh placed two large locks on our home, and took the keys. He could not quite convince himself that my father would return. Bauna Sardar's bloodstains remained undisturbed on the white sheets for a long while.

It was only when my family reached Calcutta's Amina Hotel, owned by Muslims and protected by an army picket, that my father realized that there was a woman in their jeep. "Look after her, Akbar. I leave her in your care. If this country is not safe for you, it cannot be safe for her. Protect her from the terrors of our time." Hasina's eyes were swollen, but she held her composure. She did not look back at Simon. Hasina lived with us as long as she was alive, and became my favourite aunt.

No one was in the mood for a long farewell. Simon, drained, left for Victoria Jute Mill after a quick, almost embarrassed embrace from my father. The Muslim driver of the Raj Cadillac was the only one to bid a tearful, emotional goodbye, possibly because he was a thief. Instead of returning the car to Telinipara, he took it to a garage on Lower Circular Road, sold it for three hundred rupees and disappeared to his village in Bihar.

Amina Hotel was less a hotel and more a refugee camp, an overcrowded and, inevitably, filthy, transit house for those seeking new destinations. The government imposed curfew in the city after seven as a precautionary measure, but few would have tested the hazards of darkness even without curfew. The hotel's few rooms were taken, and my family spent the night on sheets spread out in the courtyard. Who knew which sip of water, or which morsel of food, was contaminated: that night Zaigham picked up bacillary dysentery in addition to high fever. By next afternoon he was dead.

Ammijee became hysterical, my father stone cold. He

remained emotionless at the quick funeral, and then used the hotel telephone to call Colonel Hogg. The colonel accompanied my father to the offices of Air India. He purchased tickets for Dhaka, capital of East Pakistan, for the first available flight. They left forty-eight hours later.

~

Girija Maharaj lay on his bed and told Kamala a story. "The tears of Brahma's daughter," he began, "have fallen upon me."

He spoke in a slow monotone. "In the beginning of creation, Brahma was full of energy, there was no death, and life multiplied. The Earth began to complain that the burden of unceasing life had become too heavy for her, and she was sinking into the waters. Brahma, lord of thirty-three gods, was so angry when he heard this complaint that he began to destroy everything. Shiva intervened with a suggestion: could all creatures be subject to life and death? From Shiva's body rose a dark woman with red eyes, red palms, red garments, adorned in earrings and ornaments, wearing garlands of lotus. She was the Goddess of Death. But soon she too began to brood and weep. 'Why,' she wailed, 'has it been assigned to me to take away innocent children, to separate families, to divide friends, to inflict the deepest of sorrows that will scorch me eternally!' She pleaded that her dharma be changed. But Brahma was implacable. She had been created to destroy and thus it would be. The Goddess of Death tried to alter her destiny with asceticism. She went to the great yogi, Dhenuka, and stood on one foot for 15,000 million years. Brahma ordered her to stop. She refused and stood on the other foot for 20,000 million years. For another ten million years she dwelt with wild animals. For the next 20,000 years she ate only air and then for 8000 years stood in silence in water. She then went up the Ganga to the Himalayas and stood on a toe for a thousand million years. But Brahma was unmoved. Her tears became a pool in her cupped palms. These tears, cursed Brahma, will become diseases and sorrows that will kill men.

"I heard one tear fall on me, my child, when I locked my door after I heard Ram Chatterjee had come to kill my only friend, Rahmat. I denied my own dharma that moment. I used age as an excuse. What could an old man do against gangs of killers? But it is the mind that commits the sin, not the body. *Manasheshu krutham papam, na sharira krutham kurtham.*"

He was quiet now, pensive. "I brought Akbar's wife, that beautiful Kashmiri girl, into our house as my daughter. I should have been at her side when evil entered her world. If I am too weak, too old, to protect my daughter then there is nothing left to live for. Bauna was old too. But he did not surrender his pride in death." Kamala understood only this much, that something strange and fearful had happened. He placed his hand through the long beard he had played with so often, and was bewildered when in a little while the face grew cold.

Simon applied for leave. He had not taken any for too long. The war was over. Hasina had gone. The house was empty. He did not want to start drinking as much as Mathew. He needed a new life, and he needed the peace of Scotland to think.

Victor Matheson invited him for dinner on the eve of his departure. Officially, the company did not approve of officers meddling in Hindu-Muslim disputes; but Simon was quietly applauded for best-of-British behaviour.

"You are wrong, Simon," Matheson said reasonably. "The

British could not have betrayed India; only Indians can betray India, and they have done so, generation after generation, century after century, whether as collaborators of an invader, or as hoarders during famine, or murderers during vicious riots. Yesterday, we were the enemy. There was but one British official for a million Indians. Did the Indians touch a single white man when they could have massacred us all by sheer weight of numbers? The moment we leave they massacre each other in millions. What beastly religions they have – and they call themselves civilized! Gandhi's dream of a united India was the romantic inversion of a thousand defeats. He inherited an India from eighteenth century chaos and nineteenth century stupor without any answers for the twentieth century. Where is Gandhi's India now? Churchill was right. This is the chaos he predicted. Wasn't it Amery who suggested that before we gave the Indians freedom we should have put some Nordic blood in their genes?" Old Matheson, his eyebrows a sparkling white, was not given to oratory, but he had done much thinking through the traumatic loss of empire.

Simon was too depressed to argue.

Mathew was, as ever, tart. "Yes, of course; the sun was never supposed to set on Churchill's empire, was it?"

"The real mistake, young Mathew, was made in the beginning, not in the end. We took too long to establish our empire. Babar laid the foundation of Mughal rule in a few months; we took half a century to travel from Calcutta to Delhi. And then we let buffoons act their little charades on the throne of Delhi for another fifty years till the Indians were foolish enough to mutiny. Clive was right when he told the directors of the East India Company that he could have become King of Hindustan. He wondered at his race for not seizing what seemed so easily available. The Turk or the Mongol had destroyed Indian ennui with more dispatch. Perhaps we were distracted by money: Clive remarked that Murshidabad alone, the old capital of Bengal, was as extensive, populous and rich as London."

"Of course. Who on earth would want to conquer a poor country?" said Maureen in a matter-of-fact tone.

"I say, aren't Indians lucky we didn't change their names? If Cecil Rhodes could turn the land he conquered into Rhodesia then Bengal at the very least should have been Clivania, what?" said Mathew. "They're all bloody freaks," he added with a touch of bitterness. "Churchill is drunk by lunchtime everyday. Nehru screws the Viceroy's wife and Gandhi sleeps with two young virgins to test his will – or their won't, ha ha." His wife laughed. His father-in-law looked stern. (His mother-in-law was not there; she had stopped at Victoria very briefly on her way from Simla to Dundee.)

"We gave India an identity, Mathew. We introduced India to good governance."

"Three or maybe four million dead in a famine is good governance?" asked Simon. "Even the *Statesman* said that the Bengal famine was man-made."

"Which men? Hindu and Muslims stopped their politics of hatred when it was time to steal from the poor. Marwari hoarders were in cahoots with Muslims like Suhrawardy and Ispahani when they profiteered from starvation," responded Matheson.

"And we were powerless while four million died of hunger in

front of our eyes? All the talk at Bengal Club the other day was about Churchill repeatedly ignoring Wavell's requests for food."

"I wouldn't believe gossip."

"You wouldn't believe either that we actually exported rice from Bengal to Ceylon at the height of the famine, would you?"

Matheson changed the subject. "I hope you are coming back to Victoria, Simon. This is a good job, and Britain needs us. It will take a while to pay for the war."

Simon snapped. "Between Indian stupidity and British dishonesty – what a choice!"

~

The factory never paused. There was no more violence in Telinipara. There was silence, except for the pervasive hum of machinery. Even the tea shops were quiet. T.P. Singh kept to his hut, and slept with the keys to our home under his pillow. There was no anger, no bitterness, just a silence as vacant as the house that Sheikh Rahmatullah had built, now stained with Bauna Sardar's blood.

My mother, inconsolable, flew from Dhaka to Lahore. My father remained in Dhaka, in a crowded building on Bonogram Road. My grandfather's existence became mechanical. He would rise, eat, sleep, and occasionally summon my father and look at him, with very little to say. Abbaji paced the unknown, friendless streets of Dhaka, conscious that he was now responsible for the family. He took three months to make his decision. All he told my grandmother was that he would be away for a week, worried that her fears might stop him. He took Mustaqim along.

The thick mud doors on Telinipara's huts now had latches on both sides: a sliding bolt inside, and outside, a chain at the top of the door that fitted into a loop nailed to the mast. You could padlock the chain; when loose, it doubled as a knocker. It was past eight in the evening when the chain rattled loudly on T.P. Singh's door, rousing him from a sleepless reverie. "Who?" he asked, irritably, and then got up, for only an emergency of some sort could have brought someone at night. He opened the door, and looked with utter disbelief at the smile before him. The features cleared in the dim light of the low-voltage bulb. With a shriek he charged out of the hut, and screamed with all the power in his big lungs: *"Akbarwa aaa gayeee reee!"* Our Akbar has come back!

They walked over slowly, the women first, in ones, and then suddenly every person of the neighbourhood, Hindu or Muslim, was in our home. The women exhausted their sobs in sparkling smiles; the elder ones were soon scolding my father for leaving them destitute, while the young, more practical, quickly began to dust and sweep and light a fire in the kitchen. The butchers sent meat, vegetables arrived and dinner was prepared. Someone remarked that he had no idea that there were so many electric lights in Telinipara. T.P. Singh never stopped talking that night. At eleven the tinkle of a rickshaw was heard. My father raced down as workers scampered up the stairs to say that the Sahib had come. Simon smiled stiffly, but my father threw off any reserve and the workers witnessed a scene they had never imagined they would live to see: a dark man hugging a Sahib. Simon patted my father affectionately, and accepted the proffered cup of tea. "I say, Akbar," said Simon, "you must be the only goddam Muslim to leave Pakistan for India!"

The next morning, after dawn prayers, Abbaji went to offer

fateha at the graves of Bauna Sardar and Syed Ashfaque. He told the keeper of the cemetery to leave space next to these graves for our family. Within a week, Mustaqim, now an expert in air travel, had returned to Dhaka, with tickets, and escorted the rest of the family back to Telinipara. My mother had been summoned back from Lahore by telegram.

Grandfather seemed in awe of his destiny: he had been reborn twice. Bhagwan Singh would not let go of his friend Rahmat's hand. My grandfather called Kamala and told him stories about how wise and loving Girija Maharaj had been. Zulfiqar Khan, they learnt, had left for Pakistan, but his son Mustafa stayed back: he had been born in Telinipara, he said, and saw no reason to die anywhere else.

Much later, on a day when my own anguish grew slowly into uncertainty, I asked my father, one dark afternoon, why he had returned from Pakistan in 1948. His answer told a long story in a few words. "There were too many Muslims in Pakistan," he answered.

15

FRIENDS

THE FORTUNE-TELLER'S CONFIDENCE LEAKED OUT OF HIS EYES. He looked again at my birth chart, and repeated stonily, "This boy is destined for great fame!"

"Bah!" exclaimed T.P. Singh. "That is not a prediction. Even a murderer becomes famous. What do you mean by fame? I am famous on this dirt track! Is this road the child's destiny? Or Calcutta? Or India? Or the world?"

The astrologer retreated. His own fate now seemed uncertain. He wondered whether he would get paid. "The great Mughal Akbar, who ruled a mighty empire, was born in the desert when his father, Humayun, was a fugitive," he replied, without any explanation for the tangent. "Humayun did not have money to celebrate the birth of an heir. All he had was musk perfume, which he distributed to his friends. But his astrologer saw this as an omen, prophesying that the fame of his noble son would spread across the world like the smell of musk." The astrologer got his fee.

I was born on 11 January 1951, a Capricorn, with Scorpio Ascendant along with Scorpio Navamsa and Pisces Dreskana in the fourth house of Anuradha, indicating that I would have fame, travel, wealth, worldly comforts, energy, determination, and the comforting ability to convince others of a course of action while nursing an alternative idea in the quiet depths of my heart, making me practical, self-motivated and therefore successful. However, Scorpio Navamsa threatened problems in the liver, kidney and the brain. The balance sheet was positive, and my father named me Mubashshir, a bringer of good news, a name of high ambition and vaulting hope that was, for all its virtues, mis-spelt as Mobashar by Mother Michael when she admitted me into kindergarten and has remained Mobashar ever since.

When my father showed my birth chart to Simon he dismissed it as worthless mumbo-jumbo.

Mathew refused to look up from his coffee. A cold winter drizzle had cancelled golf; coffee and a three-week old copy of the *Sunday Express* were the only sensible options on the weekend. "Be careful of the terms you choose, young Simon. Do not take the name of gods irresponsibly. Mumbo-Jumbo is the legendary spirit that helps honourable African tribesmen keep a difficult wife in check. Whenever a wife sulks, or is indeed unpleasant about another wife, the husband dresses up as a Mumbo-Jumbo, appears outside her hut, and scares the wits out of her with his shrieking and hollering till she returns to dutiful obedience."

"In India," said Simon tartly, "mumbo-jumbo means astrology, and that will close the subject, if you please."

Whatever the future might have held for me, I was certainly fortunate for my father. Abbaji had brought a hamper of specially prepared sweets from Surjya Modak and four bottles of Famous Grouse whisky to celebrate my arrival. He returned with a contract to clear the ash each morning from the huge boiler of Victoria Jute Mill. In his official report, Simon explained that he had persuaded Sheikh Akbar Ali to work without cost to company. My father made decent money out of small, unburnt pieces of coal that lay hidden in the ash, which Telinipara's women sifted from a dump in the far corner of the maidan, and brought back as fuel for their home fires. They paid Mustaqim, who was put in charge of the business, a quarter of the market rate for coal. A second-hand Tata truck was bought with great ceremony, and Mustaqim learnt how to drive. The income was useful. Rent still came from the huts, but the shops had been looted and abandoned. Mustaqim set up a system. He gave two-thirds of what he collected to my father, and one-third to my mother. He did not ask anyone's permission for this allocation of resources and a question was never raised.

My grandfather, always hesitant to show his toothless gums, beamed without reserve when he learnt that his once-spoilt son had begun to earn. He could now die happy, he said, and proceeded to do so.

He agreed to sit for a portrait-photograph. There were three famous studios in Calcutta. Simon rejected Johnson & Hoffman, as well as Barton & Son, and arranged a cameraman from the best, Bourne & Shepherd. My father flinched at the bill but would not overturn Simon's decision. My grandfather wore a formal dhoti and dark jacket. The long fingers of his left hand rested gracefully on his walking stick. His left shoulder was much higher than his right, and nothing would induce him to draw them even. A copy of the Holy Quran was placed on a high table by his chair. His short beard was thick and white, and a black cap covered the head above a high brow. The round, thin-rimmed spectacles, resting on prominent cheekbones, could not dim the power of his eyes. His mouth twisted just a little to the right. He had to remain his sardonic self for posterity. After his picture was taken he insisted on a portrait of my grandmother. Jamila was shocked. "You are too old to worry about a veil," teased my grandfather.

One evening he summoned my mother, looked at her wordlessly, lifted her face by the chin and, with just a trace of mist in his eyes, gave her an exquisite pearl embedded in a golden ring. In a conspiratorial whisper he said that only Girija Maharaj knew about this pearl, for he had arranged its purchase from a Benaras jeweller who in turn had obtained it from a relative of the Nizam of Hyderabad. "When they dragged me away to the jeep, what do you think I clutched in my palm? This pearl!" He did not say anything more.

A few weeks later he called my father to his side. He was sitting in the sun, staring at nothing. He continued staring at nothing as he offered my father three bits of advice: "If you give anything to someone who has not earned it, he becomes your enemy. I learnt this from Ashfaque." He paused, perhaps for breath, perhaps for thought. "An *emir* in the morning can become an *asir* in the evening; fortune brings you wealth, and fortune can take it away. I learnt this from life." And then, with a sigh, "You have done a great many things. Who could have ever imagined that Rahmat's son would be a friend of the Burra Sahib... You have many more things to do. But as you journey through life, do not forget to pay visits to yourself. I learnt this from Burha Deewana."

~

As I may have mentioned, my grandfather died while I was playing on his chest, and that was my first stroke of luck. Even T.P. Singh, now married and father of a son named Shyam, set aside his jovial scepticism and acknowledged that Sheikh Rahmatullah's soul was now indistinguishable from mine. An infinite sadness enveloped Telinipara, a sense that it had lost its founder and its foundation. Victor Matheson and the British officers of the jute mill, including two young trainees, came to pay their respects. Matheson gave a small speech that ended with the announcement of his own retirement, and the appointment of Mathew as the next general manager. In an unprecedented gesture, the jute mill gave an hour off so that everyone could attend the funeral. Govardhan Ahir, stooping a little, walked with the cortege up to the gates of the graveyard. The next day a brat with a goatee, another graduate of Deoband, who had replaced the late Maulvi Taslimuddin as the imam of the mosque, tried to argue that a permanent tombstone and enclosure around my grandfather's grave was unIslamic for it would tempt the living to deify the dead. He kept quiet after three sharp slaps from Gauhar Ayub.

Death affects the living in different ways. My grandmother lost the desire to carry on. By the end of the year she had passed away as well, and their framed photographs were placed on the wall of the drawing room, just above the spot where my grandfather had sat for so many years. My mother slipped into Jamila's role as godmother of women, helping out when she could or when she considered necessary. She kept quiet about her generosity, for my father, now a miser, would throw tantrums over money.

Imperceptibly, life returned to a peaceful drift in which the violence of 1948, by unspoken consensus, was never mentioned. The one thing that did not survive was the kite competition. On the morning of Holi, known as Id-e-Gulabi, or the Id of Colours, at our home, T.P. Singh would appear at our door, accompanied by a small group of revellers, call out for Abbaji and fill my father's dark, thick hair with the red powder called *abir*. The kitchen got busy the instant he arrived. Tea and sweets were distributed. My father would refuse with a laugh the bhang that they brought: his share of the intoxicant, he would suggest, should be kept for TP, who did not disappoint. By noon, high on bhang and sweets, he would be asleep.

Through the gauze of half-remembered moments, and an indistinct chronology, I see the egg-dancer at the maidan on a winter afternoon, an election-campaign procession for my father on a summer night, a marriage of cats, the she-ghost with reversed feet, and the fuss on my birthdays, when I would be dressed up in a shimmering cream sherwani and tight churidar pyjamas before a visit to the uncles in the jute mill, Chowdhury and Simon, and then return to a last stuffing of cake with TP Uncle. It was good to possess my grandfather's soul.

The egg-dancer was tall, and wore a sari without a blouse so that the outline of her young, soft-firm breasts was taut against the linen. She walked with a swing of a swelling hip that mesmerized the thick ring of spectators, once around the ring, as close as she dared to the men. I remember staring up at her: perhaps it was at that moment that I became obsessed with big breasts. Her pirouette over, she went to the centre of the circle, and stood still. A man placed a wicker wheel on her head. It had a circular row of threads on the rim, each with a slip knot at the end. She began her dance with her head, slowly. The man placed an egg in the loop at the end of each thread, one at a time, while she swirled, and the ring of egg-threads rose higher to become a horizontal halo. Then the halo began to descend, an inch with every turn, and the man took out the eggs, one at a time. The last egg was removed. The dance stopped and she stood still. Not a single egg had broken, exclaimed the man in triumph. Whistles and cheers celebrated her art, and coins were tossed into a bag that the man took around.

My aunt Nasiban got the bright idea of a cat marriage. Through a mysterious process unknown to natural science, an extraordinarily lazy cat adopted our family. My mother, who considered dogs unclean, was happy with cats. When a tom began to make a nuisance of himself on the outer sill of the long window on the drawing room staircase, baying like a hideous monster on heat, my aunt decided that our cat's virginity could not be lost without pomp and ceremony. So all the children of the mohalla gathered on the verandah, and we dressed the cat up with a red ribbon, put her in a bamboo doll's house, where she promptly fell asleep, and carried her in a happy bridal procession to the river. At some point on the way back the cat woke up, looked around startled, and took a clean leap away from her palanquin. That made little difference to the happiness of the procession. We were rewarded with a feast of *murabba, sewai* and khir made by my mother, and a flour-savoury called *khajoor* because it looked like a date, cooked by my aunt, along with buckets of Roohafza sherbet. The cat did not return till late at night, so it was quite possible that she lost her virginity that day.

~

The total number of voters for the seat on the municipal council was a little upward of 800 and the excitement was contagious. My father was an active member of the Congress Party, whose symbol was a pair of oxen, but since municipal elections were technically non-partisan my father chose a bullock cart as his symbol. Benoy Chowdhury was a candidate for the second seat from Telinipara. Three days before polling, the two friends launched their formal campaign. At nine in the night, a core group of supporters gathered below the electric-light pole opposite our home. I clung to the banister of the first-floor balcony, putting my feet on the metal framework to get a better view of the scene below. The local qawwal, who practised his lungs on occasional Thursdays at the shrine of Burha Deewana, turned up with his harmonium. People began to cluster around him. There must have been much more in this vein, but all I can recall now are two lines of the campaign song:

Akbar aur Chowdhury ko vote dena doston,
Vote ke badle mein har kaam lena doston.

Give your vote for Akbar and Chowdhury, friends
Take every service in return, my friends.

On election day, Hasina (I called her Phuphu, the term for a paternal aunt) was in charge of getting the women out. She marched up and down the street, bawling at anyone who had not voted. Ignorance was no excuse. She handed out identification slips and ordered women to be flexible if by any chance the name on the slip was different from their real name. "What difference is there between Oliya and Waheeda?" she would ask, pertinently. "Wouldn't you have voted for Akbar Babu even if your name was different?" Reluctant types were told to wear a veil, to disguise last-minute jitters. With Gauhar Ayub as the chief agent inside the polling booth, and T.P. Singh in control of the volunteer corps outside, all forms of voting went on smoothly. Govardhan Ahir, who had opposed my father on the plea that he was an old man, and this would be the only election he would ever fight, did not get even fifty votes. His campaign platform was honest, for he died about a year after the election, peacefully, in bed. The returning officer looked at the numbers – over 400 for Abbaji, more than 300 for Chowdhury Uncle and less than fifty for the opposition – and wondered loudly why they bothered to hold an election at all in Telinipara.

The she-ghost must have come later, because by then I was a fixture on Mustaqim's Raleigh bicycle whenever he set out on any errand, perched on a triangular wooden seat on the front bar, ringing the bell on the left with a persistence that induced much road rage outside our little world. I was always with Mustaqim; he was my Bhaijan, or elder brother. He brought me up. My father, who always worried about my safety (refusing, for instance, to let me swim in the river), would not trust me with anyone else. I would ride with him to the maidan in the evening, when he went to bring back the truck, and it was there that I met Mustaqim's friend Jalil Mastan.

Jalil Mastan was dark, and muttered continually into a thick black beard, a mass of curls that hid a fractured skin. He spoke in flourishes, as if he had been educated at some madrasa of higher learning, and made lofty if incomprehensible remarks like "Liquor numbs the wounds of fate, but prayer heals them: therefore, do not drink but pray" and "A pregnant night gives birth to disaster" or "Sleep is the joy of illusion". He knew only a few such maxims, but used what he knew with subtle variety.

He attributed such philosophical depth to his personal djinn, an all-seeing spirit he could summon from beyond the first heaven in any emergency. A crisis arose when Ashraf, who lived in a hut directly across our home, disappeared. His mother, initially indifferent, turned frantic after a couple of days. She appealed to Jalil Mastan. It was a sleepy, mild winter afternoon. We were in the large open room on the ground floor. Jalil Mastan rubbed some mustard oil on the fingernail of my right thumb and began to mumble what seemed like an endless prayer. He asked me if I could see anything. I replied honestly: no. His mumble became more vigorous. He asked again. In slow motion, the image of a very old man with a very white beard emerged on my thumb. I was told to ask him about Ashraf. He disappeared and a beach came into view, with a vague person sitting against a palm tree. I had never seen a beach, or the sea, and described it as best as I could. Jalil waved a black hand over my thumb and said, "Enough! If I keep the old man engaged too long, he tires me out." He told Ashraf's mother that her son was safe and would return soon. And so Ashraf did, explaining that he had run away to Digha, the beach on the coast of Bengal. Jalil claimed that he was an *aamil*, blessed with the power of *kaashf*, the ability to read your heart and predict the future. Some three or four years later, when Jalil Mastan had muttered his way out of Telinipara for reasons that were never made clear, it was widely whispered that he had become impotent after being seduced by a *churail* who stalked the night in the remote parts of the maidan. A *churail* is a female ghost, a *bhutni*, who looks human and is so beautiful that no ordinary man can resist her seduction. But the price is heavy, for those who sleep with her become impotent. There is only one way to recognize her: her feet face the wrong side.

I shall always remember my fifth birthday. It was special because I was to join kindergarten at St Joseph's Convent within four days, and take the first step towards my father's limitless horizon. I was given a warm bath in the sparkle of a mother's tears, and dressed by Ammiji in a glistening white churidar and embroidered, light-gold sherwani. My aunt waved two red chillies seven times around my head and threw them into the fire to protect me from the evil eye, after which I took my father's finger and went off in a rickshaw to Victoria Jute Mill. Our first call was on Chowdhury Uncle, his affectionate but garrulous wife, Swapna Aunty, whose chatter he ignored, and two giggly daughters, Sushmita and Sumita. Chowdhury Uncle was wearing a pair of sunglasses. He did not have much of a choice. I took the glasses and decided not to return them. I held the spectacles casually-proudly in my left hand for a photograph with his new Agfa camera. Unwilling to take off my sunglasses even in the dark, I sat with a serious look in Simon's drawing room, a glass of lemonade brought by a benevolent Ghulam Rasool at my side, while the elders conversed.

They spoke and laughed about all sorts of interesting things. Uncle Simon wanted me to read a book he had just finished, *King Solomon's Mines,* as soon as I picked up enough English at school, and Mathew wondered whether that was such a good idea, for Rider Haggard's best friend was Rudyard Kipling and should a budding Indian nationalist really sup from an imperialist menu? He told the story of how, when Kipling died two days after King George V in 1936, someone remarked, "The King has gone and taken his trumpeter with him." There was much laughter. I rested my serious face on my hands, my elbows on my knees, tilting slightly forward to be part of an adult conversation.

Colonel Hogg was there, on his farewell round of visits, for British officers were finally retiring from the Indian Army. What a pity, said the colonel, that Kipling had got the Indian Army all wrong in the First World War, accusing Indians of being cowards. There were no finer soldiers than Indians, and had proved as much in the Second World War, defeating Rommel in the deserts of Libya and the Japanese in Burma. The real sorrow, he suggested, was not the partition of India but the partition of the Indian Army, an institution truly united in its diversity: the cheerful Gurkha, the reserved, aristocratic Dogra, the tenacious Sikh, the gallant Punjabi Mussulman, the intrepid Maratha, the impervious Jat, the warrior Rajput, and, from the Frontier, the mercurial Khattak, and the humorous, quick-tempered Hazara. Together they were world-beaters. Divided they were not even able to defeat each other, which was why the war in Kashmir between India and Pakistan was such a silly stalemate.

My father reminded them that Indians were world-class in other skills as well. His childhood icon, the wrestler Gama Pahalwan, had pinned the world champion, Zbysko, in less than a minute in the presence of the Maharaja of Patiala in the 1930s. Legend had it that the corpulent Maharaja sat down, turned to take off his coat, and before he could swivel back the bout was over. Gama was given the title of Rustam-e-Azam, Hero of the Heroes. What a pity, my father added, that Gama Pahalwan had settled down in Lahore, and he would never be able to see the great man wrestle. Simon pointed out that he could always visit Lahore, at which my father fell silent. He never visited Pakistan, even to meet his in-laws, after that traumatic journey in 1948.

~

I suppose I owe my familiarity with the English language to the French Revolution. Anne-Marie Javouhey, fifth of six surviving peasant children, was ten when the French Revolution broke out, and faith went underground. She celebrated her nineteenth birthday, on 11 November 1798, with a secret mass at her family farm in the village of Chamblanc, where she consecrated herself to God and dedicated her life to spreading Christian education. In 1807, she and her sisters took their vows before Pope Pius VII at Chalon. In 1819 they went international, opening the mission of St Joseph of Cluny in Senegal. In 1861 (just a few years before my grandfather came to Telinipara) the order founded the St Joseph's Convent for Girls in the French colony of Chandernagore. Since boys were not expected to provoke girls sexually before the age of ten, they were permitted to study at the convent till Class 5. My father had decided that I had to go to St Joseph's Convent so that I could learn to speak English like Simon and Mathew. The future was written in English.

Mother Michael, a tall, smiling Irishwoman was the principal when my father knocked at the massive, green, wooden doors of the convent. Thanks once again to his friends at Victoria, who had put in a word, he did not have much difficulty getting me admitted, but the miser in him pleaded for a reduction in fees, citing riots and trauma. The memory of 1947 was still fresh enough for Mother Michael to oblige. The Order had, after all, begun its mission looking after orphans of the French Revolution.

The usual things happened in school. I set off each morning on a rickshaw pedalled by Wali, in green lungi and sleeveless vest, who began life with bright eyes and luxurious beard, and ended it in glaucoma and gray scraggle. Very soon I was joined by my sister, Arfana, nicknamed Baby, and later by the youngest in the family, my brother Hashim. The three of us were a tight but comforting squeeze. I generally had good report cards, managing definitely to come second and occasionally first. The only time my father lost his temper with me was when I came fifth. I was in Class 4. He threw my report card out of the window and stomped off, leaving my mother to shame me with a severe scolding. The moment her back was turned Hasina took me to the roof and talked to me about nothing, adding, at some point, that my parents were angry because they loved me. I did not understand such logic, but I trusted Hasina. I confessed to her that I could not concentrate in class. That was the term in which I was in love with Miss Lucie Bowers, our English teacher, who wore bright red lipstick, had bobbed, fringed hair, and breasts larger than the rubber horn on Mustaqim's truck. She laughed like a filmstar and dreamt of settling down in Australia. I think the nuns found her unsettling as well, for she disappeared after one term and I came second in class again. Hasina kept my secret.

Whenever my father lost his temper he took a while to find it again. He would storm out of the house, raging at the top of his voice while my mother sobbed loudly. Later, my mother learnt to scream back, although the ratio was generally five to one in father's favour. Aunts, nephews and nieces, always around for the spectacle, watched these scenes with private glee, as if my mother was only getting what she deserved for being a swan. The fits ended with him taking a nap in a darkened drawing room, and being massaged. My mother's response to loneliness and rejection was either the comfort of the roof, or the relief of the cinema. She would put on her chadar, order Wali to turn up, and go off to one of the two cinema halls, Jyoti or Swapna, to see a tearjerker Hindi film full of daughters-in-law being maltreated. As the eldest son, I always went with her, and while I found the screen-tears too painful I delighted in the dancing and the glorious melody of the songs. I took sides in every screen conflict, and cheered the hero to vindication and triumph.

My mother refused to be defeated by the breadth of a continent between Telinipara and Lahore. Within a day of the start of our summer and winter holidays, we would get into the second class sleeper compartment of the Amritsar Express at Howrah Station. Two nights later we would be at Wagah, the crossing point on the India-Pakistan border, and Atari, the first railway station on the Pakistan side, only minutes away from Lahore. The magic of a city swimming towards you from the window of a train still fascinates. At Lahore her favourite nephew, Infishar, would wait at the edge of the railway platform, for the first glimpse of Ammiji and then run with the slowing train, whooping all the way to a halt. We would mount a tonga, smell the abundance of Lahore, and reach the badly-lit, ageing building near Shah Alam where youngsters would be waiting on the street and elders on the third floor which we reached by a perilous, winding and dark staircase.

My favourite uncle was Yusuf Khalu, named Yusuf after the

Prophet Joseph and as handsome as the beloved son of Jacob. He was the husband of my eldest aunt, Khaleda, who hid a warm heart behind a ferocious scowl. Yusuf Khalu took me out and taught me how to light a hookah for him. On winter mornings, he was not averse to permitting me an occasional puff if no one was watching. Alas, Yusuf Khalu did nothing, to the despair of his wife, but he was a wonderful raconteur. He would tell me lovely stories about the legendary Sheikh Chilli, Mullah Naseeruddin Hodja. One day Hodja, riding his donkey, met a braggart on a horse. The braggart asked Hodja: "How is the donkey?" Hodja replied, "He's fine, and riding a horse as well." A philosopher asked Hodja, "Why do some people scurry in one direction on a street, and others go the opposite way?" Hodja replied, "If they all went in the same direction, the earth would tilt and lose its balance!"

The stories were reward for filling his hookah every morning. As soon as he finished his hookah, he would leave home, pursued by his wife's curses for being so useless. His friends in the market gave him tea and a snack, and occasionally cut him in on a business deal. I would tag along. A half-smile never left his lips, and his methods of instruction were oblique. "Theft is a serious crime in Islam," he explained, "but there is no punishment for the theft of a book; since no one owns knowledge, you cannot steal it. Knowledge shrinks if hidden and expands when distributed."

My mother's favourite sister was her younger one, Rahat, who was married to Qasim, a well-built, bald, genial Kashmiri who earned money but spent it faster than he earned it, on flying kites and excellent pilau. Rahat did not mind, for she was buxom and enjoyed good food as much as her husband. A third sister, Iqbal, was married to a strait-laced Punjabi called Munawwar. Her father-in-law, known as Baba, sold second-hand oil drums, never spoke without stringing a torrent of abuse into an adjective, drank copious glasses of lassi, lifted one side of his buttocks off the charpoy to fart and was extraordinarily generous to my mother, flooding us with money on arrival and packing a suitcase with gifts when we left. The steadiest of the sisters was Shamshad, and she found the steadiest husband as well, nicknamed Maulvi Sahib because he was pious, prayed five times a day, wore his shalwar above the ankle in the preferred manner of clerics, pitied the fact that my mother had to live among infidels and sold socks of excellent quality at moderate prices in his small shop in Shalimar Market. My grandmother, Nani Ammi, was an utter dear who looked exactly like my mother, spoke Kashmiri fluently (the others, brought up in Amritsar, preferred Punjabi), drank green, salted tea and viewed life through a wry film of humour. Her favourite tale was of a group of Kashmiri Muslims who thought the Almighty had overdone it by asking the faithful to pray five times a day, so they took a delegation to Allah. At the end of negotiations they discovered that Allah had added thirty days of fasting to five prayers a day. She would chortle: *"Gaye the namaaz bakshwane, gale mein roza parh gaya."* They went to get prayers forgiven, and brought back fasting around their necks.

Ammiji began to change family life in incremental doses. Although she wore a genteel chadar in Telinipara, she changed it to a light dupatta, an extended chiffon scarf, when she came to my convent on sports day or parents' day. She found a companion in Mrs Rita Duggal, wife of an engineer in one of the jute mills: the two recognized each other instantly, for they shared the same fair skin of the northwest. When they found they shared the same language, they became friends. Her son, Rahul, was in my class, and we were soon the pair to beat at marbles during the forty-minute lunch break.

My mother raised the quality of our lives by shopping in Calcutta for Id, when new clothes were bought for the family. She made at least two trips to New Market, to the considerable annoyance of my father, who would have much preferred all cloth to be purchased from Narayan Babu's store in Telinipara. The youthful patron of Barkat Ali Brothers now got his own clothes stitched by the tall, charcoal-black neighbourhood tailor, Qurban Ali, who wore thick glasses, moaned about his eyesight if there was any complaint, and pedalled away at a Singer sewing machine all night before Id. Qurban Ali told me that pyjamas were introduced into Arabia at the time of the Prophet, became the court dress of Baghdad and were brought to India by Muslim rulers. The only indulgence my father could never resist was Henry's handmade shoes. One evening my parents were late while on an Id shopping expedition. Desperate to know what they had bought for me, I pleaded with Jalil to summon his old man on my thumbnail. I was thrilled to see my parents at Howrah Station, buying fruit before they boarded the train. I gleefully informed my father of my preview, and was astonished to discover that he was appalled. Jalil was forbidden from our home.

During that Ramadan I made a great fuss about wanting to fast. My mother had begun teaching me the Arabic alphabet in order to read the Quran, and the spirit of holiness had possibly descended upon me. Or I might have been under the influence of a popular song that was constantly on the radio. Bombay's B-grade filmmakers used to produce a spate of costume specials based on Middle Eastern legends for release during Id on the assumption that all Indian Muslims turned into closet Arabs during Ramadan. This song (*Ramzan ke mahin-e ki meshur dastan – A famous story about the month of Ramzan*) featured a six-year-old who fasted in the desert against the wishes of his parents, died of thirst and was reborn with the help of Angel Gabriel. It was sung in an affecting weepy-trembly manner by Muhammad Rafi. I was already dying to be some kind of hero. My father's response was an irritable no, but my mother found the solution. She decided that I could do a half-fast, and it would earn the same merit from Allah in consideration of my age. And so after a nourishing lunch I stopped eating or drinking water till the muezzin's call at sunset signalled breakfast. When I was seven, I fasted from pre-dawn to sunset for the last ten days and was much admired by nuns delighted to see such abstinence in an infidel. They would ask if I wanted to go home early, but that was the last thing I needed: better to fill the hours of penitence with something to do in school. One good way to ease the anguish of the final hour of dry throats was to go with Mustaqim Bhaijan to buy fresh fruit for that much-awaited minute at which the sun dipped below the horizon, a little red light on a tall pole came on, and the muezzin's call to prayer rolled out in the peaceful music of the *azaan*. The search for the new moon low on the western sky to mark the end of Ramadan was always exciting, and I was anxious to be the first to see it in the hope that it would bring me luck. By seven on the morning of Id, dressed in new clothes, we would go to the maidan for *namaaz*. T.P. Singh would wait at the edge of the green, so that he could be among the first to embrace my father after prayers, and then come home with his friend to enjoy the bliss of food and the serenity of affection. At some point during the day, everyone from near and far, friend or acquaintance, would drop by. The chatter in the kitchen never stopped. My mother changed the cuisine of festivals, adding her style of biryani and *yakhni* pilau and delicacies like *shalgam-gosht*. T.P. Singh insisted that she had brought class to a household of unworthy Biharis.

~

There was much excitement when Simon returned one year from a long holiday with a pregnant wife, Maria, a vivacious Greek girl much younger than him who he met while spending a lazy weekend among the spires of Oxford University. Both were lonely. He waited till closing time at the restaurant where she worked because he had nowhere interesting to go; and she was pleased to get company for the walk home. Before the weekend was over Simon had proposed; within another seven days they were married. Within a month Maria had risen from lonely, indigent self-exile in Oxford to pregnant mistress of a bungalow in Victoria Jute Mill. Hasina looked unaffected by the news.

Simon gave me the most prized gifts of my childhood: collections of Readers' Digest Condensed Books and anthologies like *Hundred Great Men* and *Hundred Great Adventure Stories*. There was an alcove on the side of the drawing room staircase, a cool spot where I managed to fit in if I folded my legs up so that my knees touched my chin. That was my preferred reading spot on holidays. My other pleasure was the roof when the river breeze picked up, staring at the multiple hues of red that soaked through the western sky at sunset. Saturday afternoons were reserved for football. We started a team called Azad Juniors. I was terrible at football, no matter which position I played in, but I could not be dropped from the team because I owned the ball. On Sundays we went on expeditions in support of our heroes, the Azad Club, Telinipara's senior football team, in which most of the players had boots. The star of the team was my cousin Siraj ul Haq, a handsome young man with curly hair and a wonderful smile, who played the field, defence, forward or wing as the situation demanded. The team revolved around Manna, a dark, short defender who never wore boots; Jabbar, whose good looks were mildly marred by pox marks; Ghazi, who was over six foot tall and therefore centre-forward, and of course Siraj. There were few joys greater than returning home in a group-amble after victory in the Bhagar Math at Bhadreshwar.

My father rarely left our lane in Telinipara, except to go once in a while to Calcutta to check his bank account at Grindlay's in Dalhousie Square, where he made good friends with the clerks. He never ventured into that portion of Bhadreshwar where our old farm was situated. It was now in the possession of Ram Chatterjee, who had forgotten to pass it on to the zamindar. The one exception he made was a visit to Ballia for T.P. Singh's marriage just after the troubles. TP Chacha's sons, Shyam and Bharat, were part of our gang, along with Kamala who lost no opportunity to demand the privileges of an older boy, like respect. He never managed to get it, for he laughed too much, most often at himself. The ages mixed. Mustafa was there, and Qasim, Mangu Qasai's grandson, and Ashraf, and Gauhar Ayub's son, Altaf, who clung to me because he was determined to study. I pressurized my father to get him admission to the Bhadreshwar Municipal School, and was delighted later when he went on to Serampore College on a William Carey scholarship: Carey was the missionary who established Seramapore in 1793 under the Danish flag and established the first Bengali printing press. Kamala lived with his parents, who had come to Telinipara after the death of Girija Maharaj, and I took careful notice of his pretty sister, Hilsa, as she started growing up. My father helped them set up a small shop, a *modikhana*, which stocked whatever was in demand. He increased his own income by restoring the tobacco business, but made no effort to reclaim what had been lost during the riots.

TP Chacha would often take me for walks by the river to relieve me, as he put it, of the constant pressure of being Akbar's son. The riverside was entrancing: cool, hazy and full of women in the morning; almost asleep during the heat of the day except for brief, fast surges of energy when the tide swept in from the sea and swept out, racing along the bank in a two-foot wall of water, forcing the ferry-boats to move to the centre for safety; serene in the evenings; mysterious and romantic when it nestled the moon in its lap. Boatmen told stories of ghosts they had seen, who clung to the side on the bank and waited to drag an innocent into that same silent grave that had consumed them. Jalil Mastan would hover by the river on certain nights, and summon his *mookkil*, the djinn who could predict the future – well, up to a point, he hastened to add, because a djinn's vision was limited.

Only Allah knew the future of all human beings, and only Allah had the capability to change destiny, which is why *dua,* prayer, was important as *dhal,* or protection.

Kamala did not believe in ghosts. The guru who came to teach him Sanskrit *shlokas* dismissed ghosts as the hallucination of *maili vidya,* or black knowledge. In which case, I pointed out, it might be a good idea to check the riverside in the dark. We slipped away one evening. I stopped near a banyan tree on the edge of the maidan and wondered if I had heard a noise. Kamala thought that we should return home. I felt we should investigate. A branch whispered in the gloom. I took his arm and edged warily towards a low moan. A white form seemed to drop from the branch, hang from the limb while the leaves rustled and shook, and then disappear. "What is that?!" I asked Kamala with a touch of fear.

The sequence repeated itself.

He looked at the tree, shouted, "*Arre baap re!* Help me, father!" swivelled as fast on his heel as anyone I've seen do, and disappeared.

The next morning, Kamala was still trembling when I explained that we had set him up: that was no ghost, that was Altaf, sitting on the branch with a white sheet in his hand. "Don't ever frighten me again," Kamala told me, his eyes glittering with fear embedded in mirth. "Don't you know that I am an utter coward?"

16

STARS

"*MOTHER INDIA* MAY HAVE BEEN BORN A MUSLIM, BUT SHE married a Hindu!" chortled Kamala. It was a winter afternoon in 1960, and we were gathered on the grass by the edge of the river. From the precipice of my first decade I was staring at an uncertain world outside the confines and comforts of Telinipara. The nuns had wished me a fond goodbye after five years; but my father had not been able to find an English-medium boarding school within his means that would give a place to an unknown boy from an unknown convent in an unknown small town.

The rest of the world belonged to movies, our only escape from Telinipara. Kamala had become the resident intellectual with his authoritative knowledge of film gossip ever since he began to subscribe to the Sunday edition of the Hindi newspaper *Sanmarg*, which he clutched under an armpit through the day like a trophy. I read the *Statesman* at home, entering its world through the Benji League club for children, but that did not count, for I was younger. Kamala read every word in his newspaper, to extract maximum value for the price he had paid.

The great existential dilemma that raged amidst us was: How could *Mother India* be a Muslim?

A Hindi film called *Mother India,* made by a well-known director, Mehboob, released in 1958, became an unprecedented critical and popular hit of its time. Our parents took us to the theatre with the enthusiasm of missionaries escorting children to a moral science class. The *Statesman* reported that it almost won the Oscar for the best foreign film, losing to Frederico Fellini's *Nights of the Cabria* by a solitary vote in the third round.

The narrative was constructed around the memories of an old woman, Radha, eponymous wife of Lord Krishna and therefore Mother of India, who had been abandoned by her depressed husband after he lost his arms in an accident. She had three sons: one drowned; the second was a good boy; the third, Birju, a rebel who grew up to become a dacoit. Impoverished Radha was a paragon of virtue, and spurned the attentions of a leering moneylender, Sukhilala, who demanded sex as interest on his loan. Whether this moneylender was a symbol of the World Bank or not was left unclear, but there were plenty of other allegories. In a climax that had father, mother, brother and sister India in tears, Mother India shot her dacoit-son Birju to save the honour of the village. It was an epic superhit, its peasant-patriotism and femme-nobility high on the approved agenda of a nation that still wanted to believe in itself.

Radha was played by Nargis, a Muslim. Jaipal, Kalyan Singh's slightly precocious son, thought this ridiculous. Mother Pakistan was a Muslim; how could Mother India be a Muslim as well? Could Muslims partition the motherland and still claim ownership of both nations? "You Muslims are greedy. You want everything. You take your own country, and then say India is your country as well."

"Yes," agreed Shyam Singh. "Muslims must make up their minds. They go to Pakistan when they like, they live in India when they want. We Hindus can't do that."

"My father was born in Pakistan, so he went to Pakistan. I was born in India, so I live in India," answered Mustafa, who had inherited his father's terse logic.

"Ha!" responded Jaipal, "you stayed back because you want the property that your father left behind! You go and see him whenever you want. What difference does it make to you? Only Hindus suffered in the partition of their motherland."

"What is there to argue about? Indian Muslims marry among us, so they are one of us," reasoned Kamala, who was always anxious to find balm in the most obscure cupboard, for he hated confrontation of any kind. "Nargis married Sunil Dutt just after the release of *Mother India*. Sunil Dutt was her son, Birju, who she killed. Sunil Dutt is a Hindu. She married a Hindu, so it's all right, isn't it?" Since Freud had not reached Telinipara, no other interpretation was made.

"You mean to say that I have to marry a Hindu in order to become an Indian?" asked Mustafa, with a touch of anger. "I will never marry anyone but a Pathan girl."

"Why are we taking film people so seriously? It's all fake. Which one of us is going to find anyone as beautiful as Nargis?" said Kamala, displaying his usual good sense.

"If it's all make-believe, why do Hindus keep saying Raj Kapoor is much better than Dilip Kumar?" asked Altaf, rising above his usual timidity.

Raj Kapoor and Dilip Kumar were superstars; the first a
Hindu and the second, disguised by his pseudonym, a Muslim.
Multiple identities stitched disparate imperatives, but loyalties
were absolute. A superstar both borrowed and returned identity
to his community.

I was bored by this conversation. My favourite star was Dev
Anand, the third of the men who dominated the film industry in
the fifties. Dev Anand lived on the street and beyond religion. If
he had any faith it was in himself. He would gamble with thieves,
dance with bar girls, drink to celebrate and win the day without
trying to save the nation. Dev Anand was liberation, and gave our
generation its first beautiful essay on love and adultery, forsaking
the world for the gorgeous Waheeda Rehman in that wondrous
classic, *Guide*. Dilip Kumar and Raj Kapoor carried the past in
their eyes. Dev Anand wore the insouciance of the future.

I loved the songs of Dev Anand's films.

Main zindagi ka saath nibhata chala gaya,
Main fiqr ko dhooen main urhata chala gaya.

I dealt with life as it came,
I turned worry to smoke rings.

I dreamt of the day I could start smoking.

Jo mil gaya usiko muqaddar samajh liya,
Jo kho gaya main usko bhulata chala gaya.

What I got became my destiny,
What I lost, I simply forgot.

Could philosophy be more enchanting than this?

Radio supplied the evening's entertainment, but not Delhi's

government-voice All India Radio, which confused patriotism with unintelligible Hindi. A neighbour helped out. Radio Ceylon, the official station of tiny Sri Lanka, was commercial, and listened to its audience. Two brothers commanded its airwaves. Hamid Sayani compered western music in a voice wrapped in a club tie and dipped in BBC. Amin Sayani spoke Hindi in a breezy, soft lilt that was as popular as the music he offered on the weekly Wednesday night show, Binaca Geet Mala, the garland of sixteen top hits of the week. The family clustered around a large GEC radio while a GEC ceiling fan whirled overhead like a high-speed top dancing on its head. My father remained aloof from such frivolity, but my mother was an enthusiastic, sing-along listener.

Life outside the family revolved around two sets of friends, on either side of the walls of Victoria Jute Mill. I enjoyed the affection of both, nibbling cucumber sandwiches with one and sucking mangoes cooled in a bucket with the other. My palate became multinational at an early age.

We visited Chowdhury Uncle in his officers' bungalow frequently. Calls on Simon and Mathew were more formal. Politics was part of my passive education, because it was the main subject of adult conversation. Simon was a great admirer of India's charismatic prime minister. Mr Nehru could do no wrong, whether his policies affected a crossword puzzle or a country. Mr Nehru called for a socialist pattern of society at the Avadi Congress session of 1955 and Simon called him a greater visionary than Clement Attlee. He went to the Bandung conference of Afro-Asian nations in April and Simon applauded a world leader. The Hindu Marriage Act ended polygamy among

Hindus, and Mr Nehru became a great social reformer. The Imperial Bank was nationalized and renamed the State Bank of India, and Mr Nehru was applauded for economic wizardry. The Phillips Company demonstrated a technology called television and Mr Nehru became the prophet of the media. M.F. Husain, a young painter with a startling brush, won the first Lalit Kala national award; Satyajit Ray, a young adman with unique sensibility, won the national film award for *Pather Panchali*, and Mr Nehru turned into patron of the arts. Crossword contests in newspapers, a marketing gimmick where as much as Rs 200,000 might be offered in prize money, were stopped, and Mr Nehru became a politician who respected the dignity of news. A certain John T. Bailey applied for permission to print the *New York Times* in India, inducing a blanket ban on the publication of all foreign newspapers, with the arbitrary exception (noted in Nehru's hand) of the *Statesman,* which was still owned and edited by the British, and Mr Nehru metamorphosed into a trustee of the Indo-British special relationship. Asia's first atomic reactor, Apsara, named after a heavenly nymph, went critical in 1956 and Mr Nehru was another Einstein. India entered the semifinals in football, and won the hockey gold in the Olympics, Wilson Jones became the first Indian World Amateur Billiards Champion, and Mihir Sen crossed the English Channel: Mr Nehru, photographed in Delhi, cricket bat in hand, became godfather of sports. Finance minister T.T. Krishnamachari resigned, caught with his hands in the till, and Mr Nehru became Mr Integrity. The Dalai Lama, fleeing Chinese oppression in Tibet in the spring of 1959, received sanctuary and Mr Nehru was guardian of the oppressed. My father's admiration was equally uncritical: Nehruji was the sole saviour of Indian Muslims. And so it went through the serene placidity of the fifties.

My father's mohalla friends would gather over late weekend evenings for endless cups of tea, biscuits and cards. T.P. Singh, obviously, was Abbaji's partner. The footballer Ghazi's father, Dr Liaquat Ali, was the third. A self-taught vet, much in demand from buffalo owners, he was particular about being addressed as "Dr". Shafi Sahib, a gentle, thin teacher of Urdu at the new local municipal school, was generally the fourth, and irritated the hell out of everyone else because he did not mind losing. Sometimes they corralled the bulbous, bulging cloth merchant, Narayan Babu, into the game. He never seemed eager to play but once he sat down he fought bitterly over every point and considered every successful finesse against him a personal insult.

In the winter of 1960, the card games paused, and we did not go to Lahore, because my father was consumed by anxiety. Elite boarding schools like Doon, whose prospectus he guarded like a family relic, were too expensive. Calcutta's schools wanted references; he had none. At St Xavier's School he was rejected by an apologetic Jesuit priest; at La Martiniere, by a gruff gatekeeper. He could not permit his circumstances to betray his son.

The number of nations, and ecumenical conflicts, required to put me through eleven years of school was extraordinary. The French had already done their bit. Now it was the turn of England and America. John Wesley, born in 1703, wanted some Method in the Church of England. The establishment, predictably, drove his society into a sect. By 1795 the Methodists were a separate church, and soon flourishing in free-spirited

America. James Thoburn was born in 1836, his sister Isabella in 1840. James arrived as a missionary to India in 1859, one of a flock that came to India in the belief that the Mutiny of 1857 was evidence of God's wrath upon the British for neglecting the conversion of the natives to Christianity. After stints in the Himalayas, Moradabad and Lucknow he settled in Calcutta, where he constructed what was then the largest church in India, the Thoborn Methodist, next to a new girls' school started in 1856 by a Governor General, Lord Canning, who was full of reforming zeal. It was called, simply, Calcutta Girls' School. Once Canning's term was over, the school began to wobble and might have shut down. The vigorous Isabella Thoburn, who had followed her elder brother to India, stepped in and saved the institution. In 1879, about half a mile down the road, the Calcutta Boys' School was started to correct gender bias.

My father had no idea that there was anything in the world called a Methodist Church, much less that it ran a boys' school or that Colin Hicks was its principal. That late December morning he shed his normal reticence towards ritual and offered a prayer at the grave of Burha Deewana before taking the train to Calcutta to continue his hunt. Off Chowringhee, he took an unfamiliar road to the left of Metro cinema. About fifteen minutes later, he was surprised to see a large sign indicating the presence of Calcutta Boys' School. He walked in. No one stopped him until, in the deserted anteroom of the principal's office, Jogi, the well-fed head of peons, asked him what he wanted. To see the principal, my father said. Did he have an appointment? No. Did he know the principal? No. Did he know the name of the principal? My father glanced at the nameplate outside the office and said, "Mr Hicks." Jogi asked him to leave. My father sat down and said he would wait. Jogi raised his voice. My father ignored him. Jogi raised his voice higher.

"Why are you shouting, Jogi?"

Colin Hicks was about forty, had the haircut of an army recruit, the bulk of a wrestler, the height of a basketball player and the keen, watery eyes of a committed headmaster. He entered the office and looked at my father.

"Sir, I beg of you, please give me a minute. Only one minute, Sir."

No answer. "It is a matter of life and death, Sir."

He got his minute. My father placed all my report cards, barring the one in which I came fifth, before Hicks and said, "My son is very brilliant in English, Sir. He must study English, Sir. Save his life, Sir."

Hicks' decision emerged from the look in my father's eyes. It was only after he said yes that he realized that he would have to give me a place in boarding, where the quota was exhausted. He shrugged. It was too late to say no. And so I got an unusual hostel number, 77, later marked in indelible ink by Jogi on every shirt and pair of trousers (stitched by the indefatigable Qurban Ali) for laundry identification. That night, as they went to sleep in my grandfather's four-poster bed, my mother reached out and hugged my father. He was stunned. I, however, never forgot to give fifty per cent of the credit to the residual luck in my grandfather's soul.

What else could we call him but Chicks? The name on the board outside his office said "C. Hicks, MA". Nastier boys had nastier terms for him, but Chicks was perfect because he was the very opposite of a chicken. He was six feet tall and seemed the same distance in circumference. His legs, arms and face were not fat; but his stomach ballooned from thigh to lung. He must have been hungry as a child. His wife Ruth was fleshy, with soft layers of fat between every joint of the bones, a chin that curled up like a sheet and a dimple that deepened within the folds of the cheek. Her eyes held a grim sense of power. Chicks was merely powerful. One of his great pleasures was punishing students. He bent and straightened a Malacca cane in both hands, and described its effects in loving detail as he prepared to use it on a trembling, bent child, fingers touching toes, awaiting the huge whack from an arm that swung from seventy degrees north to the buttocks in an invisible blur. If every whiplash was therapeutic then quite a bit of the therapy was reserved for us boarders who queued up in two long, neat lines in the dormitory to watch the torture. "Character! Brains! Sports!" Chicks would boom. "That is what CBS stands for!" Swish.

I was spared the attentions of the cane for I did very well in my first term examinations, and did not swear, which made me a model child. One reason for such piety was that I did not know any swear words. My initiation was complicated. My first name, Mobashar, had too many syllables, so my compatriots shortened it to Moby. Ratty Mukherjee, with a pug nose and a bully's small eyes, extended it to Moby Dick. I thought I was being compared to a whale, but when Ratty rattled off Dick Dick Dick Dick his toadies twittered. I couldn't get the joke. They laughed when I gathered up courage eventually and asked what was so funny. "Moby! I'll show you your Dick at the bath tomorrow morning!" shouted Ratty. The next morning, Ratty picked up a wet towel, stretched it taut between his hands, and snapped it hard against my bare skin. That hurt, but I could do damn all while everyone else sniggered. Fortunately it missed my dick. I began to spread the word that I would prefer to be known as MJ.

~

Telinipara was visibly proud of me when I returned for my first vacation, during Easter, for I had broken a barrier. My friends cheered my arrival at the station and cycled alongside as Abbaji and I sat on a rickshaw. My mother waited on the steps of the iron grill gate, and welcomed me home with a mouthful of carrot halwa. There was chatter and the clink of spoon on plate through the day. Simon gave me three more sets of handsomely-bound Readers' Digest condensed books; Mathew gifted a children's encyclopaedia and a hardback copy of John Gunther's *Inside Russia* which he had finished and suggested I read a little later. Chowdhury Uncle bought me a blazer, my proudest possession till I outgrew it. The happiness was infectious. We went to the riverside and chewed grass while I told my friends stories about the Big City, forgetting to mention that my only interaction with it so far had been the Sunday evening tramp to Thoburn Church to hear the utterly boring platitudes of Reverend Jim Morgan. I discovered that, aided by a little bit of truth, I could cook up quite a credible story, which was a good basis for a future career in journalism. More truthfully, I told them that I had begun to play cricket and read the Bible, and they were very impressed. Kamala decided that he had to learn English, and bought himself a primer.

We spent that summer in Lahore. Ammiji looked beautiful; a girl when married, she had grown into a lovely woman, in command of her life, proud of her family, and with enough strength to remain cool about her husband's tantrums. Or perhaps beauty is just another dimension of happiness.

There was a great deal to be happy about: her nephews were repairing uprooted lives by finding jobs. Infishar had become a clerk in a bank upon passing school; a second cousin, Asif, had pride of place among his peers for he received a commission in the Pakistan Army; a third, Atif, had started a small business making safety pins; and Zahid had joined his father in the socks-and-vests shop, protesting all the while at being made to pray five times a day. He fantasized about escaping to Birmingham in England, where, he had heard, Pakistanis got jobs at fancy salaries. We stayed with my aunts in turn so that the holiday was a continuous feast. One long weekend was reserved for a visit to Gujranwala where my mother's childhood friend, Inayat, lived. One formal evening was reserved for the Bukharis. Summer in Lahore meant eating fruit in the shade of trees, dips in the canal that crept through the city, and evening walks by the wide, patchy Ravi river. Family dinners had a festive feel in the company of pretty friends of unmarried cousins who giggled behind the shimmer of georgette till late into the night.

Yusuf Uncle would take me to busy corners of the city, dense with pungent smells, like the Bazaar-e-Hakimah near the majestic Wazir Khan mosque, crowded with herbal doctors who looked more exotic than their medicines, and faith healers who looked more important than their faith. At Mochi Gate, we bought open, leather shoes with a colourful curl at the tip that reversed like an elephant's raised trunk. They seemed the epitome of taste in Lahore and bit huge chunks of skin off the back of the heel when we wore them in Telinipara.

The best warren for a loaf was the great Anarkali bazaar, named after the dancing girl in the court of the Great Mughal, Akbar, who won the heart of his son and heir, Prince Salim. The magic of myth burnished these names from history. Anarkali, blossom of the pomegranate, made an empire tremble with the flick of an eyelash, lost her prince but won her legend, and found an immortal home in a grave in the heart of Lahore. Akbar, lord of the world, picked up his sword against a cherished but obstinate son who preferred the love of a slave to the demands of empire.

Happily, while Anarkali and Akbar heated my perennially warm imagination, they also resolved those nitpicking dilemmas of *Mother India* in a film called *Mughal-e-Azam (The Great Mughal)*.

I saw Anarkali reincarnated in the exquisite poise of Madhubala, the actress who defined beauty for a generation. Lahore, mesmerized by the movie, sparkled with her image. She soared above the Mughal skyline of Lahore on dozens of huge billboards as other faces faded in deference to her grace. At Shah Alam Gate, Anarkali looked up in prayer towards God, mysterious, haunting, bewitching, her face framed by a black dupatta and lit by the soft touch of a candle. She lived again in the protective embrace of Salim, glancing around the hem of a white muslin dupatta, her lips parted in a smile that was both a challenge and an invitation, her eyes dancing to a silent melody. And there again, alone, unencumbered by pretenders: she lifted a shimmer of a veil with fingers dressed in jewels; a large nose ring, swaying slightly, was held by a thin bridge of pearls that swept into her hair; her eyes spun gossamer traps that floated and disappeared and her succulent lips – the arc of a bow above, and lush heart of a melon below – destroyed all the laws that kept this world in place: morality, order, obedience, fear.

I saw the emperor through the looking glass of an enchanting slave.

But it was the emperor who gave me back my identity when we went, a cluster of cousins, to see the film. The curtains rose above a dark screen on which, slowly, a map of united India appeared. A deep regal baritone spoke three simple words: *"Main Hindoostan hoon!"* I am India! I am Mughal. I am Muslim. I am India. My India is not a part of India. It is the whole of India. I am not just Pakistan; I am this vast subcontinent that sprawls from the rough-diamond mountains of the Hindu Kush in the northwest to the turbulent waves of the Bay of Bengal and the sweet rhythms of the Indian ocean beyond the shores of sultry, sunburnt Kerala. I am Muslim. I am everywhere.

Through two hours of epic narrative I found myself, my past, my culture, my language, my flirtations, my loves, my rebellion, my poetry, my music, my intrigues, my art, my suffering, my sacrifice, my oath, my father, my mother, my present, and perhaps even my future. Who else could have made this film except an Indian Muslim from Bombay, K. Asif, who distilled history in a dewdrop and squandered a fortune in pursuit of an elegant glance? Who else could have been Anarkali except Madhubala, shy and erotic, in life and on screen the quintessential Indian Muslim lady? Life and art overlapped repeatedly like the streams of Muslim and Hindu cultures. Akbar's son, Salim, was played by Dilip Kumar, named Yusuf Khan at birth. Salim's mother and the emperor's wife, Joda Bai, was a Hindu: Salim's blood fed from both Mughal and Rajput genes. Prithviraj, a towering Hindu

Pathan from Peshawar, acted the part of Akbar, an empire-
builder with bloodshot eyes and iron will who bowed before
Allah while his queen worshipped Krishna. Salim's childhood
friend was Durjan, the son of Raja Man Singh, who gave his life
to save Anarkali. Anarkali, a Muslim, danced to an ancient Indian
Hindu beat, while the immaculate voice of Tansen floated,
paused, rose and fell, went back to the Hindu shastras and then
moved four centuries forward to become the music of a
contemporary genius, Ustad Bade Ghulam Ali Khan.

They did not toss their heads in the Mughal court, they
merely raised their eyes. Anarkali destroyed her nemesis when
she looked an emperor in the eye before being led away to death,
and passed an immortal judgment: *"Yeh kaneez Jalaluddin
Muhammad Akbar ko apna khoon maaf karti hai!"* This slave
forgives Jalaluddin Muhammad Akbar for taking her life!

In that summer of discovery, Anarkali turned me into a teenager.

I don't know about it being darkest before dawn, but it was
certainly brightest before sunset.

My mother, eager to sustain the moment, insisted that I write
letters to all my cousins once I returned to Telinipara. She would
stand over me as I struggled, the ink dry on the nib as the pen
hovered unwillingly over dark blue notepaper, decorated in one
corner with a flowery *Forget Me Not.* I found little to say after
"How are you?" and "We are all well" and "I am very happy in
school". She could never understand that the worlds were
parallel, not interlinked: Telinipara made little sense in Lahore,
and both meant nothing in Calcutta Boys' School. I was a
seamless chameleon: English in Victoria; Bihari in Telinipara;
Kashmiri in Lahore and Eurasian in CBS. Her letters to her

sisters and Inayat were regular and voluminous. The answers from Pakistan bulged out of badly-glued envelopes – they often seemed glued twice, which became a minor joke with the fastidious postman.

~

There was some talk, much encouraged by Chowdhury Uncle, of my father becoming a Congress candidate for the local seat in the state legislature. The third national elections were scheduled for February and March 1962. The Congress had been in power since Independence, and my father was an active loyalist. He had campaigned for the party in the 1957 elections, and had a photograph (framed and placed on the drawing room wall) with a smiling Congress president, U.N. Dhebar, to prove it. He was pleased by the attention, but when he checked how much it would cost to contest the miser in him backed out. Rumours began to seep into the bazaar that Ram Chatterjee might get a Congress ticket from Tarakeshwar, a nearby constituency. My father grimaced and kept quiet.

The Congress believed in democracy. It met for annual sessions and elected office bearers at national and state levels. But in the Bengal Congress, only one man was in power. He had curly, jet black, well-oiled hair, a mango face, a rising paunch that lifted the front of his immaculate khadi kurta, and a sedate mien. He wore square-framed dark glasses, spoke rarely, sported a small frown, and smoked Burma cheroots that became ash on one side and ragged tatters on the other, where they had been chewed to death while the cheroot was still alive. Everyone knew him, and he knew everyone, whether an office secretary in a remote district in Bengal or the prime minister of India. He was called

Atulya Babu. Every morning, weather permitting, he spent an hour in his garden, fussing over flowers. He was at his most amenable then.

His personal secretary, Bibhuti, an old man with a sour, bored expression who never looked directly at any superior and never allowed an inferior to look directly at him, stood patiently at a respectful distance of six steps. He was wearing a precautionary sweater, for it was the first week of November. Atulya Babu let him wait for ten minutes, then growled through cheroot smoke, "Tell me."

Bibhuti cleared his throat, his eyes fixed on grass. "With your permission, Sir. The Hooghly list should be cleared today."

"Why?"

"With your permission, Sir, there are only two months left for the election."

"Three."

"Yes, Sir, yes."

"So what's the hurry?'

"This time, Sir... difficult."

"Yes, that's true. This time the elections will be difficult. Jawahar thinks he can give a speech and everyone will line up to vote for him. That is how he won two general elections. By giving speeches. Ha! That drain on the other side of the road stinks more than it did when the British were here, but Jawahar believes English phrases about socialism will be sufficient. He is prime minister of India; who are we mortals to argue with him? And as for our great chief minister of Bengal, Dr Bidhan Chandra Roy: the less said about him the better. If I hadn't ordered a power failure while his votes were being counted in 1957 and stuffed the ballot boxes he would have gone back to being a doctor. He can't win his own seat and thinks he can save Bengal for the Congress. Ha! Those Communists will be in power soon, you mark my words."

"Sir, with your permission Sir, the Hooghly district list..."

Atulya Babu turned around. "Bengal is lost and all you can think of is Hooghly! Which candidates are you interested in?"

Bibhuti said nothing.

"Don't waste time, my man."

"Sir, with your permission Sir, Nirmalendu Guha is very capable party worker in Chinsurah. I can say similar for Byomkesh Mazumdar in Baidyabati and Ram Chatterjee in Tarakeshwar. They are all your men, Sir."

"You mean they are all your men. I know Nirmalendu and Byomkesh. You can tell Byomkesh to go ahead. He is good and will win. Who is this Chatterjee?"

"Very good man, Sir, very energetic, very hardworking, with full band of loyal dedicated personal cadre."

"Is he from Tarakeshwar?" Atulya Babu asked. He knew every party member of some significance and could not quite place Chatterjee.

"No Sir, no Sir. With your permission Sir, he lives in Chandernagore."

"Then why doesn't he want the ticket from Chandernagore? Why go to the rural constituency next door?"

"Sir," Bibhuti answered with a rare grin which he hid almost as soon as it appeared, "Chandernagore not back to India yet. French government gone, but bill stuck in French Parliament."

"Oh. Well, your Chatterjee can wait for the French to deliver the rest of our country back."

Bibhuti gargled air before he spoke. "Chatterjee, Sir, with your permission will not need party funds to fight election."

Atulya Babu became wary. A Congressman who didn't want money was an anachronism. He voiced a sudden suspicion. "Wasn't this chap in jail?"

"With your permission, Sir, during British time, Sir. Freedom fighter, Sir. Big fighter in Chandernagore, Sir."

Atulya Babu paused, and said slowly, "Yes, yes, yes... I know that kind of fighter. I remember the name now... used to loot railway wagons." He suddenly raised his voice. "Jawahar will not touch any money. He is so holy his nose is always in the air, raised to God; a Brahmin like him doesn't look down from his pedestal. Bidhan is worse; money never soils his gleaming white dhoti. What do they think? That elections are fought with municipal water? This is not 1952. Congress will lose if we cannot raise funds. This crook of yours, this Chatterjee. Can he give me the funds for five Assembly candidates?"

"Yes Sir, with your permission Sir, yes Sir."

"How do you know? You haven't even asked him!"

Bibhuti's eyes sank even further down.

Atulya Babu dismissed his secretary, then stopped him. "How much has this Chatterjee scum paid you?"

Bibhuti blubbered a denial. Atulya Babu looked away. It was not yet eight in the morning and he was already feeling tired. He wished he could leave politics. One part of him wanted to retire and play rummy.

Ram Chatterjee was nominated by the Indian National Congress for the Tarakeshwar seat, and won the elections of 1962 by an unremarkable margin of three thousand-plus votes.

17

OFFERING

THE BRAHMIN WAS LIGHT ON HIS FEET BUT HEAVY WITH incandescent piety. Eyes closed, folded hands raised, he addressed the tethered goat waiting to be sacrificed to Mother Durga, consort of Shiva, patron of victory, slayer of vice, with three eyes, ten weapons, ten arms, and swelling breasts, full of bounty. It was the eighth day of the Hindu lunar month of Aswin.

The fortnight of the Goddess, the Devi Paksha, begins with the new moon. Expert artisans put the last touch on her clay image, shaped with devotion over many weeks, by drawing her eyes. On the sixth day, the image is brought to the shade of a *bel* tree. In the early hours of the seventh day, she is infused with *prana*, life. Life comes from a pond or a river, in a banana tree wrapped in a new red-and-white sari to resemble a bride, seated on a palanquin. The Banana Bride is placed before the clay, as the priest chants verses from the Purusha Sukta of the tenth Mandala of the *Rig Veda*. He gives the image a ritual bath, places lampblack in the eyes with a blade of grass to give the goddess sight, and recites the *mula-mantra* 108 times. Then he puts his thumb on the heart of the clay image and utters the holy verses:

"*Om!* May Vishnu give you genitals, *Tvasta* shape your form, *Prajapati* make you fertile and *Dhata* make you pregnant!" The goddess comes to life with the Gayatri Mantra, and worship begins.

I remember the date clearly, 25 October 1962, for the world began to wither after that night. We left Telinipara to see the many images of Durga in dozens of famous pandals in Chandernagore, finally a part of India after the French Senate ratified the treaty of accession on 16 August 1962. Kamala and I slipped away into a bylane beyond Urdi Bazar. Kamala promised me mystery, not unmixed with one-upmanship. "You think only you Muslims sacrifice animals to God? We Hindus do so too!"

"Should I stay?" I whispered, feeling very much an intruder into a secret rite.

"A temple mouse does not fear the gods!" replied Kamala majestically. He had developed a good line in aphorisms. "Just merge into the crowd. No one knows your name."

"The Mother will be pleased to receive thy blood and flesh... *Om!*" recited the priest, addressing the goat. "Thou art a hero. Forgive the pain that must follow the sword, but thou art blessed, for thou shalt attain Gandharvaloka, heaven." The head rolled off, neatly severed, and the goat, with a last yelp, went to heaven. The priest turned to the Goddess. "Thou who art fond of sacrifice, O Great Goddess, accept the blood and flesh of this beast." The priest then became the voice of the worshipper: "*Om!* Give me long life, fame, sons, wealth, give me all good things O Goddess! I have done my duty, Mother, come to my abode."

"Do you believe that these goats go to heaven?" I asked Kamala, as we walked back in the shadows of the edge of the road.

He laughed. "Neither your goat nor mine goes to heaven. If it were so simple, why don't we sacrifice our fathers and send them to eternal bliss?" That evening Kamala kept us entertained with jokes whose variety became indistinguishable in the spate. "What is it that the poor man throws away but a rich man picks up and keeps in his pocket?" Give up. "Snot! Only the rich man has a handkerchief!" The joke was on me, for I was the only one in the group with a handkerchief.

The next day, the Government of India declared an Emergency. Till then, war had been a series of newspaper headlines.

The headlines had been simmering since September. At Calcutta Boys, Ratty Mukherjee brought tension to a boil in a fearfully funny way. As readers of the *Statesman*, we were familiar with details. On 8 September Communist Chinese forces crossed the McMahon Line, drawn by a British official across the Himalayas to neither India's nor China's satisfaction. Nehru ordered the Indian Army to throw the Chinese back, and patriotism crawled up our young spines like an ascending firecracker. China had other ideas. It launched a full-scale attack on 20 October. Chicks told us that the Chinese were yellow godless ants who had swarmed into god-fearing Korea ten years ago. We were confident that our brave Indian soldiers were good enough for ants.

Two days later, the Himalayas were dwarfed by America. On 22 October the glamorous John Kennedy ordered a blockade of exotic Cuba to prevent Soviet ships from placing their missiles less than a hundred miles off the United States coast. Our war in the Himalayas looked like a scratch compared to a nuclear holocaust. Ratty, unable to contain his desperation, began to mutter, "The world is going to blow up, we are all going to die and we haven't even had a fuck!" Marutpal the yodeller, who tortured Nat King Cole every afternoon, took me aside to ask what fuck meant, and, despite indulging my imagination, I could not offer a satisfactory answer. Tiwari, the tattler, who had forgotten that his father was a Bihari milk-seller and claimed that he had become a devout Christian, was worried enough to keep his mouth shut. Normally he reported everything he heard to Sassoon, who taught history and was the vice principal.

The Cuban crisis faded by the twenty-eighth and ours escalated into our first national tragedy. On 27 October we learnt that the mountain city of Tawang had fallen. No one had heard of it before, but it was clearly important if it stirred something as placid as the Government of India. Tears became an authorized element of patriotism; Nehru himself dropped one in public. Gold was collected for a national defence fund and Communists arrested for sharing Mao Zedong's ideology. Defence minister Krishna Menon resigned on 7 November. Bomdila fell on 18 November, the day of Diwali. Lamps were left unlit. The *Statesman* carefully informed us that the road to the plains of India was now wide open. Before we could conjure up a slit-eyed headmaster of CBS, China announced a unilateral ceasefire, on 22 November. I knocked on the door of Sassoon's room, and gave him a gold ring with an amber stone that I wore, as my donation to the national defence fund. It was the first important decision I made without consulting my parents.

It was a good war for me, because we were all in it together. Defeat united Indians.

~

A taunt took me towards cricket. The Maharajah of Porbandar, captain of the Indian cricket team on our first official visit to England, said Mathew, had more Rolls.Royces in his garage than runs on the board during *the whole of the 1931 tour*. I became patriotic-passionate, determined to erase the slur on my country's reputation despite a morbid fear of being hit on the testicles. Mathew again. "Heard of Freddie Trueman, my lad? You could float the British navy on the amount of beer he drank, but did he whip Indian ears with his bouncers! He sent you all home with red ears in '52. Chap called Pankaj Roy opened. Got four ducks in a row. He was both quaking and quacking by the time he got back to Calcutta!"

My ears went pink with shame.

We were back from a winter in Lahore. A week was left for the start of the first term of 1964. Colonel Ian Hogg was down for a holiday, and my father fussed over him to the point of embarrassment. Every second day he would send some gift, whether biryani cooked by Ammiji, or a pair of knee-length, calf leather boots made by Henry, or a silver cigarette lighter from Frazier, the silversmiths in the arcade of the Great Eastern Hotel. He took his three children to visit the colonel, perhaps to display those who had been saved before they were born. Baby, dressed in a pink frock of many folds, her hair overwhelmed by a huge red ribbon, was quite at ease, particularly after the cake appeared; my brother Hashim remained taciturn. Now that I was heading into Class 9, Mathew considered me old enough to tease. "You're a big boy now. We've got to start looking for a lady for you, isn't it?" He recited the limerick with great aplomb:

There was a young girl of Lahore
The same shape behind as before,
They never knew where
To offer a chair
So she had to sit down on the floor.

The colonel, his thick white moustache flecked with beer froth, changed the subject. "Should have shot that rat! Riots. No one would have known. Law and order casualty." He had just learnt that Ram Chatterjee had become an honourable man.

"At the battle of Waterloo General Blucher, the Prussian, pleaded with the Duke of Wellington to throw Napoleon into a ditch and shoot him. Wellington refused. Nine years after Napoleon's death, Wellington's carriage was stoned in London on Waterloo Day by a mob shouting 'Bonaparte forever!' That's what happens when you don't shoot them in time."

"Chatterjee," said Simon, "was hardly a Napoleon."

"Right right right. It's the principle of the thing, of course," said the colonel. "Shoot when you can."

"Can't blame you, old sport," said Mathew, "the old empire was in meltdown. You couldn't be expected to remember everything."

"We didn't melt. We weren't the Mughal empire. The politicians gave away what we had preserved," said the colonel.

"No politician is born generous, colonel, and doesn't survive if he is. The Mughals collapsed when their costs outstripped their revenue. They spent like Shah Jehan when they controlled no more than the city Shah Jehan had created around the Red Fort. When the Persian Nadir Shah destroyed their pretensions, he had 55,000 troops with 160,000 attendants. The Mughal emperor had 75,000 soldiers with a million hangers-on! It was a bloody circus. We lost our nerve after defeating Hitler. Never quite understood why."

"Nerve? One Britisher ruled a million Indians; if that wasn't nerve, I haven't seen nerve." The colonel was on his third bottle of glycerine-heavy Indian beer. "I tell you, there is no finer man than the British army officer. He has backbone, brains and bowels. By God, all three have to function!"

"But Colonel Hogg, there were more than 100,000 British. There were only 12,000 Mughals with Babar and no replacement, and they ruled an empire bigger than the British. You can only rule India with the consent of Indians." My father had spoken. Accustomed to his silence, the others were a bit startled.

"Hear, hear!" said Simon.

"Very well said, Akbar!" cried Chowdhury Uncle, lapsing into Bengali.

I rose an inch in pride. Baby was unmoved from her devotion to the half-eaten cake. Maria recognized her look and refilled her plate. Hashim refused, and I was beyond the second-helping stage of life. A secretary interrupted the evening with a note for Mathew, which he read and passed on to Simon. All India Radio had just broadcast the news that Jawaharlal Nehru had fallen seriously ill at the Congress session in Bhubaneswar and been flown back to Delhi. A faint dread entered the room.

The environment was already acrid. Riots had returned to Calcutta that winter, sparked by reports of violence against Hindus in Dhaka. Bengali newspapers began to publish lurid accounts picked up from travellers fed on rumour or refugees thirsty for revenge at Sealdah station, where the train from Dhaka stopped. Reaction was inevitable. Muslims in Park Circus, Beniapukur, Beliaghata and Taltola areas in Calcutta were attacked. Landlords who wanted to drive Muslims out of cheap tenancies, hired thugs to set fire to their homes. The biggest thug was a portly racketeer called Ashu Ghosh, leader of a Taltola gang, who set himself up as saviour of Hindus and guardian of landlords. The Calcutta Police, anxious to protect their reputation as the best force in the country, were frustrated by a class they had not encountered before: criminals with influence in the legislature. Government was undermined at its core.

Three Muslim families escaped from Beliaghata and took shelter with friends and relatives in Telinipara. Zahid Qureshi, leader of the butchers, who had not improved with age, began to talk. "If these Hindus think that they can throw out Muslims just because they have power," he said at the tea shop, "then this knife of mine also has power." Kanhaiyalal Sahu, who described himself as the local *pracharak,* or preacher, of the RSS, gave a very comprehensive report, studded with fact and embellished with conjecture, to Narayan Babu, who listened very patiently. Such patience encouraged Kanhaiyalal.

T.P. Singh was half asleep in the canvas lounge chair in our drawing room when we returned. He was waiting with bad news.

He and my father acted immediately. They sent word to Chowdhury Uncle, and the three of them went around Telinipara in the late evening with a single message. "What has Calcutta to do with Telinipara? Does Calcutta send us anything to eat when we are hungry? All that we get from Calcutta is violence. Why should we soil our hands with Calcutta's blood?" That was the reasonable part. T.P. Singh frequently threatened to wrench the head off anyone who lifted a finger against his neighbour. The three friends had the credibility to command attention. Women applauded their good sense, men welcomed their leadership. A potential conflagration was snuffed out. There is, therefore and thankfully, not much of a story to tell.

Superintendent of Police Deepak Handa drove in at about ten at night. Handa was a young officer who had been sucked up in a vacuum as the police force Indianised and expanded after Independence. His jeep stopped at our gate. Abbaji welcomed him with a confident wave of the hand. They drank tea and Handa complimented my father and his friends. "Handa Sahib," said my father, "Telinipara's people have a long tradition of peace. You can watch Shyamnagar and Jagadal burn across the river, but that will never happen in Telinipara." Handa smiled and said, "That's not what the file says, but thank you. My people have kept me informed, which is why I am here. I don't know how you stopped the gang of butchers from starting a riot, but thank you. You have been a great help to me." I got a ride out of the bonhomie. When Handa learnt that I would leave for school in a few days, he offered to come over and drive me to the railway station. It was my first ride in a police jeep, or any jeep for that matter.

~

At CBS, Torrick, dour, simple, always half-frightened he would lose his job, held his light-brown frames in one hand, the spectacles hovering near the eyes in case they were needed again, clutched his notebook with the other, peered at the notes and read in a heavy monotone: "We are going to study *Twelfth Night* this year, one of the finest comedies in the English language written by the finest writer in the English language, William Shakespeare." We looked at the first page of the Arden edition. It was remarkable how quickly Torrick could make you feel drowsy, particularly in the hour before the lunch break. "Shakespeare's longest play is *Hamlet*. It has 3,834 lines and 29,844 words. His shortest play is *The Comedy of Errors*. It has 1,782 lines and 14,415 words. *Twelfth Night* has 2,481 lines and 19,592 words. It has eighteen scenes, and the fifth act is only one scene. It was written in 1601, just after *Hamlet,* probably as comic relief, heh heh heh." That was Torrick's personal version of humour, and he lifted his eyes, closely glued to his notes till then, to observe the applause. His joke sank in silence. "71.5 per cent of *Hamlet* is in poetry, mainly of the kind known as blank verse, while only 38.2 per cent of *Twelfth Night* is in poetry. That is because the latter is a comedy, and the former a tragedy; poetry cannot be funny. The character with the most lines in the play is neither the hero nor the heroine but a chap called Sir Toby Belch." At this point the resident wit in the class, Tapan Basu, belched. Torrick, who did not see the connection, looked up and repeated a school rule: "No belching allowed in class." He paused, and continued, "The play has some of Shakespeare's most famous lines, which we shall discuss presently. You will then appreciate why they are so famous. I think you will like Malvolio," he said sternly. He shut his notebook and looked up blankly. There were two minutes left before the bell but he had nothing more to say, so he stared at nothing and waited. Those last two minutes were excruciating, for more often than not I was dying to pee.

From Class 9, moral science lessons went up a qualitative

notch: from books in large type with florid pictures of Jesus and the Prophets, we boarders ascended to compulsory Bible studies twice a week for half an hour before breakfast. In my continuing efforts to suck up to the powers, I decided to actually read the Bible. At 7.30 on Bible mornings Chicks would come to the senior section of the dormitory, ostensibly to take meaningful questions but really to provide the day's admonition. I was such a good boy that I was made member of the choir where I sang *Hosannah, Hosannah, to our Christ and King* at the Thoburn Methodist Church in a very disturbing tenor.

Choir and cricket destroyed my comfortable life as a toady.

Choir practice would take place at about six in the evening for an hour or so on Thursdays and Fridays on the stage of the school hall in the largely deserted new building. Ruth Hicks, our boss, who played the piano, would begin diligent preparations for choir practice at least three hours before we started, with the able help of our saxophone player and hi-fi wizard, P.J. Bose, a handsome young man with thick lips and thin moustache, one year my senior.

Pat O'Dwyer, our sports master, entered our lives when I was in Class 8, and provided uninterrupted entertainment for three years. He had been a sergeant in the Second World War, and avoided profanity only because Chicks would have thrown him out. The nearest he got was the frequent use of "bumpf", a short form for bum fodder, or toilet paper. His fetish was the lawn, which became immaculate under his military control. The gardeners went crazy mowing it to perfection, and the whir of the mower could be heard at all waking hours. He made me cricket captain not because of any inherent talent, but because I was very punctual at net practice. One Friday afternoon, in my eagerness to please, I went up to his apartment on the far side of the auditorium to get permission for some silly thing or the other.

This is where I must confess my guilt. It was almost obligatory before we knocked on the door to take a quick look through the keyhole, not in the hope of discovering anything sensational but simply for the thrill of doing the forbidden. Nothing irritated teachers more than the thought that they might be glimpsed in their underwear. What I beheld that afternoon was, in CBS terms, the riches of Alladin's cave. Pat was standing, nude, while his wife shaved his pubic hair. Obviously I did not knock on the door after that. But I must have made a noise in my excitement, for I heard a rustle behind the curtains covering the stage at the far end of the hall as I turned and fled.

Such truths cannot be kept secret in boarding school. Even Ratty, who hated being upstaged on matters salacious, was impressed. The cynic in him asked, "What was she cutting the hair with?" I could hardly resist the temptation to make a good story better, "With a lawn mower of course!" And thus did Pat get the unforgettable nickname of "Mnnnaaaawww". Each afternoon, as he came on the field, a low cry would start and build into a floating crescendo: *Mmmmmmmnnnnnnaaaaaawwwwww*. Puzzled, he kept asking what this was about. It is a tribute to our discipline that no one tattled, or I would have been expelled. Under severe interrogation, Marut explained it was a new war cry we had developed for the cricket team. Marut literally rolled with laughter on the dormitory floor when repeating this story to us. Chicks was not so easily appeased. He was convinced that there was something more sinister. Ruth Hicks began giving me nasty looks and, after I made my usual hash of *Hosannah* at the triumphal Easter march down the aisle of Thoburn Methodist, dismissed me from the choir ostensibly because my voice had cracked.

Was my response a form of oleaginous revenge?

You will recall that we were, in principle, encouraged to ask questions about the Bible. No one did, because no one read it, practising during those thirty minutes an art form in which the eyes remained wide open but the mind went off to sleep.

My first question trembled with troubled innocence. "Sir, Sir, it says in the Bible, Sir, in Leviticus, 16, 'And if a man has an emission of semen, he shall bathe his whole body in water, and be unclean until the evening'. Sir, Sir, should boys in such a condition go to the sick ward till the evening?" Chicks looked stunned; everyone else was shocked, partly at the thought that the Bible was such a good read. Helpless, Chicks muttered, "Sassoon will tell you," took off his frameless spectacles, opened the Bible and began to recite, in a powerful, musical baritone, for he was a natural orator: *The Lord is my shepherd, I shall not want; he maketh me lie down in green pastures. He leadeth me beside still waters; he restoreth my soul...*

His large face turned pink when I stood up the next time. "Sir, Sir, it says in the Bible, Sir, in the Psalms, that God will break the teeth of the wicked in their mouths, tear out the fangs, turn them into snails that dissolve into slime like an abortion and bathe his feet in their blood. Sir, will this happen for any sin, or will God be nicer for small sins?"

"Sin is sin!" he thundered, and turned to the Sermon on the Mount.

I think I broke him a couple of weeks later with this question: "Sir, Sir, the Bible says that Joseph and Mary were from Egypt. Sir, Sir, the picture of Jesus in the hall shows him with blue eyes and blonde hair. Sir, did Egyptian Jews have blonde hair and blue eyes two thousand years ago?"

That is when he used some silly excuse to whip the shit out of me. Boarders were lined up in the dormitory in familiar rows, the juniors in front, the seniors at the back. He walked down slowly, barking here, sneering there, his cane sometimes a walking stick, sometimes a baton. Suddenly he stopped in front of me, pulled me out by the hair, and shouted, "You!" My brains froze, and my legs began to tremble. "You were cheating!" My addled mind was perplexed because I was good in class, and didn't need to cheat. "You were giving your notes to Neogi! That too is cheating. It is what your people have been taught to do ever since your Prophet cheated Christians by calling himself the last saviour! Bend over!"

His cane went up high in the air, four hundred pounds of flesh seemed to swivel in that hand, and the Malacca came down across the bottom in a flesh-charring swoop. "All Muslims cheat!" Whack. "Do you know how many times the King of Arabia has married?" Whack. "This is his sixtieth wife!" Whack. "They've stopped counting!" Whack.

I kept my mouth shut after that. The other positive consequence of my misfortunes was that Ratty became a friend, and I became privy to his darkest secret. "Chicks doesn't fuck Ruth. Ruth fucks PJ, the saxophone player."

For the first time since I joined CBS life was more fun in Telinipara. Both Mustaqim and Kamala got married. I was the *sahbala,* the groom's brother, semi-decked up and given a place in all ceremonies, at the first marriage, a simple affair in which Mustaqim made only one demand upon his future in-laws: that the marriage party be fed and entertained sumptuously. He had no particular interest in dowry, although he was proud of the Tissot watch and Raleigh bicycle that he received. Kamala shocked his prospective in-laws by sending word that at least ten Muslims would be present for a Brahmin's nuptials, and they had better make suitable arrangements. The bride's family had never fed outcastes before, and an uncle insisted that everyone would have to swallow the five substances of a cow – milk, clarified butter, curds, urine and dung – for *panchgavya* purification if unclean *mlecchas* entered the home. T.P. Singh mediated, and two dining arrangements were made, the Muslims being offered a meal in the local school building.

"If I don't feed you guys properly, you will kill me," said Kamala. There was sober agreement all around. "You see," he continued, "you Muslims can marry four times, and can give four wedding feasts, but I can marry only once. All Hindu gods have only one wife: Brahma has Saraswati, Vishnu has Lakshmi, Shiva has Parvati, Ram has Sita, Krishna has Radha."

"Yes, but Krishna had a lot of girlfriends," I pointed out.

"Arrey! To have Krishna's girlfriends you also have to have Krishna's looks. With this face I should consider myself fortunate that someone is going to marry me as well as give me dowry." Kamala promised us a detailed account of how he lost his virginity, but never kept his promise.

~

We should have been prepared, but we do not have the courage to expect death. The newspapers had begun an eerie vigil with learned articles attempting to answer the question: *After Nehru, Who?* That always seemed to me less important than *After Nehru, What?*

At two in the afternoon of 27 May 1964 doctors confirmed what they had known from 6.25 in the morning, when they found a rupture in the abdominal aorta: that Jawaharlal Nehru would not open his eyes again. My father could not control his tears, and we cried because he was crying. Telinipara gathered on the street in front of our home as the funeral procession in Delhi crawled to Rajghat on the banks of the Jamuna for the last rites on one of the hottest afternoons of the year. We placed the radio on the balcony and hitched an amplifier to broadcast the commentary. India seemed to enter a blur, as if the horizon had disappeared. During that long evening my father had only one anguished question, to which no one could quite frame an answer: "Jawaharlal has gone. What will happen to India's Muslims now?"

He would soon find out.

The knock came like a cliché, at midnight.

September in 1965 delivered another harvest of war, provoked by Pakistan. Its Scotch-and-salaam military rulers, regretting that they had not taken advantage of the Indian Army's shattered morale in 1962, sent guerrillas to stimulate an insurrection in the Kashmir valley. They came surreptitiously, from 7 August, in units of twos and threes, through the mountain passes along the 470-mile ceasefire line, until 7000 men had crossed the border.

Kashmir's Muslims did not show much enthusiasm for such liberation. Shepherds caught a few of the intruders and handed them over to Indian soldiers. On 24 August the Indian Army moved across the ceasefire line to block the passes, occupying Pir Sahiba and Haji Pir by 28 August. On 1 September the Pakistan Army responded with a massive formal offensive against Jammu and Kashmir. Pakistani brigades broke through to the Tawi River in Jammu and sent a shudder across the Punjab to Delhi.

Ram Chatterjee read the leaves correctly. When the *Statesman* was reporting a skirmish, he was preparing for war. Ram Chatterjee summoned Bibhuti to his room in the MLAs' hostel in Calcutta.

Bibhuti did not come on time. That would have indicated weakness. Chatterjee was calm. He had the thief's ability to wait for the right moment, and the patience needed to indulge the ego of weak men.

"What is this desperate hurry?" asked Bibhuti. "Don't you know how busy I am?"

Chatterjee said nothing.

"And to come all the way here, to the MLAs' hostel!" Bibhuti grumbled. "You might as well take out an advertisement about our meeting in *Jugantar*." He was referring to the premier Bengali newspaper of the city.

Chatterjee said nothing again.

"What kind of man is this! Drags me out in the middle of a busy day, when Atulya Babu has given me so many responsibilities to shoulder, and then keeps his mouth shut. Is this a game?"

"Atulya Babu..." Chatterjee said, slowly. "Who keeps his personal notepaper, with his letterhead, on which his letters are typed?"

"Who keeps them?" replied Bibhuti, thinking he had come a long way to answer a stupid question. "The almirah keeps them."

"And you have the key to that almirah."

Bibhuti displayed his irritation with a startling grimace.

"I have a letter which has to be sent to Delhi, to the home minister of India. It has to go with Atulya Babu's endorsement."

Bibhuti sniffed. "I will have to see about that. I have to know what is in the letter before I can recommend it to Atulya Babu. Do you know what his signature means? Do you know how powerful he is? Delhi gets a cold when he sneezes," he ended dramatically.

"I am not interested in your views. You will take this letter, place it in your office envelope and add a letter from Atulya Babu to the home minister saying that he has read the contents and recommends that action be taken immediately in view of the serious national emergency."

Bibhuti sniffed loudly. "Atulya Babu does not send letters he has not read."

"I am not bothered about what Atulya Babu does or does not do. I am asking you to do something. You will type that two line letter, adding that it is an urgent warning sent by a party MLA, get it signed by Atulya Babu and ensure that it reaches Delhi."

"Who do you think I am?" asked Bibhuti hotly.

"I don't think. I know what you are. How much money have you taken from me in these last four years?"

"With your permission, Sir," replied Bibhuti meekly, took the envelope and left.

Ram Chatterjee often wondered what he resented most about those years in jail. As a professional thief he had always been prepared for a spell of bad luck. Was it the lost opportunity, the number of additional wagons that could have been looted? Or that a Muslim upstart and a Muslim policeman had stolen years of his life? A white man had saved them once. Revenge would be sweeter for the wait.

Pakistan's offensive, launched on 1 September, threw back the Indian Army in Jammu and threatened to cut off the valley. Some Indian generals became so pessimistic that they wanted to vacate half of Punjab and make a stand near the river Beas. The Pakistan Air Force threatened from west and east: in Bengal window panes were darkened and lights restricted to hamper Pak bombers on a night run. Lal Bahadur Shastri, Nehru's successor, appealed for unity across political and ideological divisions, and asked the anti-Muslim RSS to help assist the authorities in maintaining civilian security. Suddenly, every Muslim's loyalty was suspect. Kanhaiyalal reported to the police that he had seen Altaf Gauhar flashing his torch, practising future disloyalty, and Gauhar was arrested. On 6 September Shastri and Indian generals shifted the strategic balance, and attacked Lahore.

The letter would never have been opened in crisis-wracked Delhi had it not borne the authority of Atulya Babu. A director in the home ministry read it and sent it immediately to his counterpart in the Intelligence Bureau. The letter reported that one Sheikh Akbar Ali, son of Sheikh Rahmatullah, resident of Telinipara, in Hooghly district, living across the river from Barrackpore air force base, was in constant contact with the enemy, through his Pakistani wife, passing highly dangerous double-secret information to a relative, a member of the Pakistan Army, in Lahore, in thick letters. It prayed for immediate action to save India from traitors in this hour of life-and-death struggle to save the motherland, thank you, yours obediently, Sir.

Handa refused to come to our home. He was too embarrassed. He sent a sub inspector who could hardly speak through his fumbles. When no one answered the knock, he shouted. I watched the whole scene, alone, from the balcony: my father's disbelieving face, his stunned stutter, his heavy tread, one slow step after another, towards he knew not what.

The first, bewildered response of the family was that he had been called for some emergency. My mother started weeping. She knew.

The next morning, Handa formally told everyone that this was not an arrest, but something called "preventive detention".

Everyone chose his or her own response to shock. My mad aunt retired screaming to her deathbed, where she lingered for a while. My second aunt took charge of the household. T.P. Singh and Chowdhury Uncle left for Chandernagore at six in the morning, and sat on Handa's lawn until they were allowed to visit Abbaji in jail. Once there, T.P. Singh refused to leave until night. This became the unauthorized, but permitted, pattern. On the weekend, he took the gang over to play cards inside the cell. Mustaqim was the most practical of the lot. He followed my father that night, first on foot, then on bicycle. He bribed the jail superintendent, came home and went back with clean sheets, blankets and a mosquito net. Early in the morning he left again with breakfast. He was possessive. He would not allow anyone else to do anything for my father. Handa allowed him free access. Simon and Mathew called on my father at the official visiting time on the weekend and discussed every subject but India or the war. Siraj took leave from his job as mechanic in Eastern Railways and, along with his footballer friends Ghazi and Badri, took charge of the endless stream of visitors who came home to sit silently (apart from Chowdhury Aunty who was loud in her damnation of the government and promised to teach it a lesson in the next elections) and show solidarity. Jalil Mastan turned up out of the blue – perhaps summoned by Mustaqim, no one was sure – and said he had set his djinn to work to clear the cloud of evil hovering over our home. Modak's family sent a daily supply of specially prepared sweets, which persuaded T.P. Singh to leave even earlier for the jail each morning. Maulvi Ejaz Ahmad Khan Sarhadi, Taslimuddin's successor at the mosque, delivered a powerful sermon against the anti-Muslim character of the Congress Party and held special prayers for the release of my father. Zahid Qureshi, Altaf Gauhar and Ashraf met in secret and started the Zulfiqar Defence Force, named after the celebrated sword that the Prophet presented to the hero and champion of Islam, his son-in-law Ali.

In the dim light of a shaded bulb, on that terrible night, Ammiji opened the Holy Quran at the first verse and did not look up. A small group gathered, to read the holy book along with her. Day broke and she was still immersed. Others got up to work, or do their chores, and returned. There was silence in the home but for the music of the Quran. Baby nodded vigorously as she recited verses hour after hour. Hashim became totally quiet and sullen. The fires of the kitchen were not lit, so Mustaqim made arrangements for simple meals of rice, dal and a vegetable for the family and visitors to be cooked at Mustafa's home. But he ensured that the very best food was sent for Abbaji, with fish and meat and fried brinjals, which my father loved, so that the irrepressible T.P. Singh commented that he had never had such a continuous feast. I stayed with myself, neither joining the prayers at home nor the world outside. I wanted to see my father, but almost the first order he had given Mustaqim was that I was never to be brought near his cell. Kamala organized a kirtan at a Hanuman temple on the first evening in which all the Hindus of the mohalla participated, except for Narayan Babu, who said that he had to go to Calcutta to purchase goods from the wholesale market.

At about eleven on the first morning my mother's head slumped back against the wall, her finger still on a line of the Quran. She was exhausted. The others left her alone. She woke up in about fifteen minutes, looking remarkably refreshed.

She had had a vision, she said, in a very matter-of-fact voice. They would have to recite the Quran continuously for nineteen days, and on the nineteenth day my father would return home. Nineteen was God's number, the basis of the mathematical order of the Quran. The holy book had 114 chapters: six times 19. It had 6,346 verses: 334 times 19. Allah occurred 2,698 times in the Quran, or 142 times 19. *Bism Allah al-Rahman al-Raheem,* In the Name of Allah the Compassionate and Merciful, consisted of 19 Arabic letters.

On 23 September, with ammunition running low on both sides, India and Pakistan agreed to a ceasefire. At 6 a.m. on the morning of 25 September, exactly 19 days after he had been taken into custody, my father was released without a charge and my mother lifted her head from the Quran.

There was one small change in his day's routine: my father

made his afternoons his own. After lunch, he would go to the drawing room, shut the doors and windows, and lie in an armchair in the darkness. When I was at home, I ate lunch with him, then went to a shop and brought him one Scissors cigarette. He had stopped buying cigarettes by the tin or the pack, and shifted from Capstan Navy Cut to Scissors to save money. One afternoon, I asked the question that had been festering in my mind. "If this was going to be our fate in India, then why did you return from Pakistan!" I may have mentioned his reply, given after a thoughtful pause: "There were too many Muslims in Pakistan." And aren't there too many Hindus in India, I asked angrily. "Be that as it may," he said evenly, "this is my land."

By the time I returned to boarding school, I had taken my first decision. The *Statesman* had written an editorial against the jingoist victimization of innocent Indian Muslims during the 1965 war. I knew then that I wanted to become a journalist.

18

BIKINI

I SURVIVED 1967 THANKS TO SHARMILA TAGORE'S BIKINI. HER eyes were demure, but her pout, legs and curves spoke a different language. I saw her on my way from the *Statesman*, where I had graduated from child-star to minor pest to irregular freelance.

I was nine when a tale of mystery, adventure, rebirth, struggle, tyranny, escape – in other words, all the elements of a costume drama – turned me into a news addict. I had better tell the story from the beginning, in the hope of being understood.

In 1933 the thirteenth Dalai Lama, spiritual and temporal leader of Tibetan Buddhists, turned his head towards the north-east and died. It was a signal. The priests obediently headed northeast to look for a successor, who had to be his reincarnation. They found Lhamo Dhondrub, the two-year-old son of a peasant in a village called Taktser who recognized the lamas and claimed the dead monk's possessions as his own with cries of "Mine! Mine!" Further signs were sought. In 1939, they took the eight-year-old Dhondrub to Lhasa, capital of Tibet. On 11 September 1939 he was formally recognized as the fourteenth Dalai Lama and installed at the Potala Palace.

Destiny's smile began to fade when the Dalai Lama turned nineteen; in 1950 Mao's China conquered Tibet. The god of Tibet became a vassal of Beijing. At twenty-eight, the Dalai Lama, fed with visions of glory by supporters and friends like the CIA, rebelled against the Communists. China quickly crushed his hopes and the Dalai Lama fled to India.

The story did not exist until it burst upon the front page in 1959, occupying, day after day the inverted L's in which the *Statesman* laid out the news. Correspondents filed from exotic outposts in the Himalayas like Kalimpong, Bomdila, Zero Point and Nathu-la, scouring the passes for tales of Chinese torture and Tibetan sacrifice. The Dalai Lama was re-reincarnated, this time by Jawaharlal Nehru, now the preeminent deity of the subcontinent, at Dharamsala, a mountain village in the Indian Himalayas that became a town upon his arrival. By the time the drama left the front page I was hooked on newspapers. The events of 1965 took my fascination a decisive step forward.

I returned to boarding school after the ceasefire between India and Pakistan, and began writing letters to the editor. Inevitably, possibly on a light day, one letter was published. Sassoon's eyes widened, and Torrick said, "I told you he was good in English." Pat O'Dwyer winked and said that if this had been Ireland he would have bought me a Guinness.

Never short of ambition, I started sending articles to the editor. In Class 11, my last year at school, when I should have been preparing studiously for my Senior Cambridge examinations, I could only fantasize about more prominent bylines. I submitted articles on any and every subject:

The temple, mosque and tomb were the first significant achievements of Indian architecture. For those who buried their dead, the tomb linked life to eternity. The profound is best expressed in simple lines, hence the elegance of tombs. A mosque is defined by space, size, strength and stability. It must reflect the power of the collective. A temple is unity within chaos, as tempestuous as the dancing Shiva, as beautiful as the calm of prayer.

"The Editor thanks you for your contribution and regrets that exigencies of space do not permit its publication in the *Statesman.*"
That is how I learnt the meaning of "exigencies".

India is united by its people and divided by its scripts. There is tolerance in its religions and intolerance in its language. The Hindu loves Devnagari more than Lord Krishna, the Muslim worships Nastaliq more than Allah.

"The Editor thanks you for your contribution and regrets that exigencies of space do not permit its publication in the *Statesman.*"
Respectable prose having failed, I attempted something a little more risqué.

The British gave the world pornography through their empire. The word was coined, according to scholars, in the 1860s to describe the activities of a man called George Carmon. He employed laundry workers to throw publicity material over the walls of girls' boarding schools. When the police caught him in 1874, they found over 100,000 obscene pictures.

I was lucky they returned this, or questions might have been asked about how I knew what I claimed to know.

Or tamer subjects, heavily larded with textbook information:

> The balance between safety of men and security of animals has always been weighted heavily in favour of men. The British government may have saved some human lives, but it played havoc with wildlife when it offered a reward of Rs 25 for every tiger killed, Rs 8 for a leopard and two rupees for a hyena. An average of 10,000 people per year might have died of snakebite in Bengal in 1878, but was it sufficient reason for a reward of one rupee for as many as eighteen snakes?

If you had asked my personal opinion, I would have considered the reason more than satisfactory, since I hated snakes, but that would have buried the pathos. It didn't matter. The article came back.

And then, when only obstinacy could have kept my hopes alive, I struck gold. I wrote a piece on an imaginary sage who won a following in Telinipara with Kamala-style English, and, instead of posting it, took it personally to an assistant editor, Desmond Doig, who was preparing dummy runs for a new paper aimed at the young, *JS*. Desmond, with a gesture of amused pity, placed his spectacles on his nose, read three sheets in three endless minutes, looked at me, shook his head, and sank my heart: "This isn't for *JS*." He paused. "This should be a middle on the edit page." My father kept the cheque for fifty rupees that I received from the *Statesman* for years in his pocket; my joy was to see him smile again after 1965.

Once my Senior Cambridge examinations were over in early December, I began hanging around the *JS* office, watching skeletons acquire flesh and a magazine emerge. The talk that winter was of famine conditions in Bihar. I took some money from my mother, and told her I was off to Ranchi in Bihar to do a story on famine. My father forbade me from travelling alone, but my mother was more sensible. She knew I would do what I wanted to, so she agreed with what I wanted.

Ranchi looked normal. The slums were no worse than usual. A bazaar was functioning. Where does one find a famine? The state administration had little idea about what needed to be done, and less interest. A few charities were visible on the margins, but only one institution had organized practical action on a relevant scale: the Church. It had set up camps for villagers in search of any morsel. I found famine in the queues for food.

She was diminutive, a little bent, as small as a sparrow. Her face was lined with deep furrows that added stress to whatever she said. She called herself an athlete for God. She was always busy, marching up and down sternly to ensure that buckets of khichdi, a mash of lentil and rice, were evenly distributed along the long, endless rows of the hungry. She fussed over children, their stomachs bloated with hunger, with a fierce passion. I tried talking to her, but she was irritable; she had no interest in giving quotes. That evening I waited outside her makeshift hut until she let me in. The warmth of her sublime smile embraced me with a force that was palpable. A young photographer from the *Statesman* was also there; his name was Raghu Rai.

Desmond did not need to look at Raghu's superb pictures when I described her, in very guarded tones, for scepticism is required doctrine in journalism. His eyes lit up. "You met Mother, did you?" he asked. My story on Mother Teresa made the second lead in *JS* (the lead was reserved for the Beatles). I could now claim to be a semi-pro.

~

I was floating back from Desmond's office when I saw Sharmila Tagore in a bikini; it seemed divine reward for hard work. She was on the cover of the country's most popular film magazine, *Filmfare*. That bikini was a revolution. It was the first time that a star had bared as much, and punched so many holes into middle-class modesty that it died without a gurgle. Good girls from good families could now also pout.

The owner of the kiosk near Metro would not let me touch *Filmfare*. He was a fat Bihari in a loose kurta and a once-white dhoti that had turned a smelly brown. He looked at me with bored eyes when I said I wanted the issue.

"It costs five rupees."

That was ten times the cover price. I bought it. His boredom disappeared.

"You want books?" he asked.

It was my turn to get snooty. "You don't have books here. You are only a magazine seller."

He looked at me with faint contempt, which would have been stronger but for the fact that I had wasted five rupees on a photograph. "Come with me."

He took me to a junk shop in the alley next to Metro and introduced me to Henry Miller and other fine writers published by Olympia Press, Paris. The deal was this. I would have to deposit ten rupees with him, and I could get nine rupees back when I returned the book. The cover of *Tropic of Cancer* was innocuous: plain text in simple type on bland blue paper. I returned the next day, and paid the deposit. I never saw the money again, of course; instead, I read ten books. The ones by

Anonymous were better. *The Lustful Turk: Scenes in the Harem of an Eastern Potentate*, first published in 1828, became an important aide memoir to life's most difficult passage, introducing me to the potential pleasures of the kiss: in ascending order, the dove-kiss, the kiss of enjoyment, and the kiss of desire. White Victorian English girls, dreading heathen rape in the harems of Turkish Beys and Deys, discovered instead sexual ecstasy with dark men. Sometimes I wondered if I was dark enough to be good. And then there were the delights of Paris and convent schools, matters I had clearly missed at St Joseph's:

> Gretchen the Swiss was lying across the bed, and sucking Therese's breasts. Her mouth glided along and descended, lapping the brown skin. She opened with two fingers the gate, not of sodomy but of nature, and seized her clitoris between her lips. Therese cried out, writhed, and called to me.

I checked a dictionary when Kamala did not have the foggiest notion of what a clitoris was.

But there was nothing foreign that could match the intricate realism of India. Foster Fitzgerald Arbuthnot, a proper Victorian Sahib and Collector of Bombay in the middle of the nineteenth century, had translated a fifteenth century Sanskrit text called *Ananga Ranga, The Pleasures of Women*. There was no harmony, it said, more exquisite than a woman, if played upon well. I probed distant corners of the imagination in search of music.

Foster had a friend, Richard Burton, a subaltern in the Indian Army who was so thorough in investigations, ordered by Sir Charles Napier, of homosexual brothels in Karachi that he was accused of being a pederast himself, thereby ruining his army career and saving him for worldwide fame as an explorer and translator, along with Foster, of the *Kama Sutra*.

I told Kamala that as a good Hindu he had a sacred duty to practice what the *Kama Sutra* preached. He took my suggestion seriously. A woman, he said, had been created to obey, first her parents, then her husband, and, in her old age, her children. But his wife fell asleep when he began to teach her the sixty-four sensuous arts, started to laugh when he broached the congress of the cow and thought he had gone mad when he suggested that she go on top. It was his considered opinion, after a few days, that Vatsyayana, author of *Kama Sutra*, was an unmitigated idiot and I an unrepentant mischief-maker.

~

My father was ecstatic when I passed the entrance examination and was admitted to read English at the Presidency College: I had achieved what he had once wanted for himself. Chowdhury Uncle was delighted that I was going to his alma mater, and both, to my embarrassment, accompanied me to the gates on the first day. My initial lessons, regrettably, were not in English literature but in how to survive a thrashing. Having seen war, death and famine in the past two years, all I needed was a conflagration to round things off. I found one in a Maoist revolt, popularly called the Naxalite movement.

The resident comrade, Kaka Mukherjee, was a charismatic orator with a Che Guevara beard, wild hair, twisted lower lip and bulging eyes. He had entered the campus in 1961 for a political science degree and had no plans to leave. He ate in the canteen, slept in the adjoining Hindu hostel (which lived up to its name; only Hindus were admitted) and indoctrinated students from

Bengali-medium schools. He scorned the convent-educated as petit bourgeois. We English-wallahs filled the arts departments, English, history and economics and stuck to our slightly elitist world. In the third week of the first term, Naxalites closed the college for four days in a row, one day being allotted to American genocide in Vietnam, and three to the perfidies of the running dogs of American imperialism. We thought we had come for an education. It was a foolish thought. A few of us decided to clamber over the drawn steel gates to break, symbolically, the strike. That was easily done. The Naxalites did not expect any defiance, and were not around to stop us. Our mistake was to celebrate at the Coffee House across the street. When we came out we were surrounded and beaten with a couple of educative iron rods. That was the end of my counter-revolution. I spent a very pacifist, non-ideological three years in Presidency after that, writing for newspapers and seeing movies with girlfriends. Falling in love was far less demanding.

If Calcutta was crimson, Telinipara had turned a dark shade of pink. Marxists started a trade union in Victoria Jute Mill with Mohammad Ismail, a young man with studious spectacles, as the general secretary. During the 1967 general elections it was apparent that Ismail had become a power centre in Telinipara. Red flags flaunting a hammer, sickle and star fluttered outside his office, a hub of continuous activity as younger workers gravitated towards the aggressive defenders of the working class. My father did not campaign for any party in 1967.

The Congress, corrupt and stale, was thrown out of office that year and a motley alliance thrown in. It called itself the United Front. A rebel Congressman, Ajoy Mukherjee, became chief minister. A Communist, Jyoti Basu, representing the second largest bloc of seats, was his number two. It was a disparate bunch of over twenty parties, many of them overnight concoctions.

The concoctions punched above their weight. Ram Chatterjee had three members in the Assembly, and flaunted them under the label of Forward Bloc (Marxist-Leninist). He never explained how much of his outfit was Marxist, how much Leninist and how much a happy marriage of the two. He became minister of sports. The only Marxist-Leninist thing he did was to barge into the genteel Calcutta Swimming Club wearing a lungi and jump into the pool to assert that the fortunes of the proletariat had changed.

Chatterjee is the past, explained Simon; think about the future, he urged.

Simon had taken me out for lunch to say goodbye. It was a Friday and, at his suggestion, I wore a tie. We met at the Oxford Book Store on Park Street, and he asked me to choose any book I wanted. The English Language Book Society had published a collection of Shakespeare's works which I had often eyed without finding the will to buy it. My budget was no longer as stressed by porn, but movies took their toll. Shakespeare was Simon's last gift to me.

"Come on," he said, "let's go to my club for lunch. It's Poet's Day."

Bengal Club had been a "whites only" club till recently. A plaque at the entrance reminded visitors that this immaculate Raj building had once been home to Macaulay, the nineteenth century British godfather to my class of twentieth century Indians. We walked up the grand, polished teak staircase to a musty bar dull with leather sofas and full of smoke. The club motif, a black cobra, was etched on the door.

"A drink, son?"

I flushed, as Simon turned to say another hullo, this time to a certain Ivan Surita.

"Don't worry, your dad will never know!"

He gauged the feebleness of my protest, and said, "Vodka. It doesn't leave a trace on your breath. *Aabdar!*" he called out to the bearer, "My usual and vodka with lots of ice and tonic for the young man."

Simon had thought through what he wanted to say, which made that afternoon even more valuable.

"I'm glad you are reading English and not history. Historians are gravediggers; whenever they churn the soil, all they find are worms. You must build the future, your own and your country's."

Like any teenager I was indifferent to good advice. I did wonder at the purpose of the sermon.

"You must not let the Ram Chatterjees destroy your faith; he is the past. If Ram Chatterjee did not make enemies, he would hate himself."

"That's easy to preach when you are leaving India," I replied.

"I've seen India change, son. When I came to this country, Indians were not allowed to enter a tent in a British cantonment with their shoes on. Some white men called Indians niggers and trained dogs to go for them. But you can see for yourself the new confidence of this nation – yes, even in Bengal Club. It isn't a Scotsman but Ivan Surita who is the life and soul out here."

As if on cue, Surita raised a loud toast: "To absent friends!"

"I am old now, and would like to spend a little more time with my son in England."

I said nothing.

"All right, that is not the only reason. I cannot deal with the morality of Indian business. You know that a Calcutta business family has purchased Victoria Jute Mill. I am afraid they expect managers to look elsewhere while they fiddle invoices to take money out of the company. There is no salary that would tempt me to play such games." He laughed. "The Indian National Congress and the Indian Chamber of Commerce were born in the same year. I don't know which has deteriorated faster!"

I smiled, "So the Naxalites are right about one thing at least."

"Perhaps more than one thing... But enough about me. You've grown up splendidly. Your father is so proud of you, your writing. Your success adds years to his life. You'll be the second boy from Hooghly district to become an international star!"

"Second?" I asked.

"Quite right. There was a chap called William Herschel, whose grandfather discovered the planet Uranus. William discovered something much more important while he was serving as a district officer in Hooghly: the method of fingerprinting!"

"To our sheathed swords!" boomed Surita's voice.

"He's doing the Wellington toasts," explained Simon. "There are five more to go. The Duke had a toast for each day of the week. It's Poet's Day. They're all going to get drunk."

We continued talking till late in the afternoon, through mulligatawny soup, omelette and crisp toast served on a silver rack, roast beef, caramel custard and coffee: of life, and life in Telinipara; of friends who became family and family that drifted;

of passions that dimmed and moments that had endured. Simon offered advice: whatever else I did in life, I must never beg, and never hate. He hadn't forbidden shrugging, so I shrugged.

He sank into himself at one point, then broke his silence with a request: could I pass on a gift to Hasina and keep it quiet? It was a beautiful diamond ring. I did not ask him why. I gave the diamond to Hasina in the emptiness of the roof at home, and large tears filled her eyes before she smiled them away. Surita's voice drawled into the dining room from the bar: "To our wives and sweethearts: may they never meet!"

"Simon, tell me, why is today Poet's Day? It isn't Rabindranath Tagore's birthday or something of that sort, is it?"

"Ah. Poet's Day. It comes every Friday in the Bengal Club, and is celebrated by those members, all of them managers in the blue chip companies of Calcutta, who won't return to office after lunch. Acronym. P.O.E.T.S. Piss Off Early Tomorrow's Saturday."

I felt a deep sadness as he waved at the door and went back to the club, while I walked away, Shakespeare in one hand, and the tie, now off, in the other. He had tried to cheer me up by saying he would see me next when I went up to Oxford for higher studies, but I knew Oxford was out of my reach, a stride too far from Telinipara. I would not see him again. Mridula took me to a movie to console me. That's the good thing about being young. Sadness fades quickly.

~

"No spiritual progress is possible without renunciation of women and gold," said Babu Girdhari Lal Gupta. He rested against emaciated, cylindrical pillows, his legs bent forward, little glimpses of thick flesh visible through his dhoti, on the foot-high, cushioned platform that dominated the room. "That is what the great Ramakrishna Paramahansa used to say, and he was right."

Kanhaiyalal Sahu sat, crosslegged, on the uncarpeted floor, his face bowed in deference to wealth but not to status. Gupta, the new owner of Victoria Jute Mill, was rich; he was poor, no more than a recently promoted Sardar of workers, but they belonged to the same caste. "Kanhaiyalal, the Lord has brought me to that stage in life where I have renounced women," Gupta said with a laugh that hiccupped through his words, "but He has not made me fit for spiritual progress yet. I still enjoy gold."

"That is your destiny, Babu. It is your fate to be a servant of the goddess of wealth."

"Yes, Kanhaiyalal, and the goddess can be very demanding. How can I serve her when Communists encourage farmers in the villages to raise the price of jute to unheard of levels, and Communists at my door threaten to strike for higher wages in the mill? Sometimes I feel that the only way to teach these workers a lesson is to shut down this factory for a few months. When they starve, they will realize what it means to obey a rabble-rouser rather than listen to me. I pay the salaries and they pay homage elsewhere... is that justice? That Muslim trade union leader, do you know him?"

"Yes, master, I know of him," replied Kanhaiyalal carefully.

"You are a religious man, Kanhaiyalal. You run the RSS in Telinipara. How can you tolerate these Muslims who behave as if they can do what they like in our country?"

Kanhaiyalal's heart swelled with patriotic pride.

"What do I have to do?" he asked shrewdly.

"You understand, of course, that you will never suffer as long as I am alive. I have the highest respect for your selfless sacrifice and commitment, and there will never come a day when Kanhaiyalal and his family cannot light a fire in their kitchen."

The plan was simple enough. Over the next few weeks, Kanhaiyalal would instigate different levels of trouble between workers and manoeuvre to ensure that the blame was laid on the trade union. The police would be squared to confirm this version in their reports. Kanhaiyalal would also insinuate that Communist leaders were Calcutta Bengalis who had no sympathy for Biharis, especially Bihari Hindus. That was why they had put a Muslim in charge of the trade union. Now, if by some accident, during one of those scuffles, either at the gate or elsewhere, a knife came out, and a Muslim was stabbed by a Hindu... The police would make arrests, there would be tension in Telinipara, perhaps an incident or two. Someone would give a call for a strike. The management of Victoria Jute Mill, taking appropriate note of the deteriorating law and order situation, would declare a lockout till peace returned.

"Peace... It goes easily, but the return journey is so difficult... Shall we give peace about four months to return?" hiccupped Gupta. "By that time the price of raw jute should have stabilized. Some of my friends in other jute mills are going to cut production as well so that jute prices come down. But my brother Kanhaiyalal! The fires in your kitchen shall always be lit!"

~

Mathew Horne squirmed as he remembered an old antidote for a hangover; even a thought had become a burden in his benumbed head. He was alone, but that was not the reason why he had been drinking so heavily. His wife lived in England most of the time, and Simon had been gone for almost a year. He should have left with Simon. He could have left with honour. He filled a small glass with cognac, clutched his nose to shut off breathing, and splashed the cognac deep down into his throat. For a moment, fire and brimstone stormed through his head. Then came the miracle. The hangover disappeared. Grandmother was right, bless her soul. It was such a good feeling that he drank another small tumbler of cognac. He took his time over a bath, swallowed some toast with coffee, and watched himself carefully in the mirror as he sipped another cognac, slowly.

No one tried to stop him as he walked into Gupta's room without an appointment.

"Mr Gupta, you are a bastard."

Gupta was considerate and concerned. "Oh Mr Mathew, you must not say such bad things. Mr Mathew, you are I think working too too hard. You must take leave at once."

"Mr Gupta, Victoria was a beautiful jute mill. It was the mother of a community. Its workers have lived in peace for a hundred years in the shadow of its great walls; its shareholders have enjoyed the fruits of their investment and their managers' industry. In less than two years you have turned this company's balance sheet into a fraud and its workers into beasts –"

"Oh Mr Mathew, no no no. I am not a Communist. I am God-fearing, Mr Mathew. I worship the Lord in my puja room every morning. It is godless Communists who are destroying Indian culture and Indian business. You must understand Indian business, Mr Mathew. It is the dharma of money to make money."

"While workers starve?"

"Mr Mathew," said Gupta, rising with an effort from his cushions, his voice still as reasonable as ever. "Who taught us divide and rule?" Gupta's small smile grew slowly into a hiccup. "But you are right, Mr Mathew, we Indians do not know how to play that big game as well as you British... Mr Mathew, you know my secretary, Chand Gupta? He will accept resignation and clear all dues, plus free ticket to London."

19

BROTHERS

Thou shall see mankind as in a drunken riot, yet not drunk...

"IT'S TOTAL *CUNDUM*... RUBBISH! SHE IS BOOTPOLISHING YOU!"
I never laughed at Kamala's English, and always smiled at his
jokes, which had a wayward knack of interrupting a conversation
about something totally different. We were discussing love, and
his joke of the day was on cricket. A Nawab, eager to join the new
age, was batting in his garden, and heaved the ball into the house.
The obedient bowler, his servant, chased the ball, and was caught
by the caustic Begum who scolded him severely for wasting time
with her useless husband and dispatched him to buy vegetables.
When the servant returned from the market, the Nawab was
purple with breathless rage. "Where have you been, you
scoundrel!" the Nawab shouted. "I've taken 342 runs already!"

Applause over, Kamala returned to love. "She can't be good
for you if she knows only happiness and anger. To make another
person happy, she should also understand pain."

I would not have discussed Mridula at all; I prefer
discretion. But that evening I was afflicted with the instinctive

desire of a teenager to brag. I had reached Mridula's breasts through Rumi.

Her breasts, luscious, bursting, each nipple a tower above a dome, were my ambition; a Penguin Classics translation of Rumi was my means; Baron's Café, five minutes away from Presidency, the venue. Once my objectives were clear, I could be persuasive. These seven lines, with rhetorical space before the last, had set the stage.

> *Those who don't feel this Love*
> *pulling them like a river,*
> *those who don't drink dawn*
> *like a cup of spring water*
> *or take in sunset like supper,*
> *those who don't want to change,*
> *let them sleep.*

Mridula was studying geography because that was one of the few departments (philosophy was another) in which the number of applicants was fewer than the seats available in class. But she was a student of Presidency, which would rather leave seats vacant than admit second-raters. We had one class, additional history, in common during which I kept my eyes locked on her face while Prof Ashin Dasgupta carefully elaborated on the implications of sea trade between Orissa and Bali in the second century BC. After a day or two of discomfiture she began to enjoy it. Perhaps it helped that I was exotic. She had never met a Muslim on equal terms before, her previous relationship to the community being limited to a tailor who came home to her fancy bungalow on Judges Court Road and measured her chest size with his fraying tape from the back. The only other Muslim in Presidency College was a thirty-year-old Mauritian on state scholarship called Abdoul Kreme who spoke French and broke into pidgin English only to describe weekend sex in one of the many bordellos along Free School Street. He was constantly surprised at how little it cost when he converted dollars into rupees.

I milked the cultural nuances of poetry, inundating Mridula not only with Rumi but also soppy Urdu lines like

Mujhe gham bhi unka azeez hai
Ki unhi ki dee hui cheez hai.

I treasure the sorrow she gave me
For that too was a gift from her.

On a higher note, I described a ghazal as a conversation between lovers. Persistence paid off. This was the decisive Rumi couplet:

Shams, so loved by Tabriz: I close my lips.
I wait for you to come and open them.

I could hardly mention that Shams was a man; it would have rather spoiled the effect. But the upshot was that we walked to the nearby Grace cinema and in the darkness of a semi-empty hall, kissed. She told me it was her first kiss as well, and I was inclined to believe her. Neither of us was perfect. There was never any question of discussing Mridula with college mates, not even Kunu Chatterjee, who became a friend out of a common commitment to low-stakes gambling in a three-card variation of poker called flush. Mridula was less careful, paying for my coffee too often, but there was nothing by way of admissible evidence. Confiding in Kamala was a different matter, because Kamala had no access to the world of Presidency College. His sun rose in the east of Telinipara and set in the west of Telinipara.

"Why does one need to know pain to make another happy?"

"Because most of life is spent in the wrong waiting room," he said, taking another sip of tea as we stood on the balcony of the verandah of my home. I wondered which Hindi book he had been reading.

"Ah... you mean we wait for happiness and we get pain? Very philosophical."

He was drowning in enigma that evening. "There are many levels of sin. There is *upa,* venial sin, like sex during the day." He looked at me sharply. "A penance of a day's fast is sufficient to atone for it. There is *maha* sin, a great crime, like causing the death of a cow; which requires far greater penance. But this damn Telinipara is heading towards *ati* sin, beyond classification: you can chant the Gayatri Mantra for a lifetime and never atone."

"How?" Like anyone who laughed too often, Kamala could get depressed easily.

"Something is happening in Victoria Jute Mill," he said, "and I can't get beyond the curtain of rumours. There are too many people searching for a fight. Someone is poisoning the air..." He returned to enigma. "What is the point of fighting till the last man? Even if you win, there will be no one to claim victory."

~

Chand Gupta took to his teak table with acquired flair. The changes in the office that once belonged to Mathew Horne were minimal but significant. In addition to the wastepaper basket beneath the desk there was a spittoon. A large portrait of Sir Ian Butchart, the last British chairman of the company, had gone. In that space appeared a calendar image of Lord Ganesha. Each morning, Chand Gupta checked, with his personal astrologer, the exact minute at which he should enter his office and then went straight to the Lord, to whom he bowed a very reverential head before he picked up the first betel leaf of the day from a silver casket. The casket was a self-indulgent gift on being made general manager after Mathew resigned. Babu Girdhari Lal Gupta, normally addressed as Girdharilalji, could think of no better man for Mathew's job than his secretary. He placed loyalty at the top of corporate virtues.

The second order of business was to collect gossip from Kanhaiyalal Sahu, who was allowed to sit at the far end of the room, on a small bench, rather than on the ornate, velvet-cushioned chairs at his desk. He then put in a phone call to Girdharilalji, if the owner was in Calcutta, or went to the latter's office if he was visiting the factory. The new owner's minor pleasure, in a life full of inexpensive pleasures, was gossip. He had to know more than anyone he was conversing with. Gossip was invaluable, because it could be traded in subtle ways.

This morning Chand Gupta was irritable. The Marxist union had sent another set of demands and management could formulate no response apart from various degrees of capitulation. His labour officer, Benoy Chowdhury, was too correct to be of any help. Sahu had good intentions but no ideas. Ideas were Chand Gupta's responsibility. He got a good one that day.

His official duties included periodic visits to the three MLAs in the vicinity of the company's factories: the MLAs of Chandernagore, Baidyabati and Tarakeshwar. It was important to maintain cordial relations with the elected representatives of the people. In one case the relationship was more than cordial. On each visit, he picked up two thousand rupees in ten-rupee notes from the cashier (who, never taking expense for granted, double-checked with Girdharilalji each time), put the money in an envelope, sealed the envelope with a lick, and handed it without any ceremony to Ram Chatterjee the moment he was ushered into the august presence. "I pay the bastard for nothing. Time for a little payback," Gupta muttered as he picked up the black telephone from his desk and put it on his lap. Making a call could be time-consuming; it did not hurt to be comfortable. He placed the receiver tight against his ear, raised his voice and asked the long-distance operator to get him Chatterjee's number in Calcutta. He was motionless while waiting. A voice answered. Gupta stood up in instinctive acknowledgement of authority. "Sir, how are you, Sir?"

"Very good, very good. Tell me."

Gupta fumbled his way to an explanation: the Marxist trade union was getting uncomfortably strong. Could Chatterjee suggest what could be done?

"What can be done? What can I do? I am not Congress anymore. I am partner of Marxists. They will throw me out of government. Plus, I too have Marxist party."

A touch of ice comes naturally into the voice of a paymaster who has been denied his expected dues. Gupta's fumbles stopped. "Girdharilalji says that you are the only person who can help."

"How how how how? You people expect too much. I have already opened my own trade union in your factory; what can I do if I can't get any members?"

"Girdharilalji cannot understand one thing about the Marxist union, Sir," said Chand Gupta. He was now improvising. "Both Hindus and Muslims are joining it despite the fact that the leader of the union is Muslim."

"But these Marxists have no religion," explained Chatterjee with ebbing patience.

"That may be true, Sir. But the workers have religion."

I was oblivious to subtle shifts in mood, because I was indifferent to Telinipara. Life had become a comfortable pattern: up early, cycle to station, the fast eight o'clock train to Calcutta, a tram ride to Presidency, class, Mridula, regular visits to Statesman House. Home for dinner. It was my tutor, Arun Kumar Das Gupta, AKDG in college parlance, who pointed out in a polite letter to my father that whatever else I might be doing, I wasn't studying. After my father's initial rage, this letter proved beneficial in two significant ways.

First, I came to a deal with AKDG. I didn't want to study, I said, I wanted to be a journalist. He stared at his desk very carefully before he replied. He wanted a commitment from me: I would never include anything he taught in his tutorials when giving my Calcutta University examinations. I should consult bazaar notes to get a degree. He then gave me a reading list to help me with the English language: the Bible, *Macbeth*, *Lear*, the Henry histories, Book Two of *Paradise Lost*, Marvell, Dryden, Pope, Addison and Steele. I recall vividly the excitement with which I saw the serpent hiss through Milton's language, the "s's" creating subterranean waves in the text. The Bible became a very different book from the one I read under the beady eye of Chicks. AKDG was convinced that a journalist needed to know the history of ideas, war and governance. Machiavelli and Tzu Su were passé. He introduced me to a treatise hidden in the gloomy library of the college, protected by years of dust: Muhammad Mansur's *Adab al Harb wa'l Shujaat*, a treatise on the art of war written in the fourteenth century, when Il-Tutmesh was Sultan of Delhi. The first duty of a ruler, it said, was to avoid war. But if war was inevitable, then it was much better to lead 4000 soldiers who were united rather than 40,000 who could be divided by rumour. When I told him that I was going to Lahore during winter, AKDG ordered me to get half a dozen books from "abroad". I could have got all of them from across the street, but "abroad" had a special piquancy.

The second advantage was permission to stay on in Calcutta, ostensibly to study instead of doing the two-hour journey back home each evening. I could not find accommodation at Presidency's Hindu hostel since Muslims were not permitted there, and so became friendly with a chap from Maulana Azad College, Alamgir Choudhry, who lived in the Muslims-only Baker hostel. I offered to split the hostel rent if he let me keep a mattress in his room.

Alamgir was a Bengali Muslim who had lost an elder brother during the 1964 riots. I rather regretted gaining his confidence, because at night he would insist on narrating visions of fantastic revenge for his brother's death. He had read up the kamikaze missions and kept a quotation on the opening page of his notebook: "Kamikaze is not suicide. It is a moral victory over cowards who take comfort in numbers." Below it was a haiku written by a certain Vice Admiral Takiiro Onishi for his pilots:

Blossoming today, tomorrow scattered
Life is like a delicate flower
Can one expect the fragrance to last forever?

He had a wild scheme: he wanted to convert himself into a bomb and blow himself up at a puja pandal so that he might take a hundred Hindus with him when he attained martyrdom. That is why, he confessed, he had befriended me. It was common knowledge that every evening the campus of Presidency College became the Yenan of the revolutionary movement and doubled up as a Naxalite bomb factory. Could I get him a supply of bombs? I didn't tell him that those bombs, produced by students and collected in a bucket, had academic qualities: their principal asset was sound.

Alamgir collected bits of strange information and knitted them into interesting theories. All great victories, he said, were won by generals who gave their troops only one choice, between death and glory. The Mughal, Babar, had a simple message for his heavily outnumbered troops at the battle of Khanwa in 1527: if they didn't win, they would all die. They won. The last great warrior king of Hawaii, Kamehameha the Great, told his soldiers when they reached the island of Maui in 1810, "Forward, little brothers, and drink bitter waters. There is no turning back." They won. Queen Victoria had named a cross after herself and gave it to anyone ready to die for her. That is why the British won. In Vietnam, at the very moment, Ho Chi Minh was sending boys on suicide missions to defend their country against American imperialism. Ho Chi Minh would win.

Alamgir wanted me to write about him in *JS* after he died. I promised to do so, but the story has a happy ending because no bomb could be located that was large enough for Alamgir's purposes. I found a better solution; I introduced him to Abdoul Kreme who in turn introduced Alamgir to his well-wishers on Free School Street. That was the end of Alamgir's desire for martyrdom.

True to form, Alamgir was soon educating me on the history of whores: the ancient law-giver Manu included a tax on prostitution as part of general revenues, and the sage Kautilya recommended that the state employ a superintendent of prostitutes. The most famous courtesan of all time lived during the reign of the greatest of India's kings, Asoka. She was called Bindumati and treated every customer equally, irrespective of caste, as long as she was paid in gold.

My friends from Telinipara, like Mustafa or Ashraf, were much more comfortable at Baker hostel than in Presidency. They came on Fridays, and we ate beef kebabs for a rupee and drank a cup of sugary, scented tea for thirty paise at Diamond restaurant before trooping off to see Mohammedan Sporting play football.

It was not that I did not quite live in Telinipara; I did not seem to live in Calcutta either. Calcutta was wasting with violence as Naxalites terrorized the police and the police responded with mayhem. Our college echoed with slogans of a revolution that was always but one final assault away from victory. But this was not my war.

Mustafa went to see his father in Karachi and brought back an affectionate invitation from Zulfiqar Khan for mine, but Abbaji would sink into silence at any mention of Pakistan. My mother refused to be defeated by injustice to her husband. Travel resumed after the India-Pakistan peace treaty signed at Tashkent in 1966, and in 1967 she made it clear that she wanted to visit Lahore in winter. Letters had brought news that my grandmother was ill; but this may have been a simulated excuse. There were oohs and aahs when my Lahore aunts saw me: I had changed enough in three years for them to begin suggesting potential brides. I was suddenly as tall as Yusuf Khalu, and the nature of his homilies became different. He now told me of Khusrau, the king of Persia, who noted that the test of a king lay in his ability to preserve his secrets and his harem. The other great Khusrau, the poet of Delhi and father of Urdu, Yusuf Khalu pointed out with a thin smile, survived six sultans and four revolutions but not the death of his master, the sufi saint, Nizamuddin Auliya.

My mother began to shop for my sister's future. Baby had stepped into her teens, and a good trousseau takes time to collect. Ammiji bought a *nuth,* a gold ring worn on the left nostril, *kils,* a jewel-studded gold pin worn on the side of the nostril, and *bulaq,* a tiny gold pendant set with precious stones. Azam, who had fought in the 1965 war, told us stories of his superiors. Like any young officer, he believed that his side should have won, and was shocked by the absence of victory: he could not conceive of admitting defeat. Pakistan, he said, had destroyed the Indian Air Force and broken through in Jammu but strangely Field Marshal Ayub Khan, their president, had halted the offensive when the road to Delhi was open. He called Ayub Khan a traitor. I reminded him that India had nearly captured Lahore, and he called Ayub Khan a traitor twice over.

I don't know what Mridula expected as a present from Pakistan when college reopened in mid-January, but the collected verse of Alexander Pope was not it. In retrospect a colourful pair of shoes would have been more useful. I had thought about it. Since leather was traditionally repugnant to Hindu craftsmen, shoes became a speciality of Muslim artisans. Lahore had a wide range of styles. I could have got her a pair of *aughi*: pretty things embroidered in gold, silver and threads of other colours; or the *kafsh*, Persian high-heeled shoes. But there was no way I was going to answer my mother's questions about who they were meant for, so they remained unbought. Mridula started going home earlier, and circumstances forced my attention back on Telinipara.

~

Muhammad Ismail's goatee served two purposes. In front of his comrades he affected a Trotsky look. The Bengal Marxists were of Stalinist bent, but not dogmatic about looks. During Friday prayers, Muhammad Ismail stroked his beard with the care of a believer. He was a good politician and genuinely indifferent to religious identities, but he knew that Muslims were angry with the Congress and would be easier to mobilize. If a stroke of a beard kept them happy, it was worth the mild deception. His message to the local committee was succinct: Victoria Jute Mill was making record profits because competition from the mills of East Pakistan had been crippled by strikes organized by comrades across the border. This, paradoxically, made the company vulnerable, because they would be loath to close the mill at a time of high profitability. It was the moment to strike, literally. A little pressure and management would accept their demands. Once they showed the workers what was possible through militancy, every other union, including the Congress' outfit, INTUC, the only union recognized by management, would collapse. All committee members agreed enthusiastically with the man who had made them members.

Chand Gupta did not fully understand what it meant but nodded his head vigorously when Girdharilalji suggested, languidly, that Bakr' Id represented a wasted opportunity. The big days on the religious calendar were close to one another in 1968: Bakr' Id in late February, Holi in mid-March and Muharram on the last day of March. Chand Gupta was uncertain about what was expected of him. The din at the gate increased each day, and with it the threat of a strike. The Marxists had the momentum. All he knew was that Girdharilalji was not going to give workers a thirty per cent wage increase or guarantee a twenty per cent bonus.

"You met Chatterjee, didn't you?" asked Girdharilalji. It was a rhetorical question, meant to elicit details. Chand Gupta furnished them, adding that Chatterjee had found a good excuse. He was a junior minister now, he said, and it would be improper to get personally involved. Girdharilalji was famous at Calcutta Club for the cleanliness of his finesse at bridge. "Get me Chatterjee," he said and concentrated on files while Chand Gupta picked up the phone and asked the operator to put him through. Girdharilalji took the receiver only when Chatterjee was at the other end. He then asked his secretary-cum-general manager to leave the room. This must be serious, thought Chand Gupta, if even he was being kept out of the loop.

~

"Kahan Raja Bhoj aur kahan Gangwa Teli!" said T.P. Singh

acerbically when Kanhaiyalal Sahu suggested, chatting at the tea shop, that Muhammad Ismail might have become more influential in Telinipara than my father; it was an old adage that laughed at anyone who compared a king with a cook. But Sahu had succeeded in planting that niggle in the mind that becomes a persistent rash. There was a new tension in the eyes of mill-workers: they wanted a different order; they wanted more. They did not know how much, or how; but they knew they would find out.

There were no incidents during Bakr' Id, but Zahid Qureshi, who had started an office of the Jamaat-e-Islami, taunted Sahu, who was passing through the butchers' enclave on his way to the river ghat, with the suggestion that animals other than goats might have been sacrificed in secret that morning. Qureshi laughed provocatively, but nothing could be held against him because he had said nothing specific. Sahu reported the insinuation to anyone who cared to listen. Narayan Babu certainly cared to listen.

Girdharilalji fixed a beady eye on Sahu and said, with matter-of-fact simplicity, "The Hindus of Telinipara have become cowards." Sahu's head slumped in shame. "They have insulted our mother. Who should we insult?" he asked.

"The virtue of religion," said Abbaji, as he, Benoy Choudhary and T.P. Singh chatted on the eve of Holi, "is surely not what it gives to its believers, but what it offers to others. My father was an orphan, who came to Islam out of a mother's love, and became a believer when he learnt what was written in the Quran. 'He who gives to an orphan lends to God,' says the Quran. That is wisdom for all mankind." My father had, almost imperceptibly, turned to religion after the trauma of 1965. Less imperceptibly, he had grayed, but his figure remained lean and his face as handsome as ever.

"The great quality of Hinduism," said Benoy Choudhary, "is that it clothes god in beauty, not morality. A rich Brahmin who was reduced to poverty by a pernicious ruler was asked why he was smiling when everything had been taken away. 'Not everything,' the Brahmin replied, 'I still have my sacred thread.' But where are such Brahmins now? Hinduism has been taken over by acquisitive communities; if the gods don't deliver hard cash, they are resented!"

"My father, I used to call him Baba, was a devotee of a man who did not even want a tomb. Burha Deewana wanted a place in our hearts. We still have his tomb, but who remembers him?"

"He started the Muharram procession in Telinipara, isn't it?" asked T.P. Singh.

"Yes, to symbolize that Hindus and Muslims should be together in any struggle against injustice. Baba used to quote him often: 'Allah's highest reward goes to those who bring joy to the human heart... be generous as the river, bountiful as the sun, hospitable as the earth'..."

"That Telinipara is long gone. We now have the greed of the rich and the demands of the poor, and such an imbalance can only lead to trouble," said T.P. Singh.

"You've been talking of trouble too often, TP." A thought came to him. "Why not open the *faal*? Your sister-in-law is good at it."

It was a common practice among Indian Muslims to check the omens through the Holy Book, and my mother solved all her own doubts through it.

"Imtiaz!" my father called out. My mother came to the curtain and answered from behind its folds.

"Come in, come in; it's only TP and Benoy. You don't need purdah from them. TP keeps prophesying trouble. Why don't you read the *faal?*"

My mother chided him; she refused to get whimsical about the Holy Book. My father insisted that they were serious. She brought her copy of the Quran to the room, placed it on a wooden platform called the *rehal*, closed her eyes, said a brief prayer, opened the Holy Book at random, and let her eyes fall on a point on the page. There was a tremor in her voice as she read a line from the second verse of Surah 22: *"Thou shall see mankind as in a drunken riot, yet not drunk..."*

The next morning such fears seemed exaggerated. T.P. Singh came with his friends for the usual Holi badinage, and slept with familiar fervour after a morning of bhang and mithai until the quiet of the afternoon was disturbed by a cry that rose from the huts where the *gawalas* lived: *Jai Bajrang Bali!*

It was a cry of battle, raised in the name of the monkey-god Hanuman, son of the wind, general of the monkey-king Sugriva, who could swell to the size of a mountain or shrink to the width of a thumb, leap two hundred leagues across the sea in search of Lord Rama's virtuous wife Sita and set fire to a city with his tail. The group that set out from the mohalla was not very large, but it had fashioned itself on the Muharram procession. There were large banners, in saffron instead of green; the men, with Narayan Teli's elderly sons Mohan and Vishnu in the forefront, carried weapons and indulged in mock encounters. Mustaqim, who went to investigate, provided details: young Jaipal Singh was among those on the march, and Sahu seemed to be the brain behind the idea, although he did not show his face. They went, a trifle too quickly, up to the river, and then dispersed. When we asked Jaipal later why a procession had been taken out during Holi he repeated what he had been told: to prove that the Hindus of Telinipara were not cowards.

Jaipal was among the guests at a very special dinner that night; special because we had finally bullied Kamala Pande into spending money. He had been working as a teacher for two years, but no one could claim that he had got as much as a cup of tea out of Kamala. You got jokes aplenty, but no tea or cigarette or betel-leaf. He succumbed to pressure and invited us over for a festive dinner cooked by his wife, Hilsa. Although the expense must have gnawed at his soul, Kamala proved to be a warm-hearted host. He had stocked up on jokes, and re-done them around local characters, so that friction melted easily in laughter. "Did you know," he asked, "that the shawl which Maulvi Ejaz Sarhadi is wearing has only *La i laha il-Allah* (There is no God but Allah) written on it, and not *Muhammad ur-Rasul Allah* (And Muhammad is His Prophet)?" We clamoured to know the reason. "That is because the shawl was bought before the Prophet was born!" I suppose he had to impress his wife, who did not appear too often before us but kept a sharp ear on everything that was said, with an occasional display of English. "Maulvi Ejaz is a willy chap... His backside story is very murky..." His character analysis, however, could not be faulted. We were all there – Mustaqim, Mustafa, Bharat, Shyam, Ashraf, Jaipal, Qasim, Altaf – and conversation floated from the obscure to the imaginative. Mustaqim recalled, in awe, an exhibition of endurance he had seen: a champion who cycled for three days around a circle without a pause for even a pee, and exclaimed that the prize he received, of a hundred and fifty-odd rupees, was not worthy of such courage. Kamala's wife, who we called Panditain, once intervened to explain that a Hindu wife must always wear bangles to protect her husband from harm, and that gold, being a noble metal, could not be worn below the waist, which is why her hip might jingle with gold but her toe and ankle ornaments would always be in silver. Hilsa, who was alleged to have a good voice, looked towards me, but not at me, as she sang, to prove the claim, a number from *Mother India*, *"Ghungat nahin kholungi saiyan tere aage... umar tori syani, saram mohe laage."* *I shall not remove the veil before you, you have become a young man, and I am feeling shy.* Kamala explained that normally a Brahmin tucked his dhoti twice around the waist to secure it, but for a religious ceremony a third tuck was necessary. The one thing that never crossed our minds was the virulence that would consume Telinipara.

We were in such good spirits that I did not feel sleepy. I went to the roof, and was surprised to see Hasina, by herself, staring into the dark, holding Simon's diamond ring in one hand. She smiled when she saw me, and I sat beside her while she told me stories of Sahibs and the jute mill till I dozed off, when she shook me awake and sent me to my bed. I was lost to the world when the dragons stirred.

Qasim, Mangu Kasai's grandson, discovered the posters that night on his way home because he had an incurable addiction to loitering. He did not know the meaning of a straight line. And so when he noticed two white sheets pasted onto the rear wall of the mosque, he stopped to investigate. Most of the poster was taken up by a caricature: of a man with a beard, wearing the high, red Ottoman cap called a *Turki* topi, or Turkish hat, in India. Below it was a message: *Muhammad married many times, including in his old age. This is the kind of leader Muslims admire!*

It was past one in the morning, but Qasim decided to wake up Maulvi Ejaz Sarhadi, who slept in a room on the first floor of the mosque. The Maulvi examined the posters carefully, sat down for a good half hour to think, and then decided that he needed witnesses. Normally, attendance for the pre-dawn prayer was thin. He told Qasim to wake up at least a dozen Muslims, including Zahid Qureshi. His eloquence during the sermon before the prayer woke up more. A speech was never expected at this hour, but this was an unusual occurrence, and the Maulvi chose his loudest voice in which to deliver his message.

"I warn the infidels! Say what you like about Allah, but we shall not tolerate a word about our Prophet! It is a sin to draw his portrait; and may those who cast aspersions on his glorious character burn in hell for all eternity! Islam ended female infanticide among Arabs. The only basis for superiority is piety, says the Quran, not gender. Muslims honour a mother twice as much as the father! The Prophet said that whoever treats his daughter as an equal of his son will go to Paradise! We shall not rest in peace till the police have arrested the criminals who have insulted our Prophet; and if it is necessary to become martyrs in this struggle then I say to you, every Muslim child shall march to his death with head held high, a smile on his face and the name of Muhammad on his lips!"

The police tore down the six offending posters (four were

glued on mud walls nearby) before eight that morning, but that complicated the problem. Some pacifiers, like Shafi Sahib, suggested that since the caricature was wearing a Turkish hat it could not have been a portrait of the Prophet, for Arabs were a *kaffiyeh*, but Zahid Qureshi dismissed it as the quibbling of an appeaser who had not seen the originals. Moreover, no one else knew what a *kaffiyeh* was. Someone thought it might have been a caricature of Muhammad Ismail, since the beard looked like Ismail's, but that was treated as a poor, and possibly seditious, joke. A rumour spread that Mohan and Vishnu Teli had been seen putting up the posters, but they were obvious targets since they had participated in the Holi procession. As word rippled through Telinipara and beyond, Muslim sentiment began to cascade. T.P. Singh, his sons Bharat and Shyam, the ageing Bhagwan Singh and of course Kamala publicly joined the protest against the insult to the Prophet; but Narayan Babu said he had a headache and could not leave his bed. A demonstration of goodwill can last only that long, and everyone went home. I had never seen streets so empty.

Benoy Choudhury received strict orders from Chand Gupta: he was not to leave the premises of Victoria Jute Mill or involve himself in any way with disputes outside the factory. Girdharilalji asked Chand Gupta to inform Ram Chatterjee that the material had arrived and been satisfactory. He added that he was leaving for Delhi and would not be available for a few weeks. If the police made any enquiries, Chand Gupta should handle the situation in the usual way. Ram Chatterjee laughed when he got Gupta's call; they should thank Ashu Ghosh, he said; he did not have the brains for subterfuge so subtle.

In the huts behind the mosque Zahid Qureshi reactivated the Zulfiqar Defence Force.

That night Mohan Teli was dragged into a deserted backlane and stabbed to death as he walked back from the jute mill. There was outrage when his body was discovered; the police arrested eight Muslims of dubious reputation. My father, concerned, suggested that they ask Narayan Babu to calm passions. T.P. Singh asked a question in reply: "Who appeals to fire to save him from burning sand?" Bhagwan Singh looked ill when they called on him. "I don't understand people anymore," he said, "even my children don't listen to me."

Abbaji stopped me from going to college. Since the new owners of Victoria did not permit us to use the factory access anymore, the only exit from Telinipara was through the road on which Ashfaque Alam had been killed. It was widely expected that any form of revenge killing would occur there. Dr Liaquat Ali survived a scare. He was on his way to meet Shafi Sahib – again, foolishly, after sunset – when he was attacked. Fortunately, this happened near the *gawala* mohalla. The cowherds saved his life; it was their way of thanking their buffalo-doctor. Jalil Mastan had no such luck. He was muttering to the wind on the maidan when he was killed. No one could understand why he should have gone to the maidan at night. Perhaps he was confident that his genies would protect him. His confidence was misplaced. The rational assessment was that it was Jalil Mastan's fault for being so stupid, but Mustaqim was angry: "He was the victim!" cried Mustaqim, weeping as he carried the coffin. "How can a victim be guilty?"

The Muharram moon appeared on the evening of 20 March;

Telinipara hardly needed another reason to mourn. My mad aunt, on her deathbed for three years, finally died. My mother, wearing black bracelets on her wrists (black and blue are the colours of sorrow), told me that the Quran forbade warfare during the month of Muharram.

Kamala was in a mild panic the next morning. He had dreamt of the Sheesh nag, the king of serpents with a thousand heads, in whose lap Vishnu sleeps between spells of creation. What did this dream signify? I shrugged. They did not teach answers to such questions in Presidency College.

It was the death of Wali, the rickshaw-wallah who had taken me to school for so many years, that ended my restraint. He was a simple man, a poor man, an innocent trying to make a miserable living so that he might eat a few vegetables along with his rice every day. His murder was neither revenge nor accident; it was the lust of venom. In 1965 I had experienced anger beyond my comprehension. I now felt a bitterness beyond my control.

The forbearance of my genial cousin, Siraj, and his friends also snapped. Altaf Gauhar, using his father's contacts, organized the purchase of a cottage-industry pipegun, a rough metal rod that carried one bullet and heated to burn levels when fired. It was highly inaccurate, but its glamour in Telinipara was unmistakable. The only Hindu who knew about this pipegun was Badri, who visited Siraj every day and said, in a slow and unsentimental drawl, that he would rather be with his friend than anyone else.

Hindus and Muslims in adjoining huts quietly began to distance themselves. Most said that they were going to Bihar, and many of them did. Others took shelter with their relatives. My father would not let the few Hindus in our neighbourhood leave, and they remained. Men went to the mill, and women to the maidan in small groups. Nothing was said, for suspicion does not have a language. T.P. Singh would rumble across every day, and my father returned the compliment by turning the corner to his home, but both did so during the middle of the day. Talk spread that an arsenal was being collected at Narayan Babu's home. My mother made a small parcel that she kept within easy reach in her cupboard. I asked her what it contained. It was the jewellery she had bought for my sister Baby's trousseau. If fate made her a refugee a second time, that would be the only thing she would take with her.

The police placed pickets on street corners. They remained immobile. Stabbing became an expected feature of the night, and the first question every morning was usually, who? The superintendent of police, a swarthy officer whose name did not interest me, drove down from his headquarters in Chinsurah, called on all the worthies, toured Telinipara once on his jeep without stopping anywhere, declared his inspection tour successful and went back. His deputy proposed that Muharram processions be banned that year in view of the tense law and order situation. Muhammad Ismail led a delegation of Muslims to Chinsurah to protest. This astonished Telinipara's Muslims, because no one had led a delegation to Chinsurah before. Ismail became a hero after he negotiated a compromise: there would be only one Muharram procession that year instead of the usual three. Muhammad Ismail did not tell anyone that the compromise had been pre-arranged through the Communist MLA of Chandernagore.

Darkness came a little before noon on the last day of March. Clouds massed in separate formations, leaving shifting gaps for a thin pallid light to deepen the unreality: it was neither day nor night. In the afternoon, men began to gather at Burha Deewana's shrine for the sole Muharram procession. There were no Hindus at the shrine this year. Drums were heard, green banners were lifted, and they began to move. My father was not with them. There was no mock combat between him and T.P. Singh; a sense of real combat filled every mind.

Siraj took charge of the security on our street. A small group, with Mustafa, Altaf, Ghazi, Jabbar, Hakim and Ashraf at the core, was posted in the hut on the corner of the street just before the turn that led to Kamala's hut. Those who had joined the Muharram procession were ordered to return at the first hint of trouble. I asked for a role and was told to stay at home: they did not want city-slickers messing things up. My aunt boiled and stored water in cans, pans and cooking vessels, and placed packets of chilli powder near each utensil. Six young women were given charge of this mission: if any mob reached our home, they were to mix chilli powder in the water and throw it in the face of an assailant.

Around four o'clock the Muharram procession was attacked on both flanks by a series of crude bombs. We later learnt that they had been sent from Chandernagore. The man who fled the fastest was Maulvi Ejaz Sarhadi. He tripped and broke a tooth which he later claimed was a war wound.

The first casualty reached our home at five. Shahabuddin, Wahabuddin's garrulous son, had survived a spear aimed at his throat, but the weapon had bitten off flesh from the side of the neck. Mustaqim converted his room into an impromptu dispensary. Within an hour there were a dozen men being treated with Dr Liaquat Ali's buffalo antiseptic and rough bandages. My mother told my sister, who bawled occasionally, and my brother, who stayed silent, to remain in her room, near her cupboard: she was instinctively keeping all that was valuable to her within the same space. Ammiji was cool, and had found a friend in Hasina; together they gave comfort to the women of the locality who were taking shelter in our house. My father, helpless and harried, worried that I would charge off into some side-battle. Mustafa appeared, his face flush with triumph. He had driven back five armed men and chased them up to the railway line with nothing in his hand except a rusty sword.

Arson began when darkness fell, and the colour of the clouds merged with the colour of the night. There was no electricity. No one knew why; or who had cut the lines. The few policemen hanging around the Muharram procession had disappeared.

The huts built by my grandfather were secure from nature but not from men. Muslims who felt vulnerable had left their homes and taken shelter in the brick house that my grandfather built. I saw the first flames to my left. The bamboo of the thatched roof was easy prey to fire. Someone must have scurried through the warren of lanes, thrown petrol and lit a match. Who? Who knew? Anonymous Hindus were searching for Muslim blood; anonymous Muslims were thirsty for Hindu blood. The first line of defence at the top of our street held, with Siraj in control. Mustaqim kept moving between Siraj and me.

The first *takbir* did not rise like a roar, more like a placid wave that descends in natural harmony. *Allah o Akbar!* cried the

Muslims, as flames glittered in the dark. Fear was answered by fear. *Jai Bajrang Bali!* came the reply. In between there was the constant scurry of news and rumour, and skirmishes in dark corners; Hakim was killed, Ashraf seriously wounded but would survive. The air trembled; fire and slogans were locked in a macabre competition, till half the thatched huts had been consumed and men with tired nerves held the line between life and death.

Dawn began to diminish the uncertainties of the night. Too many had no homes to return to, and my father broke the silence of fear by discussing plans for a refugee camp. Some policemen appeared, and disappeared.

It must have been around ten in the morning. I was standing on the balcony of our verandah when suddenly Kamala came into view. He was at the corner of the street, perhaps fifty yards away. I realized that I had not seen him for a while. I called out to him, without thinking, as I would do whenever I saw him.

He turned towards me, startled. He was heading elsewhere, perhaps searching for a rickshaw that would take his family away from insanity. He looked at me, and looked away. His face was white, and I remembered that he had once called himself a coward.

I reacted irrationally. "Kamala," I said loudly, "come here!"

It was a test. He knew it. To reach my home he would have to walk through a totally Muslim area; each step would be an invitation to some wounded animal's ferocity.

He waited. Then suddenly, he swivelled and with fast, trembling legs entered our street. I went down, held him by the hand and brought him home. He was shivering.

His explanation was simple. "I could never have met you again in life if I did not trust you today."

I walked back with him to his hut around the corner beyond our street. I could have done no less. My mistake was to linger there, chatting unnecessarily with Kamala. Sunlight breeds complacency.

Our street dogs were the first to understand. They charged up from wherever they had been hiding and began to howl. One moment, there was no one; the next, we were surrounded. Kamala began to blubber, "No no no no no no..."

"Get out of the way, you filthy Muslim-lover! Where were you when my brother was killed?" It was Vishnu Teli. Young men with sandal paste on their foreheads and murder in their eyes stared at me; I did not recognize who they were.

Kamala stood in front of me, shaking.

I lost my temper. I think I shouted. "Let me be, Kamala. These bastards don't scare me. I am standing on my soil. Who are they to tell me..."

There was the swipe of a knife, which I sidestepped. The rest is a blur. The sharp snap of a pipegun was heard. It created the confusion necessary for rescue. Mustaqim literally fell on me, to protect me with his body. Siraj, Ghaffar, Ghazi and Badri were behind him.

"You want to kill Mobashar? Get me first," shouted Badri, swinging a heavy cycle chain.

The blur cleared. There was blood on my shirt. It was not mine. Kamala was flat on his back, moaning. Blood poured through a deep gash on the side of his body, next to his stomach.

All movement stopped, except for Vishnu Teli edging away before he sprinted as fast as his ageing legs could carry him. A sense of profound helplessness overtook us as Kamala's moaning weakened. We reacted in slow motion, as if time had outpaced us. I picked Kamala up by the shoulders, Mustaqim under his knees. Siraj, with practical sense, rushed off to get a doctor, or at least medicine. Ammiji was already with Kamala's wife, comforting her, when we reached his home. His wife looked bewildered, and frightened. It was strange; Kamala looked peaceful when he lost consciousness. I fell over his face, sobbing, when his head slumped to the side, and did not see his wife as she raised her arms and brought them crashing to the floor to destroy the bangles that had been unable to protect her husband's life.

Mustafa and Qasim did not enter the hut; they wept, outside, with other young men. T.P. Singh, his sons beside him, sat beside the body, and covered his face with his hands, unwilling to see death. "The paradise of Brahma is *Satyaloka,* the world of truth, far higher and purer than other heavens, watered by the Ganges... You have found your place there, my son," said Benoy Chowdhury, his head bowed, his hands lifted in reverence, his voice soft. He had resigned from Victoria Jute Mill just before he set out for Kamala's hut.

The rituals took time. My father presented a cow to the *purohit,* and donations were given to Brahmins for their prayers as the soul passed through the river of fire. The last bed was made: seven pieces of wood bound by straw ropes across two parallel poles. The funeral was beside the Hooghly, the child of Ganga, the river by which we had grown up. Kamala's wife screamed as the body was lifted for its last journey. Kalyan Singh opened the door when they stopped to let Bhagwan Singh, who was too ill to move, take a last look. Jaipal was not there: in a sudden frenzy, he rushed to the small hut in the *gawala* mohalla where so many schemes of violence had been born, and vandalized it with a fury that amazed onlookers. Maybe it was this that provoked Qasim, Ghazi and Jabbar: they went to the mosque, thrashed Maulvi Ejaz, the only Muslim not at the funeral, and told him to get out of Telinipara that instant. He did.

The body had just been laid on the funeral pyre when Zahid Qureshi appeared; while the world watched, he placed a cache of weapons at Kamala's feet. The *purohit* recited mantras, and sprinkled water over the pile of sandalwood. There was sunlight but no sun that afternoon, and clouds scurried through the sky. Small flames began to eat the four corners of the pyre. My father stood still as the smoke began to rise, his expression stoic. But his eyes were open, drained of everything but inexpressible anguish as the tears of Brahma streamed down his face, incessant, unable to stop.

College was not different when I returned. I was different.

"Where have you been," asked Mridula when I caught up with her. I told the story as briefly as I could. I asked her if she was free that evening. She said she was busy. She flung a sentence across her shoulder as she left: "You Muslims! You are always fighting..."

I saw the laughing face of Mridula walk away from me through the corridors of Presidency College.

I heard AKDG whisper a line from Shakespeare: *"I am a fool. Thou art nothing."*

I remembered the strain on the face of Kamala as he walked towards me on that numb morning in Telinipara.

I was seventeen. Life had begun.